THEY WERE SHIPWRECKED
ON AN ISLAND OF AWAKENING DESIRE...

His eyes were a deep winter gray and hawk-like, alert, missing nothing. She felt him looking at her intensely and sensed that he found no flaw in what he saw.

"Please—" Garlanda stammered. "I want my dress." She tried not to notice how tanned and solidly muscled his body was. He reminded her of a sleek, wild stallion—smooth, dangerous, and fierce.

But the thing that alarmed her most was the hunger that had lain slumbering secretly in her soul. She knew that once she had discovered and awakened that hunger, her life could never be the same again.

LADY
OF FIRE

Valerie Vayle

A DELL BOOK

To Freddie M.—
who won't know why

Published by
Dell Publishing Co., Inc.
1 Dag Hammarskjold Plaza
New York, New York 10017

Dell ® TM 681510, Dell Publishing Co., Inc.

ISBN 0-440-15444-8

Printed in Canada

First printing—January 1980

CONTENTS

PART ONE
FLEUR/7

PART TWO
GARLANDA/145

PART THREE
SAFIYE/309

PART FOUR
THE COUNTESS/413

AUTHOR'S NOTE

Although Garlanda Cheney is fictional, the historical background of her story has been portrayed as realistically as possible. Female pirates existed and were known for their ferocity. William Kidd left the Caribbean to marry a wealthy widow and become a New York shipowner with a house on Wall Street before returning to the sea and gaining fame as the fey Captain Kidd of lore.

A French convent-reared girl from Martinique became Grand Sultana and went on to rule her late husband's empire through her son in the latter part of the eighteenth century. More than one Turkish pasha was known to have a fetish for European women and a report is still extant describing the kidnaping of a woman from the stairs of an embassy for a pasha's harem.

Port Royal, "the wickedest city on earth," has been recreated from eyewitness accounts of its doom. Among those accounts is that of Doctor Heath, rector of Saint Paul's Church, who absolves Garlanda in this story.

PART ONE

FLEUR

CHAPTER 1

The violence of the storm met and clashed with the storm in her soul. Jagged flashes of lightning briefly illuminated roiling sections of sky—then darkness and the feverish pitch of the ship. She clutched at the rail for a moment then staggered across the deck which rose and fell sickeningly beneath her. As she reached the cabin door she was flung back abruptly before she could enter. Once inside she took a deep, shaky breath of the steamy, stale air in the cubicle.

A deafening crash and jolt told her that lightning had hit the ship. She fell heavily to her knees and in the blinding flash of light she could see her mother's pale, sorrow-streaked face. Lying motionless in the narrow bunk, Mother looked far older than her years, but that was because she was so ill.

"Garlanda?" her voice came faintly. "Garlanda, are you there?"

"Yes, Mother," she said, crawling to her side. She hadn't the strength to walk anymore and fear was rendering her legs useless. She was trembling in spite of the oppressive heat.

"Is the ship sinking?" her mother asked feebly.

"No, of course not," Garlanda said. "That's silly. It's just a little storm. Rest now and it will all be over soon." She reached across the narrow aisle and fumbled in her reticule for the comfort of her rosary. She pulled the smooth beads between her shaking fingers and whispered prayer after prayer. How many times had she done this in the last ten years at the convent school? But she'd had nothing to pray for—not really. Life had been simple and easy. Life on Grandfather's plantation had been pleasant. Martinique was a lush paradise for the well-to-do. And the school had been an island of peace with the only intervals of excitement when letters had arrived from England.

She had saved all Mother's letters. The spidery tracings had kept England and Mother and Father alive in her mind. Sometimes between letters she had found herself forgetting their faces, especially Father's. It had been so very long since she had seen him, years even before she had been sent away to school. "Where is Papa?" she used to ask and Mother, young and pretty then, never ill, would reply, "He's working for us, Garlanda. He's serving England and the King." At the age of four Garlanda accepted that explanation and was proud. But later she began to wonder. In her weekly letter to Mother she would ask about Papa, but Mother never answered her questions.

And now Papa was dead and Mother was ill and the trip back home to England was turning into a nightmare. Garlanda clutched the rosary more tightly. "Please, God," she whispered, "please save us." Hot tears spilled over and ran down her cheeks. "Don't take us now. Let us get back to England—let us go home." She choked back a sob and wiped away the tears with the back of her hand. If Papa hadn't died— if Mother hadn't come to Martinique to fetch her home—if they had taken next month's ship as they originally planned—if—if. But what use was this?

The small window above her head flew open and

flapped against the wall. She rose unsteadily and struggled to close it. Wind-lashed salt water stung her face and she was suddenly aware of the sounds of the ship. Cries of alarm swirled through her head—pained cries of men and the terrified whinnying of the horses deep in the hold mixed in a symphony of horror. Suddenly there was a soul-splitting crash and the entire ship groaned and was utterly still for a moment, then the cries broke out afresh, a new note of hopelessness laced through them.

Mindlessly she continued to struggle with the window. Suddenly there was a face near hers, just outside the window. It was a man who had sat at their table last night. His unforgettable eyes were looking into hers. "Get out!" he shouted at her and even this close she could hardly separate his words from the storm. "Get out!" he shouted again. Then as quickly as he had appeared he was gone.

Garlanda felt something pulling at her skirts. "We're sinking," her mother's voice came out of the torrid darkness.

This time Garlanda could not deny it. She fell to the floor and buried her face in her hands. "Oh, Mama," she sobbed, "what shall we do?"

"We shall pray," her mother said in a calm voice. "But there is something you must know first." She paused and closed her eyes. She breathed raspingly for a moment, then the pale eyes reopened. Her voice was now fainter as if her pitiful supply of energy was nearly gone. "You must know. I will not live to do—anything more."

"Don't talk, Mama," Garlanda begged. "There will be time when this is over."

"No. No more time. For anything. Your papa did

not die a natural death . . ." The voice trailed away and her eyes closed again.

"Mama!" Garlanda cried. "What do you mean?" She held tightly to her mother's thin, wasted hands. "What *do* you mean?"

"Murder," her mother said. Or did she only mouth the word?

Another shudder went through the ship and Garlanda felt it clear through her body. "Murder?" she whispered.

"Pray for me," her mother said.

Garlanda bowed her head and began a prayer. Her voice rose above the tumult of the storm and the chaos of her mind until she was nearly shouting. She shut her eyes tightly and continued, trying to block out everything but the prayer. If she prayed hard enough, if she could show God her intense desire to be heard, and if she could shut out her fear, her prayers would certainly be answered.

She stopped and looked again at Mama. A strange calm had come over her face. She looked peaceful. The years and illness had dropped away. The cabin door was wrenched open and Garlanda found herself being violently pulled to her feet. At that instant she realized that the illumination in the room was no longer the cold blue of flashing lightning, but the orange flicker of flames.

"We're sinking. Get out of here!" It was a man's voice—the man who had been outside the window a few moments ago. He tried to pull her to the door.

"No!" she screamed. She clung to the side of the bunk. "I can't leave my mother. She's ill. Help me take her first."

The man bent over Mama. He put a thumb on her

eyelid and eased it open. "She's dead," he said. "We can't help her now. Come on."

"No! No, she can't be dead. She's sleeping. She's very ill and tired and she's just sleeping! She's *not* dead. She's not!"

"You fool," the man said, desperately grabbing Garlanda as the ship lurched. "She's dead as we'll all be in a few minutes. And she's probably better off." Garlanda's long copper hair had come unbound and he grasped a large handful of it and dragged her to the cabin door.

She tried to free herself and managed to brace her elbow at the side of the narrow opening. She would not be torn from her mother this way. He couldn't be right. The man chopped his hand brutally against her upper arm and as she pulled it in toward herself with a cry of pain, he hauled her through the doorway and down the hallway.

"No! No! Let me go! My mother. I can't go!" she cried as she was dragged across the slippery, fire-studded deck. She twisted her head around and in animal desperation she bit into his shoulder.

"You stupid bitch," he exclaimed and slapped her face. "I ought to let you stay in there and die." He grabbed her wrist and savagely twisted it until she turned in his direction. He shoved her toward the rail where the black sea yawned malignantly beneath her. "Here she comes!" he shouted and suddenly she was being picked up and slung over the side of the ship.

The water hit her with a solid force that robbed her of breath. She struggled frantically for a moment; then there were more rough hands on her. She was pulled up and backward and her spine was scraped against a hard edge. She was dumped on the floor of a small boat, and as she looked upward at the fiery ship looming over them, the ship seemed to tilt again. No, not the whole ship, only the mast was tilting. With horrible slowness the burning pillar cracked and splintered as it fell to the deck.

The man who had thrown her overboard was still standing at the rail. He was a black silhouette against the curtain of flame, an eerie satanic figure framed by hell. She saw him whirl as the mast fell and throw his arms in front of his face.

She saw no more of him. The air was full of flying timbers and burning sail floating down with deadly grace around them. She was enveloped in pain and darkness. The ship blurred and faded, the pain ebbed, and she was a child again, rocking in the old wooden chair she had loved. She was being rocked to sleep, humming the lullaby her mother used to sing. Her throat constricted and she fell into a deep oblivion.

Garlanda was late for Vespers and the Mother Superior was gently scolding her. "Now, my child, we must not be tardy."

"I'm truly sorry, Mother, but there was an accident."

Accident, accident—the words echoed in her head. Salt water filled Garlanda's mouth. Why was she being forced to drink it? Was this a part of her punishment?

"Mother Superior, I'm sorry, I'm sorry, I'm—"

Garlanda returned to reality with a frightened cry. The next wave broke over her with a roar. She pulled herself to her elbows, choking. At first all she could see was sand, everywhere, on all sides of her—sand and the rough piece of wood she was clutching. Sharp rocks bit at her hands and knees as she tried desperately to stand amid the booming surf. The wood, waterlogged as it was, had left splinters buried in her hands and arms. Her face felt hot and tight.

She teetered and nearly fell, but the taste of salt water in her mouth and the sting of it in her nostrils and the back of her throat served to remind her that she must not fall. She *must* not! Another wave hit her and drove the plank into the back of her knees. She gasped with pain and surprise as she fell, face first, into the churning surf. Too exhausted to fight, she held her breath until the water began to recede then clawed at the sand to keep from being swept back out with the tide. She rose again, and with trembling legs and pounding pain in her head, she fought her way to dry land. The next wave came only to her thighs but knocked her down again. And once more she got up and kept going.

Finally she was on dry sand. It was searing hot on her feet. As she looked down the length of beach the very air rippled with the heat. She fell to her hands and knees in the burning sand and stayed like that for a long time, unmindful of the heat, of the circumstances, glad only for air to breathe without having to fight for it. Finally the incoming tide began to lap at her feet, and she forced herself to get up again and walk farther up the beach. There were trees and shade ahead, but she could not get that far—not now. She must get away from the deadly sea. Only far enough to elude the lethal waters that pursued her.

What had happened? Garlanda peered around, almost too tired to focus her eyes. She remembered all too vividly the storm battering the ship mercilessly while her sick mother prayed weakly. Her mother, dying, telling the shivering girl at her bedside that Sir

Robert Cheney, renowned diplomat, Garlanda's long absent father, was dead and not of natural causes.

Both parents were dead now—gone forever—while she stood uneasily alone on the shore of an untamed jungle island. Garlanda covered her face with her sea-crinkled hands and cried. She cried out of sorrow, out of fear, and out of the knowledge that she, carefully convent reared, knew nothing about survival. How would she live—eat? What if there were wild beasts?

She looked about her, squinting against the blaze of sun on sand. The beach was deserted except for a few pieces of wood and ragged clumps of seaweed. She could go no further. She buried her sunburned face in her arms. Her last thought before oblivion was that this was the beginning of death and she did not care. Soon she would be reunited with her parents.

She slept.

It seemed fated that she should live—even against her will.

When she awoke it was dawn—or was it sunset? Dawn, she guessed, for the sand had cooled and she was trembling. Joint by aching joint she got to her feet. Thirst constricted her throat and her lips were cracked and dry. The trees were outlined against a feeble pink sky, the sea behind her was black, trimmed with pink wave crests. She forced herself to walk toward the trees and actually had to concentrate on how to walk—right foot, then left, then right. She promised herself a rest after ten steps, but when she had gone the ten she knew she dared not sit down for she might not be able to get back up and she must find water. Death would be a relief, but not this kind of death, not with this horrible, sea-parched, consuming thirst.

Ten more steps—then ten more—she was almost to the line of palm trees. Her senses, sharpened by desperation, did not fail her. She could hear water now, even above the perpetual slap of tide on sand she could hear an irregular splashing undertone. She must find the source.

She reached the trees and the mossy undergrowth that thrived in the shade of its giant protectors. Pink light filtered down through the rustling leaves far above, but she did not need the light nor care about it. She was relying on her ears to lead her to the water. She stumbled through lush tropical plants, ignoring the sting of thorns that tore at her legs and skirts, ignoring the maniacal cries of birds frightened by the human in their midst.

Finally she found a small clearing in the tangle of plant life. A small pool was there—blue and fresh and fed by a tiny rivulet trickling down the slope of the hill. She fell to her knees at the edge of the water and scooped up handfuls of the lifegiving liquid. She drank and drank and drank until she felt almost ill. Then she leaned down and put her face and head in the pool. She sat up and pushed her wet hair back from her face, cooled now and somewhat refreshed.

What in the world was she to do? With her thirst satiated, hunger had come to the fore. What could she eat? She looked over the plants growing around the small clearing. They were full of fruits, strange fruits unfamiliar to her and possibly poisonous. But then, did it matter?

She picked a handful of red berries off a bush and after a moment's hesitation, put them in her mouth. They were sweet and tart at the same time—

quite good, really. At least they were good to someone who hadn't eaten for a long time. How long had it been? she wondered. She picked some more and ate them, then she found some nuts with soft shells and she devoured them as well. Some more fresh water, then she settled down by the side of the pool to see if she would become ill. But she didn't feel any discomfort, only a slightly renewed energy. After a while she ate some more of the berries and the nuts and went back to sleep for a while. Being awake would mean thinking and she could not face thinking about her situation—not yet.

When she awoke again, near noon (if she gauged the sun correctly), she had to face reality. She had saved her body, provided it with nourishment and water and rest. How could she save her mind? What was there here to nourish it? She had heard of people who had been locked in solitary confinement in prisons and gone mad for the sound of another human voice. How much the same this was. She was free to walk about, to eat what she could find, but how could she stand being alone?

She was still unable to comprehend it, to consider it. Her mind shut down. Every time she tried to think rationally about her situation, rational thought eluded her. She would feel a horrible, nameless fear well up inside her, stifling her breath. To combat it she would venture out for food, for something practical to occupy her mind, or she would sleep and escape that way.

Finally the shock began to wear off a little and she could think more clearly. First she made long mental lists of the things in her favor. The island: It was apparently not cold at night, just pleasantly cool, and the days were not uncomfortably hot if she stayed away from the wide stretch of sand at midday. Of course, the seasons might change that, but she could not be very far from Martinique, even considering that the storm had blown the *Valiant* off course. She had adjusted to the climate of Martinique over the years; the island she was on now could not be very different.

The island was rich in other resources—she had an abundant supply of fresh water and the jungle growth was insanely fecund. She would never lack food, only variety of food. Eventually she would need some sort of shelter against bad weather, but that shouldn't be too much of a problem.

But her own resources? What of them? What had she in her own soul to sustain her? For the first time in her life she had to look into her own heart and mind and assess what she found there. Not an easy task. What did she know about Garlanda Cheney? She had been told that she was very pretty. That would have been an asset in the life she had been prepared for—the life of an English lady. It made no difference here.

She was accomplished at the lute and harpsicord and loved music. Well, there were no lutes and harpsicords here, but she could make her own music, her own songs. That would exercise her mind and cheer her spirits and that would be useful—even though there would be no one to hear her or sing with her.

She had been among the best girls at needlework at the convent school. There would be no more daisy chains and lover's knots to sew on fine lawn chemises, but she could certainly improvise some sort of protection from the sun with leaves and grasses. But these were talents, not traits.

She was patient, even the nuns admitted that, and

patience would serve her well. She was curious. The sisters had regarded that as her greatest failing and tried to cure her of it. Being inquisitive about her surroundings might help her, but she was most curious about people: how they came to be how they were, what they thought, and what they had done. That was closed to her. There was no one here but herself. No one that she knew of.

That led her to start thinking of her disadvantages, which were overwhelming.

She was alone.

Alone!

Was that not, above all other misfortunes, the worst that a human being could suffer? Never to exchange opinions, experiences, victories, and challenges with another person! Never to have someone tell you of his love and support when you're unhappy. Never to have another to help with a difficult task or share a joke.

And yet, it might be even worse to contemplate if she were not alone. What if there were natives on the island—hostile natives? She had no idea of the size of the island, nor had she gathered the courage to explore any farther than necessary to obtain food. She had never heard voices or drums or seen fires, but that didn't mean there wasn't someone just beyond the curve of beach or on the other side of the hill that sloped down to the pool.

And animals—she often heard furtive scurryings in the brush. There might be larger animals, dangerous creatures, or deadly spiders. And she knew so little of survival against such odds. What could she do for herself if she became ill or injured? The advantages she had so carefully enumerated to herself withered and faded in the despair she felt now. She wept with fear and loneliness and the prospect of years of deadly boredom. She wept for most of a day until she made herself sick with it in her mind and body and finally she found the answer.

Suicide.

That was the solution. She would no longer need to fear *how* she might die, nor how long she might have to exist this way before death took her at its whim. She would give herself willingly now. She felt strangely cheered by this decision, glad that she would no longer have to wonder what was going to happen to her.

She went down to the beach to die. She would cut her wrists and then wade out into the sea. She made herself walk briskly and with purpose along the beach as she searched for just the right instrument. Then, glinting in the sand was what she wanted. A flat shell, paper-thin and brittle. She picked it up, examined it, then knocked it against a water-rounded rock to make a sharp edge. *Sharp enough?* she wondered, running her finger lightly along the break. *Yes.*

With her right hand she held the shell to her left wrist. She made a tentative stroke across the skin. Beads of blood formed instantly along the line, and she stared at them, petrified at the enormity of what she was doing. She must not look—it must be done quickly before her resolve failed her. She held her arms close to her body and looked blindly out to sea. She took a deep breath and prepared to plunge the sharp shell into her own flesh.

But before she could do so, she thought she saw something. No, it was a trick her eyes played on her. There was nothing out there—or was there? She stood up and the shell clattered, useless and forgotten, to her feet.

It was a sail, the tiny white tip of a sail on the horizon! Maybe it would come closer. Perhaps she would be rescued!

It was possible! She screamed, knowing she could not be heard but unable to simply stand passively and wait for fate. The sail seemed to dance lightly on the sea, dipping out of sight, now seeming nearer. She screamed until her voice gave out and all sight of sail was gone.

She went back then to her clearing and soothed her aching throat with the cool water of the pool. She was unhappy, of course, that the ship had not come nearer, that she had not been seen, but nevertheless she had gained something very worthwhile.

She had acquired hope.

Hope and the need to survive. If one ship had sailed close enough to the island for her to see it, others would sooner or later. She would survive!

CHAPTER 2

Once hope returned, she was appalled at herself. Her dress was tattered and as crusted with sea salt as was her fire-colored hair. When she further examined herself, she found that her arms and legs were scratched from the foliage she had been blundering through, and her skin was bright pink from the sizzling tropical sun. In Martinique she had never gone walking without lacy mitts and a headkerchief to protect her skin and keep it fashionably pale. Now she itched and burned all over. When she scratched the tip of her turned-up nose she discovered flakes of peeling skin.

She plunged into the clear blue pool. The cool sweet waters were kind to her parched skin. Salt floated away. She combed twigs and leaves from her hair and cleaned her dirty, broken nails with a piece of bark.

Her gown was salvageable, but her underwear was not. She stripped off the dress, wrung it out, and hung it over a low branch. Her delicate petticoats and chemise with the tiny tucks and braided ribbons were in shreds. There was nothing to do but remove them and heap them on the bank. She crawled out of the pool physically and mentally soothed.

From then she went on to an almost defiant existence, refusing to let the jungle defeat her. Her petite frame held a more resolute spirit than she would have guessed. But still, at night she huddled, terrified, on the upper reaches of the beach. There were too many chattering things in the bushes, too many snakes slithering in the undergrowth. The beach seemed safest at night. Sounds that had amused her coming through the open window at the convent now sent her cringing in fear. At night she was most acutely aware that she was utterly alone in her small world.

She began to explore during the day. She found traces of long dead fires during her wanderings. An island with fresh fruit, small game, and a spring—it might be a stopping point for sea-faring natives. She could only hope European vessels knew of the place. She returned to her beach several times a day to scan the horizon for ships.

She thrived on the open air and sunshine. After a cloistered life she felt adventurous. She ran barefoot in the hot sand, wearing rags, eating berries, and knowing that there was no one to scold her for her wanton ways. She swam, sang to herself, and took long walks, but she always returned to her section of the beach before the sun sank over the ocean. Her copper hair became gilded by the sun and her skin bronzed. She was not happy, but neither did the breathtaking despair grip her as fiercely and frequently as it had at first.

One afternoon the tide brought a round wooden barrel ashore, bobbing amid a tangle of ship's rigging. She wrestled it up on the beach. *I hope it's salt pork or biscuits*, she thought, noting how tightly sealed the cask was. The fruit and berries she ate every day no longer left her feeling full. She rolled the barrel to her "home" by the pool.

It took awhile, but she finally pried loose the lid

with the aid of a sharp stick. When the top finally popped off she peered inside anxiously. Liquid! It was only sea water in the cask—or was it? No, it was too dark to be water and the barrel was too tightly constructed to have absorbed anything. She dipped cupped hands in and brought them up. Mellow Madeira wine met her lips. It tasted strange after days of nothing but water. She drank eagerly.

Later, pleasantly glutted on berries, nuts, and wine, she settled back against the gnarled roots of her favorite tree. The barrel nodded lazily from its place in the shallow end of the pool. She had decided that Madeira would keep better in the cool water with the trees shading it from the sun.

It was nearly time to leave the jungle for the beach. Garlanda yawned, wiggling her feet. She let her head drop back until it rested against the rough bark of the tree. At that moment she saw a wispy trail of white drifting across the sky, framed by leafy branches. Her heart thudded madly. She sat up clutching her throat. Smoke from a fire! *Merciful Mother of God,* she thought desperately, *savages on the island! I haven't left a trail they could follow, have I? Any tracks or meal scraps?*

She crouched down among the massive roots. Fear of being alone was replaced by the sinking knowledge that she wasn't. It seemed inconceivable that she could be in this situation. She was what the nuns called "gently reared," the daughter of a diplomat too often absent from home and his soft-spoken French wife. Garlanda's life until now had consisted of childhood in the London countryside, followed by years at the convent school in Martinique. She had never known strife or grief or even real fear. Kindness was all that had ever touched her. She had been trained to be a gentle wife and mother someday and she knew nothing else. Nothing in her education had prepared her for a moment like this. She had nothing but her own resourcefulness to depend on now.

She could not move. Minutes ticked by with agonizing slowness. When no shrieking cannibals came rushing at her from the brush, she forced herself to relax. The smoke was gone now—not a trace of it remained. She shivered. Had she imagined the entire thing?

She climbed a little way up the ancient tree. There was a hollow where it branched and she would sleep there. She drifted in and out of consciousness until well after sunup. She woke stiff and cramped from her fetal huddle. A painful stretch brought a snapping sound from her back. Garlanda wrinkled her forehead thoughtfully. Odd—she had dreamed of the dark man who had saved her life against her will. *He tore me from Mama*, she thought, *and flung me into that little boat.* But the boat hadn't survived—as far as she knew none of the other passengers had lived—only her. *That man would have lived if he had not taken time to save me.*

At the time he had seemed brutal and cold to yank a sobbing girl from her dying mother. She tried to imagine his thoughts. He must have seen her mother as past help while she herself had been alive and capable of surviving. What he had done was actually a very Christian thing, an act of great self-sacrifice. Then why did she hope he was condemned to eternal hell fires for tearing her away from Mama? Mama who was dying. *Dead, not dying*, she rebuked herself sternly. *Dead. Think back. She was beyond earthly aid before he burst in the cabin and forced me to the boat. He gave his life. He gave me mine when I would have squandered it. Judge not—*

She rubbed her forehead. She wished she had her rosary; it would have helped her sort these strange thoughts. Her courage faltered then returned. She decided to sneak down to the beach to see if a ship was in view or whether anything useful had been brought in by the tide. The jungle was ominously quiet as she reached the edge of it and looked out at the expanse of burning sand. A warm wind stroked her face.

She was about to step out when she saw something unusual in the sand. Garlanda shielded her eyes with her hand. Revulsion crept over her at the realization that what she saw were the battered bodies of two who had not survived the storm at sea. She turned and fled back into the jungle.

She rose early the next morning, determined not to waver about leaving the pool to search for food. It was difficult but she managed to force her feet to the clearing that led to the beach.

The bodies were gone. She felt a queer dryness in her mouth. Pitiful corpses, mutilated by fish and the rough sea. They had been too far away for her to be fully aware of the damage, but she had seen enough to know the ocean had been merciless. Had they been fellow passengers on the *Valiant*, or were they human flotsam from another vessel? She said a quick prayer. In the midst of the hastily babbled plea for the souls of the dead, she remembered how far up the beach the water had washed the bodies. The ocean could not have reclaimed them!

Men must have taken the bodies—cannibals, the

savages whose fire she had seen the smoke from the day before. She ran back to the safety of her favorite tree.

Three days passed before the need for shelter drove her back to the beach to seek driftwood. Sleeping in the jungle was frightening, but she felt safer there than out on the beach, under the stars, vulnerable to the world. But if she was going to stay in the jungle, she would need some kind of hut to protect her from wild animals, the noises in the night, the things that slithered and crawled and cried out in a hunting lust. Night after night she had climbed up her tree, hoping that whatever was floundering around below wasn't a skillful climber. She needed a shelter.

Waterlogged pieces of wood littered the ocean's edge. She began gathering them, glancing over her shoulder from time to time to make sure nothing was creeping up on her. Her slender fingers met an unusually smooth piece of wood. Garlanda gripped it tightly. It was a plank, still stained with the remains of once-gray paint. It said *H.M.S. Valia* . . . It had been part of a lifeboat! Perhaps the very vessel which had carried her to safety.

It was a blazingly hot afternoon. Garlanda remained in the shelter of the jungle, sorting the wood she'd gathered to build a hut. But she'd never constructed anything in her life and she didn't know where to start. She sat, trying to picture the workers on her grandparents' plantation. The dusky giants had had tools, great hammers and winches, but perhaps she could find a rock to pound with. It occurred to

her that she'd have to whittle wooden nails or hope
for twine or rope to be washed ashore.

How disheartening! She tore loose a fat splinter of
bark from a broken branch and dug at the dirt under
her nails. *Delicate little hands*, she thought wryly.
Who could have warned me of their uselessness? She
had not been prepared for a struggle for survival. She
was meant to marry some nice young man and settle
down to managing a household and a flock of well-
bred children. How her friends would stare if they
could see her now, dirty and dressed in rags. She
stood swiftly. There was no reason to be dirty!

She stripped off her tattered dimity frock and hung
it on a branch. She walked into the pool, letting the
water soothe her as it always did. She was so relaxed
that at first she thought she had dreamed the sound.
Then it happened again. A twig snapped loudly in the
underbrush. She was afraid to look, to know the truth.
Had natives found her? Slowly, she turned, but she
saw nothing at first.

Then a man stepped out from the shadow of a tree.
Garlanda stifled a scream. But it was *not* a native, it
was a white man—the man who had saved her life on
the ship. He too had survived and was here!

He had been dark to begin with, now his skin was
as bronzed as a savage's from the sun. He was lean
and well-muscled, face fringed with an uneven growth
of beard. His torn clothing clung to him with disheveled dignity. Everything was primitive about him except his pleased expression of surprise.

"Well," he said and she thrilled to the sound of a
voice other than her own. "So there *is* someone else
here. I thought I was going to have to wait it out on
my own and I'm getting sick to death of my company. You're the girl from the ship, aren't you? You

made it after all. Come out of the water little—what was your name? Something flowery—not Rose—Fleur? Was that it?" He came closer. "Come out, Fleur, I won't hurt you."

All she could think of was her dress hanging out of reach on the branch. She stared at him dumbly, arms crossed over her breasts.

"Speak up, Fleur. You were vocal enough when I dragged you from the ship. You cried and screamed and tried to beat me. I seem to remember getting bitten as well. Come out of the—oh, I see." A low laugh escaped him. He tilted his crudely hewn spear up, caught her dress and dropped the garment to her. She yanked it on and crept from the water, embarrassed at the wet fabric clinging to her body.

"I'm not going to hurt you, Fleur, stop cringing," he said. "Are you hungry? I've caught a fish. Damn you, speak!" He reached for her. She dodged under his arm and fled for the beach. She had no plan, no reason, just surprise verging on fear and terrible confusion. A branch slapped her shoulder, knocking her off balance. She screamed as the branch caught her long hair and held it fast.

He was beside her. His fingers were kind to her lacerated scalp as he freed her from the barky tentacles. The liberation was no sooner complete than she bolted, leaving him with a faceful of branch. "You crazy little animal! What the hell's wrong with you?"

The sand was hot under her bare feet as she scrambled across the beach. He brought her down in a flying tackle that knocked the breath from her. They grappled fiercely for a moment. He pinned her arms down and knelt over her, victorious. "I'm not going to rape you or throw you into a cooking pot! Will you stop fighting me? What's the matter with you?"

Garlanda hesitated, then relaxed under him. "I'm sorry," she said softly. "I don't know why I did that—it seems so long that I've been alone and you frightened me. I must be losing my mind!"

He released her. She sat up rubbing her wrists. "No, it's a perfectly natural reaction, I guess," he said. He looked her over. "By God, you're a pretty thing!" He leaned forward and caught her chin with his fingers. Steel-gray eyes met her violet ones. She was too bewildered to make any move to stop him. When his lips touched hers, it wasn't what she expected. Accustomed to the chaste sparrowlike pecks on the cheek her mother and aunt had always given her, she was nonetheless aware that when a man kissed a woman it involved direct contact with the lips, but his mouth bore down on hers, forcing her lips apart. His warm tongue thrust into her mouth, invading her, making her feel warmth and a strange excitement.

He drew back and gave her a sharp glance. "What the devil's the matter with you? Get that look off your face or I'll—I'll—" He leaned back and smiled. "What were you doing on that ship, anyway?"

"Returning from convent school in Martinique. It was to have been my debut season in London."

He smacked himself on the forehead. "Sweet *Jesú*, of all the women in the world I find myself stranded with a child nun!"

"I'm not a nun, sir," she said. "Is there something wrong? Are you ill? You seem to have unusually high color, perhaps it's the sun. I'll fetch a shell and bring you some cool water to drink."

"Damn it, forget the water! I'm not ill. Ah-h-h, sweet innocence. What an undeserved fate this is," the man said with a hearty groan.

He wasn't so frightening now that he'd quit scowling.

On board ship he had been a satanic beast of prey, swooping down on her. Now he was human, a little addled perhaps, but human. And he was interesting with his aristocratic nose and the white scar dissecting his right eyebrow—interesting and handsome with his black hair, gray eyes, and wide shoulders. Above all, he was another person with whom she could share the small daily victories over the jungle and in whom she could confide her fears.

CHAPTER 3

"How did you get here?" he asked. "Is there anyone else?"

"Not that I know of," she answered. "And I don't really know how I got here. The last thing I remember is seeing you on deck and the mast falling. Then I was on the beach, clinging to a piece of wood."

"Funny the things we can forget if we need to," he mused.

"I haven't any idea what happened to the boat or to the rest of the people in it, although I must have been conscious at the time or I'd have drowned. How did you get here? How did you escape?"

"The same way you did. I jumped overboard and hung on to anything that would float. In my case it was a barrel—"

"How long have you been here?"

"Three—four days. I've been looking over the island in the meantime."

"Are there natives?"

"I haven't seen any," he said, picking a handful of berries from the bush next to where they sat. "But I think there are some on the island somewhere. I've found stumps of newly cut trees and some burned out fires that haven't been rained on yet."

"Do you think they might be friendly?" Garlanda asked.

"Not bloody likely. Why should they be?"

"Why shouldn't they be!" she said, a little angry at his attitude.

"Ah, well, you might be right. But if they find us I wouldn't count on a welcoming feast if I were you. You're likely to find that you're the main course."

"What a horrible thing to say!"

He stared at her for a minute. "Where have you been hiding from life? Oh, yes, in the convent."

"I wasn't hiding. And where have you been hiding? What are you—I don't even know your name," she said, anxious to turn the conversation away from the subject of her naiveté.

"My name is Roque."

"Roque what?"

"Roque is enough. I'm not planning on having calling cards printed here and you won't have need to introduce me to anyone. As for where I've been hiding, that's truer than you know."

"Are you hiding?" What an interesting man he was. Or was he just saying that to entertain her—or himself at her expense.

"Well, I hadn't planned to hide quite this well," he said, making a gesture that included the whole island.

She looked at him speculatively. Was he a gentleman? He seemed to be. His speech was well-bred although there was the tiniest hint of an accent that was not solidly British. "Are you English?" she asked.

He didn't answer at first and she wasn't sure he had heard. Then he said, "Half English, half Portuguese— the dangerous half."

"What do you mean?" she asked, but he ignored this question. "Are your parents living?" She was deter-

mined to find out about him, to make him talk. She
was hungry for information about him.

"My mother's dead," he answered so quietly she had
to lean closer to understand his words, "and my father's worse than dead." With that he got up and
walked away.

"Don't go!" she cried out. "Don't leave me here."

He turned back and smiled. "I'm not running away
from your nosiness. I've faced worse interrogation. I'm
going to get us something to eat. I can't face another
of those damned little berries and I lost the fish I had
when I chased you."

"You must not ask so many questions," the nuns had
told her over and over. "It is not polite." She must
curb this impulse to turn people's lives inside out and
examine them with a magnifying glass. This man,
Roque, obviously resented it and since he might be
her only companion for a very long time (maybe forever—no, don't think about it!) she did not want to
offend him.

After a while he came back with a long stick and a
sharp shell. He sat down by the side of the pool and
started whittling a sharp point on the stick. He
hummed a sad tune to himself while he worked, but
he didn't look sad. He looked—he looked, what was it?
Haunted? Perhaps that was it. From time to time he
made the slightest move to glance over his shoulder,
not moving his head far, just darting a quick look. It
had the appearance of an instinct, a long-standing
habit of caution.

Finally he finished and went down to the beach.
Pretty soon he was back with two fish. He offered her
one which she declined. Hunger had not yet con-
quered fastidiousness to the point that raw fish
seemed like a fit food to eat. Roque ate both fish and

then, as the sun started to set, he said, "Where do you sleep?"

She pointed up at the tree. "You sleep in a *tree?*" he said incredulously. "Don't you fall out, or do you hang upside down like a sloth?"

She had to laugh at the mental picture of herself hanging from a limb. "No, there's a flat space up there where the first big branch grows. I curl up there. I don't like all the invisible things that come out at night. I feel safer up there."

"Well, I don't want you falling out on me. We'll sleep down here. Now, don't look all wide-eyed like that, I don't mean together—unless you—no, never mind. Go on, my little arboreal nun, climb your tree, if you want."

He picked out a place by the side of the pool, fluffed up a bed of dead leaves, and lay down. He was asleep almost immediately. Garlanda stood around for a few minutes, trying to decide what to do, then she made a similar bed of leaves on the other side of the pool. Some conventions would have to be sacrificed to life on an island, she decided.

He did not try to kiss her again. She knew she shouldn't want him to, but really—hadn't it been harmless and interesting? He hadn't hurt her. She knew the nuns would not have approved and she tried to erase the reminder of that kiss from her mind. She failed.

He seemed amused by her. She was surprised at the ease with which he coaxed details of her own life from her. There was not much to tell. Garlanda feared she was boring him, but he kept asking her questions. She suspected his childhood had been unhappy and he was eager to hear of hers. There were few facts with which to entertain him. As a child she had lived in the country home outside London with occasional visits from her mother's sister, Aunt Althea, and even more infrequent visits from her own father. When she was six she and her mother had crossed the sea to Martinique to visit her grandparents on their plantation. Her mother had left her there to attend the convent school.

She told him endless details about the nuns and he laughed when she told him how she had climbed a tree to spy on an important visitor. The nuns had scolded her thoroughly and made her spend hours at penance. "Just think, Fleur, if they'd permitted you to climb trees, you might know a great deal about clambering about this island. What good are all those years of learning embroidery work doing you now?"

She giggled. "But, Roque, I cannot picture the sisters teaching us to fish or hunt."

At that they invented descriptions of the sisters trying to reconstruct their habits to suit travel in fishing trawlers. Garlanda experienced a guilty sense of pleasure at the image of her nuns scaling cliffs and loading guns to hunt dinner. It was so ludicrous she couldn't help but laugh until she remembered that she would never see any of the dear nuns again. At that point she dissolved with a torrent of tears while the mysterious Roque comforted her. She suspected that he even enjoyed her weeping because it offered a break in routine.

"Are you through?" he inquired after she had saturated his shirt front. She nodded, letting him dab at her tears with his sleeve. "Homesick, little flower?"

"Dreadfully. I never saw my father after I was six because he was always away when I was home, but hearing of his death hurt me all the same. And then losing Mama in that shipwreck—and now this horrible place."

"It's not so horrible. We have food and water and each other for company. After a while I'll know all your little convent stories and I can tell them to *you.*"

"You think I'm funny! You're laughing at me. You have been all along!"

"I'm not laughing at you," he said, trying to repress a broad grin. "I'm laughing at the remembrance of being young and full of life. You're so innocent and excited. You remind me of a frisky colt suddenly set free in a huge field. You love this freedom, but it makes you feel guilty."

"It's just that this is all so pagan!"

This time when he laughed it infuriated her. She hammered at him with her little fists, which brought a further burst of hilarity from him. Suddenly she hated him! He was sarcastic and cruel, pretending to be her friend and all the while laughing at her! He was a monster. She got up with terrible dignity and stalked off to the woods.

"Fleur!" he gasped, still laughing, "Oh, little flower of religion, come back. Forgive me for being so—so pagan." His laughter started up again.

Oh, that abominable man, she thought angrily. *I hate him, I hate him!* He was still calling her to come back between gasps of laughter. She kept on walking, determined not to see or speak to him for the rest of the day.

Later, as the sun sank over the molten sea, turning everything the color of her hair, she noticed a hot, pungent aroma. He was cooking fish! She tried to ignore it, but her mouth watered. *He won't lure me back to be the brunt of his humor,* she insisted to her-

self. *I'll show him! I'll stay here all night and prove I
needn't put up with his ridicule.*

She set to work fashioning a rosary from nuts and a
piece of vine. She'd fight his enjoyment of her sheltered ways. He'd cease his laughing when he saw that
she was serious and not to be altered by his opinions.
Making her laugh at the nuns! What a wicked man!

The fish scent was growing stronger. Tears of self-
pity and hunger mingled in her eyes. She returned to
the pool to splash away every trace of her misery. Her
stomach rumbled traitorously. How long since she'd
eaten anything but the monotonous berries and fruits?
Hot fish, cooked over an open fire, was too tantalizing to ignore. Garlanda knotted her strand of "beads,"
slipped them over her head, and crept stealthily toward the beach. Roque sat near a small pit dug in the
sand. He was wrapping a fish in wet leaves and carefully laying it in the smoldering pit. She watched as
he used his sharp stick to spear another fish that was
already cooked. He put that one on a pile of leaves.
"Want some food? There's far too much for me to eat.
You'll have to help me, Miss Fleur."

Still snickering at her, was he? She waited, but he
said nothing else. At last hunger overcame her. Seething with resentment and reluctance, she nevertheless walked to where he sat. He looked on expression-
less as she stiffly bent and picked up the hot fish and
carried it around to the other side of the fire where
she could eat undisturbed. It took every bit of control
she had not to rip the leaves away and cram the
smoked food in her mouth. She unwrapped it daintily,
then hunger triumphed. She turned her head away
from him so he could not see her devouring the fish,
savoring the tender white flesh as she wolfed it down.
When she had finished, he wordlessly crossed to her

side of the fire and handed her another. She took it.

"Did you make that necklace while you were off in the woods just now? You certainly are resourceful. I should like to see you in pearls someday, but for now everything suits you. Do you have any idea how lovely and wild you look with your incredible hair and all that tan flesh peeking through your rags?"

"I—I—you mustn't speak that way! It's sinful."

He took hold of her crude necklace. "Pretty. Very pretty. And unspoiled by anything or anyone." His fingers left the beads, trailing down to the torn neckline of her gown. She stiffened. His damp mouth covered hers in another of the unexpected kisses like the one he had given her the other day. She made a whimper of protest and felt it hushed under his mouth. His fingers traced the full line of her breasts, sliding the material down from her shoulders.

"Roque, no. We must not, I—what are you—oh!" He had freed her breasts from the confines of her gown. She flinched a little as he gently stroked her nipples. He slid the dress down over her hips, gave a sudden rip, and flung the scrap of dimity to the sand. Garlanda cried out, pushing at his broad, bare shoulders. He caressed her back—lightly, ever so lightly and tantalizingly. He cupped his hands over her firm buttocks and pulled her closer to his own rigid body. Then he drew back a little and stared into her eyes. She felt like a bird, transfixed by the hypnotic gaze of a snake. She wanted to look away, to pull away from him, but her body would not obey. He dropped his hand to her quivering thigh then slowly, very slowly, slid his hand between her legs. She heard a small moan of pleasure—a pleasure she had never suspected—escape her own lips. Then he was kissing her again. Garlanda felt her knees buckle. He sensed it immediately and lowered her to the ground.

No, she thought dizzily. *What is he doing? What am I letting him do? This is wrong. It must be!* She pushed ineffectually at his hairy chest. Roque's hands glided over her expertly, making her body arch against his. Her pink nipples rose, rigid with throbbing excitement and anticipation of unknown pleasure. He touched her with practised ease, exploring her trembling body intimately, making her writhe with delight and guilt. She knew what they were doing must be a mortal sin, but she seemed to be on fire, craving more and more of this splendid torment. He continued to bring her closer and closer to—to what?

He cupped her breasts and tortured them with wet tugging kisses using his teeth and tongue. His fingers coaxed fevered responses from her moist, pulsating flesh.

Suddenly Roque's body was on top of hers. He plunged into her and she was filled with a piercing pleasure-pain that made her gasp and clutch frantically at his dark hair. "No, no, stop!" The spiraling sensation gripped her entire body and she could not escape it. She was drowning in sensation. She was vaguely aware of her fingernails digging into his shoulders in an awful tangle of enjoyment and fear.

Sin was gone—there was nothing in the universe but this man—filling her, driving her mad with ecstasy. She wanted time to stop so that it would never come to an end, and the two of them could be entwined forever this way. She closed her eyes and floated on a tide of exaltation. Wave after wave of bliss crashed over her body and she was swept away.

At long last it began to subside. Garlanda remained crushed under Roque, her breath shallow and unsteady. She wondered limply at the voracity of her own needs—powerful needs she had known nothing of—allowing her to do such a thing. Gradually the love-mad woman was gone and was replaced by a frightened schoolgirl listening to a man she hardly knew croon odd foreign endearments in her ear. He kissed her soft, wounded lips with great gentleness.

"Roque—oh, no, what have we done? It was wrong. It was—"

"Hush," he said, smiling down on her. "No more of your religious quandaries. Worrying won't bring back what I've taken from you. You're lovely and you're mine now, and you know what it means to be a woman. Are you injured?"

"No, but . . ." she surrendered herself to his hungry kisses. With her still under him, he propped himself up on his elbows. She really saw him closely for the first time. His eyes were a deep winter-gray and hawklike, always alert, seeming to miss nothing. She felt him looking as intensely at her and she sensed that he found no flaw in what he saw. Her hands sought his thick black hair then she stopped. "Please, I want my dress."

"Fleur—" he began then stopped. "I can see it will do no good to try to talk to you now. Go on, little nun, fetch your dress." He rolled off her. She tried not to notice how tanned and solidly muscled his body was. He reminded her of a sleek wild stallion, smooth and dangerous and fierce when it suited him. She had to restrain herself from reaching out to stroke his glistening bronze skin.

Abruptly she dived for her gown. Where was it? A cry of dismay escaped her. In their frenzied lovemaking, her dress had been kicked onto the coals of the fire Roque had made to cook the fish. The charred mass that was once her dress was recognizable only by a familiar flowered pattern showing through the soot.

"Oh, no! What shall I do?"

He sat up, smiling, but he didn't laugh. "Take my shirt, Fleur, it's right there by you. I don't understand that it matters now, but if it makes you feel better—"

She seized the shirt. He looked on as she plunged her arms into the sleeves and clutched the front of it in belated modesty. Her print dimity frock was a charred skeleton beyond all repair. She dragged it from the fire and let it drop on the sand. She fought back tears as she looked at the wreck of her last worldly possession. Roque continued to study her intently, all trace of a smile gone.

She stood up and with head dropping, she began to walk toward the sea.

"Fleur!" His voice cut through the perfumed air. "If you feel the need to wash the taint of me off your skin, use the spring water. The ocean can be dangerous at night. The tide is unpredictable and there are hungry creatures out there—hungrier even than I am."

How had he known? She turned and walked up the beach toward the clearing. She looked back at him sitting staring out to sea. What was he thinking? Would she ever know? She doubted it.

Garlanda spent a long, dream-filled night struggling with her conscience. She knew what she had done was wrong—she knew that she had not been forced. She also knew that she would have been forced to submit, had she not done so willingly. She tried to imagine what the sisters would say to such a situation, not that she would have had the courage to discuss it with them. This was a moral dilemma that she would have to deal with herself.

Her thinking was becoming too clouded by her emotions. She was here alone and except for Roque she would have been condemned to a solitary existence, completely alone for the rest of her life. But Roque was here; he was the only other human being in her entire future. It would be insanity to insist on a morality that created an unresolvable conflict between them. She really had no choice.

The thing that disturbed her most was that a hunger had lain secret and overpowering in her soul—a need that she had never been aware of. Now awakened she could never forget the passion she had discovered within herself.

Days passed quickly. Garlanda submitted to Roque, knowing it was wrong. But it was reassuring to wake in the sun-splashed mornings and find his strong body curved against hers. But she had learned something. She could share her body with him, but not her mind—not her precious memories. She no longer spoke of the times her family had been intact. She kept private the recollections of her frail, birdlike mother and the dimly remembered, gingery-haired father who brought her dolls from foreign countries and who occasionally wrote her long letters full of questions about her life and no return addresses.

She could not bring herself to speak of her father nor of her mother's dying words. The thought of that kind man, her father, being murdered haunted her. If she hadn't been shipwrecked, if she had been a son and not a daughter—why, if she had been a son and found out such a thing she would have been free, in fact expected, to track down her father's killer and wreak vengeance.

Poor Papa, there was nothing she could do about him. Nothing but grieve and pray.

CHAPTER 4

Life, however absurd the circumstances, tends to fall into patterns and so Garlanda's life became a long, relaxed cycle of eating the game that Roque caught and the berries she picked, sleeping under the tranquil moonlight, and making love. She had set aside her guilt and regrets. Guilt was no longer functional. As for her natural concern that Roque had ruined her virtue for the man who would someday want her to be his wife—why, that was laughable. She would never see another man—never meet another human unless the hostile sea threw another victim onto their beach.

She had come to accept the fact that they might never be rescued, but Roque had not. She found that she could face peacefully the future with only him for companionship even though she would not yet admit to herself that this was love. But she could sense that Roque did not feel the same way about her. He was fond of her, that was true. He was pleasant and considerate and had genuinely worried when she got a cut on her knee that became infected. He had bathed her leg in cool spring water and held her in his arms and comforted her at night when it was especially painful. When the swelling went down he was pleased. But that was kindness, not love. Perhaps, she told herself, with time he would come to feel about her as she did about him.

She tried to restrain her curiosity about him but didn't always succeed. "What were you doing on the *Valiant?*" she asked one day.

"Traveling," he said with a half smile and a raised eyebrow.

"I'm sorry. I guess I shouldn't have asked."

"Dear Fleur, I have been asked more pointed questions than that by big ugly men with clubs in their hands. You may ask all the schoolgirl questions you like without fear that I may break into weeping and lamentations. I just don't intend to answer them," and with that he bowed over her hand and strode away humming to himself.

That night, like most, they made love by the side of the pool, and there were no more questions in her mind about his past. She lived for the present and his gentle touch. He was a tender lover, seeming to care as much for her pleasure as his. Or perhaps it was just that her pleasure intensified his. She worried, at first, that she would conceive. This disturbed her more than anything else. She could resign herself to the fact that God's design had put her on this island, but she could not imagine having children here, children who would never know civilization. Roque told her not to worry. There was a sort of seaweed that the native women in this part of the world boiled and drank the broth. As long as they drank a quantity of this brew every day, Roque told her, legend said they would remain childless. Garlanda had no idea whether this could be true, but she did as he suggested.

Part of each day they spent doing the things necessary to life. Garlanda gathered food from the trees and bushes while Roque fished or found turtles to eat.

They made a sort of hut out of the wood that Garlanda had gathered and some large rubbery leaves that grew deep in the inland part of the island. She found some other leaves that remained very soft and pliable when they dried. With sharp shells and vine tendrils she sewed them together to make herself a skirt.

Sometimes late at night she would lie in his arms in the moonlight and he would tell her stories. Not stories of his own invention usually, but stories born of an excellent education and brought to life by his vivid imagery and enthusiasm. His use of the language was extraordinary and he could slip in and out of accents like other men did hats. Garlanda wept over Ophelia's death and laughed at Roque's Shylock when he realized how Portia had tricked him.

Sometimes she found herself almost wishing that they would *not* be rescued, but no, that wasn't right to think that way. Even if she could be content with only him, Roque hungered for the world. She would see him sometimes pacing the beach, his shoulders hunched angrily as he watched the empty horizon.

Their only disagreement came about over the permanency of their living arrangements. Garlanda wanted to take the time to build the hut very strong and rainproof. "Don't waste the effort," Roque told her. "It's only temporary."

"How can you say that?"

"Very easily. We'll be rescued." He looked at her defiantly as if daring her to dispute his optimism. "They'll find me."

"Who—?" she began, but he wasn't listening. He was going back to his most frequent occupation—the accumulation of piles of firewood along the beach, just above the highwater mark. He really believed that they would be found. She didn't, but she got as excited as he did when the occasional tip of sail appeared on the horizon. Roque said they must be near a shipping lane and that sooner or later someone would sail close enough to see their fires. Every time they saw a ship, or Roque imagined he saw one, he would hurriedly rub bits of rock together and start his great piles of wood on fire. He spoke with an odd familiarity of ships. "That must have been the *Great Harry*," he would say. "Her captain is a blind fool. He wouldn't see us if he'd run aground right here on the beach." Or, "I'll wager that's the *Lucinda* going into Port Royal for careenage."

"You know so much about the sea," Garlanda said. "Are you a captain too?"

"Ah-ha, we're back to questions again. Yes, I'm a captain."

"What country do you sail for?"

"Country? I don't sail for a country. I command my own ship, for my own benefit—"

"You mean you're a—"

"Let's get some more firewood," he said, cutting off her speculations.

After they had eaten that night Garlanda wandered out onto the beach a little way. It was a languid moonlit evening with gentle tropical breezes cooled by the sea. Garlanda looked up as Roque approached. He smiled and sat down next to her in the fine white sand. "Isn't she beautiful?" he murmured, staring fixedly out into space.

Garlanda turned toward him, her bright hair stirred by the caress of the wind. "Who, Roque?"

"The sea. She's a dangerous mistress, dangerous and beautiful and unforgettable. I remember coming down the Gulf of Lions in the Balearics for the first time—that fierce wind and the waves like sheets of molten glass rising."

"You have spent a lot of time at sea, haven't you? You speak of oceans as if they were people."

"They have personalities. The Mediterranean is my favorite. She isn't tempermental like the Caribbean. The Caribbean is a wildcat, docile and lazy with all her sunny islands, but without warning there are earthquakes, hurricanes, even volcanoes. But the Mediterranean is a lady despite the deadly bora of the Adriatic or the Gulf of Lions, when the fury of the north wind falls shrieking and rips shrouds, rigging, and sails, as if the world is ending. Then there's the meltami of the Aegean—but most of the time it's blue and steady. Sailing is a law unto itself with its own odd brand of peace."

Garlanda stared lazily at the sapphire waves gently slapping the shore with a half-hearted froth of snowy foam. "It is beautiful, Roque." Then after a long silence she said, "You're so well-educated. It's odd you should have turned to the sea."

"Everything serves its purpose," he said firmly.

"But—"

"Everything, Fleur."

There was no arguing. She stretched out on the accommodating sand and stared up at a thousand stars.

Sometimes they explored the island. Garlanda had no idea how large it was, but Roque seemed to care. After each of their explorations he would get a charred stick and add what they had learned to the map he was making on a large dried leaf. Each time they went a little farther. Once they walked a long way down the beach as far as Roque's map showed, then turned and started walking inland.

They struggled through the thick tropical growth. Roque, as always, was muttering to himself and constantly turning to take note of the position of the sun. He always carried a long pointed stick and he would lift it from time to time and sight along it. This walk was particularly tiring and pretty soon Garlanda got weary of trying to keep up with his energetic, long-legged stride. She sat down in a little clearing to get her breath. She looked out to the sea spread beneath them. They had climbed quite a bit, no wonder she was tired. She sat gazing sightlessly at the white-capped blue expanse when suddenly two facts exploded in her mind at the same instant.

The first was that she wasn't sitting in a natural clearing—it was a path! A path meant humans.

The second realization was that there was another ship on the horizon and this one was headed directly toward the island!

She was on her feet looking frantically for Roque. She could hear sounds of movement farther up the hill. Did she dare call out? What if it were not Roque at all, but the beings who had made the path? She swallowed back the hysteria she could feel rising through her body. Her teeth chattered with fear and excitement. "Roque?" she whispered.

The rustling sounds stopped abruptly. She stood silent with terror. It was someone, or something else making the noise, and she had alerted them to her presence. What could she do? If she ran along the path it would silence the sound of her flight, but where would she be going? Running, possibly, right into a settlement. If she tried to run back down the hill, she would make noise and be caught. Even if she could get back to the hut, what protection was that? The only thing they possessed that approximated a weapon was the pointed stick that Roque carried.

She could not just stand here. She must take some action. As important as the threat of savages was the fact that the fires must be lit. This ship could not be allowed to pass them by. She screamed, "Roque! A ship! Where are you?"

Suddenly the underbrush was alive with noise. The towering bushes in front of her parted. Out stepped a lethally exotic savage, naked except for a reptilian loincloth and the brilliant plumage of a green and scarlet bird in his long straight blue-black hair. Intricate indigo designs were tattooed on skin the hue of old copper. His eyes were merciless as he raised his bow and arrow, calmly training them at Garlanda's heart.

Her head pounded insanely, throat dry and constricted. He made no move to kill her, only stood waiting—for what, she wondered frantically.

"Don't move, Fleur," came Roque's calm voice from somewhere behind her. "He's too close to loose the arrow. When I make my move, fall to the ground. They never travel alone, there must be more somewhere near. Their blowguns are deadlier than the arrows and for all we know there could be a dozen aimed at us this very moment."

She turned her head slightly. Leaves fluttered stealthily behind Roque. "One of them's creeping up on you," she said.

The savage aimed his arrow at Roque. Garlanda, momentarily freed from danger, thought fast. Cornered—surrounded! What would Roque do? *Roque?* she thought. *But he's the one they're watching, not me. He's dangerous, I'm not. Or so they think.*

It would depend on her whether or not they lived long enough to signal the approaching ship. Freedom! Her hands clenched at her sides. She would not come this close to salvation only to lose it.

She took a step, pretended to stumble, then came up, catching the tattooed native in the stomach with her shoulder. "DOWN!" came Roque's shout. She obeyed as the arrow was loosed. A quick roll and she was on her knees in time to see the man behind Roque stagger and clutch at the feathered end of an arrow shaft protruding from his chest.

Garlanda had fallen against a rock, and pain was bursting through her. She was fainting—she must fight it. With enormous effort she focused her vision on Roque and the remaining savage. They were circling each other, both crouched and sweating and parrying with their primitive weapons. The native's feathered plummage swung with the tilt of his powerful shoulders and he keened a gruesome wail. Whether this was an expression of sorrow at the loss of his comrade or a call for more help, she could not guess.

"Run, Garlanda. Light the fires!" Roque shouted at her without letting his eyes leave his adversary.

She couldn't run. She didn't think she could even stand without fainting. But she had to do something—something. She looked around the ground where she knelt. There was a sturdy branch on the ground next to her. She picked it up. Roque and the bizarrely tattooed Indian were still circling each other. As the savage neared her, she gathered her strength and swung the branch in a wide arc.

It hit him across the shins with a splintering crack. He paused in pain for the merest second, but it was enough. Roque lunged at that moment and Garlanda saw the man's glistening brown body roll in agony at her feet. Green nausea gripped her stomach as she stared at the man's blood spattering her legs. Roque grabbed her arm and pulled her up. "Quick! The fires!" he said, dragging her down the hill.

They struggled ever downward until they reached the beach. Roque half dragged, half carried her all the way. Her head throbbed with pain and there were ugly scratches all over her skin. Her feet were bleeding and her only clothing, Roque's shirt and her leafy skirt, were torn. Roque dropped her unceremoniously and went to work on his fires.

Garlanda sat on the gritty sand, panting with pain and exhaustion. The ship was still out there, still heading in their direction. When Roque finally got one of his fires going, she limped over to it and took one flaming stick out. She carried it carefully down the beach and ignited the next pile of wood. Satisfied that it had caught, she carried her stick on to the next fire, the last in the row.

She ran back to Roque and stood by him as he shaded his eyes and squinted out to sea. He had forgotten her, all he could see was the ship moving majestically closer. Roque began to shout, cupping strong brown hands around his mouth. Garlanda followed suit. Finally there was a tiny puff of smoke at the side of the ship and a moment later the sound of the cannon fire reached them. "They see us!" Garlanda screamed. "They see us!"

"*La Doña del Fuego,*" Roque said reverently. "I knew they would find me." But he wasn't speaking to her, she realized. He was talking to himself. Why had it happened so suddenly? She wanted time to talk to him, to tell him how she felt, to discuss their future— or did they have a future off this island?

Why was there no time! The ship was near enough now to start lowering a small boat over the side. Garlanda could see sailors struggling for the chance to get on it, to be part of the rescue party. She turned to Roque and touched his arm. He tore himself away from contemplation of the ship and looked deeply into her eyes with unfathomable intensity. "Eden is over, little flower," he said.

Was there sorrow in his voice? The strange, unreasoning sorrow that she felt too? Or was it simply dismissal of the months they had shared together?

Suddenly the past swept over Garlanda in a tidal wave of lost respectability. She had buried the past in the present—put aside her convent morality, her English manners, her womanly reserve. And now in the space of an instant, the time it took to say, "Eden is over, little flower," she was again what she had been only a few months before—an Englishwoman stranded here with a strange man who had robbed her of her honor, her virtue. Everything that had made her valuable on the marriage market—her innocence, her untainted past, her creamy white skin—all was gone.

She was suddenly ashamed of her long brown legs showing beneath her leafy skirt, of her flaming hair haloing her face in wild disarray. She turned and ran to the hut. She had to have one more precious moment of this life before she surrendered herself to the strong arms of civilization.

She watched as the small boat was pulled up on the beach and the men jumped out to greet Roque. They knew him and it was apparent that they were all pleased to see him. It seemed that they were all in awe of him as well. There was something slightly obsequious in the way they regarded him. Backs were slapped, rough language was bandied carelessly, and a stone jug was passed from mouth to mouth. She had been forgotten.

As she watched them they suddenly got quiet and several of the rough sailors pointed down the beach. Then suddenly Roque was running toward the hut calling her name—no, not *her* name—he was calling for "Fleur." The men were quickly pulling the boat back into the sea. Roque dashed in the doorway and grasped her arm. "The natives are back. Hurry!"

They ran for the boat, all Garlanda's modesty and reserve set aside for the moment. Strong arms helped her into the boat and for a fleeting instant she had a strange sense of déjà vu before she realized that this had actually happened before. The sailors ignored her as they frantically pulled at the oars. Others raised muskets and fired at the wild savages on the beach. Roque barked out orders which were instantly obeyed. No question about it. He was the master of these men, just as he had been her master. Most of the natives fell back at the sound of gunpowder, a few waded into the water and tried to follow them, but the small boat quickly outdistanced them.

As they neared the large ship, Garlanda could see the figurehead and understood the name of the vessel. The figurehead was a carved lady with high, white breasts, classic profile, and a wreath of red hair. *La Doña del Fuego*—the Lady of Fire. Hadn't Roque called her that once?

A rope ladder was lowered to them and they followed Roque up and onto the deck of the ship. Roque was immediately enveloped in the arms of his comrades and Garlanda was left standing at the rail with two or three of the sailors eyeing her lecherously. Then a silence fell and the men surrounding Roque fell back a little. A woman appeared at the door of the captain's cabin.

She was a dark beauty with reddened lips and night-black eyes. She had on a blouse that cut very low, exposing large firm-looking breasts. She wore a short bandana fabric skirt that emphasized her tiny waist and voluptuous hips. "Well, cap'n," she said in a low voice, "we were about to give you up for dead."

Roque put his hands on his hips and laughed a throaty chuckle. "Would you have been faithful to my memory?"

A red-haired giant in a threadbare kilt called out, "Aye, captain, the fair lass wore herself out praying for ye—on her back!"

"Shut up, McGowery, 'tis a celibate Scots bastard you are," the woman mocked his accent.

"Come here, Sabelle," Roque said over the roar of the sailor's laughter.

The woman sauntered boldly to where he stood. She twined her plump, smooth arms around his neck and kissed him long and passionately. He didn't move. She drew back, smiling and stood beside him with one arm around his waist. "The master is back!" she shouted.

The sailors cheered and someone rolled out a keg of rum. One of them started squeezing music out of a small accordion and an impromptu dance started up. But no one payed any attention to Garlanda. She stood staring at Roque, who now had his arm over Sabelle's shoulder and his hand resting carelessly inside her blouse. Garlanda felt herself flush with shock. The woman did nothing! She just stood there in front of all those men as if it were nothing out of the ordinary. Roque too seemed almost unaware of it. He laughed and talked with the men and went on caressing her like a man might handle a key ring—absently and without notice.

Garlanda's stomach churned. She had prayed to be rescued and now that her prayers had been answered she was miserable. She had been wrenched from her tropical paradise and now her lover, her friend, her man was in the arms of another woman. *It is plain that he does not care for me*, she thought with hurt bitterness. *He used me. It's all over, the warmth, the fun, the caring. I'm used goods, used and discarded. God only knows what will happen to me now. I'm little better than a prisoner.* She held her head very high and blinked back the tears that threatened to spill over.

Finally Roque bent and whispered something to Sabelle. She drew back and looked around. Then her eyes found Garlanda. "Her?" she asked. "I will not!"

"You will," Roque said coldly, "or I'll put you off on that island. The natives would find you delicious."

"Yes, master." Sarcasm dripped from her voice. She pulled away from him and strolled arrogantly over to Garlanda. "Follow me," she ordered, leading the way to the captain's cabin. As they neared the door of the cabin a young man with rotting teeth reached out and touched Garlanda greedily. Tears of dismay came to her eyes and she cringed away from him.

"She's mine!" Roque barked and the man froze in place. Silence came over the ship as Roque went on, "There's a cat-o-nine-tails waiting for anyone who touches her. Do you all understand?" The men nodded dumbly and the man melted back into the mass of men.

The music resumed as Sabelle opened the door and rudely shoved Garlanda inside. The room was beautiful, it was hard to believe that just outside was a rough wooden deck and dirty sailors. The walls were paneled with rich, chocolate-colored wood with a linenfold motif. The fittings were burnished brass that shone of years of daily polishing. There was a wide desk with maps and charts rolled and neatly filed in pigeonholes. Across the opposite wall were the sparkling leaded windows of the aftercastle. The afternoon sun shone hotly on a large bed with a luxurious red taffeta quilt.

There were cabinets and drawers built into the walls with porcelain Tudor roses for pulls. Sabelle was rummaging in one of the drawers. She flung some worn garments on the bed and went to the door. Three men stood outside with a large copper tub and other men behind them with buckets of steaming water. They pulled the tub into the room and the men filed through, each pouring in his bucket of water and leaving without looking at either of the women.

When the tub was nearly full Roque came in. Sabelle had been standing aside with her arms folded and an expression of distaste on her beautiful face. Roque walked past her and looked at the clothes she had gotten out. "These are discards, Belle. Selfishness ill becomes you." He smiled at her, but there was something cold and determined in the smile. "Get out the best."

"Get it out yourself, you lily-livered Episcopalian deck-swabber," Sabelle said.

In spite of herself Garlanda let escape an indelicate snort of laughter. She bit her cheeks to keep from smiling. She didn't dare meet Sabelle's eyes for fear of bursting into laughter. Roque looked from one to the other of them, drew himself up with offended dignity, and went to a small drawer. He started selecting soaps and scents. He handed them to Garlanda without looking at her. Opening a silver-encrusted glass bottle, he poured the sweet smelling powder it contained into the bath water. "You—out," he said to Sabelle, "—and you, in." He gestured to Garlanda and then the tub of water.

Sabelle strolled out with a defiant toss of her raven hair. Roque followed her to the door. He stopped and turned back to look at Garlanda for a moment. "Fleur," he said quietly as if savoring the word, then he was gone.

Garlanda was beyond thinking, beyond considering what was happening. She stripped off her skirt of which little remained. She pulled Roque's shirt over her head and stepped into the tub. Vapors of steamy exotic perfume enveloped her and she slipped deeper into the soapy water. She sat there for a long time, mindlessly reveling in the clean English smell of hot, fresh water. She washed her long hair and scrubbed every inch of her slender body. Finally the water began to cool and she realized what a long time she had been there. She stepped out and wrapped herself in the heavy, absorbent length of toweling that had been left beside the tub. She was looking over the clothing that Sabelle had reluctantly put on the bed for her when she remembered the shirt—Roque's shirt—the one he had given her when—

She dipped the tattered shirt into the bath water and washed it carefully, as if it were fine silk. It was the only tangible memory she had of the last few idyllic months. She would keep it and later, when the re-

membrance of "Eden," as Roque had called their island, had faded to scrapbook yellow, she could look at
the shirt and recall the taste of mangoes and moonlit
lovemaking.

She looked longingly at the bed. It was too tempting to resist. It was barely dusk, but she was so tired!
She pulled back the red quilt and the soft wool blanket and slid naked between the soft sheets. She was
exhausted now that the fear of the natives' attack and
the thrill of rescue had ebbed. Her head hurt and
there was a heavy weight in her chest.

I've got to think, she told herself sternly. *I've got to!
What will I do now? I had resigned myself to life on
the island. I had to live the way I did when we were
stranded there. I thought we would never see other
people again. But now—*

But now what? Garlanda sat up, knuckles to her
mouth. Roque had been *her* man and now he was an
efficient stranger with the mantle of command riding
regally on his shoulder. She wanted to cry for him and
for the loss of what they had known together, but she
was too weary. Tears would not come.

*But I—I think I love him. He can't be gone from me
like this. What will I do? If he does not want me, then
I am ruined for a future husband. Where will I go?
Who will want me now? Oh, he must marry me. He
must or I am lost! He'll come back and we'll talk
about this*, she tried to convince herself. *He's a good
man, he'll do the proper thing by me, won't he?*

But she knew he wouldn't marry her. He was a man
of the sea, his women were oceans whose beauty he
loved and spoke of so eloquently. He had been fond
of her on the island, perhaps he still was, but then she
had been the only other person there. An artificial
bond, now broken.

She couldn't think anymore. Her body sagged and she slid down under the covers in the bone-weary sleep of one who had come a long distance and had farther still to travel.

CHAPTER 5

There was a discreet tap at the door. At first Garlanda incorporated it into her dreams, but it repeated and she was suddenly awake. She sat up and pulled the covers up to her chin. "Come in?" she called timidly.

A man she had not seen before came in the door. He was bent and gray-haired yet somehow spritely. He carefully did not look at her but said to a point just above her left shoulder, "I'll have the men remove the tub now, if that is satisfactory, Miss Fleur?"

"Yes, that would be fine."

"I'm Sebastian Sim, Miss. I'm the ship's surgeon. If you need anything, just let me know. Have you had anything to eat?"

"No," Garlanda admitted. She was surprised at the dignity and education apparent in the man's demeanor.

"I'll see that something is sent up for you. We've been at sea for a long time. I can't guarantee that there's anything edible on board. But we're making for Port Royal, there'll be fresh food then."

When he'd gone, Garlanda decided that she really should dress, no matter how much she was loath to wear Sabelle's garments. She forced herself to leave the feathery comfort of the bed and put on the dress. It was shocking, truly tasteless to her convent-trained

mind. It was blazing red crushed velvet—sinfully flamboyant—and the plunging neckline forced the tops of
her breasts to spill over the edge of the bodice. She
was startled by the way the gown reduced her waist
to nothingness before flaring out alluringly over her
hips. Yards and yards of opulent fabric had gone into
making the splendid ball gown, and she found herself
wondering why Sabelle had parted with something so
obviously treasured by a woman of that nature.

Then she remembered Sabelle's overly voluptuous
figure and giggled. Half of that painted female
wouldn't fit in it. There was a full-length mirror near
the bed. Garlanda had never seen such a treasure before and she stared at the woman reflected in it. The
only looking glass she had been allowed at school had
been a small, age-speckled oval which was wavy and
distorted her reflection. She looked at the woman in
the red dress across the room. Why—she was pretty!
Actually pretty, even in this garish dress. Of course
she was much too brown, entirely unfeminine, and
lacked the plump proportions that were the ideal, but
there was nothing to do about that. She wondered
what Roque would think of her in this dress.

She would wonder for a long time. A sailor brought
her a tray of breakfast. The tray was rust and black
cloisonné, elaborately scrolled and detailed. The plate
was delicate white bone china and the glass was a
feather-light crystal goblet, but the food was practically unrecognizable. There was something leathery
and highly spiced that Garlanda supposed was salted
beef strips, and a glutinous lump of white stuff that
must have once been rice. A dried up wedge of lemon
completed the meal. The wine, fortunately, was delicious and it had to serve as breakfast.

A different sailor came back an hour or so later to

retrieve the tray. He looked surprised that the food was untouched but said nothing. She almost asked him where Roque was but decided against it. She had an idea she knew where he was. Her vivid imagination, now schooled in the intimacies between man and woman, told her he was with Sabelle, doing the same things he had done with her. She felt a sharp stab of something that a wiser woman would have labeled jealousy. Her chin went up. She must appear brave despite her inner turmoil. She had to talk to him. Find out what he intended to do with her now that she had been ruined for decent men. Would he do the honorable thing? After all, what they had done was a sin. She tried not to remember the eager way her body had responded to his during those hot tropical nights.

She passed the long morning examining the cabin and when lunchtime passed without any food arriving she took a nap. She felt like a prisoner in an invisible cell. She could, of course, walk out onto the deck. But what might greet her? Another boy to try to embrace her—more leering sailors? No, she would wait here. Eventually Roque would remember her or someone would recall that she was here.

It was late in the afternoon before the door opened and Roque strode in. No knock—no warning. The "bath" entourage trailed in behind him, filled the familiar copper tub, and disappeared. Garlanda was thirsty enough to drink the bath water and was pleased to see that Roque had a bottle of wine with him. He ignored her, rummaging through drawers and whistling to himself. Finally he turned up two glasses and set them and the wine on the table by Garlanda. "Pour us some," he said. Then he began undressing. He peeled off his filthy, worn clothing as if she weren't even there. She sat staring at him with disbelief.

Had the man no modesty at all? Did he think they were still on the island? She found herself almost admiring his strong brown physique. Suddenly in the luxurious but compact ship's cabin he seemed larger— his shoulders seemed broader. He walked over to her and picked up his glass of wine. He threw his head back and drank deeply.

She had learned to accept his body using hers, she knew that his touch released something sinful and untamed in her, but for the first time she found herself craving his touch—more than that—wanting to touch him. Without conscious volition she put her hand to his strong neck and could feel the pulse pounding in rhythm to her own heart.

He finished drinking and set down his glass. He took her hand and kissed the palm but as she drew closer to him he backed away. "Not now, Fleur. No time." He stepped into the tub without regard to the water that slopped over onto the floor.

She couldn't bear it! She had never felt greater embarrassment. She must be hopelessly steeped in sin. She went to the window and sat staring out gritting her teeth to prevent the tears from flowing. What had happened to her? He splashed and whistled and she refused to turn her head. There was a knock at the door. "Come in!" Roque bellowed.

A man Garlanda hadn't seen before entered. He wore a yellow silk waistcoat with filthy lace at the cuffs, an oversized tricorne hat, and more jewels than Garlanda had ever seen in one place. He was thin-lipped and intense and Garlanda involuntarily shivered a little at the sight of him. "Port Royal sighted, cap'n."

"Thank you, Kidd. Tell the men we'll be here for a

week for provisions and whatever they fancy. Only half the crew off board at a time. It's very near dead calm so I don't want to risk anchoring too near the harbor. Might not get back out."

"There's a French fleet out there, too. At least they look French from here," Kidd said.

"Wonder what those bastards are up to now? Well, all the more reason to keep our distance. You and I'll go in tonight, leave Sebastian and Sabelle in charge. It's up to you who goes in first."

"I've got my eye on a few that's getting a mite friendly with the cabin boys. I'll send them in first. They need it."

"No women on board, you know," Roque said.

Kidd cast an appraising eye over Garlanda, grinned and said, "Aye, sir."

Roque ignored this jab. "I meant bawds, not ladies. Now, go on."

"Who was that?" Garlanda asked after the man had left.

"That's our quartermaster, William Kidd," Roque answered.

"But why is he dressed like that?"

Roque shrugged. "It suits him, I guess. Next to the captain, the quartermaster is the most important man on the ship. He likes to make sure everyone remembers it, I suppose." He got out of the tub and Garlanda averted her eyes.

The door flew open and Sabelle came in. "Port Royal," she said breathlessly. Neither she nor Roque seemed to particularly notice that he was naked, but Garlanda was burning with embarrassment.

"I know. Kidd's been here," Roque said, taking some clothing out of a drawer.

"I've got to go in and get some clothes," Sabelle said, eyeing Garlanda in her red dress.

Roque pulled on tawny brown breeches with silver buckles at the knees. "It'll have to wait. I'm leaving you and Sebastian in charge while Kidd and I go in."

"Then why don't you just leave Kidd there and let me—"

"Belle, we've been through all that before. I can't sail with a woman quartermaster."

"Don't you think I know as much as he does about running a ship?"

"Of course you do, probably more, but it just wouldn't work. Where've you put my shirts?"

"Guess," she said and walked out. Garlanda peered out to sea. It was getting dark and she could see tiny glimmers of light from the port. When she looked back at Roque he was dressed in a white satin shirt and had a yellow bandana tied around his dark hair. A gold earring adorned his left ear. Garlanda had never truly realized that he was a pirate, not a gentleman captain, until she saw him this way.

"Is there anything you want me to bring you?" He asked.

"Can't I go along?" she asked.

"To Port Royal—? A convent girl—? No. It would be too much for you." He walked out the door without a backward glance.

It was a very long week. Garlanda stayed in her cabin, or rather, Roque's cabin, as she reminded herself. Sabelle stopped in a few times to get items of clothing out of the drawers. Sebastian checked on

Garlanda's welfare twice, and she thought he was probably responsible for the improvement in the menu. Fresh fruit began to appear on her tray. She heard McGowery singing drunken Scottish ballads late one night and was tempted to invite him in to sing them to her, but she refrained. Who could tell what a drunk McGowery might do with such an invitation?

Finally, after six of the longest days in her entire life, Garlanda looked out the window and saw the small boat nearing them with Roque on board. She hurriedly brushed her hair and pinched some color into her cheeks. She was smoothing a few of the worst wrinkles out of the skirt of the red dress when he came in the cabin.

"Roque, I have to go in town!" she announced.

"No, I told you."

"I don't care. I haven't even got one chemise, and I haven't had any decent food since we left the island. You can blindfold me if you want, but I must go in town."

"She's right," Sabelle's voice cut in. "Roque, you can take us in now. We aren't leaving until tomorrow and probably not even then if there's no more wind than there is now." She walked in and sat down on the bed. "If I don't get a new dress, I'll have to wear McGowery's kilt—if I could get it off him," she said sourly.

Roque laughed. "I give up. Is Kidd back?"

"Yes, he came back just before you did," Sabelle said.

"I'll tell him he's in charge. Is he sober?"

"Sort of."

"Get ready, we'll go as soon as I clear a few things with him."

Sabelle let out a whoop and started rummaging for something to wear in one of Roque's drawers. "Say, let's take McGowery along."

Garlanda stepped timidly from the small boat. Port Royal, "Sin Capital" of the Caribbean, unfolded before her like a decadent tapestry. The strident voices of vendors filled the air as they hawked their wares. One brandished a large crustacean under her nose.

"Ugh! What is it?" she cried as the wiggling creature waved clenched claws at her.

"Fresh lobster, my dear," Roque told her with an amused smile. "Haven't you seen a live one before?"

"No. I had no idea where lobster meat came from."

"Come see the fighting crabs," Sabelle urged. "The loser goes in the pot."

The black-haired woman leaned over the fighting pit. Garlanda joined her, staring in horrified fascination as two enormous crabs circled each other warily. The smaller of the two, a battle-scarred veteran, seized the unmarked challenger in his pincers and tore a tentacle off, gouging out an eye. The half-blinded crab staggered about madly, finally running into the side of the sand pit. The smaller crab moved in with fierce dedication. Garlanda closed her eyes. When she opened them the scent of boiling crab filled the air and the victor was being lowered into a wooden cage. He caught his owner's forefinger in a bloody grip and was struck with a heavy stick. At last he surrendered the finger and dropped down to the dank confines of his cage.

Sabelle threw a few coins to a vendor and took a lobster tail from him. She tore at the steaming white meat with strong teeth, then stopped the vendor's assistant, a ragged urchin, to dip the tail in his bowl of hot, spiced butter. Garlanda looked on.

"M-m-m, delicious. Want some, cap'n? Or you, McGowery?"

The Scottish giant backed up a bit. "Ach, no, lady. But thankee kindly. I fancy a stiff tankard o' rum more 'n anything at the moment."

Roque signaled to a hawker selling steamed scallops. He handed some to Garlanda, then took an ample helping for himself. "Hoot, mon," Roque said, cheerfully mocking McGowery's thick brogue, "dinna ye crave some food, laddie?"

"I dinna crave noothin' bu' rum, sir," McGowery informed him.

Roque slapped him on the back. "Come, then. Let's find you some liquid fire to liven up those sea-weary bones of yours. Sabelle! Stop haggling with that urchin and come along or we'll leave you."

Garlanda picked at the scallops fastidiously. She was too excited to fully appreciate the hot, tender scallops in their wrapping of bay leaves and lemon. Grease soaked through the thin paper holding them all together. Sabelle told her to eat quickly before the grease completely broke through and ruined her gown, at which warning Garlanda made a face and shoved three of the scallops into the partially denuded tail of the other woman's lobster. Sabelle grinned and popped them into her mouth.

Muscular Jamaicans passed them, wearing the bright trousers that distinguished them from the wharf slaves. Merchants bellowed at tardy captains as heavily laden ships were unloaded. Sailors freed from duty came racing down the unloading ramps, whooping and shouting in anticipation of the town's entertainment. Women waited at the end of the ramps—gaudily dressed, painted females who minced and twirled lacy parasols to signal their availability. Garlanda was shocked at the readiness with which the women accepted the dirty, unshaven men. Several of the fancier prostitutes had smart carriages waiting, with liveried Negroes holding the reins to spanking pairs of bays.

"Your eyes are as big as saucers, little one. Haven't you ever seen a businesswoman at work?" Sabelle asked tauntingly. Garlanda didn't answer. Roque roared with laughter while McGowery gave Garlanda a pitying look.

They went on, weaving through the dock workers until they found their way blocked by a drunken privateer sitting on a great cask of rum. He doffed a tricorne with a crippled plume at the women. "Ladies, you may pass for a kiss, but I'm afraid these gentlemen must drink at least one round with me afore I'll see them on their way."

"We would be mightily honored," Roque said. He was no doubt swayed into a comradely show by the brace of pistols aimed at his abdomen. He took a hearty swig from the earthenware mug on the cask, then passed the mug to McGowery. The Scotsman not only drained it, but asked for another.

"I ain't feeling *that* friendly," the drunk snapped, yanking the cup away. McGowery shoved him, which sent the big man sprawling. He was unconscious before he hit the ground. Sabelle stooped, slashed his money purse from his belt with a dagger, and placed his hat on her head. She stepped over the snoring hulk. "To the taverns, *mes amis!*"

They followed her. She took them to a bustling pub where a blue sign with a crudely painted dragoon

proclaimed the place to be Kingsman. Roque pushed
his way in first, the rest of the entourage trailing
along in his wake. He and McGowery walked over to
a table where two drunks were sleeping with their
heads on the table. Roque and McGowery deposited
them roughly on the floor and took over the table.
"Four tankards of your best rumfustian!" Roque
shouted. A buxom barmaid ambled over to them.
Roque glanced at Garlanda and said, "Make that three
rumfustians and some Madeira."

"Rumfustian," Sabelle said in a scornful voice.
"Fetch me a stout rum and gunpowder, lass, and make
it sharp or I'll have your ears."

"Back off, bawd, or I'll float a dead rat in it."

Sabelle gave an indignant "harumph," but seated
herself at the rough oaken table. A teetering, eye-
patched rogue approached their table. "Pardon meself, mates, but I ain't seen women this purty in many
a year."

"They're not up for barter," Roque said calmly, but
his hand was playing along the hilt of his Toledo cutlass.

"I ain't lookin' to buy 'em, mate. I'm willing t'pay to
plant a quick kiss on this bonny beauty's brow, and
then another from the little 'un with the fire hair."

"Whaddya have to barter for such a kiss?" Sabelle
demanded. The wobbling sailor held up a leather
pouch. He jiggled it, but there were no clinks of coins
inside. Seeing their expressions, he poured the pouch
out in his cupped hand. A queen's ransom in jewels
sparkled up at them.

"First the kiss, my full-rigged lass, then you take
your choice." Sabelle flung her arms around his neck
and kissed him enthusiastically. She rubbed against
him, backing him against the wall and sliding her

hands over his trembling form. Her companions grinned among themselves as her deft fingers entered his pockets, cleaned them out and deposited the goods in the startled Garlanda's lap. She scooped her skirts over them in fright, remembering the penalties thieves paid back in England.

When Sabelle released her prey, he was red-faced with pleasure. "Well worth it, me beauty. Now take yer pick." He held out the hand full of jewels. The smiling woman selected a walnut-sized emerald and clenched it in her fist. Then she gave the drunk another quick kiss that left him reeling. He finally turned to Garlanda. "A lady, ain't you? You ain't no pirate wench, not all purty and fray-jile like that. I seen ladies like you once, they was in a carriage comin' from court."

"She's a disguised duchess," Roque told him in a conspiratorial whisper. McGowery nearly gagged. Garlanda turned a furious glare on Roque then blushed as the rum-glutted rogue went down on one knee with a clumsy flourish of a nonexistent hat.

"Permit me to kiss one a' them lily-white hands, duchess." He did so as respectfully as if paying homage to a great lady. Garlanda felt humbled as he rose and held out the hand with the jewels.

"N—no, I couldn't," she stammered.

"I ain't got no use for them. I'd just spent them on a pack of doxies. Take them to get ye home, purty little lady." He dumped the jewels in her hand, set the pouch on the table, and tottered away.

"Don't look so impressed," Sabelle sneered. "In Port Royal gems like those can be gone through on drink alone before sundown. Maudlin old sot! Personally, I would have gotten a riding horse or a fine brace of swords and pistols with the loot. Pass me my goods under the table, little one. Here's a bandana to tie it up in."

Garlanda obeyed. Their drinks arrived as she poured the gems back into the man's pouch. There were stones of all sizes and colors, but she had no time to look at them now. She put them in the pouch, then glanced about her uneasily.

"Hang it around your neck so that even if some cut-purse slits the strap, it'll fall down the front of your gown and be caught in your chemise."

"I—er—"

"Haven't got one?" Sabelle asked unconcernedly. "Don't fret. Finish off that swill they're passing off as Madeira and let's be on our way before the good captain changes his mind about our expedition. Jump, girl! We've got to get to Master Browning's by noon to find what we need before the whores run over there on siesta and get all the best gowns.

Garlanda had little choice but to do as she was told. She grimaced at the bitter dreg-laden liquid, then put it down with an emphatic bang. "I'm ready."

Roque pitched a bag of coins at them. "Here's to help with your buying."

"No, thank you, we've got our own," Sabelle told him saucily. She took Garlanda by the arm and steered her toward the door.

"Queen of the Caribbean at sundown," Roque shouted. Sabelle tipped her purloined hat at him, slipped her plump arm through Garlanda's, and started down the street.

"What's the Queen of the Caribbean?" Garlanda asked. "Is it a ship?"

"No, little one, it's a tavern where they serve the best food available in this scum pit."

"You don't like Port Royal? I find it—interesting."

"It may be interesting, but it holds bad memories for me," Sabelle said.

"Bad memories?"

"Watch your port side, child."

A pair of hands closed over Garlanda's left breast as if they considered it a handle to carry her off by. She screamed and lashed out indignantly. One of her feet caught her molester on the shin with bruising force. She scrambled away from him and latched onto her companion's arm.

"We must get a dagger for you to defend yourself. Methinks Captain Roque would be unhappy with me if I allowed some lusty buck to sweep you off your angelic little feet. Come along, girl. Is that the fastest you can move?"

CHAPTER 6

They strode along in the dust kicked up by passing carriages. Flashily clad prostitutes glared at them from open buggies and urged their drivers to go faster. Shrill laughter and loud male voices blared from the doorways of the taverns facing the dirt lane. The two women crossed to a cobblestone lane, hot beneath their feet, then around the corner to a brick street.

"I've a fancy to take a carriage, what say you?" Sabelle asked with the first honest smile Garlanda had seen on her.

"Yes, let's." They flagged down a red leather uphol- stered dog cart driven by a disreputable lout in a uni- form trimmed with drooping gold braid. Sabelle poured the required number of silver pieces from her stolen purse into the grubby outstretched hand. Gar- landa gasped at the fee. "Everything is five times higher in Port Royal than the rest of the world," Sa- belle explained. "Driver! To Master Browning's ware- house at once."

They settled back against the worn cushions, and Sabelle began to point out various landmarks. "There's Saint Paul's Church, the one with the great spire, and over there, if you strain your eyes, you can see Fort Carlisle. Look, there's Madame Pomparo's sporting house. They say she has mirrors in pewter frames as tall as a man in each room, and her girls wear the latest velvets and watered silks. Fort James is out of view, but it's over there to the right. Hurry, driver, I saw a ship pull up to Browning's wharf not two hours ago, and that means he has jewelry and bolts of fabrics for sale. If we're lucky, he's brought some stolen gowns that might fit us. I got some beautiful underdrawers from him once. They were maroon satin and had rows and rows of pink lace."

It was reassuring to know that even though Sabelle's behavior sometimes bordered on mannish, she still had a love of fancy clothes and adornments. Garlanda felt herself warming to this strange, roughly feminine pirate. They put their heads together, discussing what the latest fashions might be. Garlanda, cut off from the world at the convent, was as ignorant of the latest modes as Sabelle, who probably hadn't seen a European city in years.

"One thing I do know is that lace is more stylish than ever," Sabelle said. "Everything drips with it—gowns, shifts, hats, even the men's shirts. Venetian is considered the best and lace that comes from Flanders is also high quality. Of course, it wouldn't do us much good to be decked out in the latest rage from Paris, considering the louts we're sailing with. Even if we did find some lovely fabrics or gowns—well, I can't sew a stitch, let alone alter a ball gown."

"We can be pretty just for us," Garlanda cried, inspired. "After being on that island I crave a silk dress and silverware instead of wearing rags and eating with my fingers."

"And a tablecloth of the finest damask that rascal Browning has in stock," Sabelle added. "Ye Gods, but I am tired of living like a savage."

They were in perfect accord by the time they got to Browning's huge storehouse. "We'll get ourselves the latest fashions from Paris."

It was the second time Garlanda noticed the other woman pronouncing "Paris" with an "e" sound on the end rather than sounding the "s." It was a French pronunciation, not English. She wondered about Sabelle's background. It must be at least as colorful as her clothes. But Garlanda had learned better than to ask.

"If you were serious about not knowing how to sew, Sabelle, I could teach you."

"I don't take favors," the female buccaneer said with a haughty toss of her raven curls.

"It wouldn't be a favor, it would be a trade. There's so much about shipboard life I don't understand. You could teach me, you're so well-versed in the ways of sailing. Please would you? I could be your protégé." Garlanda wondered at her own charity. She had no desire to do anything but cower in the hold during the Atlantic crossing, but if she could soothe Sabelle's touchy pride with a lie and thus make life more pleasant for herself, she would do it. Besides, it was too late to back out now.

They examined bolts of exquisite watered silk and selected lengths of it for dresses. Garlanda pointed out that they would be foolish to buy anything but durable material for underfashions, but nonetheless, along with bolts of sturdy muslin they purchased flowered satin and silks from the Orient. Garlanda bought bundles of lace, embroidery thread, heavy sewing thread, and needles. She haggled over the price of two pairs of scissors and bullied the clerk into accepting a low bid on some linen. Both women were pleased with their purchases.

Master Browning himself showed them into a smaller room. The walls were hung with dresses. Garlanda forced herself not to think about where they had come from and selected a lavender brocade gown. There were traveling chests full to overflowing with chemises and petticoats. Sabelle emerged from one of the chests with a combination that made Garlanda wince.

The noonday rush of amply ornamented ladies of misfortune had begun. Garlanda and Sabelle, package-laden and happy, left the coolness of Master Browning's warehouse. Sabelle took a bottle of wine from a street vendor, tossed him a few pieces of eight, and they continued to the next warehouse where they spent hours selecting shoes, hats, and gloves. It was well past sundown by the time they arrived at the Queen of the Caribbean, recklessly attired in their new finery and mildly intoxicated.

Street loafers scrambled to help them down from the rented buggy in hope of earning a few coins. Sabelle sent them flying with a shower of blows from her Japanese parasol. They entered the inn with a swish of full skirts, arms full of purchases, essence of rose clinging to their garments. One of Roque's servants was near the door. They thrust their packages at him and told him to take their things back to the ship. Roque, seated at a table by the door, signaled the man to be on his way.

Garlanda was surprised at the change in Roque. His hair had been neatly trimmed and was drawn back at the nape of his neck with an inconspicuous ribbon. A freshly laundered linen shirt, obviously new, and not a proper fit, graced him as did slim black breeches and high boots. She wondered if he was as hot as she was in the swelter of this sultry Jamaican evening. "A toast to our lovely ladies," he said. McGowery staggered to his feet.

"Drat, the Scotsman's drunk. It's little action I fear I'll be seeing this night," Sabelle complained.

"Don't worry, Belle," Roque said. "That dress is enough to sober anyone up."

"What do you mean by that?" she asked belligerently.

"Nothing. Sit down and let's eat."

They seated themselves to an oddly constructed meal. Some of the eating utensils were gold-plated, the rest were silverware with ivory or mother-of-pearl handles. Garlanda particularly admired Roque's place setting—enameled Oriental porcelain with crystal-handled silver. When he saw her face he exchanged things with her, commenting on the trivialities that amused women, and how vital it was to keep women amused. Garlanda said nothing, but smiled at being relieved of her clumsy pewter plate and hefty silver tankard, which she could hardly lift. The etched glass goblet was light in her fingers and if she ignored the mismatched settings on the table and only looked at what she herself was eating with, she could almost believe she was at one of the finer tables of Europe.

The smells of spicy broiled seafood filled the air along with the mouth-watering aroma of roast pork and hot mutton. Food was served heaped high on pewter platters—lamb on beds of seaweed and basil, veal sautéed in rosemary, butter, and white wine, lobster whole in the shell, fat crabs, turtle soup, scallops on mountains of steaming rice, spiced wine, rum punch, cheap port disguised as Madeira, chunks of just-baked bread, and a pyramid of lemon and lime slices.

Garlanda applied her fork with the best of them.

Delicious odors wafted through the damp air, filling her nostrils and blotting out the stench of sweat, moldering trash, and cheap cologne. She let the uninhibited gluttony of the others infect her. The sheer sensual pleasure of not having to go hungry overcame her other senses. She gave her hunger free rein. The rum punch flowed freely.

Several hours later she was under a star-spangled night listening to McGowery at the other end of the dog cart tripping over the resonant syllables of an old Gaelic fighting song. Her head was cozily cushioned against Roque's shoulder, then he was kissing her with those deep irresistible kisses she knew so well. His fingers slid down the front of her fancy gown, unlacing her stays and loosening the ribbon holding her chemise together in front.

"Wait till we're alone," he whispered in response to her soft protests. She abandoned herself to his tingling caresses, letting the rhythm of hooves on cobblestones lull her into a dreamy sense of security. But they weren't to be alone.

Soon they were at an inn, Sabelle lustily bartering with the innkeeper for a room. Garlanda could barely stand. She had never had this much to drink before and she had to let Roque support her, the spicy masculine scent of him teasing her nostrils as she leaned against him. The four of them climbed a rickety staircase to a dark room.

"Zounds, this place produces evil effects upon one's nose," Sabelle complained. She unfastened the wooden shutters and flung them open to admit the fresh night air. A faint breeze stirred the ghostly lace curtains. In years past they would have been fit to grace the boudoir of a countess, but now, filthy, stained with spittle that had missed the nearby spittoon and faded from the flaming Caribbean sun, they were sad reminders of their own past glory.

McGowery stepped on the mattress and there was a rush of scurrying sounds along the splintery wooden floor. Roque turned to the other mattress and spread his light traveling cloak over it. "Come on, Fleur, it's the best we can do under these circumstances."

"But Roque," Garlanda protested, "where is our room?"

"Right here. They only had one room available," he said matter-of-factly.

"I'd rather sleep out on the lawn than in here," Sabelle interrupted, arms akimbo.

"I seem to remember the pair of you nagging and begging and tormenting my ears with pleadings of how badly you wanted to come ashore. Do you want to go back to the ship?"

Garlanda was about to agree to this idea when her legs finally gave out. Roque lowered her to the cloak-covered mattress and weighed her body down with his. Behind them McGowery seized Sabelle for an ardent kiss he no doubt considered to be his own idea.

"Roque, not here. Roque, please, you'll tear my new gown and I shall have nothing to wear back to the ship tomorrow."

"Damn the dress. I'll buy you a hundred others!"

He had her bodice open. Greedy, searing kisses covered her throat and breasts. She pushed feebly at his broad shoulders. His hands were under her lavender brocade skirts, shoving them up around her thighs. She moaned as the flocked ribbons of her shift tickled her. Roque's dark head nestled in her damp neck, then his hands were under her, lifting her and pressing her body against his. A cry started in her throat, but his mouth muffled it.

He filled her. Her head was against the dirty stone wall, but she didn't feel it. All she was aware of was the passionate, unfathomable man making torrid, achingly sweet love to her. Against her wishes, her spirits soared. A gutteral sob of exhilaration crept from her wet lips as he brought her to the peak and left her shattered and powerless. She was vaguely aware of the street vendors calling out their wares below. Carriage wheels and steel-shod hooves clanked on the cobbled streets, accompanied by the rustle of stiff silk skirts and low voices drunkenly stumbling over late night conversation. Presently she slept.

Blazing sunlight bathed her face in heat.

Garlanda stirred from her blissful torpor with great reluctance. Her senses were sluggish with lush sensation. She wiggled her toes. Her head felt like it was floating. She sat up, trying to get her bearings, and discovered to her horror that she was bare for the most part to the waist, shift skirts well up over her knees. The lavender gown was flung across the bottom of the bed. Sabelle and the Scotsman were tangled in a fevered embrace on the next mattress, Sabelle's full moire skirts hiding whatever position they'd fallen asleep in. A stockinged female leg showed from under the spill of lace and an edge of kilt was visible at the other end of the bed.

Roque was gone. Garlanda tilted her head to one side. The streets were queerly quiet. After her initial acquaintance with the brazen depravity of the Jamaican port, she was amazed that anything close to peace should prevail on a workday morning. The faint stench of garbage festering in the distance entered the room as she stood up to replace her undergarments.

The hot acrid air brought with it the tinny voice of a bell down the lane. It tolled less mournfully than comically, due to its falsetto whine. A man was shouting, "Repent, Port Royal! Your hour of doom is at hand! He shall judge ye and your foul crimes. The Lord knows your crimes and you shall be punished."

"Shut up down there, you crazy old man!" A woman cried. This was followed by the unmistakable splash of a chamber pot being emptied on the prophet's head.

Garlanda almost giggled, but it caught in her throat and turned into a whimper. She was one of the sinners he was raving about. She looked at herself, half-naked, sweaty. She was standing like that in a room that was worse than a pigsty. She was heartsick at what she'd sunk to. How disappointed her parents and the loving sisters at the convent would be if any of them had known what she had become. She was repulsed at herself. She hurriedly put on the lavender gown and ripped off the expensive, gaudy trim with a shudder of distaste. Her hands shook as she tore off the pearl buttons and dropped them into the bag that still hung on a long string around her neck. The plain black fasteners holding the gown together would suffice for where she was going. She leaned over Sabelle's sleeping form.

"Sabelle, wake up. I need to borrow some of your hairpins. I'm going to Saint Paul's Church."

A pink-nailed female hand came out from under the mountain of silk, lace, and moire. Garlanda took the long, sharp pins capped with uncut amethysts that were offered. "Saint Paul's, Sabelle, the one with the spire. I'll be right back."

She gentled her unruly copper hair, pulling it tight at the nape of her neck to form a twisted bun. She jabbed the pins in almost savagely, spearing the glossy locks and holding them in an imitation of respectability. She walked out of the room and across the inn floor to the street. The air was still, the blue sky utterly cloudless overhead. The wet heat of the day beaded her with perspiration before she had taken a dozen steps. She had never seen a day so unstirred by any breeze. Buzzing insects stung her arms as if starved for the taste of human flesh. She swatted them and kept walking.

There were no rental carriages on the street. She forced her feet to carry her onward through the stifling scorch of the Port Royal morning. Sweat soaked through her new gown, matting her chemise to her figure in clammy folds. She regretted having to bring her lace shawl.

A weary band of men passed her without so much as a backward glance, carrying long poles with bell-shaped metal ends. She recognized them as lamplighters returning from their daybreak rounds of snuffing out the street lamps. The sun was climbing quickly. Judging from its position in the robin's egg sky, it was nearly eight. The lamplighters must have stopped at their favorite tavern for a round before heading home. "Is this the way to Saint Paul's?" she called to them.

"Aye," one of them said, "Soon the spire'll come into view if you keep going and then you can't miss it."

Garlanda kept on. The city was already producing faint smoke from its brick chimneys, smoke flavored with bacon and mutton and fresh bread. She walked on purposefully, passing through the produce market on High Street and trying to ignore the delicate rumbling in her stomach. She couldn't eat with what she needed to do. Fasting was essential. The loaves of bread in the baker's windows were almost more than she could bear. Greasy merchants in splattered aprons pointed out bushels of vegetables and fruit—luscious mangoes, dates, beans the same color as Sabelle's enormous emerald, long orange carrots, bunches of bananas, waxy lemons and limes, corpulent apples fairly bursting out of their scarlet skins.

She kept walking despite her stomach's loquacious whining about this delicious torment. A large shadow blocked her path. She looked up to see a portly farmer and his equally plump wife smiling at her from the front of their produce wagon. "Land o'Goshen, this is no place for a young girl to go wandering alone!" the woman cried. "You must be a newcomer to this wicked place. Might we give you a ride somewhere?"

"Thank you, good lady. I was just on my way to Saint Paul's."

"Why, that's right on our way, isn't it, Bess," the man said. "Climb aboard, little lady, let's get you to that church. Only safe place for a god-fearing citizen these days. Where's your folks?"

"Waiting for me at the church." She clambered in the back of the wagon and sat down on the empty feed sacks. The next thing she knew someone was gently shaking her shoulder to waken her.

"Miss, we're here."

"Bless you, you're kind people." She climbed down and waved at them until they were out of sight. So, Port Royal had some decent people after all. She was nearly to the door of the church when she remembered her head was uncovered. She pushed her jewel bag further down in the cleft between her breasts and

draped her soggy shawl up over her head to hide her
bright hair. Then she stepped in the doors.

The church was empty. She knelt in the last row
and made the sign of the cross. She lowered her head
until her chin nearly rested on her collarbone.

"May I help you, my child?" A kindly little man in a
religious collar was gazing down at her from over the
tops of his folded hands.

"I have come to confess and make my peace with
God."

"Then come, child, I shall fetch Doctor Heath, the
rector. He was about to leave, but when it comes to
helping a troubled soul, the good man has time
aplenty. Come."

She rose and followed him to where Doctor Heath
was saying his prayers.

Garlanda stepped out into the smoldering morning.
She made the sign of the cross once more and lowered
the damp shawl from her hair. Tendrils of coppery
fringe escaped the pins and curled about her face. She
was cleansed, forgiven. She would not return to *La
Doña del Fuego*, but rather seek sanctuary with the
good Christian family Doctor Heath had given her
the name of. She could sell her jewels and thus pay
for a vessel to include her among its passengers and
go back to England. She was forgiven, brightened in
the sight of God once more. She could return home
with a conscience scrubbed clean as a schoolboy's
slate at the end of a day's lessons. The steeple of the
church, towering overhead, seemed an added gesture
of blessing.

Her stomach reminded her she had not eaten. Gar-

landa shielded her eyes from the sun with her hand,
trying to figure out which direction High Street was.
She glanced about in confusion, then began to walk.
It was some minutes later when she realized that instead of nearing the shops, she seemed to be going
farther from the sea and food. Oh, well, perhaps the
doctor's friends could feed her. Salvation—a good
Christian home bereft of sin and corruption, and soon,
a journey home at last to Auntie Althea.

Her legs were beginning to ache from climbing
uphill. She paused to rest against a shady tree. A furtive rustling above caused her to crane her head back
to see what had caused the noise. A tattered urchin
grinned down at her. It was an appealing grin because
he was at the age that he was missing every other
tooth in front, which gave the effect of smiling
through a dilapidated picket fence.

"Hello," Garlanda said. "I'm lost. Can you give me
directions?"

"Naw. I don't know nothing 'bout streets and such.
You kin use me spyglass if ya want t'see street signs
and such. Come on up, ma'am. I've a view of a ship
they're careening."

*I certainly can't go clawing my way up a tree in
these full skirts,* she thought piously. *Then again, I'm
as lost as I can be.* Secure in her refound piety, she
seized a branch and scaled the tree. Her over-the-
garden-wall expeditions to the nun's orchard had finally paid off. She seated herself next to the boy.

"Lookee there, she's the *H.M.S. Swan*, up on the
sand and stripped for careenage. They're cleanin' 'er
up and removing the barnacles and such."

Garlanda took the heavy brass-bound telescope he
offered her. He proudly showed her how to adjust it,
then pointed it at the *Swan* for her. She felt an emo-

tional constriction in her throat. A British warship! A wave of patriotism washed over her. God save King William and Queen Mary, ruling judiciously over her beloved England. Sentimental tears blurred her vision momentarily. "She's a fine, big ship, isn't she?"

"Aye," the boy said eagerly. "They've already got her cleaned and patched with pitch, and they ought to be getting ready to reload the guns."

"Won't she topple over, resting on her side in the shallow water that way?"

The boy laughed heartily through his spaced teeth. "Cor! You're green as grass about ships, ain't ya?" He reached for the glass, but she kept it out of his reach for a moment more.

There was Thames Street, Lime, over there, Cannon—ah-h, High Street, with the markets. She was looking for New Street when the urchin reclaimed the spyglass. "Thank you for the use of your glass," Garlanda said. She handed him a silver coin which he pocketed instantly. She had learned enough to know that no one ever did anyone a favor here for the simple pleasure of aiding their fellow man. Everything had a price and an impatient owner awaited his payment.

She climbed down out of the tree and set off in the direction she'd come from, back toward High Street. Hunger was affecting her again. She craved the hot foods peddled by the seaside merchants. Roast parrot or lobster tail followed by a cool draught of Madeira sounded like a perfect remedy for her internal turmoil. She was nearing the market when she swayed and nearly lost her footing.

I must be more affected by hunger than I thought. Am I about to faint? she wondered. *Odd, I don't feel at all giddy.* She clung to the side of a brick house for support. It was not until she felt the bricks tremble under her fingers that she realized that she was not delirious. The ground was moving. An ominous rumble issued from the earth and roof tiles fell around her accompanied by leaves, small branches, and some bits of railings from the balcony overhead.

Earthquake!

CHAPTER 7

It slowed and churned to an uneasy halt. Garlanda pounded at the door of the building, begging admittance, but it was bolted tightly against intruders. Her breath came in wretched gasps as she stood straight once again.

Without warning the second tremor hit. Garlanda was flung to the cobblestones. The earth opened around her, swallowing small trees and outbuildings housing kitchens and smokehouses. It seemed as if the end of the world had come.

An infuriated roar came from the very bowels of the earth. Garlanda's shrieks were drowned among the frantic cries of trapped animals and crumbling buildings. She rolled about helplessly while whole sections of the cobbled street sank around her, never to return to sight. She saw a woman run screaming out the front door of a nearby house and drop into a chasm where the street used to be. The house fell in after her. Garlanda dug her fingers into the exposed dirt to keep from sliding to the bottomless abyss nearest her. The ground gave a spastic heave and rose to an incredible height. The abyss—mended abruptly—became a hill towering over her. Broken shafts of a captured buggy emerged from its grasp piece by piece.

She heard a shattering cacophony of bells and

turned to see the massive spire of Saint Paul's topple and disappear behind torn trees. Chunks of brick battered the ground around her and sparked off shards. Jumbles of twisted railings flew past her as if aimed by vengeful hands. The mad seer was right—Port Royal's hour of doom was at hand.

A deafening *rip* accompanied the screams of a group of people on a balcony. The fragile structure gave way at one end, spilling the people onto a deadly pile of broken masonry below. Towering palm trees snapped at ground level and toppled, crushing everything in their path. Another crack in the earth opened ahead of Garlanda. It snaked its yawning way toward her with deadly accuracy.

She tried to roll away, but the earth opened under her. Flailing madly for anything solid to grasp, she slipped deeper and deeper into the widening trough. Then for one horrible minute, everything stopped. The earth seemed to slam to a halt.

Garlanda started to claw her way up the side of the hole. She could not get out! Everything she got hold of—every stone, every clod of earth—came away in her hand. Then there was a face above her. "Here, take my hand," a man called to her from far above. He must have been on his stomach at the edge of the crevasse. He stretched his hand down as far as he could reach, but it was not anywhere near! She flung herself madly against the dirt, scrambling insanely, determined to climb high enough to grasp his hand.

Suddenly the man above looked up. His mouth opened in horror. Then everything was falling— Garlanda, the earth around her, the man above—the whole earth was falling. Garlanda screamed as she saw the wall of water coming over the top. A great, glassy wall of death fell in on her.

Everywhere it was the same. The sea closed over broken houses and broken bodies alike as entire sections of the city sank, plummeting downward to their inescapable tomb beneath the relentless waves. Ships were trapped, their anchor cables snapped by the fury of the sea. As the first tidal wave took them, the ships flipflopped like turtles, helpless in the grip of a mighty hand. Vessel after vessel was doomed by the weight of its cargo and ballast shifting to one side and upending it for all time. Only the *Swan*, freed from her load for careening, rode atop the waves.

Garlanda struggled against the angry waters covering her head. Bodies and houses sank past her into the crevasse as she shot through the sea with wild strokes. Why hadn't she surfaced yet? Her lungs were near the bursting point!

She kept going upward—ever upward as the ocean boiled furiously about her. Wide-eyed corpses brushed past her, arms outstretched, forever frozen in their painful last throes as death had found them. A small boat sank like a stone, nearly dragging her with it. White-cold fire engulfed the inside of her head. Her lungs felt as if some mammoth monster had her in a grip of iron and was squeezing her to death.

With a final feeble stroke she surfaced. The stale, heavy air of Jamaica had never tasted so sweet. She gulped it in with a primitive relish at having cheated death.

Hands clamped down on her arms. "Here, lass!"

She looked up to see the bulk of the *Swan* towering over her. Dozens of people were clinging to it where it rested, impaled on the peaks of sunken houses. Two men had caught her but could not hold her in the swirling maelstrom about them. She was torn from their grip.

Beams and rafters swirled past and were sucked
down to the sea floor. A child with golden hair and
half a face went by. Garlanda retched. She was being
sucked back down when a sharp piece of something snagged her sleeve. She clung to it desperately
and saw that it was a broken board projecting from
the side of the *Swan*. She hung there limply.

"That's my house," a voice from the doomed ship
cried out. "My God, my house. Everything I own—
gone—gone."

"I was making the bed and the next thing I knew I
was in the kitchen—'"

"The Lord is my Shepherd—"

"Robert—Robert! He was here a minute ago."

"I can't see the fort or the church! Are they both
gone? Is everything gone?"

"What will happen to—"

Minutes or hours passed, she did not know which.
Sharp, slimy objects jolted against her underwater.
Triangular fins broke the surface of the water nearby.
Sharks had already moved in as macabre clean-up
crews.

Garlanda took a deep breath and hauled herself up
out of the water to sit astraddle the board she'd been
holding onto. She was none too quick. Screams issued
from the prow as a determined hammerhead shark
dragged a man from his sanctuary. She closed her
eyes and prayed for mercy to be granted to his soul.

Agony became numb unknowing. She kept her eyes
closed unfeeling of anything except retreat to a warm
place in her mind where the shocking calamity could
not touch her.

"Girl? Are you alive?"

Her eyes fluttered open. A man in a small boat was
offering up his hand. Wet, huddled forms cowered at

his feet. "Are you Charon come to take me away?" Garlanda asked.

Someone in the boat laughed a little hysterically. "Hardly that," the man said. "I'm on my way to seek my wife and family. There's a bit of ground that hasn't sunk yet. I'm hoping they're there. Come along, little one." He lifted her down to the solid, reassuring planks of the rowboat.

"Let me help at the oars, John," one man said. " 'Tis good you are to stop and think of the welfare of others when your own family's outcome is dubious."

Garlanda passed into cloudless oblivion, far beyond the reach of pain.

When she regained consciousness there were people hauling her from the boat onto solid land. Only one part of Port Royal was still above water and everyone who could swim or find something to hang onto had paddled there, the one safe haven. All around them were submerged buildings with an occasional slate roof or battered weathercock visible above the water.

Garlanda staggered up the cobbled street that now dipped eerily into the sea at one end. She wanted only to collapse against something solid and dry and sleep. Maybe then, when she woke up, this would prove to have all been a nightmare. She could hardly make her legs move and she kept twisting her ankles painfully on the slippery cobblestones.

Few of the buildings were intact. Some were missing the front face and had upper floors exposed like giant dollhouses. Men and women were digging through rubble and the bodies they found were being removed to one area where new arrivals could see if

their loved ones were among the dead. A woman, suck-
ling an infant, sat on the ground in front of a clock-
maker's shop. Her eyes were blank and dirty tears
made rivulets down her pale cheeks.

Next to her a crowd was gathered at a bakery. It
had miraculously been spared and the heady aroma of
fresh bread filled the air, momentarily blocking out
the smell of death. Garlanda stepped to the back of
the silent line of mourners. One by one these survivors
went in the door and came out clutching rolls or small
meat pies. Garlanda was almost to the door when a
large woman with knobby hands and artificially red
hair walked up to her. The woman lifted up Garlanda's skirt and looked over her petticoats. "You're not
hurt, are you?" the woman demanded in a hoarse
voice.

"No, I don't think so," Garlanda answered lethargic-
ally.

The woman's eyes blazed. "Then what are you just
standing here for?" Garlanda stared at her dumbly.
She couldn't think. Why was the woman screaming at
her? She hadn't done anything wrong. "Take off those
petticoats! Tear them up and start bandaging the injured. Don't you hear me? Don't just look at me!" The
woman drew back her arm and slapped Garlanda—
hard.

Suddenly a door opened in the back of her mind.
One small, organized part of her inner being awoke.
"Yes, yes. Of course." She stepped out of the bread
line and started untying the laces that secured her
soggy skirts. An hour later, as she was tearing off the
last strip of ribbon-trimmed muslin and making a
sling, she saw a fishing boat coming toward the tiny
island that was now all that was left of the city. The
boat was full of people. At the helm, barefoot with

bloodstained green moire skirts tied up around her hips, was Sabelle. She was shouting orders for landing the craft without damaging it—and she was being obeyed, instantly, unquestioningly.

Garlanda ran to where the boat was unloading and helped people off. "You're alive," Sabelle said matter-of-factly to Garlanda.

"Yes. What about Roque? And McGowery?"

"McGowery's dead," Sabelle said with a toss of her head as if she didn't care. But the gesture didn't quite work and Garlanda knew that Sabelle did care.

"What about Roque?" Garlanda asked, forgetting than an hour ago she had intended to never see him again.

"I don't know. He had gone looking for you at Saint Paul's."

"But Saint Paul's collapsed! I saw it!" Garlanda said.

"Maybe he hadn't gotten there yet," Sabelle offered by way of calming her.

But it didn't help. "What shall we do now?" Garlanda said, an edge of hysteria creeping into her voice.

"What do you mean 'what will we do'? We're still alive, and we'll try to stay that way. That's what we'll do. Get in here and help me. We'll go pick up some more of them." Garlanda clambered aboard while Sabelle shouted for some able-bodied young men to come along and help them hunt for survivors.

It was almost dark by the time they came back for the last time. Many boats like the one Sabelle had commanded had been plying the shark-infested waters all day and the pile of bodies waiting to be claimed had grown to grotesque proportions. The woman who had slapped Garlanda earlier met them and helped unload their stricken cargo. She untied a dirty handkerchief and took out a gray, soggy loaf of bread. "*Now* you can eat," she told Garlanda with a smile as she handed it to her.

Garlanda and Sabelle sat down in the street and shared the sad little loaf. They tried to eat it slowly and make it last. Suddenly there was a low, subterranean growl and the earth began to shake again. Garlanda threw her arms around Sabelle and screamed.

"Stop it!" Sabelle ordered, disentangling herself from Garlanda's grasp. "It's just a tremor. Let's get out in the open space over there. That's right. Now, sit down. We must figure out how to get out of here."

Garlanda took a deep breath and willed herself to stop trembling. "What about the ship? *La Doña del Fuego*? Do you think it sank?"

"I heard some sailors saying they thought she was still afloat, but I don't know if it's true."

"It has to be. I must get back to England."

"England!" Sabelle scoffed. "We'll be lucky if we ever taste fresh water again. Don't talk to me about England, Fleur."

They fell into an unhappy silence and sat gnawing on their bread as darkness fell. Every boat that hadn't been reduced to splinters in the tidal wave was still out on the water—searching, endlessly searching. Some of the people manning them were bringing in survivors, some were bringing in bodies, and some were simply looting. In the part of town that remained above water there were the sounds of crying, of drunken hysteria, of quiet sensible discussion, of babies bawling for food that wasn't available. Women grieved for lost children, men talked about lost businesses, sailors bemoaned lost ships. Sabelle and Garlanda finally managed to blot out enough of the noise to fall asleep on a mattress that had fallen out of a tumbling house. The next thing Garlanda knew Sabelle was shaking her arm. "Listen, Fleur!"

"What?"

"Listen for a minute. I think I heard someone call McGowery's name. It must be someone from the ship. Didn't you hear that?"

"Sabelle, you're dreaming it," Garlanda said, hope rising in spite of herself. Could it have been a mere twelve hours before she had been happy in the knowledge that she would never again meet anyone from the ship? Now there was nothing in the world she wanted more.

"*La Doña del Fuego.* Over here," Sabelle began to shout.

Garlanda joined her. "*La Doña del Fuego.* Here we are. *La Doña del Fuego!*"

"Sabelle?" A voice—male, faintly heard under all the other sounds.

"Here! Here we are!" Sabelle shouted in the direction the voice had come from. She and Garlanda jumped to their feet and started running. Garlanda tripped on her skirt and grabbed Sabelle for support. They went down in a heap. The next thing they knew they were being helped up.

It was Roque! "Thank God," he was saying, gathering them both in his arms. "I've looked everywhere. Where's McGowery?"

"Dead," Sabelle told him.

"What happened?"

"He fell carrying out a bottle of rum. Glass cut his throat. If the silly bastard had tried to save me instead of his liquor, it wouldn't have happened."

"How did you get out of the church?" Roque said to Garlanda. Suddenly the relief had gone out of his manner and been replaced with anger. "And what the hell inspired you to go out roaming around Port Royal of all places?" He was shaking her shoulders. "When I saw the church collapse—"

"You saw it?"

"Saw it? I was nearly in it. I tried to dig through the rubble, but the wave came over it all and I had to give up. I was hoping you'd already left and I guess you had. I've been back here, though, several times looking for the three of you."

"We must have been out in the boat picking people up," Garlanda explained. She found herself slightly flattered at his anger.

"Never mind how we all got here," Sabelle cut in. "What about the ship?"

"It's seaworthy—just. Pretty badly battered, but intact. Most of the crew were back on board and ten or twelve of them washed over. Sebastian's been busy trying to patch up the injured ones. Willie Gorman and LaFierre were in the hold when the cargo shifted. They were crushed."

"That's too bad. Nobody can load a gun as fast as Willie," Sabelle said.

"Your friend Freddie's been asking for you, Fleur," Roque said.

"Freddie?"

"The cabin boy who waits on you with such doglike devotion," Roque replied.

"Let's go back to the ship," Sabelle said.

"No. There's too much debris in the water to get through safely that far in the dark. I brought along some fresh water. We'll sleep in the fishing boat I've got so that no one else takes it. We'll go back in the morning."

Suddenly it seemed so utterly *sensible* that it was horrible. How could they just sum up a man—an individual human being—as "a good gun loader."

"Where is this boat?" Garlanda asked coldly.

CHAPTER 8

La Doña del Fuego had been ready to sail when the earthquake struck—ready even to the point of Sabelle and Garlanda's shopping treasures put away in Roque's cabin. There was food and fresh water aboard, and Roque had recruited replacements for the crew before they returned to the ship that morning. All they needed was a wind. The ship appeared to be in good condition to Garlanda, but she understood that there were problems that were not obvious. The ship would have to undergo repairs. It couldn't be done at Port Royal—Port Royal didn't exist anymore—and it apparently couldn't be worked on at sea. "What will you do?" she asked Roque when they got back on board.

"There's a group of islands south of here where we've careened the ship before. If we ever get a wind, we'll take her there."

"When will we get back to England?"

"England?" He looked at her incredulously. "Do you think this is a hire carriage? You'll get to England, if you really want to, *sometime.*"

There was a knock on the door. Quartermaster Kidd came in. "Captain, I want to talk to ye." Kidd's yellow waistcoat had accumulated additional stains, the origin of which Garlanda didn't care to guess at, and his lace cuffs were hanging in tatters. One side of his knee breeches was torn and a long gash showed on his leg. He didn't even look at Garlanda.

"Sit down, Kidd. Rum?" Roque said, pouring two generous portions.

"Cap'n, I want ye to know that I thank you mightily for taking me on after me own crew deserted. It's not every man would do that, but I'm fed up with this life. I've been through more hurricanes than I can count, and I even got through an earthquake before this one, but that damned wave—! I've never seen the likes of that. Me heart damn near stopped."

"What are you going to do? You can't leave the sea," Roque said. "She's in your blood. You'll come back to her again and again—just like you would a good woman."

"A pox on good women," Kidd said wryly. "Give me a rich one." He leaned forward conspiratorily. "I've been thinkin' for a long while of trying to make me money—well, legal." He said the word as if it were embarrassing. "There's a lot of money in owning ships, so long as they don't get stolen from ye. And I'd like to see the man who'd try to take another ship away from William Kidd.

"I've been talking to the cap'n of an English merchantman sitting out there. He's setting sail for a place called New York when the next wind comes up, and I thought I'd go along with him and try my hand there. There's a big shipbuilding business in that part of the world. I think I'll get me a fine house and not taste salt water spray again—unless it suits me to. If I get bored I'll return to the sea and be Captain Kidd again instead of Mister Kidd."

"Well, I wish you luck, Kidd. But you're leaving me without a quartermaster."

"I know, but there's lot others want to take me place."

"Sure, lots *want* to, how many *can*? Stay with us then, until the crew chooses a new man."

"Alright. I think they'll choose Hawkins. I'll call them together on deck at sundown."

Roque left the cabin with Kidd. Garlanda sat by the windows for a while watching the flotsam from Port Royal that was now washing clear out to sea. She saw chairs, tables, ceiling beams, and finally a body. At that she left the window.

Roque didn't come back to the cabin. Toward sundown Garlanda could hear the sailors gathering on deck to decide on a new quartermaster. Garlanda opened the door and slipped out to observe. A youngish man in striped trousers and a beard that flowed halfway down his chest was walking—no, strutting— from group to group. *That must be Hawkins*, Garlanda thought.

When it finally appeared that no more men could fit on deck, Roque and Kidd appeared on the poop deck. "You know why we're here," Kidd said brusquely. "Who do you want?"

"Hawkins!" A man clinging casually in the shrouds shouted. A noisy response seconded this.

"Sabelle!" A shrill voice cut through the cheer, neatly cutting it off as they all turned to look for who said it. Sabelle stood at the other end of the deck. She had her fists on her hips and her face was flushed. "Yes, me!" she said into the stunned silence. One brave soul murmured encouragement and his fellows turned on him with snickers. "What do you find so funny?" she asked as she strode across the deck and joined Roque and Kidd. She leaned over the railing and surveyed the men below. "Who are you laughing at, Smith? Who taught you to load a musket?"

Smith looked at his feet and stopped laughing. Sabelle rounded on all of them. "Who told you to look on that island for the captain? Who got us out of Lisbon that time they were firing on us and Hawkins and Kidd were both drunk in some brothel in town—"

"Who sleeps with everyone on the ship?" a humorist called out.

"Not quite everyone, Thomas. I like my men to have teeth, not just gums. And your gums aren't even much good," Sabelle laughed.

Sebastian Sim had joined them on the poop deck. He stepped forward and signaled for quiet. "She's right. There's no reason she shouldn't be considered." A hoot met this. Sebastian waited for silence. "I've seen the results of the patching up she'd done on some of you before I joined the crew. It's damned good. I've seen her bail you all out of trouble. I've seen her be mother, sister, and father confessor to all of you." No one was laughing anymore. "Jamie, remember when your brother fell overboard and you went on that long drunk and tried to kill yourself? Who took the rum away and sat up with you for two days and nights?"

"I remember," the man called Jamie answered. "She's a good lady. I vote for Sabelle."

"Wait a minute, you old butcher. Those aren't the right reasons. I ought to be quartermaster because I'm the best sailor on the ship—next to the cap'n, of course," she added without much conviction.

"But that's not all there is to the job," Sebastian countered, "and we all know it. Quartermaster has to be judge and jury in disputes and know the strengths and weaknesses of every man on the ship. Sabelle knows us better than we know ourselves."

Garlanda was watching Roque's face. How well he hid his emotions. There was no trace of agreement or disagreement on his features. *What does he think of this? Why doesn't he speak up?*

Hawkins stepped forward. "Cap'n, how long we gonna listen to this rot? You can't be paying no mind to this bawd's nonsense," he said and topped it with a cackling laugh. A few of the men joined him. "Really, cap'n, can ye think how we'd be laughed at if anyone heard we'd even listened to this?"

"Hawkins, we'll only get laughed at if we deserve it," Roque said.

"I remember laughing that time Hawkins misfigured the tide and nearly got us run aground," a voice near Garland said.

"Yeah, we damn near ripped the sails apart putting back out to sea," someone else called out.

"It was just a mistake!"

"Yeah! What a mistake!"

"Sabelle doan make no mistakes wi' the charts. I seen her working over 'em. Careful as ever. I cast me vote for Sabelle."

"She's gawd-damned WOMAN!"

"So what? She saved my life the time that musket backfired on me."

"She shouldn't have!"

"You wanna taste o' the musket rammed down your filthy throat?"

"That's enough!" Roque shouted into the din. "Enough! You all know what you think without drawing daggers. We'll vote *now*! Hawkins's men to port—Belle's to starboard."

Suddenly the whole deck turned into a madhouse. It was as if the entire crew was trying to braid itself into a single knot of humanity. Men pushed and swore and tripped each other. Garlanda got an elbow in her stomach that forced her to step back into the cabin until they had sorted themselves out. When it seemed to be quieting down a little she crept back out. The crew had neatly aligned themselves into two equal camps between which there was an animated group discussion going on that seemed to consist entirely of obscenities. Sabelle and Hawkins were with Roque and Kidd above the melee.

"Alright men, it looks like a draw to me," Roque said.

"Then we'll settle it ourselves," Sabelle said. "I propose a duel."

Hawkins took a moment to absorb this. When his brain finally caught up with his ears he started laughing. "A duel?" he sputtered.

"Yes, damn your scurvy hide. "I'll run you through."

"I'm not dueling with a *woman!*"

"Don't be afraid," Sabelle goaded.

"Afraid!"

"You are, aren't you?"

"No whore's calling *me* a coward!" Hawkins said with his hand on his dagger.

"No coward's calling me a whore!"

"Sabelle," Roque began.

"Look, cap'n. How would this be settled if we were both men? A duel, most likely. Well, there's no difference. I'm willing to get what I want in a man's way."

"Belle, I can't allow this."

"Why in hell not? I'm the one taking my own chances. I've never asked for any of you scummy barnacle brains to protect me or take care of me on this ship. I'm not asking now for anything I don't deserve. I ought to be quartermaster and at least half these sots know it. I'm gonna show that other half, and I'm gonna show this bastard Hawkins a few things about fighting."

"I'll fight her," Hawkins said. "Ain't no whore gonna beat me!"

"Look, Belle," Roque said. "If I go along with this and you don't win, there won't be any more nagging or arguing about it. Agreed?"

"*If* I lose there won't be anyone to nag you. This isn't some prissy-pansy first blood game. This is win or die."

"No!"

"What if we were both men?" she repeated.

"But you aren't," Roque said.

"This isn't really your decision," Sabelle said sweetly. "It's up to the quartermaster and that's still Kidd. What do you say, Kidd?"

William Kidd considered Sabelle and Hawkins for a long moment then raked through the crew standing below. His eyes narrowed. "I say win or die. If she wants a man's job, she has to get it like a man would or she won't be able to keep it."

"Agreed," both Hawkins and Sabelle said as one voice.

"Sand the deck." Sabelle added, "I don't want to be slipping around in Hawkins guts."

"I'll try not to carve yer dainty head off too sloppily," Hawkins sneered from the depths of his unkempt beard. "What'll it be, milady? Rapiers?"

"Heavier arms, laddie. If the captain's willing, we'll borrow that nice matched pair of Toledo cutlasses of his. You, Smith, fetch them from the cabin."

Smith turned to Roque, who gave an angry gesture of agreement.

Garlanda took advantage of the momentary calm to rush to Sabelle's side. "Sabelle, you can't be serious! You'll be—"

"Victorious, little one. And if not, ye can keep the captain." Sabelle gave her a granite smile, then the expression softened for a moment. "Don't look so damned sincere. I don't want your landlubbing Roque. Too much of an accursed gentleman for my tastes. *Merde*, where's that man with the blades?" She shoved Garlanda back toward the cabin.

Smith brushed past her with the twin Toledo blades. Hawkins took his and struck an *en garde* stance, but Sabelle turned her back on him. She rummaged in a small ammunitions bag hanging from her belt. From the depths of it she extracted a vial of oil, abrasive paper, a small lump of dark stone, and a flannel rag. "Don't stand there staring, you knuckleheaded rapscallions! Sand the deck!"

They scrambled to obey. Sabelle coolly oiled her blade. She ran the paper over a few minor nicks, followed with the stone, and rubbed out the imperfections in the cutlass. A satisfied "hm-m-m" issued from her suddenly taut mouth. The flannel piece was applied until the sword gleamed. She tested it, one hand raised, the other gripping the hilt, and gave a few exploratory slashes at nothing. A frown marred her face. She shifted the blade to her other hand, tested it, and smiled.

The onlookers waited. The buxom woman neatly tucked her skirts up with the excess caught in her belt. She signaled for the bandana Sebastian wore around his neck, took it from him, and used it to catch her ebony locks and keep them out of her face. There were lecherous glances in the direction of her nicely plump brown legs, but these ceased as she advanced on her opponent. "Avast, you scummy cur. I'm ready when you are."

Hawkins lunged without warning. Sabelle side-stepped it easily, sand providing traction for her bare feet. As the bearded sailor's sword flashed, she met it on the upswing in a skillful parry. The force of the impact sent a minor shock wave through both of them. Sabelle slashed at Hawkins, but he ducked. Her cutlass bit deeply into the cabin door.

Garlanda had seen the blow coming and slipped inside quickly. As soon as the doorway was clear, she emerged, hands to her mouth in an effort to keep from crying out. Roque caught her about the waist and pressed her to him. She turned her face to the shelter of his broad shoulder. The clash of metal on metal was too much to take. She had to look.

Hawkins lunged. The tip of his blade caught the black-haired woman on the arm and left a red stripe. His supporters howled with glee—Sabelle's groaned. Sabelle countered his next strike. Her cutlass arced, catching his and pointing it straight up. With their swords skyward, she drove an unexpected fist deep into her foe's stomach.

He roared with rage and pain and stumbled back. "Bitch!" he spat hoarsely. Sabelle took advantage of his position and shock and slashed. Her weapon cut a path across the man's glistening shoulder, evoking another animal cry from him and a gush of crimson from his flesh. He turned for a fraction of a second to look at the damage. She sliced at his other arm.

Hawkins didn't stop to look this time. He spun and brought his gleaming blade up. It caught Sabelle on the ribs just below one of the shapely breasts that showed through her thin muslin blouse. A bright scarlet splash instantly colored the white material. Garlanda made a move toward her, with no idea what she was doing, but Roque pulled her back.

Sabelle clutched at her wound, swore a fierce oath, and lunged. They collided with a thud of bodies and a clang of sword on sword. It was obvious that Hawkins was expecting another assault on his abdomen. He side-stepped as fast as possible. His fellow combatant was too quick for him. The spectators gasped with appreciation as she stuck her foot out. Caught from behind the ankle, he stumbled and had almost recovered himself when Sabelle's fist cracked across his jaw. An ugly white patch began instantly to redden.

Garlanda shook. Roque's grip on her tightened. "She won't be killed, will she, Roque?"

Hawkins kicked Sabelle on the shin and made her hop back in a clumsily executed jig. "You foul, cheating whore! It's no clean fighter you are!" Hawkins bellowed.

"It's not claiming to be that I am," she mocked. Suddenly both of her hands were on the hilt of her sword. She brought it down with crushing force. Sparks flew. Tempered steel, worked by the finest craftsmen in Toledo, met its exact duplicate. Hawkins's blade slid along Sabelle's from the strength of her thrust. The blade bit into Sabelle's fingers even as she saw it coming and tried to ward it off.

"Aye, you're a poor excuse for a sailor, but you handle a sword passing well," she said through gritted teeth. The sword was shifted to her other hand. She snapped her fingers to Garlanda. It took the girl a moment to realize what she wanted. Her eyes were drawn to the gorey groove across Sabelle's knuckles. She caught the unsaid message, pulled a handkerchief from her bodice, and thrust it at the other woman. Sabelle took it and tied it about her injured hand as she and the bearded sailor circled each other like wary cats.

The end was near. Their breathing was labored, their chests were heaving. Sabelle leaped without warning across the short space that separated them. Hawkins took an inadvertent step backward from the ferocity of her attack. She ran him down, slashing, attacking, while he could only parry limply. The bandana slipped from her thick, raven curls and left them floating about her shoulders like a dark cloud. With her blood-spattered clothes, mass of hair, and grim, earthily beautiful face smudged with sweat and blood, she looked like an avenging goddess. Her sword flashed in the sun.

Hawkins returned to life with an angry shout. He parried, feinted skillfully, and caught her with her sword up. She swung down, trying to deflect the blow. His cutlass smote hers at an angle. There was a flash of silver sparks, then her blade neatly broke halfway down.

Hawkins gave a keen cry of triumph as he swept the crippled sword from her hands. It clattered to the deck noisily. "Admit defeat and I'll spare ye," he said with a cruel laugh.

"I'll see you in hell first. You're not fit to be quartermaster."

Garlanda screamed as he lunged. Sabelle slid across the sanded deck, neatly diving under the arch of descending death. As she came up a tiny gleam of steel shone in her bandaged hand. Her arm swept up.

Hawkins staggered and collapsed, clutching his side.

Sabelle, triumphant, stood over him with her dripping dagger. "Quit yowling like a wet kitten. You'll live," she said, planting a bare foot on his stomach.

"You were a better fighter than I expected and I cannot cold-bloodedly kill a man so good with a sword. We'll allow you to ship out with Kidd."

She surveyed the speechless crowd. A frown creased her comely features. "What the devil are you dim-witted knaves staring at? Clear the deck of this sand! Sebastian, fetch your doctoring bag. You, Billy, clean the captain's remaining blade and return it to its place. Move, you idiots! We have work to do! Act alive, you swabs. Haven't any of you noticed that the wind's up? Man the wheel, we're off to Los Roques. We have a ship to careen and a pair of cargo vessels to meet. Put Hawkins off with Kidd just as soon as he's patched up.

"Step lively, lads!" And she laughed, a full, throaty Sabelle laugh.

CHAPTER 9

Los Roques came into view, small verdant patches seeming to float tranquilly on an azure sea. Garlanda, still in a minor state of shock from Sabelle's battle and new job as quartermaster, leaned on the rail and watched the black-haired woman shoot off orders.

"Heave to, you dastards! Bring 'er into the wind! You up there in the crow's nest!" Here she cupped her hands around her mouth and shouted. Whether it was that or her furious waving a moment later that brought a response, Garlanda never knew. "Are our ships in sight?"

The few members of the crew not scurrying under Sabelle's verbal lash shielded their eyes with their hands in order to look up at the crow's nest. The look-out held out both arms. "Both! He's sighted both of our cargo vessels! Who has another spyglass on this lousy bucket of barnacle fodder? Give it here, Freddie. Step it up there. Brian, get those nets stowed. John, Roger—one of you bring me the charts and the other take the soundings. Move!"

Roque leaned on the rail next to Garlanda. "She's stepped right in, hasn't she?"

Before Garlanda could answer, Sabelle joined them. "Both ships are in, cap'n, and that means the small sloop must be with them." Garlanda shut out their conversation. Land again! Fresh fruit and solid ground under foot. She could hardly wait. Once she got back to England she would never go out on the water again, not even a lake or stream.

Soundings were called as *La Doña del Fuego* neatly skirted the coral reefs off her starboard. Roque gave her a sidelong look that she could see boded ill for her dedication to avoid intimate contact with him. So far he had been too busy to seek her out in the mad haste to get to the island and careen the ship before sailing for Europe. His long, undressing look gave her chills. She clasped her shawl tighter about her, unconsciously outlining her high, firm breasts. She dashed off, sliding on the pitching deck.

"How many fathoms of water, Roger?" Sabelle yelled. Garlanda collided with Sebastian Sim, sending both of them crashing against the side.

"Easy, child," the man said. "What's pursuing you?"

"The captain!"

"Come with me and help me roll some bandages." She thanked him with a bright smile. His air of imperturbable calm steadied her no matter what the situation. Garlanda had learned not to question anyone on the sea about his past, but that didn't keep her from wondering. She questioned in her own mind once again what had brought a man of such learning and polish here. He was a tall man in spite of a slight stoop and his graying hair still held traces of tawny color. He must have been quite good-looking. Perhaps he had committed some crime—but what could a kindly man like this have ever done?

Sabelle appeared and interrupted her thoughts. "Sim, do you suppose there are women on this island?"

"Native women," he said.

"Friendly?"

"Yes, why?"

"I could use a decent night's sleep," Sabelle said and walked away, calling out for the men to bring the ship about. A minute later she was scaling the shrouds and climbing up to straighten a frayed section of rigging.

"Helluva sailor," the man nearest Garlanda said to no one in particular. Garlanda turned to watch Sabelle. It stung her to see Roque staring at the curvaceous new quartermaster with open admiration of her bare legs.

"It won't do you buckos no good to look up my skirts," Sabelle said with a laugh. She held a piece of rigging in her teeth as she sliced off the worn length and braided in a new one.

"Why not?" Roque asked loudly. She grinned down at him and sassily flipped up her skirts to show vividly striped red and white satin pantaloons. Garlanda's hands flew to her mouth in horror. She didn't know what would have been worse—Sabelle with or without the outrageous garment. Women simply did not wear divided garments; they were mannish, outlandish—and useful. The thought made her quiver at her own shocking opinion. This life was beginning to affect the way she thought, even against her own will.

Los Roques. Were the islands named for the enigmatic captain or was Roque a *nom de guerre* he had taken from this place? How little she knew of him. What was it that Sabelle had said about him just before the duel with Hawkins? Something about him being too much of a gentleman for her tastes. There was something to that. Not that he was Garlanda's idea of an *English* gentleman.

Garlanda set down the bucket of fresh water she had carried from the spring. Her hands were nearly blistered from the rough wooden handle of the bucket. Roque took it from her, greedily drank as much as he could in one effort and slopped several handfuls over his head and face. Garlanda set the bucket down and wandered around the beach trying to get a better look at the cargo vessels. They were massive next to *La Doña del Fuego.* She sat down in the meager shade of a palm tree. The trim little brigantine was on her side, and men were busily scraping off barnacles and seaweed. Since the ship was made of worm-proof Bermuda cedarwood they did not have to drill out the wood-boring creatures. Sabelle had told her that *La Doña del Fuego* was a very valuable ship, built for speed and maneuverability on the high seas. There were few privateers who had managed to capture such a ship.

Garlanda looked on as hot tar was applied to patch the hull. In this heat, it was an unenviable job, to say the least. Garlanda felt sweat break out on her own forehead as she watched the sailors drag iron pots of tar from the fire to the boat and, straining, carry them up ladders. Garlanda shifted around so that she could watch the other ships—the bigger ones that floated at sea.

The *King of Rhye* and the *Phoenix* were at anchor, having already been repaired for the long ocean trek before the fighting vessel had arrived. They faced the open seas sideways, guns ready in case of attack from the water. *La Doña del Fuego*'s guns, removed for the tedious cleaning operation, were aimed inland. Roque took no chances. Garlanda wondered where he had

gained his experience. Nothing could take them by
surprise with lookouts manning the guns at all hours.

She leaned back, feeling melted by the blazing sun.
Oh, to be back in fair England! The stench of heated
pitch and human sweat made her stomach uneasy.
They had been on the island too many days. Who
would have thought that careening a ship could take
so long? She wished there was some way to hurry
them so they could be on their way.

Auntie Althea must think I am dead by now. Certainly they will have presumed the Valiant *shipwrecked by now. Auntie Althea will be mourning for Mama and me. Flamboyantly, perhaps, but nonetheless sincerely. I must send word ahead when I get to a civilized port. I can afford it.* She touched the bag of
jewels around her neck. *In Port Royal they were mere baubles, pay for a week's lodging. Back home they must be worth a small fortune. They'll see me safely from wherever we dock in England to London and no doubt allow me to live comfortably without imposing on Aunt Althea's generous nature. Surely there is something left from my parents' estate. Poor Mama, and oh, Papa.*

Surely they would leave this place soon. She fanned
herself with a broken palm frond. The cargo ships
were heavy with spices. When the wind blew in her
direction, she could smell them. Cloves, nutmeg, cinnamon, pepper—most waylaid from Spanish ships returning. Some of the spices had been traded for and
bought, but the majority had not been come by honestly. They would bring enormous sums in Europe.

Sabelle was hard at work with the other sailors.
When Garlanda had asked her to come aboard the
ships to see what they had, her answer had been a
look that made her feel as small as a terrier. Sabelle

had work to do. Finally she had coaxed Sebastian and two of the off-duty sailors into coming with her—once Roque had given his permission.

The *Phoenix* and the *King of Rhye* were laden not only with spices, but rare silks, medicinal drugs, incense for churches, civet and ambergris to be made into perfume, and fat pearls from the coast of Brazil where bronze-skinned boys dove to find the oysters that yielded the jewels. The holds of the two ships were lush with treasure. She knew now why they were so heavily armed and why *La Doña del Fuego*, trim fighting brig that she was, would accompany them on their long ocean voyage. No ship could stand against this fleet despite the fact that they were only three ships. Each was armed as heavily as a small fort.

Will we never get underway? she asked herself with gritted teeth. *I long to be in England and out of this heat.* A trickle of perspiration began at the cleft between her breasts and ended lost in the folds of her gown. She leaned her head against the smooth palm trunk and slept.

Eventually the ship was repaired to Roque's exacting requirements. The captains of the other two ships, who seemed to be subordinate to Roque, came onshore and the three of them and their quartermasters sat in the blazing sun and went over maps and charts, planning the journey. The other quartermasters refused at first to have anything to do with Sabelle, but some less than honeyed words from Roque's crew convinced them that it was in their best interests to accept her on equal footing.

The *Doña* was loaded and as the hold filled, the

ship slowly righted herself in the shallow water. The cannons were brought on board and carefully remounted. Everything on the ship was painted, polished, cleaned, sanded, and tarred according to its need. With the first wind they set sail. Garlanda stood on the deck and admired the majestic beauty in the billowing sails of the *King of Rhye* and the *Phoenix* as they led the way into the vast Atlantic. The day was brilliantly clean and everyone was infected with the carefree relief at leaving behind the tragedy of Port Royal and the backbreaking labor of careening.

Garlanda was more excited than any of them. She was going home! At long last she would get back to cool, green England. England—where rain meant gentle drizzle instead of wind-whipped water that pelted you like gunshot then steamed off in torrid tropical sun. England and hedgerows and primroses and crisp-looking half-timbered cottages. How long would it be? It would take weeks, probably months, to cross the ocean.

She wished there was some way to warn Auntie Althea of her arrival. The news that her sister and niece had died at sea would be shock enough. To follow that with the arrival of the niece, entirely alive, would be worse. But Althea would be glad to see her, she was sure of that. Althea was a childless widow and had always been kind and generous to Garlanda, who had always looked forward to her visits with a strange mixture of anxiety and anticipation. Althea always had the newest in fashion, witticisms, and diversions. Even though Garlanda didn't always understand some of her eccentricities, she always enjoyed her visits. Althea had even come to Martinique once with Garlanda's mother to visit their parents, Garlanda's grandparents. She had come to the convent school that time and Garlanda suspected that the nuns had never quite gotten over it. Althea liked scandalizing people and had underrated the sisters' susceptibility to her technique.

Sabelle broke in on her thoughts. "We're on our way, Fleur. When do we start our lessons?"

"Lessons?" Garlanda said, her mind still in England.

"Yes. Sewing and fencing. Remember?"

"Yes, of course. But you'll be too busy, won't you?"

"Not so long as the weather holds fine and nobody gets in any trouble. I ought to have an hour or two a day of my own."

Sabelle threw herself into the lessons with the same brawling enthusiasm she had for everything she took on. By that night Garlanda was stiff and sore from the athletic workout that Sabelle had subjected her to and Sabelle was walking around sucking on pin-pricked fingers. Garlanda hadn't really been interested in fencing to begin with but had quickly become intoxicated with the feeling of grace and power in the rapiers Roque had loaned them for their practice. She loved the sound of the thin steel whistling through the hot salt air. Sabelle had even been grudgingly complimentary about Garlanda's progress in one lesson.

That night, their first at sea, Roque came to the cabin. Garlanda hadn't been alone with him for more than a few minutes since the night they had gone ashore at Port Royal. She knew this night was coming and although her resolve was firm, she had been dreading the confrontation.

He came in and fixed himself a tall glass of rum and stood for a long time gazing out the windows at the frosty wake that trailed behind the ship, delineating their progress. Then he walked over to where Garlanda stood frozen and enfolded her in his arms.

He kissed her neck and nuzzled her ears. "No," she whispered. He ignored her. With expert fingers he began to slide the shoulders of her gown over her soft skin.

She trembled a little and pulled away. "No," she repeated.

"Why not," he said, pulling her to him.

She struggled, but he did not relax his grasp this time. "Roque, please don't. This isn't right."

"Of course it is."

"No, it's not." She gave a final shrug and freed herself.

"What's the matter with you all of a sudden?"

"It's not sudden. It's been wrong all along, but I've been weak and wrong. Please understand, I'm not the girl on the island anymore."

"You are to me," Roque said, flashes of incipient anger lighting his eyes.

"But not to me. I'm going to England—home. To be what I was meant to be if this had never happened."

"But it *has* happened. How naive you are. You can't turn time around by force of will. You can't go back and be someone you used to be. None of us can do that. Not very many of us would want to."

"You're only making it harder for me to explain. I—" He crushed her against him in a searing kiss. There was passion as well as confusion in the embrace, a stirring of the things they each could not comprehend in the other. The heat of their bodies seemed to scorch through her clothing.

"No, Roque, we mustn't! I've confessed and I don't want to sin again. Oh, can't you see? This is wrong, it was wrong all along, but we were alone on the island and I never expected to see another person. I thought that excused it. It didn't. Let me go, Roque, please!

No matter what you choose to do to me, I—I will not respond."

He drew back and stared at her. "Do *to* you? *To* you? I was always under the impression that what I did was *with* you, not to you. You won't respond? We shall see, little nun!" He laughed and slung Garlanda down on the bed. "Deny it as you may, Fleur, you are still a lady of fire."

"I—I don't deny that there were times when I wanted this but—"

"Times? All the time, little Fleur," he said and laughed again. "Your show of virtue is so feeble, so pale. Come, my dear, admit you are being a prig and a prude far too late in the game."

"You don't love me."

His mouth was on her neck, making unwilling ripples of fire trickle along her body. "What the devil does love have to do with it? Are you still so incredibly naive that you think love justifies all? I could tell you that I love you, but it would be a lie. I do, however, my befuddled darling, like you a great deal."

"*Like* me?" Garlanda burst out, struggling to a sitting position. "Like me? You devil! After you have ruined me for decent men."

Roque dissolved in a helpless paroxysm of laughter. "Decent men?" he sputtered. "What do you consider decent men? Milksop virgins who fear that you know more than they do?" He kept on laughing. "Fleur," he gasped when his hilarity was finally under control. "Fleur, you are a marvel! I didn't rape you if you will recall. I only coaxed you and you responded time and again with the excitement of a real woman. Why do you suddenly decide it is a sin and attempt to stop what we've had? You cannot turn back time. You can't be a virgin once again simply because you wish to. And God only knows why you'd want to!"

She laid back down, rigid. "Very well, you despicable pirate, have your way with me, but I warn you, I will be as if dead. I don't want your attentions, and if you attempt to force yourself on me, I shall ruin it for you by being as cold, unresponsive, and grim as possible. I will not move."

Roque's mouth was still curling at the corners with amusement. "Very well, my determined lady," he said and yanked his shirt off. "Unresponsive, is it? I'll prove to you just how unresponsive you are. You're a poor liar, Fleur, unless the problem is that you truly believe your own words. You're made to enjoy and be enjoyed and I shall prove it to you."

"You're a cad!" Garlanda cried. "You're not only going to rape me, you're going to laugh at me!"

At that he laughed even harder, all the while removing his long, scarred boots and belt. "If you persist in being so funny, I shan't be able to, as you call it, rape you."

She was so angry and humiliated that it took her by surprise when he pinned her down and tried to kiss her. She stubbornly kept her teeth clenched. He called her a cloistered little hypocrite and when she tried to reply, he kissed her. She bit him. He retaliated by yanking a handful of her long red-gold hair until tears sprang into her eyes. "Behave like a savage," he said, "and I'll treat you like one. Bite me again and I'll bite you back. Any way you hurt me, I'll hurt you."

Garlanda went limp under him. *I will not give him the pleasure of battle. I will be as stiff and cold as a slab of uncooked mutton.* Roque was kissing her with maddening skill and leisure—long, tantalizing dips of his tongue in her mouth. One of his legs was between hers, rubbing slightly. His fingers roamed through her hair, then down her throat and the plunging neckline of her gown. *I will not respond, I will not respond.*

"Place a wager on that and lose," Roque murmured between kisses. To her horror she realized that she had been repeating her thoughts aloud. She forced her mouth to remain slack under his. His lips moved on her creamy throat next, then the expanse of soft skin above her gown. He removed her dress with lazy skill, as if he had all the time in the world. She remained where she was, clad only in her thin muslin chemise.

Roque casually untied the ribbons at the front of her undergarment. Garlanda forced herself to remain still and not to knead or caress his hard, smooth body. She would not move, she reminded herself. He must not know the wild chords of response he struck in her trembling body. She shut her eyes.

He kissed her again, longer and harder this time. It took all of Garlanda's will power not to writhe. His mouth was at her ear, nibbling, whispering, then on her throat, the front of her chemise—he pulled the material back and hesitated. "Your body betrays you, Fleur."

She opened her eyes and saw the stiff hot pinkness of her nipples, then Roque's lips touched them and she forgot all else. Her chemise was stripped from her and with it went her defenses. Roque's strong hands slid over her body, increasing the quiver she fought, and failed, to conceal. He was stroking her, kissing her, searing his mouth to hers while his fingers sought the soft insides of her milky thighs and above. A gasp fled her kiss-bruised lips. He kissed her harder and harder and she dimly realized through her haze of mindless need and want that he was naked too.

Fevered moans escaped her. Every touch was enflaming, every kiss an improvement on the wonderful one before. She was aware of her own irregular breathing, little gasps and cries stifled under Roque's relentless mouth. Fire and pressure built in her. All at once the weight of his well-muscled body was on hers, crushing her down against the taffeta coverlet and downy quilts beneath.

She cried his name. Their bodies came together with a wild surge. He entered her and she clung to him, heedless of her determination not to do so. All that mattered was the two of them—the one of them. Her fingernails dug at his broad shoulders and she wrapped her legs, vises of passion, around his narrow hips. The world seemed to come to a shattering end. It was several minutes before Garlanda, gulping air, could speak. "Roque?"

He raised himself up on his elbows. "So much for sin. You not only failed to remain limp, you tore half my back bloody in the process. You are not a convincing nun."

She jerked away from him. It was true. She had failed and her sole betrayer was herself. "Leave me. Get out," she said in a low voice.

"Oh, Fleur," he said in a tone that was beginning to show genuine exasperation.

"Get out!" she said.

"You don't mean that."

"I do mean it," she said through clenched teeth. "I hope I never see you again. Who are you to tell me what I mean—you, a pirate, a man with no loyalties, who doesn't care about anything but himself, not even his country."

He stood, dressing with angry swiftness. Garlanda was frightened by the expression. She had never seen him really angry and it was as if he were a stranger to her. She threw herself down, face first in the pillows.

But he seized her by the hair and forced her up. "You're a spoiled, naive, whining little bitch, and you don't know what you're talking about. Grow up, Fleur, face real life because it's all there is. Find some other man to marry you—some addle-brained, spineless fool who knows nothing about the person you are, the real woman burning under the surface of that whey-faced little nun you try to be. Have his children and go to church and live by the accepted rules. Never mind that they're absurd. But, by God, you won't be happy. You'll be miserable and you'll deserve it."

"What—what are you going to do to me?"

"Nothing," he said savagely and let go of her hair. "Absolutely nothing. Cover up and say your prayers, little nun," he said. His voice was acid that stung more deeply than a blow.

"Roque, please."

"There are warmer beds than yours, Fleur. I have never been one to force myself on a 'lady,' if that's what you think you are."

"Roque," she sobbed, "please understand."

But he was gone.

Roque did not come to the cabin again except when someone else was there. Sometimes when Garlanda had been on deck she would come back to find that he had been there in her absence to get a change of clothes or a chart. Her impulse was to seek him out, to make him listen to her explanations. But she knew that she would not convince him that she was right and that her morality was not a judgment of him. When they met on deck he was polite in an icy, remote way and she quite had his attention. She longed to touch him, to reestablish not the physical relationship, but the simple companionship she had felt with him. But she could not do that, for she knew that it was both or nothing.

She filled her time during the long crossing with sewing, fencing, and reading and endlessly rereading the meager supply of books in the captain's cabin. Sabelle spent some time every day with her, but her responsibilities as quartermaster kept her busy most of the rest of the time. Sabelle didn't have the leisure to do the sewing she had intended to do and even if she'd had all day, Garlanda despaired of Sabelle ever learning. Within two weeks they both gave up any pretense that Sabelle would ever be a seamstress and Garlanda started making the older woman a dress out of a bolt of chartreuse taffeta she'd bought in Port Royal.

Garlanda made a better student than teacher. The leg and shoulder muscles that had been so painful when she started her fencing lessons firmed and gained a smooth agility. Every afternoon she and Sabelle sanded a section of deck and worked with an audience of sailors who never seemed to tire of the spectacle of one woman teaching another to duel. When Sabelle was too busy, Garlanda would practice with Freddie, who was another of Sabelle's protégés. Freddie was about thirteen and had all the gangly qualities that went with that affliction, but when he had a sword in his hand he became the personification of grace. Garlanda enjoyed practicing with him and the rest of the crew enjoyed harassing Freddie good-naturedly and giving them both tips and even-shouting encouragement when Garlanda did particularly well. Sometimes she caught a glimpse of Roque watching her, but he never spoke.

She hadn't realized how much she was going to miss his company. It was lonely, especially at night, but she tried not to think about it. She would hear Roque laughing and talking with the crew, to Sebastian or Sabelle, and would long to be part of their conversation and to laugh with them. But she could not. She had made her decision and she knew that she was right.

She was practicing with Freddie as she thought about this. "Hold your arm up higher, Miss Fleur," he said. She responded to the name now as if it were really her own. It might as well be. No one on the ship had ever heard her real name, except Roque, and he had forgotten it by that first day on the island. She sometimes had an aching feeling that when she got back to England there would be moments when she missed this life. How strange to have been two people. She would leave "Fleur" on this ship someday soon and they would all forget her.

One afternoon she went on deck and couldn't find Sabelle. She sensed an air of suppressed emotion in the movement of the crew. Everyone seemed unusually intent on what he was doing. Finally she saw a flash of red and white high in the riggings. "Get back in your cabin, Fleur," Sabelle shouted down at her.

"What's wrong?" Garlanda asked the sailor closest to her.

"We're in for a bad blow, Miss," he said. "You'd best get secure."

Oh God, not again! Garlanda thought frantically. *I can't endure this again.* She fled to the cabin as if there was safety there. The ship began to rock with the motion of the wind and rain began to pelt against the diamond-paned windows. She threw herself on the bed. The door banged open and Roque stood there. "So, you're here! Stay in this room!" he barked and the door closed. Garlanda flew after him and caught his sleeve as he was mounting the steps of the poop deck. "I told you to stay below," he shouted above the increasingly ominous sounds of the storm.

"No, please. Let me stay by you," she cried. She could not be left alone and she was too terrified to be coherent.

"I don't need you by me," he said bitterly, "and as I recall, you don't need me. Now get back in there." He pushed open the door and shoved her roughly into the cabin. "Why don't you pray? You're good at that."

Garlanda took refuge in the corner of the room. She ripped the spread off the bed and bundled herself into a blanketed ball of fear. She stayed like that for hours that seemed like years. Once again she was forced to listen to the sounds of men fighting for their lives (and hers, incidentally) against the awesome power of nature. She pressed her hands over her ears and took Roque's sarcastic advice.

She prayed.

Finally the storm abated and Garlanda crawled in slow stages from her cocoon. She could hear sounds of pain and anger. She went on the rain-slick deck. Roque was at the far end of the ship shouting orders. Sabelle was nearer, taking inventory. "Has Sebastian got Varning patched up? We need him up here to get that sail loose," she said to one of the men. To another she barked, "Get that rigging down."

Then Garlanda noticed her fencing partner, Freddie. He was sitting on the deck, bent over forward, and his hands clasped tightly against his stomach.

Everyone else was too busy to attend to him. "Freddie, what's wrong!" she said bending over him. "Is it your stomach?"

"No, Miss Fleur," he said shakily, trying to hold back tears of pain. "My hand."

"Let me see," Garlanda said. He held out a knobby hand with bitten-down nails and two swollen, blackened fingers. "I think they're broken—no, don't bend them that way. At least it's not your sword hand," she said and got a slight smile out of him. "Come on, I'll see what I can do." The boy stood up, swayed, and nearly fell. His face was chalk-white with fear and shock. Garlanda put her arms around his waist. "Lean on me. That's right. I've got some bandages in the cabin."

"Oh, no, Miss Fl-Fleur, I—I couldn't."

"Don't be silly. You need that hand splinted and Sebastian's far too busy to stop and do something I can do just as well. Now, get in there." She got the boy seated on the bed and took a pair of scissors to some of the muslin that had been destined to become petticoats. Suddenly she felt like she was worth something. She blushed with shame at her earlier actions. Imagine her thinking that Roque, with all those lives at stake, would have had time to comfort her. She had behaved abominably! Somehow she would make up for it even if it was too late to take back her foolishness.

She bandaged Freddie's hand gently and as he looked like he might still faint she told him to lay down for a while. He didn't want to obey her, but he was too weak to disobey. Garlanda went to the cupboard and got out Roque's rum bottle. She poured some in a glass and sat on the side of the bed and helped the boy lift his head to drink some.

"What are you doing?" Roque bellowed from the doorway. "In *my* cabin!" He strode over and yanked her to her feet. The rum spilled down the front of her dress. "And with *my* liquor! How dare you be such a little nun with me! Couldn't you have even picked a man, instead of this—this boy!"

Garlanda was incensed. She slapped him with an arm now strengthened with sword play. "I was bandaging Freddie's hand. He broke his fingers."

Roque stood there stiffly, anger fading to embarrassment. He opened his mouth to speak, thought better of it, and walked to the door. He pushed his wet hair out of his face and said, "There are plenty more that need help in the hold. Get down there."

He cared, she thought, *he was jealous*. She was amazed to find that she was pleased at the realization. But there wasn't time to gloat. She checked the wrapping on the boy's hand, poured him another glass of rum, and went down to the hold to help Sebastian.

CHAPTER 10

Three weeks later land was sighted. A ripple of excitement ran through the ship that wasn't transmitted by
words. *England, at last,* Garlanda thought, and began
to gather her few belongings. Sabelle came to the
cabin. "Plan on staying up late tonight," she advised.
"We're going to slip by Gibraltar in the dark. It's a
real sight."

"Gibraltar?" Garlanda gasped. "But I thought—"

"Thought what?"

"Well, I thought we were going to England."

"Why would we go to England?"

"That's where *I'm* going."

"It may be where you're going. It's not where *we're*
bound for. Fleur, you're real smart about some things,
but how can you think that three pirate vessels are
going to travel hundreds of miles out of their way to
drop you off safe and handy to home? Why, we
wouldn't do that even if you were being ransomed."

"Ransomed? What do you mean?"

Sabelle put the heel of her hand to her forehead
and took a deep breath. She spoke slowly and clearly,
as if to a slighty stupid child. "Ransomed—that's when
we capture rich people along with a valuable cargo.
Their families have to pay to get them back. Understand? Surely that convent of yours didn't hide every-

thing about life from you? The one I was in sure didn't."

Normally Garlanda would have pursued this intriguing hint of Sabelle's past, but her disappointment had raced ahead of her curiosity. "You don't think Roque would try to hold me for ransom, do you?"

"You?" Sabelle considered this. "I don't know. Are you worth something?"

Tears started to burn Garlanda's eyes. "No, I'm not. How will I get home?"

Sabelle shrugged. "Why do you want to? I imagine the cap'n would just as soon have you stay here, even though it isn't usual to keep a woman on ship."

"No! I want to go back. I belong in England."

"You won't like it," Sabelle predicted smugly.

"Why do you say that?"

"I've seen those English 'ladies,' all prim and powdered and lookin' like stuffed birds. No spirit in 'em. No life. You're not like that, nobody who can handle a sword as natural as you do belongs in hoops and wigs. Now if you were wantin' to go back to France—I could see that! Not that I'd want to live in Paris again, but—"

"Sabelle!" Garlanda cut in, "Please help me. How can I get home?"

"Fleur, I've got my hands full running this ship for the cap'n. I can't run your life as well. I say you ought to forget about goin' back."

Garlanda thought all afternoon about what Sabelle had said. One word kept coming back to mind— "ransom." What if Roque did intend to hold her? She had told him enough about her family that he must know they had money—not a great fortune, of course, but enough to spare. He knew that she had grandparents with a large plantation in Martinique and an aunt in London. She didn't think he remembered her true name, but that would be easy enough to find out, if he wanted to know.

Before the long journey across the Atlantic, she would not have even suspected him of such a thing, but now— things were different. And it was her own doing.

Was she letting her imagination run away with her? Perhaps, but Sabelle seemed to consider it a possibility worth thinking about. It was her own fault! She had denied the captain her bed and her body and he had changed in his regard for her. He never spoke to her, and after that one night he never approached her again, never tried to force his attentions on her. She had thought before that he actually cared for her a little. It even seemed so that night of the storm when he had misinterpreted her helping Freddie. But that meant little with a man like Roque.

She had a feeling of certainty that even if he did care for her, he would not let it get in the way. He had cared in a gruff, male way for McGowery and had hardly batted an eye at the news of his death.

Garlanda felt a surge of anger. She would not let this happen. If Roque was considering taking Aunt Althea's money to ransom her, he would have to think again. She wouldn't let him have the chance. She would get off this ship somehow! Roque must not know that she suspected him. Garlanda went out on deck with a sense of calm confidence. She didn't know how she would escape, but she knew that she would manage.

Sabelle had been right. Nobody else could run her life for her as she had been allowing—no, expecting— them to do. She had been permitting others to toss her life around like the storms did ships. No more!

In the dusky twilight sailors were scrambling through the rigging like obedient monkeys. She looked at the *King of Rhye* and the *Phoenix*. Their sails were quickly disappearing, being taken down as were *La Doña del Fuego*'s. All evening the three ships sat out at sea, bobbing placidly, waiting for nightfall. When at last it was completely dark, the lanterns on deck were doused and the sails unfurled invisibly; only the gentle *thwack* of wind on canvas gave away their presence. Orders were given and acted on in whispers.

There was a powerful feeling of invisible acceleration as the wind cupped the sails and propelled them toward the narrow entrance to the Mediterranean. There were clouds covering the moon and Garlanda could barely make out the shadows—black on black—of the other two ships. She stood at the rail watching the darkness slip by. Sabelle came and stood beside her. "Now it's up to the wind," she said leaning her plump, strong arms on the rail and trying to look relaxed. She turned around and then hissed, "Damn that bastard Williams, I'll break that lantern over his lumpy head!" She disappeared. A tiny pinpoint of light was extinguished a moment later with a repressed, "Ouch!"

The clouds thinned and a tiny slice of melon moon cast a shimmering light on Gibraltar. Garlanda gasped at the sight of the sheer gray monolith rising like an enraged god from the sea. "*Yebel al Tarik*," Roque said. He had silently joined her.

"What does that mean?" Garlanda said. It was odd, standing here chatting as if they were old friends, each trusting the other, when it wasn't true.

"An Arab named Tarik made the rock his fortress a thousand years ago. Mountain of Tarik, *Yebel al Tarik*," he said quietly. "The Phoenicians called it

Abila—that means 'stop.' It's beautiful in a stark way, isn't it?"

Garlanda nodded. "Go on, tell me more about it."

"I don't know much more. Behind us is Ceuta, the beginning of Africa. They say Spain and Africa were once connected here and that men and animals crossed freely. There's a story that Hercules made the division in the land and set the rock up as an entry pillar."

"Who does it belong to?"

"It belongs to anyone who can hold it. It's changed hands many times. It has to be taken by land, though, there is no way to scale the sides." He didn't touch her and he spoke impersonally, but something of the old feeling of affectionate companionship was in his voice. In spite of the decision she had made, everything seemed so peaceful and simple on a night like this that she was drawn to him. She had almost moved into the shelter of his strong arms when a voice interrupted.

"Captain, I've got a man in the hold with a belly-ache," Sebastian was saying. "I don't like to disturb you, but I can't keep him quiet. I think he's burst something inside and he's vomiting blood."

"No symptoms of plague?" Roque asked.

"No, it seems to be his stomach, but I've tried to get him drunk enough that he'll sleep and be quiet. It doesn't work."

"I'll have a look at him," Roque said and left without another word.

Garlanda stood for a long time watching the gray, stone sentinel disappear behind them, then went to her cabin. She did not sleep for a long time. Was she really doing the right thing? she wondered. But what choice did she have? Suppose she could have put aside her conscience and stayed with Roque. She couldn't spend a lifetime this way, living in one room on a hostile sea that had taken so much from her and terrified her with its force.

Finally she slept. In her dreams she was on the island again. Only it wasn't quite the island, it was a ship with trees. It didn't matter. She and Roque were making tender love on the hot sand, but there was something wrong. There were other people there. A man kept calling her name, but even though she could hear him clearly, she didn't know if he was calling her Fleur or Garlanda. Then Roque was suddenly gone and she was wearing the chartreuse taffeta dress she'd made for Sabelle. Someone was walking down the beach toward her—a man—tall and dressed in rags. His head was bent and he kept running his hands through his sandy red hair in a gesture of wild despair. There was something familiar about his clothing.

"Dead—dead—" he chanted quietly. "They've killed me. Dead—dead—"

Suddenly Garlanda recognized him. It was her father! Just as he'd been when she was a child. Tall and handsome, but now he wasn't smiling Papa, he was wracked with sorrow. She ran to him and threw her arms around him, but he seemed not to know she was there. "Papa!" she cried out. He kept on walking, hardly impeded by her entreaties to stop. "They've killed me," he repeated.

"Papa!" she screamed. Finally he stopped and looked at her as if he didn't know who she was. "They've killed me and no one cares," he said, carefully prying her fingers from his shirt and discarding her.

She sat in the sand where she'd fallen. Now it was

night and she was cold. "I care, Papa. I care. Please, Papa, come back. Please don't go," she called out to him, but he kept on walking. Farther and farther from her then he turned and came back. But he wasn't the same. There was a vengeful fire in his eyes. He pinched her arms with bony claws and shook her violently, wordlessly. She screamed, "Papa, stop! Please stop!"

But he wasn't Papa anymore, he was Sebastian, and he was saying, "Miss Fleur! Wake up. Are you alright?"

Garlanda realized where she was. What was Sebastian doing here? What was happening? "Wake up, Miss Fleur. There now, it's just a bad dream, isn't it. You're not sick?"

"No. No, I don't think so," she said groggily. "What are you doing here?"

"I was passing your door and I heard you calling out. I thought perhaps you were hurt or ill. Sometimes fever victims act like this."

"Thank you, Sebastian. I haven't a fever. I'm just sick for home."

He patted her head paternally and handed her an extra blanket. "Get some sleep, little one. There's a bit of chill in the air tonight. We'll be in Marseille tomorrow."

Garlanda burrowed into the covers and fell back into a deep, dreamless sleep.

They dropped anchor off Marseille late in the morning.

Garlanda waited in the cabin, hearing hurried footsteps racing past her door. Sabelle was shouting and

Roque's deep bass roar joined in to give orders. It sounded as if half the crew was disembarking. There was a knock at the door. She opened it to admit Freddie. Garlanda was glad to see that his hand hadn't been permanently damaged. "Miss Fleur? We're in the bay of Marseille. I—I thought you might want to know that."

"Thank you, Freddie."

"Miss? Is there anything I can do?"

"No, I—yes, there is something you can do!" She gripped his shoulder and turned pleading eyes on him. "Your clothes would fit me—if you have a spare outfit I could have—I must get off this ship and go home."

"You mean they won't let you?" He sounded shocked.

Garlanda decided that the truth was her best card. "Look, Freddie, my father's dead and my mother died in the shipwreck that stranded me on the island with the captain. I've got an aunt back in England. I must go to her. Don't you see? I'm not meant to live like this. I'm not a whore! Do you have sisters? Imagine what it would be like for them in this position. Won't you please help me, Freddie?"

He hesitated. A quick expression of worry and sympathy creased his youthful countenance. "Aye, I'll help you. The doctor would surely lend a hand as well. Mr. Sim's a good man. I'll see what I can do. Don't worry, we'll get you off."

When he had gone she sat on the edge of the bed and covered her face with her hands. Was she wrong to trust in a young boy and an old man to come to her assistance? And yet, without knowing a thing about either of them, she had sensed that they were not like the rest of the riffraff that made up most of the crew.

Sebastian had obviously been a man of substance at one time and even Freddie showed occasional hints of breeding and education above the normal level.

Supposing she could trust them, but they got caught. What would Roque do to them for trying to free her and perhaps costing him a ransom from Aunt Althea. She could picture Althea receiving a ransom notice and promptly charging cross-continent armed with a butter knife, minus the money, a real weapon, or anything remotely useful.

A groan escaped her. Oh, what would she do? It was maddening to sit here bewailing her fate and having to depend on other people for help, but she didn't dare leave the cabin. Who could tell what fate Roque might subject her to if he realized she was trying to escape?

I long for the earth under my feet, she thought. *The pitch and sway of this ship is getting on my nerves. I wonder how I shall look making my debut in London with the swagger of an old sea dog, struggling along as if I'm still on board a ship. I'll have to learn to walk all over again. That's if I ever get there.* Her heart gave a patriotic leap. England! She remembered how Roque had satirized both her convent life and her fervent patriotism. He had no sense of decency, that man! But at least he did not believe in taking a woman against her will.

A clinking sound made her look up. Someone was turning a key in the lock. She ran to the door and threw herself against it, trying to pull it open before the lock fell into place.

"Calm yourself, Fleur," said the voice of the very devil. "It's for your own protection. You'd be risking that much-vaunted virtue of yours with the crew going out drinking and carousing. When they return wine-sotted and ready for more of what the town whores gave them, I rather suspect you would not want to receive them with open arms. Perhaps I should lock your little boyfriend up with you to protect him as well."

Was this some cruel jest? Her heart seemed about to leap into her throat. Did he suspect or was he merely toying with her? Had he caught Freddie and tortured the truth from him? Was this his sadistic way of telling her he knew all?

Garlanda waited, frozen. The next sound was that of heels clicking across the wooden deck. *He must be wearing his dress boots,* she thought glumly. *Off to have a splendid time in port while I'm incarcerated like a common criminal.*

"Roque! What the devil d'you mean, locking the child in like that?" came Sabelle's voice from outside the door. Garlanda brightened. Despite their multitude of differences, she had grown rather fond of the female buccaneer and suspected the feeling was returned, if only a little. Sabelle could be curt, rude, critical, and downright deadly, but there was a certain rough camaraderie about her, a willingness to accept everyone no matter who or what they were. She made no moral judgments, asked no questions, only took people as they proved to be.

"None of your business, quartermaster—or should I say quartermistress?" the captain asked sarcastically. Garlanda squinted through the keyhole but could see nothing.

"Quartermistress! Ha! I'm no fourth of a woman—" Sabelle shot back. There was a low laugh from Roque, then footsteps fading off into oblivion. Garlanda hurled herself down on the bed with a vengeance. That despicable man! She wished she could let loose with the kind of colorful obscenities that Sabelle adorned the air with when in one of her rages. As it was, the best she would think of was, "Oh, drat!" That sounded so feeble even to her own ears that she followed it with a short, self-mocking laugh. *Oh, drat won't get you home,* she thought. *You must be stronger, tougher. You must keep your wits about you and not lose your sense of identity. If it takes swearing and brawling to get home, then swear and brawl I shall!*

She stood up straight, took a deep breath, and said loudly to the empty cabin, "I won't let that bloody bastard do this to me!"

PART TWO

GARLANDA

CHAPTER 11

There was no escaping that night. She waited long hours in vain, but no one came to release her. Dawn came, a pale streak of light in the window. She could hear drunken voices and loud stumblings on deck. Chorus after chorus of "The Keelhauling of Black Jack Bowers" rang out, piercing the still morning calm.

Her hopes fell. Not today. Tonight, perhaps. She prayed that her accomplices had not been caught in the act of preparing to free her. There was nothing she could do but wait.

It was evening before one of the other cabin boys unlocked the door and brought her a tray. "Where's Freddie?" she asked nonchalantly.

"In town helping buy supplies."

He went out. So that was it! Had he even had time to tell Sebastian of the plan? She lifted the ragged cloth covering her food. Fresh! No more salt pork and sea biscuits. The tray was heaped with golden chicken, fresh crusty bread, wine, orange slices, spiced apple rings, and a cup of evil-looking brew. She took a sip and discovered it to be cocoa, thin, watery, and dusted with nutmeg and pepper as the French drank it. As she set the heavy tankard down, she noticed something queer about the bread.

A sharp white corner seemed to be jutting out of

the brown crust. She dug at it with her dull knife and extracted a tiny slip of paper. "Tonight at midnight. Clothes will be brought to you before then. Be dressed and ready. Destroy this," it said. There was no signature, but as she passed it under her nose she caught a faint whiff of medicinal herbs. So Sebastian knew of the plot and was assisting! Dear old man. She had finished her meal and set it on the captain's table when the door was unlocked again. This time it was Freddie. He gave her a quick, conspiratorial smile and threw her a bundle of clothing from under his jacket. Garlanda seized it and hid it under the red taffeta coverlet on the bed. No word passed between them until he took the tray and prepared to leave. "The message?" he asked.

"I ate it," she said in a whisper equal to his own. "It was the only way to destroy it." Freddie went out, trying to restrain a laugh. *Tonight! Escape from this mental anguish*, she thought joyfully. And then there was a small crash and the breaking of glass near the door.

"You clumsy dolt! Oh, it's you, the boy I caught on the bed with Fleur. I'd better not find you waiting on her again. Let Roger or one of the others do it next time. Look lively!" Garlanda winced. Roque's voice was slurred with drink. She heard the sound of a blow landing on flesh, then a muffled cry from her little friend. Roque kicked the door open.

"Good day, my little nun. I've come courting." The door slammed shut behind him. Garlanda gave a shocked gasp and backed up against the wall. The lean, hard-muscled man sat down on the foot of the bed, directly over the concealed clothing. Her heart hammered madly. Had he found out or was he only feeling lecherous? "Fleur, my dear—"

He came at her. Garlanda took refuge behind the desk, keeping it between them. He lunged with speed despite his drunkenness, and she found herself sweeping his astrolabe off the desk and clutching it behind her back.

He seized her about the waist. "What's that in your hand, little one?"

She showed him on the back of his head. The dark man's knees buckled. Garlanda struggled to get him across the bed before he completely collapsed. He was out cold. She dumped him and looked at her work with satisfaction. It wouldn't do for her to try to walk out now, even though the door was unlocked. It would look suspicious to anyone on deck, besides she had to be here at midnight.

An hour or more passed before the captain began to stir. Garlanda had been becoming worried that she had done Roque serious injury, although his sloppy snoring sounded merely drunk. Finally he was waking. She took hold of the front of her gown and tore it down between her breasts, nearly exposing them. She hitched her skirts up and crawled partway under Roque to lie there in a disheveled heap under the weight of his body. A quick rummage through her hair with frantic fingers furthered her ravished appearance.

He was nearly crushing her. She unfastened his trousers with an inner quiver, then lay still. Before long Roque gave a troubled groan and propped himself up on his elbows. "Fleur? Fleur?"

She gave a convincing moan and let her eyelids flutter open. At the sight of him she gave a cry and frantically hammered at his broad shoulders. "Leave me alone! Haven't you done enough harm already? Let me go, let me go! Beast! Savage! And you said you wouldn't harm me!" She managed to squeeze out an actual tear or two before shielding her face in the torn shoulder of her gown. Feigned sobs shook her slim body as if in the throes of grief. Roque rolled away, fumbling with his clothing.

"Fleur—Fleur, I—"

"Get away! Brute! I hate you!"

He practically ran out. The door remained unlocked although he had slammed it. A moment later she heard him bellow for an oarsman to fetch a rowboat. He was going ashore.

It was almost going too well. She remained where he had left her until she heard the watchman on deck call out that it was half past eleven. That had been cutting it close! Garlanda brought out the clothes the boy had given her. She struggled into the knee breeches and rough woolen overshirt, baggy enough to almost obscure the full curves of her figure. Clunky shoes, thick socks, and a worn jacket were yanked on. But her hair!

What to do with her hair? She dug in the pockets until she located a knit hat. It took some doing, but she managed to wind her glossy sweep of copper hair up in a tight bun on top of her head, then yank the hat on over it. A glance at the mirror told her she had done well. She turned the collar of the jacket up, hiding the dainty point of her chin. Not bad at all. With her hands crammed in her pockets she fancied she didn't make a bad little cabin boy at all. There was nothing about this urchin in the mirror to suggest that the daughter of a diplomat was hiding behind his naughty grin.

She looked around the room for the last time and on an impulse she got out the shirt of Roque's that she'd worn on the island. She used the sleeves to tie it around her waist under her jacket and tucked the ends into her waistband. She considered leaving Sabelle a note. She could pin it inside one of the dresses—but she didn't know what she could say. No, better to just disappear. Sabelle wouldn't approve of her leaving sweet little farewell messages anyway.

There was a stealthy tap on the door. Freddie slipped in with a cabin boy dressed much as she was. "Sebastian's waiting outside. He stole the key from the captain, but I see we don't need it."

"Roque was drunk. I broke an astrolabe across the back of his skull and avoided any trouble. He has gone, hasn't he?"

"Yes, he's off to town. We're pretending to be on an errand as well."

The other boy sat down on the bed. "Get away with ye now. Once the watch has changed I'll come out and no one will ever notice anything amiss until the captain comes back tomorrow."

Freddie and Garlanda left the room. "I'm coming with you," he told her in a low voice, then closed the door with a decisive bang. "Good night, Miss Fleur," he added in what amounted to a shout. He pretended to lock the door, took her by the elbow, and waved to the man on watch.

"Wait, lads!" Sebastian called. He came hurrying across the deck. "If you two aren't assigned other duties, I need some medicines. Here's the list and here's some money. Use it and hurry back. I don't want you gambling it away on fripperies." He took Garlanda's hand and in a low voice said, "Do you need money?"

"No," she answered softly, touched by his concern. "I have my jewels." She touched the cord at her neck that held the pouch containing the jewels the sailor had given her at Port Royal.

"Good. The medicine list is instructions for getting to the English embassy. Good luck, the pair of you." He winked at her in a boyish fashion signifying partnership. "Shove off, lads. I need those supplies," he called loudly.

They hurried to the rope ladder left hanging over the side. Garlanda had to be helped down it. Once they nearly fell. She looked down to see the turbulent ocean snapping what seemed miles below her. Her eyes shut and she climbed the rest of the way down by feel.

"Miss Fleur! Please, we must hurry," the boy pleaded. She nodded weakly and continued the descent. At last the creaking boat was under her feet, a wobbling vessel, hardly seaworthy. They seated themselves, cast off, and took the oars. Garlanda rowed like an old hand in her hurry to flee. She looked up as they emerged from the shadow of the trim battleship. The lovely figurehead smiled down at her benevolently, red hair gleaming in the lights reflected in the waves. *La Doña del Fuego* bobbed serenely on the cold water, then Garlanda ducked her head and refused to look back.

A welter of emotions boiled up inside her. Why were her thoughts so full of Roque—the passion and friendship they had shared? She had to leave and yet she didn't want to. How could such thoughts be hers? The pirate's woman Fleur struggled wildly with the girl who had once been the chaste, meek Garlanda and neither won.

"Freddie, why are you coming with me?" she asked, trying to get her mind off the turmoil in her heart.

"You'll never find your way through town alone and I've been here before. Besides, I'm sick of sailing."

They were approaching the shore. "Then why did you join the crew?"

"I didn't, Miss Fleur. I was kidnaped on the streets as were many others. I ended up in Tortuga where I jumped ship and was caught again. I was sold to Miss Sabelle. She signed me on this ship."

They scraped the shore. The boy leaped out, pulled the boat in, and tied it. Garlanda hopped out nimbly. "Freddie, that's awful! Surely that kind of barbarous behavior isn't common."

"More so than you'd think, Miss. Watch your step." Was he serious? Kidnaping boys and forcing them into service at sea. Freddie must have been no more than a child when he was taken. She had no more time to wonder. They set off for the glow of the nearest streetlight and stopped to unfold the map.

A cluster of drunken sailors leaning on the shoulders of gaudy prostitutes teetered. Garlanda forgot herself and smiled. They were the type of women she'd seen all over Port Royal and she knew they had endured the same hardships she had.

Her smile was misinterpreted. "Ow, lookit the boys. Hello, little ones, want some fun?"

Freddie grabbed Garlanda by the arm and bolted. Raucous laughter chased them down the twisting cobblestone alley. When they came to a halt near a deserted storefront, they were both panting and laughing. Freddie took the map from her and squinted at it in the dim light. "We're going the right direction. Up this street and then left, and we'll be on the main road. It should lead us near Embassy Row."

They set off, shoulders squared determinedly. The street seemed deserted until they rounded the corner to the left. A group of men stood there conversing in low, terse voices. "Look," one said, "New recruits."

"And you thought I wasn't serious, Miss Fleur," Freddie said in a disapproving murmur. "Quick, back up this way and we'll run for it."

The men came toward them. Garlanda caught the boy's hand and they ran—straight into a cul-de-sac. Cornered!

"C'mon, boys, no trouble now. We're just needin' a few more hands on our spice trader. Come along quietly and there'll be no untender tunes tapped out on your young heads."

Garlanda wished for a weapon, even the most nicked and battered cutlass on board *La Doña del Fuego*. What she could do with a chance to apply Sabelle's lessons! They'd be out of this situation already. No ruffian was going to confront cold steel to gain a pair of unwilling deck hands.

The men closed in on them. She forced herself to give a good appearance of limp fright as a bony hand closed on her wrist. He wore a sword! She gave a bleat of fear, sagged as if about to faint, and got a hand on the cold hilt. She had it! It sprang from the scabbard and flashed to life in her hand.

"Behind me, Freddie!" she shouted trying to mimic not only Sabelle's manner of speech, but her throaty roar as well. "Now, me mates, the first 'un among ye'll taste metal." For emphasis she gave a flick of the sword that neatly sliced the brass buttons off her ex-captor's dingy vest. She backed out of the alley only to feel a fist in her back. An arm circled her neck, then the sword clattered and clanged to rest on the cobblestones.

"Hold the bloke—or is it a bloke?" the leader of the men sneered. A rough blow landed on the side of Garlanda's head. Greedy hands seized at the front of her shirt and tore it open down to her waist, exposing the creamy roundness of her breasts. "Feast your eyes on them beauties," the leader said, gripping them. "Hold her while I get her breeches down."

Just then the prostitutes Garlanda had smiled at blundered down the alley with their clients. "'Scuse us, mates, we—"

"Help me," Garlanda screamed. She kicked out, catching a pockmarked man in the groin. He fell back with a breathless curse.

"Hey," a yellow-haired doxy said, "Hold on, lads. There's no need to rape when there's so much around that's willin'."

"Leave, you diseased trollop. What you've got can't compare to this little ivory creature. She ain't all used up and scurvy."

"And I *am*?" The yellow-haired woman's parasol crashed down on a greasy head. All at once the alley exploded into a pitched battle of sailors and clawing, spitting whores. Garlanda was released. She stooped to retrieve the sword, brought her knee up in a man's crotch, and was pleased to see her friend Freddie belting thugs for all he was worth. He shouted to her, pointing up the street. They struggled free from the crowd and ran for the open end of the alley.

"Stop them two! They stole a sword and started this all!"

Thus it was that Garlanda and Freddie found themselves racing up Embassy Row with a dozen infuriated rogues and a passel of whores dogging their footsteps. The women were still swearing at the sailors and trying to cuff them into submission, the men were determined to punish Garlanda, and the two leading the entire bizarre parade only wanted to find a place to make a final stand.

Garlanda's cap slipped, letting her copper hair

stream down her back in a flood of color. Freddie stopped long enough to heave a rock at the nearest sea dog, which felled the brawny fellow with a loud thud.

"The English embassy! Which is it, Freddie? Which building is it?"

"This way, Miss. Hurry!"

The gates were locked. She boosted him up and told him to release the latch and go for help while she held the crowd off with her sword. Suddenly the mass was upon her. She cleared a path with her blade as the gate clanked shut behind her. Lights flared up, dogs barked, and voices mumbled in the distance. Loud swearing and angry, dirty faces ringed her.

The gate opened. Garlanda backed up the walk, facing a circle of cold steel in front of her and—she knew not what behind her. She could only hope that the boy had gone for help—and that the embassy dogs hadn't been loosed on her. A rapier deftly wielded in the hand of a man not as drunk as he looked left a bloody trail across her thigh. She had lost her shoes and now in the din closing in on her, faced death or at the least a brutal gang rape and merciless beating.

Her stockings were torn, the woolen shirt she wore was slit to expose her breasts, and her breeches were ripped and bloodied. Her hair was a red-gold flame falling about her face in wild disarray. She gasped for breath, stabbed a man, and watched him fall back. *I have killed.* Sick realization. *I have broken the Commandments and committed murder. And I'm only sorry he wasn't three of the swine.*

There was no time for regret. Shouting and flashing swords assailed her with terrifying accuracy. A dozen cuts laced her sun-bronzed skin in crimson stripes that would drain her strength—her very *life*—if aid didn't arrive soon. She was aware of Freddie backing her up in the turmoil, ducking under a sword and punching someone with more aim and daring than she would have credited him with.

"They're coming! We'll be saved!" he told her through the uproar. "Hold on, Fleur! Hold on!"

The tip of a foil pierced the tender flesh over her left breast just enough to draw blood. She realized as if from a distance that she held one hand at her hip in the accepted duel stance, the other wielding her weapon with little grace and no style, but enough enthusiasm to keep the crowd off her throat another few seconds. She was tired—so tired. The power was seeping from her in a dull, aching haze.

All at once there was a shout behind her, the crash of steel meeting steel. She stood still, gasping for breath as the embassy staff took over the fight. A hand fell on her shoulder. She turned, heedless of her open shirt and bloodied fingers, putting one hand out in a "back off" gesture while the other brought up the sword in a defensive move.

Two men regarded her, one stocky and bluffly, Britishly solid. The other man was ten years his junior, a tall golden Apollo in the full bloom of arrogant manhood. The elder of the two held her shoulder, face unperturbed as if he came to the aid of half-naked, sword-brandishing young countrywomen every night and was actually a trifle bored by the entire procedure. In contrast the blond, mustached man was pale with shock, concern—and suddenly Garlanda was aware that her shirt was open.

Her knees felt as if they had become liquid. She neatly slid to the ground and fell across their feet.

CHAPTER 12

Garlanda awoke staring up at a lacy canopy. She held quite still for a long time trying to figure out where she was and how she got there. Then, drip by drip, information fed into her sleepy brain. Last night—it must have been that long for now it was light—she and Freddie fighting off the street women and the sailors intent on rape and kidnap. She remembered the fight at the embassy gates and felt a little flash of self-congratulation at her handling of both sword and language. Sabelle would have been proud.

The last thing she recalled was falling at the feet of two gentlemen—one of them, at least, distinctly English. She must be in the embassy mansion. How had she gotten in this elegant bed? Good heavens! The men hadn't put her to bed—had they? She looked down and saw that she was wearing a soft, lavender-sprigged nightshift. She raised herself on her elbows to look around and felt arrows of pain stab through her head and echo in various parts of her body. The sword cuts, of course. She looked around the tapestry-hung room—a beautifully furnished guest room.

"Good, you're awake," a soft voice said. Garlanda craned her head around in spite of the pain it caused. There was a pretty young woman sitting in a low chair beside the bed. She had wispy brunette hair

tortured into the latest fashion and a plump little
body stuffed into a gray dress that did terrible things
to her complexion. But she had a lovely, sweet smile
that made up for it.

"Am I at the embassy?" Garlanda asked.

"Yes. I've dressed your wounds and you've had a
nice, long rest."

"Freddie?" Garlanda said, sitting up suddenly.

"That young man who was with you? He's fine too.
All patched up. He's downstairs. I can send for him if
you wish."

"No, no, not now," Garlanda said. "I suppose you
would like to know who I am."

"I admit to some curiosity," the girl said with a
pleasant twinkle of understatement.

"I'm Fl– uh, Garlanda Cheney."

"Cheney! Are you related to the late Sir Robert
Cheney?"

"He was my father. Did you know him?"

"No, I didn't, but my husband's friend, the ambassador, has spoken often of him. He was highly regarded in diplomatic circles. His death was a great
loss. By the way, I'm Elaine Ridgely. My husband
Renwick is a friend of Sir George Young–Brookes."

"That's the ambassador?"

"Yes, Sir George is. They have been great friends
for a long time and Renwick often visits here. This is
the first time I've been here, though. We were only
married last year." She seemed inordinately proud of
this fact. Garlanda only vaguely remembered the two
gentlemen from last night, but if Elaine Ridgely's husband was the tall, blond one, Garlanda could appreciate her attitude. "We were to have left tomorrow,"
Elaine added.

"Where are you going?"

"Back to England. Sir George is making a report to the King and Queen and we were going to travel with him."

"Then why did you say you 'were to have left'? Oh, no—don't change your plans because of *me*. I'm so sorry to have imposed on you this way, but I—"

"Please, Miss Cheney, do not distress yourself. I shall be glad to stay here with you until you are fully recovered. Are you—well, are you bound for England?"

"Yes! Most assuredly. You see, I've been—I don't know quite where to start—" Garlanda said. It was literally true, she had not given serious, specific thought to what story she was going to tell of her adventures. It would be very difficult to assume her proper position in society if anyone suspected the full truth. No decent man would ever have anything to do with her if her relationship with Roque were even guessed at. She must be very careful about what she said.

"Please forgive me. I've tired you and I certainly don't mean to pry into your personal affairs," Elaine Ridgely said, her pretty face falling into a distracted expression.

"Not at all. I owe you an explanation. I owe all of you an account of why I appeared on your doorstep in such—such shameful condition. It's just that I'm still a little unclear. That last day has been—"

"There. I *have* tired you. No, I won't hear another word. Let me apply a little more ointment to your injuries and you shall be left alone. Perhaps if you feel like coming down to luncheon you would like to join us and explain then, although I assure you that absolutely *no* explanations are the least necessary."

Yes, I must make an explanation and it must be the right one, Garlanda thought. She allowed Elaine

Ridgely to doctor her wounds and expressed gratitude
at the frumpy-looking dress that the other woman provided for luncheon attire. As soon as the door had
shut behind her Garlanda was sitting up in bed, thinking frantically.

Sir George Young-Brookes was a florid-faced Englishman of thirty-five or so. He looked like he belonged in hunting clothes, huffing as he tried to mount
an oversized horse. He was the sort of man who probably took great interest in dogs and partridges.
Elaine's husband, Renwick, was not so easily catego-
rized. Or perhaps he was, Garlanda decided. Very
wealthy, very handsome, and very aware of it. His
blond hair swept his forehead in a manner that would
make him appear boyish for another thirty years and
his eyes were the penetrating pale blue that made
women think he was looking at them fully clothed and
seeing them naked.

Garlanda found it hard to keep from looking at him
and harder yet to meet his searching eyes. He devoted
his attention to her in a manner that neglected everyone else in the room, including his wife, who appeared even mousier in his august presence.

"Mistress Cheney, we are charmed to have you
among us," he said in an intimate tone that seemed to
hint at more than the actual words.

"I am more than charmed to be here," she said between bites of a luncheon she was trying to eat daintily. Her true impulse was to fall on the delicious food
like the starving escapee that she really was. But she
had her plan well in mind and gobbling her food
didn't fit in. She washed her fingertips in the silver

bowl of almond water by her plate and left little portions of each food. A servant took it away. Conversation lagged and Garlanda knew it was time.

"It has been more than generous of you to help me, Sir George," she said with an inclusive nod to the Ridgelys. "But I feel I must impose on you further to explain the unfortunate circumstances that led me to your door." There were polite murmurs from the men to the effect that such a course was unnecessary, but she went on, "My mother and I sailed from Martinique last spring for England. My mother was very ill and became more so aboard the *Valiant*."

"The *Valiant*!" Sir George barked. "But the *Valiant* went down in a storm. Everyone perished. We heard all about it a few weeks ago."

"Forgive me for disagreeing, Sir George, but everyone did not perish."

"By Heaven, George, hold your tongue and let the poor girl finish!" Renwick Ridgely said.

"Thank you. You see, the *Valiant* did go down in a terrible storm, but I was saved."

"A miracle!" Elaine Ridgely interjected. "But what about your mother?" she asked softly.

"My mother," here Garlanda sniffed lightly and put a handkerchief to her eyes. All the sorrow and horror of that day washed back over her. "My mother died on board before the ship sank. A nice man on the ship took me from her and threw me overboard. That dear soul saved my life and I shall be eternally grateful to him for that. I only wish that I could have expressed my thanks to him before—"

"Miss Cheney, please don't trouble yourself to relive this," Elaine implored. "Come along to your room."

"No, it's alright," Garlanda said holding her head high. Perhaps she was overdoing it. *Be careful, this*

story has to be told at least once to stop speculation,
she told herself. "Forgive me and please indulge me
and allow me to continue. I was thrown overboard
and taken aboard a lifeboat. I was unconscious and
the next thing I knew I was on an island all by myself."

"How awful!" Poor Elaine looked ill. "You must have
been terrified!"

"I was at first, but I was so glad to be alive and
there was plenty of food."

"Weren't there wild animals or savages?" Elaine
asked, ignoring the look that Renwick gave her.

"No, nothing like that."

"Was no one else with you?" Sir George asked.

"No. Not a soul. Two bodies washed in later." For
the first time since that day she recalled the bodies.
She hadn't meant to mention them. What did happen
to them? Of course, Roque must have buried them.
Roque—what had he thought when he discovered her
absence?

She pulled herself back to the present. "After a
while, I gathered big piles of wood and lit fires whenever a ship passed near. Finally one of them noticed
me and I was rescued."

"An English ship?" Elaine asked.

"Elaine, please!" Renwick said repressively. Elaine
clamped her lips shut and looked an apology at her
husband.

"No, it wasn't an English ship. It was a—a pirate
ship."

"Pirates!" Elaine gasped.

"Elaine!"

"Yes, pirates. But I was fortunate. The captain was
a rather pleasant elderly man in spite of his horrible
profession and he had his wife on board."

"His wife?" Sir George asked. "Isn't that rather unusual?"

"I suppose it is," Garlanda said. *Am I going to get away with this?* "Of course, I know very little about these awful privateers that ply the sea and terrorize decent people. Anyway, the wife took charge of me and kept me in her cabin. I never saw anyone else the entire time, except the cabin boy who brought our food. I did the mending for the crew and read my Bible and the time passed quickly enough." *Surely they can see in my face what lies these are.*

"Then who was chasing you last night," Sir George asked.

"When we got into port I discovered why the pirate captain was willing to treat me so well. He had apparently intended to ransom me to my family."

"The fiend!" Renwick said. "What's to be done with this sort of thing going on in the world?"

"They couldn't have gotten ransom for me anyway," Garlanda went on, determined to complete the story without losing the thread of it. "I gave them a false name. I told them my name was 'Fleur.' You probably heard the cabin boy calling me that last night?"

"Why 'Fleur'?" Sir George asked.

"Oh, I don't know. It just popped into my head. The young man, Freddie, helped me escape. He's a good person. He had inquired about the location of the embassy and helped me get here."

"Were those the pirates following you?"

"No. Those were just some thugs from town who were trying to capture us for enslavement on another ship."

"You were doing a capable job with that cutlass," Renwick said. Was there an undercurrent of lazy sarcasm in his voice or did she imagine it?

"Cutlass? Oh, is that what that big knife is called. Freddie gave it to me and I was just trying to defend myself."

"Just a sort of natural ability, I guess you might call it?" Renwick said. Definitely sarcasm. She cast a quick sidelong glance at Sir George. He looked skeptical, but Garlanda knew he couldn't disprove her story and suspected that he wouldn't even try. Of course, there wasn't much chance that he actually believed it, either. "Now all I want is to go home to my dear auntie Althea."

"We'll certainly see that you get back. Never fear, we'll do that," Sir George said.

"I understood Mrs. Ridgely to say that you are all planning to leave tomorrow?"

"Yes, that's true. I have dispatches that should be delivered to our gracious sovereigns in person."

"Is there any way that I might accompany you? I would be more than happy to pay my own way, of course, if you could allow me to do so when we get to England." *It would be difficult to explain the bag of jewels around my neck. I hope Mrs. Ridgely didn't take special note of that bag.*

"We'd be charmed to have your delightful company. I'm sure you and Mrs. Ridgely would greatly enjoy each other's company on such a long journey. But are you sure that your health will permit—"

"Sir George, I want more than anything in the world to go home. My health is quite adequate, I assure you. As for holding up your plans for leaving tomorrow—I would prefer to leave at the first possible moment. I could not feel safe here. The pirates are probably still in the harbor, and I couldn't consider leaving this building without being in danger. It's not

as if I have any packing to do," she said with a light
laugh.

"If you're sure?"

"Quite sure. There's one thing. What about Freddie?"

"Oh, yes. The young man in the ragged clothing. I
interviewed him this morning. He would not discuss
you at all. Not that I questioned him about you, of
course, and I thought that admirable. He told me he
dare not return to his former 'job.' I have given him a
post here as an errand runner for the embassy. Our
boys must present a respectable appearance and the
boy does. I've given him fresh clothing, and I think
you'll be surprised at the change. Do you wish to have
words with him before our departure in the morning?"

"If you don't mind, sir, I would. He helped save my
life, just as the old man on the *Valiant* did, and I don't
wish to miss another opportunity to express my
thanks."

"Hm-m-m, yes. I see. Well, it can be arranged."

"Thank you. Now, if you don't mind, I am really
quite tired."

"Of course, of course. Didn't mean to wear you
out." Sir George clearly didn't approve of her desire to
speak to Freddie, but that was too bad. She did have
an obligation and she intended to fulfill it.

Later in the afternoon Freddie came to her room.
"You asked to see me?" he said. Garlanda was astonished at the change in him. He had been cleaned up,
his hair neatly cut, and he was dressed in the livery
that all of Sir George's servants wore. He was indeed
a respectable-looking young man.

She smiled at him and he smiled back. "How nice
you look, Freddie."

"Thank you, Miss Fleur."

This wouldn't do with Elaine sitting chaperone. "Mrs. Ridgely, I'm a little chilled. Do you have an extra shawl I might borrow?" Garlanda asked.

"Surely," Elaine answered. "Just a moment," she said rushing out and nearly tripping in her eagerness to do small favors for Garlanda.

Garlanda stepped close to Freddie. "Hold out your hands," she said in a quick whisper. "Let me see how you've healed." He did as he was told and she put a fat ruby in his palm, folding his fingers back over it. "They look fine to me."

"Miss Fleur! I can't take this."

"Yes, you can. I want you to have it. I have no other adequate way to tell you what your help has meant to me. You risked your life for me." Freddie looked at the floor and scuffed his toe on the rich Persian carpeting. "Freddie, I must depend on you for more yet."

"Anything, Miss Fleur, anything at all . . ."

"I have told some lies—only you know the truth. I want you to back me up." She told him the story she had told Sir George and the Ridgelys.

Freddie nearly gagged with laughter when she got to the part about the old pirate's wife. "Miss Sabelle would tear your tongue out for that." He laughed.

"Wouldn't she, though," Garlanda giggled. "Sir George told me that you wouldn't talk about me."

"No, ma'am. He was trying to find out who you were. I didn't know except that we called you Fleur, and you were on the island with the captain. But I didn't even tell him that. Do you think he believed what you told him?"

"I don't think so, but unless you tell him otherwise, he can't really dispute my story."

"You can count on me, Miss Fleur."

"I'm grateful for your discretion. Please, Freddie,

don't tell anyone on the staff anything but the story I just told you. I'll send you my address in London when I get there. You must write me and tell me—oh, you *can* write, can't you?"

"Yes, Miss. I've had a lot of schooling."

He offered this information about himself willingly enough. Although Garlanda knew the code well, she had to ask. "How did a boy like you end up getting kidnaped by pirates?"

"Oh, it's a long story." She had overstepped, but he would excuse it, his tone said.

"Well, you must write and tell me how you're doing. If there's anything you ever want, please let me know. I owe you a great deal and I would be glad to help you."

"I know that, Miss Fleur. But I don't need any more help than this." He held open his hand for a moment and looked at the ruby. "I've got a nice enough job here. Nobody to box my ears or make me climb around in riggings on cold nights. I think I'll like it here."

"Don't you have family? Someone—somewhere to go home to?"

"Not anymore," he said. Just then Elaine came back in.

She got the shawl tangled in the door latch, unsnarled the loopy yarn, and handed the shawl to Garlanda. "Freddie," Garlanda said formally, "I've told the ambassador how much help you've been to me and I expect you to be as useful to him. I shall look forward to hearing of your progress."

"Yes, Miss Fleur," he said and bowed politely.

* * *

The trip to England seemed interminable to Garlanda. There were two other couples from the English community of Marseille traveling with them and near Paris an elderly woman and her daughters joined them. No one asked Garlanda about her experiences, at least not directly, but the other ladies watched her speculatively. Did they think she might burst into tears or break out in intimate confidences at any moment, Garlanda wondered.

Sir George sent a courier ahead to alert Aunt Althea to the fact that Garlanda was alive and due to arrive in England shortly. Elaine had two black dresses that she loaned Garlanda to wear since she was still in mourning for her mother's death less than a year past. No matter what she wore, however, she wore a small bag around her neck on a long ribbon. No one asked about it, not even Elaine, who must have noted it the night she put Garlanda to bed at the embassy. Garlanda's only possession that was her own and not borrowed from Elaine was a worn man's shirt, carefully folded at the bottom of Garlanda's traveling case.

Elaine proved to be a pleasant companion. She had developed an instant affection for Garlanda. She was, appearance aside, just what Garlanda would have been if it hadn't been for the shipwreck. She was shy, well-bred, and totally innocent of the baser aspects of life. She just barely missed being pretty, however, and everything she did to improve her looks misfired. Her soft, thin hair refused to curl and when she had it crimped, it fuzzed dramatically. Her complexion was sallow and when she applied the most infinitesimal bit of paint, it showed up like gaudy-colored lanterns. Then she had to scrub it off and that made her face blotchy for hours.

She was so soft-spoken that people were continually

having to ask her to repeat what she'd said, and when she was genuinely excited enough to speak loudly, she stammered. If there was a puddle for anyone to step in, Elaine stepped in it while the others walked around. Drinks that got spilled, always got spilled either *by* her or *on* her, usually both.

Renwick was a different matter altogether. He had social graces enough for both of them. Everything about him was studiedly perfect. He was handsome, sympathetic, and extremely courteous. Elaine's fumbling ways could very nearly be smoothed over by his cool suavity. Garlanda was embarrassed by the extravagant attention he gave her, plying her with compliments, talking to her a little too often while poor Elaine stumbled about in the background. More than once Garlanda caught him gazing at her in a way no gentleman should have, and yet there was nothing specific that he did that she could criticize without sounding foolish, even in her own mind.

His outward conduct was irreproachable. He was never less than courtly and at all times he oozed good British breeding. She hated herself for wishing he wasn't married, and to dear Elaine of all people—Elaine who had been so very kind to her. Garlanda always felt a sort of guilty excitement in his presence and wondered if she would have felt the same way if she, like nice young ladies protected from the realities, did not know what could happen between a man and a woman.

She decided that once she got back to England she must avoid him as much as she possibly could without insulting Elaine.

CHAPTER 13

She peered into the fog at the ghostly outlines of South-ampton harbor and found herself wishing for the spyglass the little boy in Port Royal had let her use just before the earthquake. But that was part of the past and she must put it forever out of her mind. The only things that remained with her from that life were Roque's shirt and the jewels in the bag she kept con-cealed in the bodice of her dress. *I earned them,* she thought coldly. *The fact that I have survived entitles me to them.*

She thought she heard Renwick's voice and she ducked quickly behind some cargo piled on the deck. She had to be alone right now. She didn't want Ren-wick's flattering, solicitous attention. Private time was necessary—time to completely set aside what re-mained of "Fleur" and become totally "Garlanda" again.

The docks came into clearer view. She could see people now, tiny animated dolls, awaiting their loved ones. Among them was Aunt Althea. Dear Auntie—she wondered if she would recognize her little niece, grown up now, not the skinny little convent girl of Martinique. Garlanda was so excited that her teeth were nearly chattering.

Closer yet and she could finally see Althea standing

calmly in the center of a little storm of waiting relatives. As tall and beautiful as Garlanda remembered her, Althea didn't seem to age and Garlanda had never been able to guess her years. As she watched, a small girl ran past Althea, apparently trod on her toes and got a sharp rap on the top of her head with a folded fan. The girl ran back to her offended-looking mother and clung to her skirts.

"Look, Leon, there she is," Althea's melodious yet piercing voice cut through the fog. "Gar-lan-da," she called out like an opera singer in full voice.

Garlanda waved back enthusiastically. She wondered who Leon was. Another of Althea's never-ending supply of suitors, no doubt. Garlanda's mother had once said of her sister that she did with suitors what our Lord had done with the loaves and fishes. Of course, Mama had tried to take it back later as a blasphemous remark to make to a young girl, but Mama's embarrassment had made it stick in Garlanda's mind all the better. Althea had been married in her youth to a Monsieur Pasteau, about whom she had very carefully never said anything at all. All Garlanda had ever known about him was that he had died early and left Althea a very wealthy young widow.

The ship kept up its snaillike pace and Garlanda found herself mentally weighing the efficiency of this crew against Roque's quick, snappy sailors and determining that this was definitely inferior. *Will I ever forget what I've learned?* she wondered. *Will time dim my memories—and do I really want it to?* Probably so, and yet a small part of her pictured an elderly Garlanda scandalizing grandchildren with tales of her exciting youth.

Grandchildren? What was she thinking? Grandchildren obviously came after children and that meant marriage first. She must clear her mind of everything that had happened since the day she and her mother set sail from Martinique. No respectable man would have anything to do with her if he even suspected her experience. One particular aspect had bothered her a great deal, and there had been no one to ask, except perhaps Sabelle. Garlanda wasn't a virgin—would a man know? Could she deceive a husband on her wedding night?

She would have to, that was all there was to it. Somehow. Still, she wished she knew how. Finally the plank was down and she had to restrain herself from knocking over the other disembarking passengers in her excitement.

Then she was in her Aunt Althea's arms, enveloped in a cloud of jasmine scent and pleasant little yelps of greeting, nearly smothered in ostrich feathers and yards of lace. "Darling little Garlanda, look how you've grown," Althea said, holding her at a graceful arm's length. "Look, Leon, she's all grown up."

The man addressed as Leon stepped forward. He was, like Althea, lean and ageless. He was dressed as for fashionable mourning, almost entirely in black including his unpowdered shoulder-length hair. His thin face reflected cool amusement, but there was nothing condescending about it. "My dear Miss Cheney," he said, bowing over Garlanda's hand with practiced ease. "Your aunt has spoken of nothing but your miraculous return for weeks. She's quite bored all her friends, in fact."

"Leon! I never bore anyone."

"My dear, were it not for your great beauty half the population of London would have perished of ennui long ago."

"Half the population of London *is* dead and they

don't know it," Althea said smugly. Leon bowed to her in tribute. "Oh my, I've forgotten my manners again, haven't I? Garlanda, my sweet, this is my dear, dear friend Count Leon Jareski–Yanoviak and this is my darling little Garlanda. You don't mind if the count calls you Garlanda, do you? He's practically one of the family."

"God forbid," Count Leon muttered.

"What was that?" Althea demanded.

"Nothing. I was just saying that your niece is not quite the 'child' you have led us all to believe. She's a grown-up lady, and an attractive one at that."

"Hm-m-m." Althea held Garlanda off at arm's length and surveyed her carefully. "Yes. I see what you mean. Well, of course, her mother was *so* much older than I—we're more like sisters, aren't we, Garlanda?"

Garlanda looked at the count who was shaking his head behind Althea's back. "Yes, of course, Auntie," Garlanda answered, trying to suppress a smile.

"About that, Garlanda, wouldn't it be much nicer if you would just call me 'Althea' from now on instead of 'Auntie'?"

"Better for you, certainly," Count Jareski–Yanoviak said to Althea.

"Oh, Althea, there are my friends who brought me back," Garlanda said. "Come over here and let me introduce you."

Althea swept through the crowd which Garlanda observed parted for her in some mysterious manner. Count Leon sauntered along in her wake. "Aunt Althea, I would like you to meet Sir George Young-Brookes, our ambassador to Marseille," Garlanda said, ignoring Althea's slight flinch at the word "aunt."

"I'm delighted, Sir George. I've heard all about you

from your mother. She has visited my home—a gifted woman at the harpsicord."

Count Leon leaned closer to Garlanda and whispered, "Althea wouldn't recognize Sir George's mother if she was served up on a silver platter with an apple in her mouth and sprinkled with watercress. But she is charming, isn't she?"

Garlanda was determined not to get sidetracked from her introductions, "Sir George, this is my aunt, Mrs. Pasteau and this is Count Jareski–Yanoviak. Oh, here's Renwick." She made her round of introductions again and Althea inspected Renwick approvingly.

"Garlanda has been very fortunate to have two gentlemen such as yourselves to look out for her on this journey. Such handsome gentlemen, I might add." Just then Elaine joined them and Althea's disappointment was evident when she found out that Elaine was Renwick's wife. "I'm having a party to celebrate Garlanda's return to us on Tuesday next. You must all be there, n'est-ce pas? Now I must get Garlanda home and arrange for dressmakers."

They made their departure in a great flurry that Garlanda was to discover was Althea's trademark. Once inside the high-wheeled coach that Althea had hired for the journey Garlanda looked back at the quayside crowd and realized that Renwick was still staring after her and there, beside him, was Elaine watching him with such sad understanding that it made Garlanda's heart contract for a moment.

The coach started up with a lurch. "Leon, darling, may I have my pipe?" Althea asked. Count Jareski–Yanoviak fished in his pockets and turned up a delicate little clay pipe with fancy carvings. He filled it with clove-scented tobacco, tamped it down with a gold tamper, and lit it. Then he handed it to Althea who took a few little puffs before turning attention to her niece. "I hope this doesn't shock you, my dear." *Yes, you do*, Garlanda thought with an inward chuckle.

"Not at all, Auntie—I mean, Althea."

Althea looked a little disappointed. "Now, you must tell us all about it—your—uh, adventures. That is, if you feel like talking about it. You know how sorry I was about your poor mama. We were never very much alike but I did love her too."

Garlanda found that she could hardly bear to talk about it, but she managed to tell about Mama's illness. Althea seemed perplexed as Garlanda's story unfolded, but she said nothing for a while. "Mama was anxious to get back home. That's why we took an earlier ship than the one we had planned to take."

Althea exchanged an alarmed glance with Count Leon. "You took an earlier ship? When did you leave?"

Garlanda told her, wondering why it made any difference.

"Oh, no!" Althea cried. "Then you don't know."

"Know what?" Garlanda asked. What *more* could there be?

"Oh, Leon," Althea said. "I can't!" she pressed a lacy handkerchief to her mouth.

Count Jareski–Yanoviak sat forward and reached across to take Garlanda's gloved hands in his. "Miss Cheney, the first your aunt heard of this entire unhappiness was from Martinique. Your grandfather's solicitors informed us that there had been a native insurrection, and the plantation house had been burned to the ground. The letter said that everyone had died. Your aunt assumed—everyone assumed—that this included you and your mother."

"Grandmother and Grandfather—dead?" Garlanda said in spite of the great painful lump in her throat.

"Yes, I'm afraid so, child. You see, your aunt has been thinking that she lost her entire family in this tragedy. This is the first we have heard of your early departure." Garlanda felt the blood draining from her head. She leaned against the side of the rocking carriage.

Count Leon went on, thinking, no doubt, that it was best to get the conversation over at once. "When Althea received word from Sir George that you had been rescued and were on your way home, we assumed that you had been rescued from Martinique. You see the misunderstanding?"

Garlanda nodded, but could not speak. Everyone gone now—everyone but Althea. It didn't seem possible!

"My dear—my own dead sister's child—tell us what happened," Althea sobbed. "Oh, you must."

Haltingly, Garlanda told them of the shipwreck— the same version she had told to Sir George. That gentleman had seemed skeptical, Count Jareski-Yanoviak looked downright disbelieving. ". . . And then I escaped through the streets and ran to the embassy where Sir George rescued me."

"It is extremely fortunate that those knaves did not mishandle you, Miss Cheney," Count Leon said with detached calm that left her feeling that the state of her virtue either way was of no concern to him— except in a purely academic sense. She felt that if she blurted out the entire sordid tale, he would neither flinch nor gasp, but rather continue regarding her in his inimitable, carefully calm manner.

"Yes, I—"

"Mishandle!" Althea screamed. She sat up, gripping

her sodden handkerchief. "Mishandle! Leon, don't jest! Garlanda, my own dear girl. Oh, the brutes didn't—they wouldn't—!"

Garlanda froze.

"Althea, calm yourself. Of course they didn't harm the child. They would have been worse than fools to misuse one they doubtless hoped to ransom for a high price. Privateers are businessmen, you know," the count interjected smoothly. Garlanda turned grateful eyes to him. Garlanda remembered her initial reaction months before when thinking of Auntie Althea receiving a ransom notice and coming to rescue her with a butter knife. She had been entirely correct.

"Oh, Leon, what a comfort you are to have as a friend. Of course, they didn't abuse the lamb. They knew I would come right after them."

"Flourishing a parasol and making Valkyrie noises, no doubt," the slim man said dryly.

They left behind the busy docks and fell silent. Leon and Althea seemed to sense that Garlanda had much to absorb and idle conversation would make the process more difficult. *Grandmother and Grandfather, gone! How could it be? And killed by the army of sloe-eyed natives who had always served them with apparent devotion? Certainly not old Margy, the cook. Or Adam, the head gardener, who had spent hundreds of afternoons on his knees working beside Grandmother in the terraced tropical gardens.* Her grandmother had taught him the French songs she had learned as a girl and Garlanda had often heard them in the garden, Adam's voice booming out French lullabies and Grandmother's thin trilling weaving through.

Garlanda blinked back tears. Impossible! Dead now—like Mama and Papa. Another heavy door of life slamming shut behind her, making memories that would have to be preserved as they were and never visited again. There was only the future now. She straightened her shoulders. Her future. To make for herself—to mold and shape and live as she chose. And she chose to be an untarnished English lady!

The autumn countryside flew by the window as they bounced along the dusty roads. Other high-wheeled carriages with liveried drivers passed them from time to time and they had to put handkerchiefs to their faces to breathe until the dust settled.

It was harvest time and the fields were full of peasants in drab clothing stripping the hop vines off their summer stakes and cutting down rippling fields of ripe rye. Children played along the hedgerows with little baskets for the berries they were supposed to be picking. Garlanda drank in the sights as if they were actual nourishment. Home at last! How many times had she dreamed these very scenes, fearing that she might never see such ordinary sights again. How many times in Martinique had she tried to conjure up the cider tang of crisp English autumns?

It took three days to get to London. Every evening they would stop at an inn and Leon would get rooms for himself and the women. Althea was quiet during the first part of the trip and Garlanda sensed that it was a strain on her, that she was merely curbing her exuberant nature for the sake of her bereaved niece. Althea had known about the tragedy at Martinique for longer and had had time to adjust to her losses.

Leon occasionally pointed out sights along the road and discoursed in a bright, impersonal way on interesting aspects of what they were passing. Garlanda found his company a great pleasure. Gradually Althea began to talk. She gossiped with a remarkable lack of malice about the King and Queen, the Queen's sister Princess Anne, and her friend Sarah Churchill. Only in regard to this lady did Althea sound bitter. "Pushing the poor little dumpling princess about and starting disputes between her and her sister. It's not right. She's just trying to further her own husband's career, of course. William and Mary will never have children and Anne, poor dear, will be Queen someday. Duchess Sarah sees her husband as the premier peer in the next reign—which God forbid should be soon. I hear that Queen Mary is not well, however. And so young—not yet thirty and married to that pompous Dutchman we have had foisted on us as a king."

"Isn't that treason?" Leon said languidly.

"Oh, fiddle! It's not treason, everybody feels that way. At least he's gone half the year doing those silly little military drills in France that he presumes to call a war. A fair weather war, that's what it is."

"We're at war with France?" Garlanda said. "But we saw nothing of it and no one stopped us or questioned our movements in France."

"That's what kind of war it is," Leon said. "No one but King William and a few of his favorite generals know it's going on. They only have it on pleasant days."

By the time they reached Althea's fashionable London house, Garlanda's spirits were reviving somewhat. They arrived late in the afternoon and she had a leisurely hour to accustom herself to her new surroundings before it was time to dress for dinner, not that dressing presented any problems. She had the bor-

rowed black dress of Elaine's that she had on and the
other borrowed black dress of Elaine's to choose from.

Garlanda had not been to Althea's London house
since she was a very young child and a great many
changes had been made since then. Althea had the
latest in everything that was stylish. Her home was
furnished to the bursting point with tall, stately chests
and chairs that came in matched partridgewood sets
with caned backs and seats. The slim, dignified furniture suited Althea perfectly. Instead of the dark paneling that had been the fashion for so long, Althea's
house had fabric panels on the walls in light, airy colors and hanging everywhere were multitudes of bright
paintings. Her living room had a carved Grinling Gib-
bons ceiling and an inlaid parquetry floor that fascinated Garlanda with its smooth intricacy.

Garlanda's own room was the size of a small ballroom and was filled with exquisite pieces of furniture
and knickknacks. There was a wide marble dressing
table with elaborate powder boxes and perfume vials
marching in casual precision across the width. The
mirror above it was hinged and could tilt to give a
full length view. The walnut cabriole legs ended with
dragon feet holding pearls that rested in a deep Persian carpet. It was the most luxurious place Garlanda
had ever seen and she reveled in the sensual pleasure
of elegant surroundings.

A pert little maid entered in a few minutes with a
pitcher of steaming water, a soft cloth, and cakes of
scented castile soap. She introduced herself as Jolee
then left Garlanda to wash off the travel grime and
don the fresher of the two black dresses.

Dinner was a quiet affair consisting of seven expertly prepared courses. Count Leon joined them

which rather surprised Garlanda, who had assumed that once back in London he would return to his usual pursuits—whatever they might be. Now that she was over the first blow of the grievous news of her grandparents' deaths, she was beginning to come out of her own sorrow and take more note of those around her. She was intrigued by the relationship between Althea and Leon. It was very strange. They were obviously extremely fond of one another, though loving words never passed between them; in fact, civil words rarely passed between them. There didn't seem, however, to be the tiniest shade of romance in their feeling for one another.

They were a little like a clever brother and sister who, through long association, have come to appreciate one another's wit above all others. No jealousy, no conflict, no protestations of affection—just a comfortable comradeship. This struck Garlanda as odd in view of the fact that they were both extremely attractive people, both in appearance and personality.

"I don't think you would wish to be presented to society before you had time to rest and get fitted for a proper wardrobe," Althea said, "So I only invited Leon to dine with us tonight."

"The tactful distinction being made between my august self and 'society', you see," Leon said with the expression that seemed to pass for a smile with him.

Althea made a face at him.

"I appreciate that, Althea," Garlanda said. "I do need some time to adjust to being back."

"I've made an appointment with the dressmaker for the first thing in the morning," Althea began.

"Rest quickly, Garlanda," Leon said quietly.

". . . Even though all we can get now will be black. Of course, we can begin selecting your wardrobe for when our mourning period will be over. And then there's the hairdresser in the afternoon, and I think I'll have a quiet little dinner next."

"Please, wait," Garlanda interrupted. "There is something I must do first before any of this."

"Frankly, my dear niece, if you could see yourself in that dowdy tent you're wearing, you would run to the nearest seamstress. What could possibly be more important?"

"I have to go home first."

"Home? You injure me." Her hands fluttered to her face, illustrating, Garlanda presumed, her injury. "My home is yours. You are home!"

"No, no," Garlanda protested, trying very hard not to laugh at Althea's theatrical response. "I know what you mean, but I must go to my parents' home and settle things."

"No need. Minette, your mother, put the entire household in my care when she left for Martinique. I put most of the servants out to pasture or moved them here and spent two positively *agonizing* days down there supervising getting the covers over the furniture—"

"It quite prostrated her," Leon interjected.

"Leon, you make it sound like I'm complaining. I'm not at all. Minette was my own dear sister and I didn't mind at all. I'm just trying to convey to Garlanda that she need not bother about the house. Everything is taken care of."

"I'm sure it is," Garlanda said soothingly. "I would just like to go down there and see it again and sort out some of my mother's things. She intended to come back, of course. Since she hasn't, there are things that should be properly disposed of and there are some things of mine still there that I would find a comfort

to have with me." All of which was true but it wasn't
the real reason.

Garlanda didn't want to tell Althea about her mother's dying words—not just yet, anyway. Whatever
made her mother think that Papa had been murdered
might be there at the house. A letter, perhaps, certainly
a communication of some kind. It might be recorded
in a diary, if her mother had kept one.

It was possible, of course, that Althea already knew
of the entire matter, but Garlanda seriously doubted
that her mother would have discussed it with her sister. Mama had only mentioned it to her because she
knew she was dying.

If only she'd had time to tell her more. To say why she
thought such a horrible thing. Mama had been
slightly inclined to pessimistic fancies about some
things, but not something this serious. Mama worried
about missing coaches and flowers not blooming in
time for parties and soaps that might not get the bed
linens sufficiently clean. Silly, domestic things—she
was not a woman to imagine murder.

Althea was still protesting. "Next month will be
plenty of time to go there. I'll send some servants
down ahead to air the house and—"

"I'm going tomorrow," Garlanda said as politely as
possible without losing the impact of determination.

"She's going tomorrow, Althea," Leon interpreted a
shade more loudly.

"Well, if she's going, she's going," Althea said with
an insincere little pout. "But I do insist on sending
some servants ahead." She rang a dainty silver bell
and gave instructions to the butler that it summoned.

Garlanda was aware of Count Jareski–Yanoviak
watching her speculatively. Even so little as a year
ago, she would never have considered standing her

ground against ⌐
She felt a strang
tory over her y
feeling that the

CHAPTER 14

Garlanda woke early with a strange mixture of dread and anticipation of going back to her childhood home. She was nearly dressed when she realized that she was still wearing the bag of jewels around her neck. She had worn it for so long that it had become natural and unnoticed. There was no reason anymore to keep it with her at all times. In fact, there were several reasons not to, the first being the possibility of losing it if by some horrible misfortune she should meet with highway robbers. Not that this happened often, but it was certainly possible.

She cast about for a safe place to put the jewels and settled on an inlaid box that was meant for beauty patches. She poured the glittering stones out on the dressing table and they sparkled and winked in the morning sun. It was the first time she had examined them at leisure and she was astonished at their number, size, and beauty. There were several tawny topazes, marine-blue sapphires, and small emeralds. But the bulk of the jewels were pearls, almost a handful of equally sized teardrop pearls. In the middle of all this treasure was a ruby—an enormous uncut pigeon-blood ruby. She picked it up and felt the rich, smooth weight of it. It was a beautiful stone, but what would she ever do with it? It was far too showy to wear. She

put it in the box with the others and closed the snug
lid.

She had a light breakfast, which Althea enlivened
with a running commentary on why Garlanda
shouldn't be going so soon. It was easy to see that it
was a half-hearted attempt to stop her, however, as
she also discoursed on her own plans for a day of visiting, card playing, and shopping. Garlanda left
shortly in Althea's richly upholstered black carriage.
Garlanda felt it was almost sinful riding in it with its
glass windows instead of leather flaps and springs
that cut down on the jostling effect. She took along
her maid, Jolee, and the coachman and his son.

Garlanda felt a small, traitorous tinge of relief when
they got outside London. She had been remembering
the rural England of her youth, not the filthy London
that was now her home. The air was nearly black and
rancid-smelling with the coal smoke of fires newly lit
against the fall chill. The streets were dirty and
crowded and there were unexpected glimpses of true
poverty when one looked too carefully up side streets.

It was nearly nightfall when they arrived at the
home where Garlanda had grown up, a lovely brick
and stucco country house on the road to Canterbury.
As they rounded the last bend in the long, tree-shaded
drive she saw the house. It was just as she remembered it—sitting with patient dignity on a slight rise
overlooking golden meadows where she'd once run
and played with imaginary friends.

She tried to draw out and prolong the pleasure and
the pain of her return as long as possible. She strolled
around the flagstoned walkways that meandered
through the now neglected gardens and visited the
empty stables before going in the house itself. She
was nearly overwhelmed with nostalgia the moment

she passed the front door. This house, like most, had its own distinct smell—a mixture of furniture polish, wood fires, and the mysterious scent of violets that Garlanda had always associated with her mother. Strange, even in mother's absence, the house maintained the delicate scent in memory of its onetime mistress.

The servants had aired the rooms, removed Althea's furniture covers, and started fires in the hearths in every room. Dinner was already being prepared and its aroma mingled with that of the house. Garlanda wandered through the downstairs rooms, remembrances of the past assailing her in unsortable waves. She went into the drawing room and sat for a moment in her favorite chair. How much smaller it had become! She ran her hand over the top of a tiny mosaic-topped table beside it and realized that if someone had blindfolded her anywhere in the world and let her touch it, she would have recognized that table. The edge tiles were slightly elevated and when she was very young she had played on it with some pretty marbles her father had sent her. They ran around nicely in the grooves between tiles, without falling off the edge. It had been a wonderful game until she stuck one of the marbles in her ear, just to see if it would fit—and it did, very snugly. Mama had extracted it and the marbles disappeared.

On the far wall a heavy buffet covered the section of paneling that Garlanda had embellished with the aid of a kitchen knife. That had been when Mama had some carpenters working in the dining room and Garlanda had admired their work and sought to reproduce it. Mama had put the kitchen utensils off limits after that.

In the windows were the lace curtains that Mama

had stitched herself the summer she was ill and could not ride or do her gardening. And there, by the fire, was the little footstool done with ragged crewel work that was Garlanda's first adventure in sewing. Garlanda realized for the first time what a sacrifice it had been for her mother to allow the sad little item of furniture in her elegantly appointed drawing room.

Dear Mama. All Garlanda's memories were of her. None—well, almost none, of Papa. But then he had been here so seldom when she was a child. A month or two in the summer sometimes, two weeks occasionally at Yuletide. Often he was in London making his reports and Mama would excitedly pack a few dresses and go up to stay with him, but Garlanda was too little to make the trip to the city.

"Miss Garlanda, cook says dinner can be served whenever you are ready," Jolee said from the doorway.

"Thank you, Jolee. Tell her a quarter of an hour would be satisfactory." Garlanda went up the wide stairway feeling the familiar smoothness of the oak bannister. Her mother's room was at the head of the stairs and she went in. It was exactly as it had always been except that some of her favorite things were missing—missing for all time now at the bottom of the Caribbean.

Garlanda blinked back tears and went purposefully to the clothes press and looked in. Mama had been nearly the same size as she was; there might be something in there that she could wear for the time being. She took out a black wool dress with Flemish lace undersleeves and a crisp, white collar. It had always been Garlanda's favorite dress on her mother. She slipped out of Elaine's dress and carefully pulled her mother's over her head. Yes, it might fit.

She tugged on the bell cord that would cause a bell to ring in the servant's quarters. When Jolee arrived to lace the back of the dress, Garlanda had put on a pair of her mother's shoes (after placing a folded handkerchief in the toe of each). She had Jolee quickly dress her hair in a simple twist on top of her head then dismissed the girl. Standing in front of the pier glass in Mama's dressing room she realized what she was doing—she was playing "dress-up"! But now Mama's subdued grown-up clothing fit her—belonged to her.

She put her face in her hands and allowed herself five minutes of wracking sobs. Then, exhausted and strangely relieved, she dried her eyes, splashed a little cool water on her puffy face, and composed herself for a solitary dinner at the head of an empty table.

Garlanda woke late and luxuriated in the morning sun bathing her room. She dressed lazily and had breakfast brought up to her so she could look over her dolls and childhood treasures while she ate. She had determined to put all sadness from her mind—not an easy thing to do—and be too busy to dwell on unhappy thoughts.

"Jolee, call the staff together in the kitchen in an hour. There is much to be done to make the house habitable."

"Will you be living here, ma'am, instead of London?" Jolee asked. Her pretty, cherubic face looked crestfallen. She was a country girl who had finally made it to London and considered it the best place in the world to be. She was obviously afraid that she, too, might end up back out in the country.

"No, I think not, but I would like this house to be

kept up so that I may visit anytime. The air in London is stifling and I may feel the need to get away."

"Ah-h-h," Jolee breathed. "Would you have me do your hair now?"

"No, I'll do it myself. But I want an inventory made of the linens. You may begin that now." Garlanda brushed out her hair and twined it into two gleaming braids to wind about her head. She flew into a flurry of activity. She wrote and dispatched a letter to Althea asking that the rest of the staff be located and returned. She informed her aunt that she would be absent for a week and that Althea's dinner for Sir George and the Ridgelys would have to be postponed.

By noon most of the carpets and tapestries had been taken out and hung up to have the dust beaten out. The furniture was being polished, the linens washed and pressed, the fireplaces were being cleaned out, and the tiles scrubbed. Jolee was hard at work at the big oak table in the kitchen cleaning the silver. The gardener had pressed the coachman's boy into service to tidy up the gardens. Everyone seemed pleased to be putting the house back in order.

Once the operation was organized, Garlanda was free to begin the search she had come home to conduct. With some trepidation she began carefully looking through her mother's drawers in her bedroom. They yielded up the expected—tortoiseshell combs, powder boxes, a packet of Spanish Paper, which when wetted was used to impart an additional rosiness to lip and cheek. As she went along, Garlanda set aside those things of her mother's that she wished to keep. The rest would be distributed among the staff and the villagers.

There were a great many semiprecious jewels. Some

very attractive, none of any great value, either sentimental or monetary. The best pieces her mother
would have taken with her or deposited with her London banker before leaving on her fatal journey to
Martinique. It occurred to her then that if Mama had
proof (or a concrete suggestion) that her father had
died an unnatural death, she might have locked up
any pertinent documents in the London bank as well.
Well, this has to be done sometime anyway, Garlanda
thought, *and I'll need to see the banker soon whether
I find anything or not.* She went on with her search.

By evening she had found nothing. She had completely gone through everything in her mother's room.
She had spent a full hour examining every piece of
paper in a large japanned lacquer writing box only to
find that it contained nothing but party invitations
and polite notes from friends. For some reason she
couldn't explain to herself, Garlanda had carefully replaced the box with its contents on the high shelf on
the wardrobe. They were merely papers, she told herself, but she felt that since her mother had so carefully
kept them, they shouldn't be lightly thrown away.

She settled down in front of a toasty fire after dinner with a little leather-bound book of poetry she had
found among her mother's things. She flipped through
the parchment pages, reading some of the poems out
loud to herself. She came to one she particularly liked
and decided to copy it out to keep with her. She went
to the desk and got out paper, pen, ink, and sand. She
wrote out the poem in careful schoolgirl script, and
when she finished she held it arm's length and admired her work.

She folded it carefully and put it in the pocket of
the apron she was still wearing. *No, it might get dirty.
Or crumpled. I'll put it in an envelope. There must be*

some in the desk. She rummaged around fruitlessly in the top drawer then went on to the second. It stuck slightly as she pulled on it and she remembered the secret compartment that she and Mama used to hide notes to each other in. It was at the back of the drawer and papers tended to get stuck in it and make the drawer difficult to open.

She reached in the partially opened space and fished about blindly with her fingertips for the obstruction. Yes, there was something at the back. She tugged lightly at the paper and she could feel it come away. She laid the folded paper on the top of the desk and went on looking for an envelope. Finding one, she slipped her poem in and went back to the fire and her book. She had been reading for some minutes when she found her mind wandering from the words on the page.

She went back to the desk and picked up the paper that had been stuck. Probably a list of household chores or a receipted bill or something. She unfolded it and her father's familiar handwriting sprang out at her.

My Dearest Minette,

Pressing businesse compels me to be brief, but there are Certayn Matters which I feel it is Imperative to convey to you now, Before it is to Late. I shalle be out of touch with you, but Please, my Own Love, know that tis not of my choice. My Employers (you know of Whom I speak) are sending me on a New and possiblie Perilouse asignmente. I leave within the Quarter Houre.

Minette, tis of vital Importance that no one, not

even our Friends—speciallie not our Friends—
knowe of my whereabouts. You must burn this
lettre and envelop and any others I mighte be
able to Smugle to you. *Do Not* let anyone know
from whence this lettre has come or, indeed, that
you have Received it.

I do not mean to distres you and my Heart is
near to Breaking at the necessitie of this, but
there are Divers Matters and a great many Person's safetie at stake, possiblie even Yours, dear
Love. If you are oblig'd to procure new Staff, be-
tere to hire Strangers offe the Streete than take
the recomendations of Those we Know.

This Matter wille, by Grace of God, be settl'd
soone and I wille be home with you to Stay. I
shalle explane alle then. Bye the tyme I return
Garlanda's Sojourne in Martinique shoulde be
complete and I wille be able to settle into the
Pleasante country Life we have always wanted
with my Beloved wyfe and daughter.

My Dearest one, I must rushe, but you and
Garlanda wille be in mye thoughts dayly, Wherever I am. Pray for me, My Darling, and forgive
me for the Unhappines I greatly fear this Epistle
mae be causing you. I woulde Spare you any-
thinge I coulde, But it is Vital that you take Care.
I should bee the Most Miserable man on Earth
shoulde the Slightest of harme come to you. I assure you of my Esteeme and Devotion.

> Yr. Loving Hsbd.
> Rbt. Cheney

Garlanda groped for a chair and sat down heavily. This was what she had been searching for! There was no postmark, no return address, or date. She yanked out the drawer where she'd found it and dumped the contents on the floor. There was no envelope, but there was another paper, from Lord Bramson, the man to whom Garlanda's father had reported when in England. At least, she assumed, that was what he met with him for. The letter was to her mother saying that her father had died in the service of his country and expressed the government's sympathy. It praised him as a great patriot who had made the ultimate sacrifice for England. Lord Bramson went on to say that he had been one of her father's staunchest admirers and if there was anything he could do for his friend's family, they should call on him without hesitation. Finally there was a paragraph regarding a generous sum of money that was being deposited in their London bank. ". . . As token of Their Majesties' esteeme for Sir Rbt. Cheney and recompens for yr. most grievous losse . . ."

Garlanda folded the two documents and put them in the envelope with her poem. She slowly gathered things from the floor and replaced them in the drawer while her mind whirled in frantic circles. Lord Bramson's letter told nothing specific about her father's death. He seemed to have carefully avoided mentioning what he died of or even, for that matter, where he died. Surely that was odd. Or maybe not—maybe she was reading mischief into the letter where none existed.

But her father's letter—That was something different. She could hardly sort out in her mind what it could mean. It appeared to her to signify that he might well have been murdered. She tried to reread it with a completely open mind, pretending that she had not been suspicious before she found it. If she had seen this letter and her mother had said nothing of her belief that he had been murdered, would Garlanda think so? She could not tell for sure.

It was obvious that he was doing something dangerous and secret. This surprised her to begin with. She had always thought he was engaged in rather routine diplomatic work—taking messages, negotiating treaties, representing Englishmen who got into difficulties in other countries—that sort of thing.

It was also clear from the letter that he feared that he, if not Garlanda and her mother as well, could be in danger from someone they knew. Someone, then, was a threat—and apparently it had been a true threat against his life that had been carried out. Someone they knew? How would she ever guess who he might be? It was her father's business to have a wide circle of acquaintances and because of her long years away from home Garlanda had no idea who they might be.

But she was forced to agree with her mother's interpretation. Papa had been murdered. And Lord Bramson was either unaware of the true circumstances of his death or unwilling to discuss them in the condolence letter to Mama. That was entirely proper, of course, but she needed to speak to the man in person. That would be her first responsibility when she got back to London.

CHAPTER 15

"Something in a moss green or a violet velveteen to match your eyes, perhaps?" Aunt Althea asked, trying to steer the lavender muslin from Garlanda's hands. "You can't really plan on wearing drab colors when you come out of mourning."

"No, I really prefer this and the dove gray and the tan cloth."

"But, my dear! Bright, deep colors are the vogue! Crimsons, cloth-of-gold, topaz damask, and brilliant blues! Surely this violet velveteen or some of this lovely green moire—"

"No," Garlanda said firmly. She tried to push the memory of her shipboard gown, the lowcut, red-crushed velvet beauty that Roque had so admired on her, out of her mind and failed. "These fabrics," she told Aunt Althea's dressmaker firmly. "And starched lacy collars. None of those indecent necklines or I'll refuse to wear them."

"Going gownless would be a definite improvement over what you're about to do with that charming figure of yours," her aunt argued. "Garlanda, Garlanda! Be reasonable! You shall look terribly out of date, like a priggish schoolgirl next to the other debutantes!"

"I have come from a convent school in Martinique. I do not wish to dress myself like a fatted calf with all my flesh available for the highest bidder to gaze upon."

"Merciful heavens, where did you learn to talk like that?"

"It's only the truth, Auntie."

"Now, you promised not to call me 'Auntie.' Oh, well, in the meantime, mourning suits you. Black is lovely with your bright hair. And it isn't too bad on me either."

The dressmaker patiently wrote down Garlanda's instructions. She had already been measured within an inch of her life—standing about in her shift for hours while long, marked pieces of tape were applied all over her body and the results were called across the shop. Corpulent matrons in starched silks stared at her through gauzy curtains separating the dressing room from the rest of the shop. She had endured it all with good grace, she thought, for she knew this was part of the price she must pay to become a part of the respectable society she wished to enter.

She had come back to London in a fire of curiosity to see Lord Bramson only to find that he was out of the country for an unspecified time. His assistant offered, by messenger, to meet with her in his master's stead, but Garlanda felt that there was nothing to be gained by that. When Althea insisted once again upon an immediate shopping foray, Garlanda agreed, first taking just enough time to run off a quick note to Elaine who had called in her absence.

She debated telling Aunt Althea about Papa, but decided, for the time being, not to. She wasn't quite sure why, it was a combination of things. First of all she feared that Althea would laugh at the entire thing. Worse yet, she might take it seriously in her own strange way and embark on solving the mystery as if it were a party game. If she could find out some real facts she would confide in her aunt, but for now it would remain her secret.

"All of London knows my vital statistics," she growled at Althea under her breath. "Jolee, fetch those parcels I brought along."

"Ah, yes, the secret parcels," Althea said. "Are we now to see what is in them?"

"There was nothing secretive about it, I simply didn't want you strewing the wrappings around in the coach on the way. They're Elaine's dresses," Garlanda said, receiving them from Jolee. Althea shuddered delicately. Garlanda gave the seamstress instructions to make exact duplicates of the two dresses, but chose pretty colors and ribbons for their construction. When they left the shop the liveried coachman assisted them into a coach marked with the gilded Pasteau coat of arms. This was Althea's town carriage—smaller than the other and without springs, but more sumptuously decorated.

I wonder if I should have brought Freddie to London with me, she thought as they rolled through the streets. *He might have preferred it here to Marseille. Then again, the stench of London really is incredible.* She sunk back against the upholstery. The cushions, like most of the ladies in the shop, were overstuffed. She fanned herself languidly while Althea waved a clove-studded orange on a stick under their noses.

"These gutters are beyond belief," Althea complained. "You know my dear girl, when your mother left she extracted a promise from me that if anything ill were to befall her, I should see you enter society and find you a husband. Believe me, you won't find one running about in a gray gown with—well, your hair is lovely, but we must do something about it. You can't wear it just pulled up like that and completely unadorned. We must call in a hairdresser. I certainly hope your natural color returns before your first ball. You're a bit—er—sun-browned. Not that it isn't lovely."

"Why did mother tell you that?"

"Tell me what? Oh, to take care of you? It was the natural thing, wasn't it?"

"No, that's not what I meant. Althea, tell me the truth. Do you think Mother thought there was any danger that she might not return?"

"Why ever do you ask? Her health wasn't good, of course, but then she was never really robust. Even as a child—"

"Did she say anything to you about my father's death?"

"My dear, you mustn't dwell on unhappy things. She talked about how much she missed him, naturally, and she stayed here for a while, seeing people—tying up business details and such before leaving to bring you back from school."

"Did she say what he died of?"

"No-o-o, I can't recall that she did. I didn't ask. Why are you asking now?"

So Mama had not confided in Althea. "No reason especially. I was just wondering and I can't ask Mama anymore."

Althea's eyes narrowed. "You *are* asking for a reason. I can tell. I want to know what it is!"

"No, no," Garlanda tried to laugh lightly, "you are much too suspicious. Who is Count Leon?" she asked, thinking she could lead Althea to a new and less important subject.

It worked. "All I know about Leon is that he comes from a fine Polish family with whom he has severed connections. He has several homes all over Europe though he spends most of his time in London. He must be fabulously wealthy and has a tendency to be quite lavish with his vinegar wit. Dear Leon, odd sort, isn't he?"

"Is he married—I mean, has he ever been?"

"Who knows?" Althea shrugged. "I like to think that he has had one great tragic love in his life, but I have no idea. He may have a fat wife and six children in a mountain shack somewhere."

"Oh, you don't really think so, do you? I think he's very nice."

Althea looked like she might gag at this sweetness. "Fresh out of a convent school! My dear, how can you be so knowing about some things and so utterly steeped in naiveté concerning others?"

It takes work, Garlanda admitted to herself and smiled.

Waiting the month or so for Lord Bramson to return to London didn't seem as long as Garlanda had feared. Between Althea and Elaine, her days were filled with activities. Althea decided to expose Garlanda to society in slow stages. The elegant dinners increased by Noah-like twos from four to twenty guests and were received with return invitations in profusion.

Elaine introduced Garlanda to all her friends and planned luncheon after luncheon. There was a strange, subtle difference between Althea's friends and Elaine's, however, that Garlanda couldn't quite put her finger on. Althea's friends, mostly of the older woman's age group, seemed to accept Garlanda unquestioningly, much as Althea and Leon did. But Elaine's friends were a different matter.

They were very proper young women which sometimes made Garlanda a little uneasy. They were charming to her, but their occasional gossip about missing members of the group made Garlanda fear what they might say about her when she was not present. She gave them absolutely no ammunition. Her dress and manners were so subdued and self-effacing that Althea made fun of her and called her a Puritan— the worst criticism she could level.

Elaine played completely ignorant of Garlanda's experiences and would not reveal so much as a word of the watered-down version Garlanda had told her. When the young women questioned Garlanda about her adventures, she played it down so much that it was no more exciting than a fishing excursion to the Isle of Wight and acted as if the very recollection made her quite, quite faint. They didn't ask for long, apparently satisfied that she was not going to slip and provide them with some delicate tidbit of gossip.

Sometimes they were great fun, especially Elaine. Garlanda learned many card games and a great deal of the young set's time was taken up with shopping and comparing hair styles. After a while Garlanda sometimes found herself letting her mind wander during these sessions and had to chide herself that if this life *was* a little dull, nevertheless it was what she had chosen, what she preferred to the exciting life of pirates and earthquakes. Every time she found herself thinking of Roque, she immediately got busy with something to divert such thoughts.

Eventually Lord Bramson returned and sent Garlanda a note saying that he heard she had inquired after him in his absence and he would be delighted to call on her whenever she chose. She did not choose. If Lord Bramson turned up at Althea's home, there would be no way on earth to dislodge Althea herself from the center of the conversation. Garlanda returned a message that she would call upon Lord Bramson at his office instead. This was not strictly proper—in fact, it wasn't proper at all—but until she knew more about the matter of her father's death, she didn't wish to reveal her thoughts to Althea.

The next morning Lord Bramson's carriage arrived to pick Garlanda up. Althea nearly went to pieces. "Why didn't you tell me? I can't possibly get dressed this quickly!"

"You don't need to go with me," Garlanda assured her.

"Why, certainly I must. I can't have you running about London visiting strange men and riding in their carriages!"

"Althea, Lord Bramson must be two hundred years old, and besides, I'm taking Jolee along with me."

"Well!" Althea sniffed. "I'd think you'd be more cautious with all those nicey-nicey friends of yours. What would *they* think?"

This was a valid point that Garlanda had overlooked. "They won't know," she asserted. She must be very circumspect. She considered putting off her appointment until she could take Althea along, but she was impatient and taking Althea along would necessitate discussing the whole thing with her. "I'll be back shortly," she said as she hurried out.

When she arrived at the government offices, she rushed through the corridors fearing any minute that she might meet someone she knew. She felt enormously relieved once she was in Lord Bramson's waiting room and his clerk ushered her directly into his private office.

Lord Bramson was a little dry stick of a man who almost rustled as he moved. Even his voice was dry and papery. "Ah, m'dear, m'dear. Come in. Miss Cheney, I cannot adequately express my grief at your untimely losses of both parents. Such a tragedy—tragedy! But your recovery—amazing! Sure your aunt is delighted to have you back—snatched from the grave as it were, snatched from the grave," he chuckled. It sounded like cornhusks being rubbed together.

"I have come to inquire about my father's death," Garlanda said. She didn't know quite where to begin. "You see, my mother passed away before she could tell me much about it."

"Don't suppose there was much to tell—not much to tell." He got up and rummaged through a file. "Got notice from the ambassador in Paris," he said over his shoulder. "Yes, here it is. No, that's something else. Maybe in here—"

"If you could just tell me something about his death."

"Not much to tell. I was informed by Sir James Wilton that your father had died in the service of his country—yes, service of his country. Ought to be proud of that, m'dear—proud!"

"I am," she said, almost falling in with his cadence and repeating herself for emphasis. "But I wonder what else you might know."

"Nice sum of money put into an account for you and your mother—nice sum."

"Yes, I know about that and I'm grateful, but tell me, what did my father die of?"

"Die *of?*" he said as if he didn't quite understand the question. "Die of? Can't say that I know. Probably the ague or old age."

"Old age?" It was Garlanda's turn not to understand. "My father wasn't that old."

"No," Lord Bramson said, looking down from the height of uncountable years, " 'spose he wasn't actually, but his job had aged him a great deal—a great deal. Hard on a man—traveling so much—hard!"

"Where is he buried?"

"Buried? Oh, buried, I see what you mean. Well, don't think I know that either. Sorry."

"Certainly whoever reported his death to you mentioned it," Garlanda said more sharply than she intended.

Her tone seemed to take him aback. "I'm sure they did. Just can't find the communication at the moment—can't find it. Silly clerks, stupid about filing things so a man can get his hands on them when he wants. Silly clerks—"

He dashed back to the files to make another foray. Garlanda considered him. He wasn't the fool he appeared to be. She knew that he held an important post because he was well able to hold it. Was he simply too busy to want to take the time? Or was there something he was trying to hide? *Don't be foolish,* she told herself, *perhaps Papa was truly in poor health and it had affected his mind. That letter to Mama might have just reflected his mistaken idea that someone was after him.*

An even worse thought occurred to her. What if he had taken his own life? No, that couldn't possibly be, but something like that could explain Lord Bramson's apparent reluctance to discuss his death.

"Know it must be in here somewhere—somewhere,"

Lord Bramson was muttering as he riffled through another stack of files.

"Perhaps your clerk could find it," Garlanda suggested.

Lord Bramson waved away this possibility. "New here. Only had this one for a week. Doesn't know where anything is—anything. I'll have it in a minute. Perhaps over here—" he tore across the room and attacked another cabinet. When nothing came of this he subsided, breathing wheezily, in his chair. "Tell you what, m'dear, I'll find the letter and send it on to you. Yes, send it on. That's what I'll do. Sure to turn up in a day or two. Sure to."

"Very well," Garlanda said. She was disappointed, but there was nothing else she could do. Perhaps he would actually find the letter. If not, she could always come back later and nag him about it. "I'm grateful for your time, Lord Bramson."

"Delighted, m'dear. Delighted. Best advice is forget all about this. Lovely young girl, life ahead of you. Get married, have children, and let the past be the past. No point in prolonging your distress—no point."

"But you will look for the letter from—from?"

"—Sir James Wilton, English ambassador to Paris," Lord Bramson supplied on his way to the door to see her out. "Certainly. Send it along to you."

"Lord Bramson, are you sure you know nothing else about my father's death?"

"Positive. Now, then, I'll have my carriage sent back around for you. Give my regards to your dear aunt—charming woman! Spirited, but charming."

Garlanda left Lord Bramson's office more convinced then ever that there was something strange about her father's death, but more unsure of what it

was. The idea of suicide had taken root and she could
not dismiss it.

Elaine had a dinner party in Garlanda's honor the
next night. It was typically Elaine's party—the soufflé
fell, the soup tureen broke just before the guests were
seated, and the lukewarm soup had to be served in individual bowls. The silver polish hadn't been adequately rinsed off and all the dishes had the same eerie, metallic taste.

Even as Garlanda, Althea, and Leon had arrived
there was an argument going on upstairs about
Elaine's inability to manage her staff. Snippets of the
conversation drifted down the stairs for a few moments before Elaine herself descended, red-eyed and
self-consciously overcheerful. Renwick joined them in
the drawing room for sherry.

Garlanda had been going out of her way to avoid
Renwick since they got back to England; he had a
distinctively bad effect on her. Handsome, attentive,
witty—he was all these things and he was obviously
very impressed with Garlanda's charms. Under other
circumstances Garlanda would have found herself en-
couraging his attentions, but he had one other quality—he was married—and married to her closest friend
at that.

Elaine, in her usual fashion, had seated Garlanda
next to Renwick at dinner. "Miss Cheney, that is a
particular lovely dress you're wearing," he said to her
once everyone had taken their places.

"How kind of you to think so, sire. It is, you may
have noticed, cut in the same pattern as your wife's

dress. Merely the color is different, since I am in mourning for my parents."

"I fear there is more difference than mere color," he said.

"I'm afraid this discussion casts aspersion on either myself or your wife, sir."

"Not at all, Miss Cheney. I would never meaningly cast aspersion on any lady. Forgive me if I have offended you—especially so early in the evening."

"Why, Renwick," she said with her gayest forced laugh, "does this mean you prefer to offend only late at night?"

Those seated closest broke into polite laughter at the exchange. Garlanda noted that Renwick was not joining in the merriment; instead, he was regarding her with a deep, searching expression, the kind of expression Roque had often had when he was planning to enjoy her favors later in the evening. It alarmed her.

She turned away to see what Althea and the count were doing to amuse themselves. Leon was being prevailed upon by a fluffy blonde, too-deliberately girlish young woman who wished to know if the Poles were really as barbaric as rumor had it. Leon was insisting that he never went in for pillage before breakfast and frankly, burning cities and carrying off screaming females was a bore. He then added that his people, dark-haired for the most part, were fond of a dish consisting of—well, the principal ingredient was blonde English females, but he did not wish to go into details.

By this time the fluffy bit at his elbow was nearly swooning with excitement and cooing that she had never met a real Polish count before. Althea, across from the calm Leon, was trying not to have convul-

sions. She choked quietly into her soup and turned
blue in the face, but did not explode with laughter.
Garlanda found that quite admirable. She moved to
one side and let the maid put a slice of charred roast
on her plate.

The bread was lumpy and hard enough to qualify
as a lethal weapon. Elaine's eyes met Garlanda's over
it. Her mismanagement had extended to everything in
the meal, even the scorched spot on the littlest maid's
frilled apron. Garlanda managed a smile as watery as
the soup.

There was a handsome young man of some distinction seated across the table from her. He had wavy
brown hair and a small moustache that drew attention
to his charming smile. Garlanda looked over at him
and realized that he was watching her every move
with kind, brown eyes. He raised his glass to her, but
she pretended not to notice since they had not been
formally introduced.

Renwick was sitting too close. She could feel the
hard muscles of his thigh pressed against her leg
through her heavy skirts. She tried to inch her chair
away from him, but only succeeded in bumping the
table and making everyone's claret dance in the cut-
glass goblets. When everybody looked around to see
from whence the disruption had risen, she looked
around too.

"Pray, are you uneasy?" Renwick asked, the model
of decorum and perfectly bred manners. Garlanda
could not reply. Should she say, "Sir, we are touch-
ing," or try to move away again or what? His touch
was starting a line of goose bumps up her spine. Even
such light physical contact was exciting and frustrating her. It made her very angry with herself.

The meal progressed. A whisper was passed between Elaine and a maid and the food that then graced the table was better, by which Garlanda guessed that the kitchen staff had started over. She wondered how a man of Renwick's refinement could have married such a sweet, naive bungler as Elaine. They seemed so mismatched. *Probably an arranged marriage*, she thought, picking at her sliced pheasant.

The flounced and ruffled blonde creature was still besieging the count for any idiotic details she could get her dainty little hands on. Leon was trying to eat and hold her at bay at the same time. He was succeeding at neither. Althea was chatting with a lovely woman in a blue, flowered gown. *Poor Leon*, Garlanda thought, *this isn't the first time he's been assaulted by a husband hunter, to judge from his face. Doesn't she realize how silly she looks? The woman has no pride.*

The young man with the moustache was watching her again. This time she could not hide a small, shy smile that crept across her face before she looked away. She should not smile. In this rigid society, such a thing could be mistaken as flirting.

It was a relief when the women retired to the parlor and left the men with their pipes and snifters of fine old brandy. What did the men talk about after the women left the table? Garlanda had always wondered. Probably talked politics and religious reform and pretended to know more than they did about each. She followed her aunt from the room. Althea was dressed demurely for once. No plumes waved from her chignon and no jewels glittered about her throat and fingers. It was almost as though she were in disguise.

The ladies seated themselves around the room, many pulling bags of embroidery from behind their chairs and beginning to work. Elaine was attempting to unravel a mass of murky blue wool, so Garlanda offered her hands to wind the yarn on as it was untangled. She sat passively, glad to be of even such a small help to Elaine. Next to her, Althea was fidgeting uneasily, making it quite obvious to her niece that she craved a smoke. The scent of flavored tobacco filtered into the room under the door. Althea breathed deeply from time to time. Garlanda wondered if she was trying to live on fumes.

The ladies were gossiping already. Katherine Mendenhall had gone out without a chaperone! Wasn't that disgusting? Imagine what trouble she could get into! Shocking!

"Isn't she a widow?" Althea inquired with a sharp edge to her voice.

"Yes, but a young one. Therefore, she must be all the more careful of her reputation."

"Speaking of reputations," began the woman in the blue flowered dress who had been Althea's companion at the dinner table. "Is it quite proper for a young woman to visit a widower at his place of employment—without an escort?"

Everyone agreed it was not. The woman turned to Althea. "I only say this out of affection for certain of those who are no longer with us and would want to see their children brought up in the proper manner—and she is fresh from Martinique and everyone knows they live like barbarians there with no emphasis placed on propriety."

Garlanda's mouth went dry. She felt an ugly tightness in her throat as she realized she was the one the woman was talking about.

"Yes," another woman joined in. All eyes were swiveling back and forth between Garlanda and Althea.

"You see, Elizabeth Wentworth's husband saw your niece coming out of Lord Bramson's office the other day and she was quite alone. Alone! He has only men in his office, you know, and he is a widower—shocking, my dear."

The room was creeping with deadly quiet. Althea leaned back in her chair with a panther smile. "Then Elizabeth Wentworth's husband needs to have someone else do his seeing for him. *I* was with my niece, naturally. Not that it is a matter of concern to anyone among you, but the child has recently lost both parents, as have I. Lord Bramson is an old family friend as well as business associate of my late brother-in-law's. My niece and I went to his office to settle some business matters having to do with her estate—matters which I do not choose to confide to anyone here." Althea could be splendid when, as now, righteous indignation shook her. Garlanda hardly dared breathe. The lie had been delivered with such aplomb that it would surely be believed.

"Now, Althea, we were not suggesting anything. Only warning you of what some vulgar people might say," soothed one woman.

"Some vulgar people *have* said it!" Althea shot back.

Garlanda, genuinely overwrought, gave a dry sob of confusion. Elaine burst into tears. When the gentlemen came out of the dining room they found that the hostess had retired with a headache, and the guest of honor had been taken home by her chaperone. The rest of the ladies were sitting about in sullen knots, hashing over whose fault it all was.

CHAPTER 16

"And these are the people you want for your friends! Jealous, greedy, grasping, ready to talk spitefully—come, Garlanda, let me introduce you to some real people."

Garlanda shook her head. "Elaine's circle is the epitome of gentle society."

"If a wolf dons a sheep's pelt, is he then a sheep?"

"I don't know what you mean."

"You *do*. Mark my words, Garlanda, you are not making the kind of friends who will do you any good. They'll be at your throat like this at the slightest breach of decorum."

Garlanda snuggled deeper in her cloak. "Auntie, thank you for lying."

"I did not lie. I was right there in the office with you, at your elbow. We visited Sir Whoever together and if the old rascal doesn't remember it, I'll thrash him with my parasol until he comes around to my way of thinking."

"Althea, you are an angel."

"No, I'm not. I'm going to help you get what you want. I'm going to go to all those wretched social functions with you and sit and smile through inane chatter and moon-eyed glances thrown at you by young men. And when you come to your senses and see that it's not worth it, I'll cackle like an old witch and scream 'I told you so' from the rooftops.

"Speaking of young men, are you aiming for any particular rank for your husband? Because that nice young man seated across from you tonight—the one with the spaniel eyes and moustache—gave me his card and asked if he could call sometime next week. I don't think he meant to visit me. Of course, he's only a baronet, but—"

Garlanda pounced on the card. A baronet, and his name was Lawrence Jennings! A gentleman—a handsome *young* gentleman wanted to call on her. Her first real suitor!

"If I ever see another rosebush, I shall die." Garlanda surveyed her handiwork. She was not meant to be a gardener. There must be some other hobby she could take up. The roses were pitiful. They looked as though wild horses had trampled through them.

She stood up, leaning on her hoe. Terrible—sloppy! Perhaps the real gardener could salvage them. She picked up a long stick from the ground and dropped the hoe. "*En garde*, rosebush! You have insulted my honor by refusing to stand up of your own accord!" She stabbed it with a quick thrust. The entire bush fell over. Garlanda looked at the stick in her hand. *A dangerous weapon*? she asked herself wryly. Memories flooded over her. She rubbed her red hands together and blew on them to restore circulation in the brisk air.

Her game with the stick had reminded her of sword-fighting—of her lessons with Sabelle and Freddie—and of the night of the wild chase through Marseille when she had put the lessons to good use and fought for her life. She threw the trailing edge of her skirt up over her left arm and aimed the "sword" at an imaginary foe. Her flat-heeled slippers allowed her almost as much ease of movement as bare feet. She thrust, feinted, parried with her invisible foe, cornered him against the stone garden wall, disarmed him, and stood over his body, triumphant!

"Grant clemency, fair lady! Surely he did nothing so grave as to deserve death!"

She gave a panicked start. Leon was behind her and he could have come from nowhere but straight over the wall. "G-good morning, Leon, I, uh, this isn't as it looks, I—"

He walked around her. "Your wrist action was stiff, but I'd say your instructor did an excellent job. You're light on your feet and seem to have a natural aptitude for fencing. Yes, I think we could complete your education nicely."

"B-but ladies don't fence!" she said. The black-haired man gave her a cool, evaluating look.

"I do not intend to tell anyone you can defend yourself, but you do have an excellent sword arm and it would be a waste not to make use of it." He turned toward the house in a swirl of dark brown cape. Garlanda gaped after him. He was going to teach her more about fencing whether she wanted to learn or not. He was not shocked by a woman knowing the basics of dueling. It would be their secret—theirs and Althea's.

She made another lighthearted jab at the wall, then looked up. Count Jareski–Yanoviak had already vanished. She shivered. There was something uncanny about that man!

* * *

Baronet Lawrence Jennings was undoubtedly a gentleman. Garlanda allowed herself to gloat over that fact. He never tried to see her alone. He was content to obey all society's rules and call on her with Althea in the room pretending interest in her embroidery work, or go for carriage rides with Elaine chaperoning. He was young, dashing, handsome, attentive, and only slightly boring. He never so much as suggested that he wished to take liberties with her. No one who observed the courtship had a doubt that he would propose marriage to Garlanda before the New Year.

"You don't like Lawrence," Garlanda pouted one afternoon as the count fenced with a friend twice his size.

"Have I ever said that?" His opponent's blade sliced off the bottom half of a curtain due to Leon's spritely duck to one side.

"Aren't you using foils? What are you doing? Your blades are uncovered!" she shouted, forgetting to keep her voice at a ladylike level. Leon backed up the stairs, calmly and efficiently mastering his rapier.

"Dear girl, be quite patient. We would not be swordsmen if we knew that every strike would be nothing but a chalk mark on protective padding."

"You make *me* wear padding and use a foil!"

"Thomas, I insist you keep your guard up, or I shall be impelled to do this—" The slender count disarmed his opponent.

There was laughter all around. "Good show, Count. Smashing good show!" the Englishman congratulated him. They shook hands.

"Now, dear girl, what is it that you wish of me?" Leon asked, swiping at his forehead with a linen handkerchief.

"I'm here for our lesson."

"Oh, yes, I had quite forgotten today was Tuesday." He rang for the butler and ordered cold lemonade. Garlanda was not introduced to the other swordsman. She seated herself as the count saw his friend to the door. The lemonade was good—tart and fresh and only slightly sugared. When Leon returned he was in a clean shirt. She looked at him with a tiny frown. How old was he? There was a touch of gray at his temples, slight dashes against his black hair. He never curled or wigged himself as did other men. He was as slim as a boy of fifteen and yet there were lines of wisdom and patience in his noble face. Leon escorted all the fashionable ladies in London and attended hunts and balls, but he never seemed to fall in love or confide in any of his friends. And he did have many friends, despite his odd temperament.

"Trying to guess my age again?" he asked, fastening a button on a white cuff trimmed with the barest essential of lace.

"Yes, sometimes you seem hardly more than my age and yet at other times you seem old enough to be my father."

He bowed with what was as close to impishness as he ever got.

She scowled at him. "You delight in shrouding yourself in mystery, don't you?"

"Yes, it gives the gossips plenty to talk about and yet no ammunition with which to attack. By the way, you will notice that I was being rude with good reason. I dared not introduce you to my friend without blighting your reputation. Dressed as you are for practice, with your hair covered and in that servant's dress, it's unlikely he'll ever recognize you."

"I was careful to keep my face half hidden in the collar of my cape."

"Good. Ah-h-h, refreshment first, then work. You are progressing well, your initial style would have been sufficient to hold attackers at bay, but there was no finesse involved. You must not only be capable, but stylish as well. And you need to be able to take the offensive."

"Count—"

He looked up from his lemonade, one black eyebrow raised. "Yes, Miss Cheney?"

"You've never asked me where I learned to fence in the first place."

"It is none of my business."

"I learned from a pirate. A lady pirate."

"Yes, I have often wondered if there might not be such a thing," he said amiably, no more excited than if they were discussing a mild change in the weather.

"You're not going to ask me any questions?"

"If you consider the information worthy of sharing, you will volunteer it someday. In the meantime, are you ready for your lesson?"

She stood up. "You don't like Lawrence," she began again, unable to keep from smiling.

"I don't *dislike* him. I merely said that were I to find myself locked in a room with him for any length of time, they should find me dead of causes other than starvation."

"Namely boredom, but he's sweet and kind and a gentleman."

Leon's look was almost pitying. "As might an adoring puppy be. There is a being of no little fire beneath the surface of you. It is a shame you suppress it so rigidly; it is a shame you have to. But I'm not here to advise you. I do not care for people who force their ideas on unwilling ears. Marry the young man if he pleases you."

She had not meant to, but she reached out and gripped his wrist. "You don't understand! If he proposes I *must* accept!"

"Why? Because you no longer qualify as a maiden? Any man so narrow-minded and bigoted as to judge a woman by standards directly in opposition to those he himself lives by—"

"You know! How do you know?"

"I have dealt with pirates," he said drily, "and know a good deal about men. Your story was a Swiss cheese of a tale, poked through with holes in any number of places. I didn't mean to upset you."

She sat down, weeping quietly. "I was raised to live this kind of life, to be a good woman, a wife, a mother. There is nothing else for a woman like me, except to be a maiden aunt to my friends' children. I dare not think back on my days at sea. God! It seems decades away now! I was so happy for a little while. I even thought I was in love with the pirate."

"Ah-h-h, so it was only one and it was an affair of the heart. Very well, then, if you want to be a proper Englishwoman, by all means, proceed. Only do what pleases you, Garlanda." He handed her a clean handkerchief.

"You are so good," she sobbed.

"No, my child, only impatient to make a respectable swordswoman of you."

She glanced up. His dark eyes were twinkling just a little.

*　*　*

Althea was still howling with laughter late that night when Garlanda returned from the opera she had attended with Lawrence, his formidable mother, and Elaine. Renwick had left the country on business and Elaine was sticking to Garlanda like a small, insecure burr.

The house was not dark. Garlanda smiled as Jolee admitted her. "What's that cackling?"

"Your poor aunt. She's been carrying on like this every few minutes since you told her you thought that she should marry that Polish count."

Althea was in the parlor, trying to embroider. An occasional "oof" of merriment escaped her. She had removed her stays and gown and was lounging in a chair by the fire, wearing a loose dressing gown of Oriental design over her shift. Her pipe was clenched in her teeth. Blonde hair, unbound after a hectic day at the hunt, cascaded over her shoulders. She looked young and carefree and very pretty. "Auntie, are you still laughing at me?"

Garlanda hugged Althea and sat down on the needlepoint hassock at her feet. Althea shook her head. "Marry Leon! That would be like incest. We would satirize each other to death within a fortnight! Really, Garlanda, there is no touch of the physical in my feeling for Leon."

"Don't you think a marriage can be perfectly happy when there is no spark of physical attraction?"

"No! You mean to tell me that nice baronet hasn't managed to so much as kiss you yet—or maybe he has and you didn't like it? Spare me your maidenly blushes—I know you young women all sit around comparing notes on your beaux."

"Please don't be vulgar," Garlanda pleaded.

"Vulgar! Oh, turn around and let me help you loosen your hair."

"That's Jolee's job!"

Althea yanked a copper-colored curl a little harder than she might have meant to. She grumbled under her breath about suitors and weddings and a suitable trousseau and which dressmaker made the finest wedding gowns. "How do you know so much about weddings?" Garlanda asked.

"I've been researching for yours. We must do this up right. Let me think—as soon as your year of mourning is over, you can marry. Of course, that'll only give us a very short engagement if he proposes soon, but it's enough time."

Lawrence did propose as expected. He did it in the expected way as well. He sought out Althea and said that since there was no surviving male member of the family, he appealed to his beloved's aunt for permission to offer his hand. Althea said that she supposed it was alright and steered him to the library where her niece was reading a volume of Milton. He insisted Althea accompany him, at which suggestion she grimaced and told him he'd best learn to do his courting in private. She shoved him in and shut the door.

He went down on one knee and made a very pretty speech, kissing Garlanda's fingertips from time to time as he spoke. He informed her that she was not only the most beautiful woman on earth, she was the purest, brightest, wittiest, kindest being he had ever met. He admired her—dare he say it—he worshiped her. Would she do him the honor of being his wife?

He hoped he was not being too bold, suggesting

matrimony so soon after her bereavement, but he could no longer live without knowing whether there was a chance she might consent to marry him. She was all he had ever wanted in a woman—pure, but not overpious, lovely but not prideful about it, well-educated but not too well-educated for a woman. In short, she was the perfect wife for a baronet.

And thought Garlanda, clenching her teeth behind smiling lips, *he thinks I will be a good mother for his children—a good moral example. If only he knew that I have been deflowered—and not exactly unwillingly.*

"Sir Lawrence, I am flattered at this attention, but I am still in mourning and—well, if you would be so kind as to allow me to think this over, I would give you my answer soon." She lowered her eyes, thinking what an attractive man he was. But why wasn't she happier? He was considered a great conquest. So young a man and already come into his inheritance and title. She knew he would be a good husband, generous, kind—a warm father to their children. He cared for her. And yet she could feel nothing but a cold, numb sensation inside.

She permitted him to kiss her cheek before he left. Althea came to the door. "When might we expect the joyous occasion?"

"I haven't said yes—yet."

The tall woman sat on the edge of Garlanda's chair. "What is it, dear? I hate to see you looking so distressed. Tell me and let's see if I can help."

"I don't know what it is. I should be happy, but I'm not. Althea, you were right. He proposed one day before New Year's Eve. You said I'd find myself betrothed before the next year was upon us."

Althea gave her a quick hug. "Let's have Jolee fetch you a warm mug of milk, then off to bed and sweet dreams. In the morning perhaps your thoughts will be better sorted out."

When Lawrence called on her the next afternoon, she accepted his proposal. Since her year of mourning was not yet over, she could not wear the big emerald and diamond betrothal ring of the Jennings on her finger. It was given a place on a dainty filigree chain about her throat. As soon as her mourning was over, their engagement would be announced. Balls and dinners would be held in their honor. But for now, the ring was in plain sight, though not officially recognized. Lawrence was insufferably proud of himself.

Now that she was engaged it was harder than ever to slip off to Leon's for fencing and riding lessons. She was practically imprisoned. Althea must be dragged everywhere with her and then it was not quite right that there was not a male member of the family to escort them. The butler was then dragged along on every shopping trip and forced to stand by like an impassive stone statue. But things would be easier once she was married.

She decided that she really liked Lawrence. He was unusually good-looking, dashing, full of the spirit of youth. It pleased her to look at him, but it was the kind of pleasure that she imagined a mother might take in seeing her son grown to manhood. When it dawned on her one night, alone in her four-postered bed, that someday soon he would be next to her under the covers, hold her, make love to her, she froze.

What if he could tell? What if something in her response told him she was not inexperienced? Would he know she was not a virgin? Should she remain motionless? No, that was what Roque had hated, the times she had tried not to respond. He had said it was like wooing an end table. Then he would tease and cajole and caress her until she responded. Except for that last time in his cabin on the ship. That had not been in the spirit of fun, deliberately making him lavish more of his skillful fondling of her.

Roque. Dark, mysterious, masterful Roque. Fiery, capable of flashes of dangerous temper, and yet he had been a gentle lover and friend, crooning foreign phrases in her ears that were surely affectionate, getting angry that she had risked her life by going to Saint Paul's Church in Port Royal. Surely his anger that day had been born of fondness. He was virile, clever, impossible to comprehend.

And she loved him.

Still, after all this time! Every day without him was less sunny than it could have been. Remembrance of long island nights swept over her—lying in his strong, sun-browned arms while he told her stories, comforted her fears, protected her from night noises. She longed for the sound of his voice, the reassuring sight of him, the feel of his hard body on hers, driving her to peak after peak of shameless ecstasy. The remembrance of their impassioned embraces made her blush. She slid down under the covers, hot with longing and embarrassment. Her body throbbed for want of a man. Not any man—*her* man. A pirate who might be plundering ships from her own country as well as those from Spain and France.

She tried not to think of him. She tried to turn her thoughts to her future husband, but the picture of embracing him, yielding up her body to him as she had done with Roque, was beyond her imagination. Lawrence was still a boy—a charming boy. Roque had been a man. And in that realization of their difference was the knowledge that she would never know with her betrothed what she had known with Roque.

It was not only what had happened physically to her when she had been with Roque. It was a feeling beyond their animal attraction. She loved him—madly, deeply, completely. And her heart was heavy with the knowledge that she must never think of him, must put him from her mind forever. She would not see him again. The path of an English gentlewoman would not cross with that of a lawless privateer, not accidentally, not deliberately.

Lawrence was marrying her, giving her his name, his home, his heart. She owed it to him to be a good wife.

And yet, she could not help remembering her dark lover and the island where she had discovered love.

CHAPTER 17

Elaine asked Garlanda to accompany her to meet Renwick's ship when he returned. Garlanda was surprised that the sight of him affected her as it did. He was so mature, so aloof, so cultured. She found herself contemplating what a difference he would be from the eager-to-please Lawrence. Renwick would be such an interesting husband. She wished Lawrence had more of his grace, style, bearing, golden good looks, and his sensual mouth.

She choked when she realized what she was thinking. Looking at Renwick with something very like lust! He was married to her best friend at that! And yet the way he looked at her, the tone of voice in which he addressed her, all started her heart hammering wildly in her breast. He, like Roque, was a man. Poor Lawrence looked twice as boyish in her eyes. She was going to feel like she was marrying her younger brother despite the fact that the baronet was three years her senior.

It wasn't just how she saw them—it was partly how the two men regarded her. Lawrence idolized her as a perfect girl—sweet, innocent, and pure. Which she wasn't, but worked hard at being. Renwick, on the other hand, managed to very subtly suggest that he regarded her as a woman—and a worldly woman at that. Of course, he had seen her in torn boy's clothing, fighting and clawing for her life in the dirty, night streets of Marseille. He had a better understanding of what she really was.

Whatever she was experiencing, Renwick seemed to be a victim to it as well. She could see in his eyes that he felt more than friendship for her. Suddenly she realized that her eyes were betraying her as Renwick's had done him. Was it only because he reminded her of Roque in some ways? Was it his sharply marked difference from Lawrence, the man she was going to spend the rest of her life with? Or was it the man himself? She wondered at the twisted emotions seething in her own soul. She had imagined that life, when she got home, would be simple and uncomplicated. How wrong she had been!

"I am in the planning stage of an adventure," Count Leon Jareski–Yanoviak announced, then followed it with a yawn politely, if inadequately, covered with one thin hand.

"How exciting," Althea said and went on dabbing at her canvas with a long paintbrush. She added another splotch of blue as if inspired by Leon's remarks.

Garlanda perked up. She set her embroidery on a side table. "An adventure, count? What kind of adventure?"

"I am not yet sure. Later this year I think I shall journey to Marseille and reopen my villa there, but for now I need something to kindle my interest."

"The only interest you need to kindle is in food, Leon. You grow more emaciated by the day," Althea said tartly. "In fact, I am on my way to supervise the making of some cherry pastries at this very moment."

She stalked off, paintbrush in hand. Garlanda scrutinized the canvas. "What is it?"

Leon joined her in front of the half finished painting. "The first thing that comes to my mind is that it's your aunt's interpretation of the sea—or perhaps it's a carriage wreck."

Garlanda laughed. "Oh, really! It could be either one, couldn't it?" She seated herself while the count reached for the brandy decanter. "What is this adventure you're planning?"

"Oh, I was thinking of traveling incognito—going horseback and camping on the road and mingling with the various gypsies and low life. I'm thinking of writing a book."

"Gypsies and low life? If you need any information on pirates, let me know," she said jokingly.

"That's an idea! Perhaps I'll go to the Mermaid and gather impressions on the buccaneering way of life," the count mused. He poured just enough brandy to put color in the snifter.

"The Mermaid? Is that a ship?"

"No. It's a smuggler's inn. It's in Rye, a pleasant enough ride if the weather permits."

A smuggler's inn! Visions of Roque and Sabelle came to mind. She would never see either of them again, but perhaps there was some news. She could find out whether *La Doña del Fuego* still roamed the seas or if she had been halted forever, captured or sunk. Sunk! She had never stopped to consider that Roque might be dead or serving in the galleys.

"The Mermaid! Rye! Oh, Count! you must take me with you! I must find news of their ship, I—"

"Calm yourself. What ship? Oh, I see—*his* ship. There is no way you can go adventuring with me. Not even Althea would consent to that and she's had adventures in her life you could never even dream of! You are going to be married shortly, you cannot go traipsing across the countryside with a man who is not related to you."

"I must know!" she cried out, springing to her feet. "Don't you understand? I won't slow you down. You said yourself that I rode as if born on horseback and there was no one my age—not even a man—could approach my skill with a sword. I must go! The man I lo—" she stopped. "Leon—" she pleaded.

He was wavering.

"Please don't misunderstand me. I'm going to marry Lawrence and be a good and faithful wife. I will respect our vows and honor him all the days of my life. But before I do so I must know how the pirate fares. I would not wish to see him again or have anything to do with him, but it would soothe me if I could know he was well. After that I intend to put all thought of him from my mind. Please, Leon!"

"I will not lie to Althea," he warned.

"That's alright," she said brightly. "I will."

Garlanda had to laugh inwardly at Count Leon's conception of pirate garb. He wanted his adventure to be authentic so he had procured (God knew where!) his idea of what pirates wore. The clothes were sufficiently rich and gaudy, but they lacked the flamboyant shabbiness necessary to be absolutely convincing. All the lace was intact and there were no stains on the quilted taffeta. It seemed unlikely, however, that there was any field of knowledge that he was not familiar with, so Garlanda had to conclude that absolute accuracy would have offended Leon's delicate sensibilities.

According to Leon's scenario, they were a retired pirate and his young wife, living well on the spoils of his years at sea. He invented a head injury to account for his indistinct recollection of particular names, either of ships or people. Leon was regarding the whole trip as nothing more than a lark, something to fill his days and expose him to some new knowledge. To Garlanda it was something else, a chance to momentarily relive, at a safe distance, a part of her life that was exciting and fearsome and—and romantic, yes, romantic.

Even though she knew better Garlanda half expected Rye to be something like Port Royal, but it was no such thing. It was a proper little English village that just happened to have a port that was frequented by pirates, and smugglers. The land around was flat, but Rye itself was on an impressive rise and most of the cobbled streets were steep and exceedingly narrow.

Leon seemed to know where he was going as they rode along on the nondescript horses he had borrowed. "What's up here?" Garlanda called ahead to him as they went single file up a street to let a dogcart coming down pass them.

"The Mermaid," he called back. "Right here. There's a place to tie up the horses in back." They rode through an alleyway into a courtyard. *Poor Althea*, Garlanda thought, *I should have told her the truth. She would enjoy this. But then, she would probably enjoy herself too much and give away that we are pretending to be what we're not. That might be actually dangerous.* As it was, Althea was safely back in London believing that Leon had driven Garlanda down to her family home to sort out some household matters. That kind of jaunt was something Althea was only too glad to miss.

A fat man was dozing in the corner of the stable yard with his generous rump firmly resting in a cut-down barrel. He was leaning back and delicately balanced against a drain pipe.

"Ahoy!" Leon called in a suitably bluff manner. "Are you working or sleeping?"

A sound that was more of a rumble than a word escaped the fat man. "Aaaaayeeee," he said, opening his eyes, one at a time, and looking them over—especially Garlanda. Apparently he approved, for he pulled himself upright and out of the barrel with a sucking noise.

Garlanda dismounted and adjusted the scarf that barely covered her hair. She thought of what a difference there was between "Fleur" the pirate's woman with tanned skin, long straight hair, and tattered clothes and this sham pirate's wife, fashionably pale with short, crimped bangs. Fleur's friends would never have recognized her—at least she hoped not. Not that there was the slightest chance of seeing anyone from that life. Or was there?

They went in the back door and Leon had to duck to avoid striking his elegant head against the age-darkened beams that were not very far over Garlanda's head. The air was thick with tobacco smoke, alcohol fumes, and sweat. Garlanda wondered in passing if they had opened the windows anytime in the last ten or fifteen years. Probably not. The sounds were as thick, garbled, and primarily unpleasant as the odor.

"Damn place must be siltin' in. I damn near scraped off me rudder—"

"Get that ale over here—"

"—And then he ups and vomits, right on my new boots. I killed the bastard for it. Nobody can—"

"Barney, Ah dinna ken ya werrre herrre—"

"—So I told 'em, if you don't get your arses out of my place—"

Garlanda looked at Leon. His eyes were positively glittering, but even now he didn't smile, at least not what anyone else would consider a smile. He gestured toward a pair of stools and a tiny round table in the far corner. She nodded and they made their way through the crowd. There were a number of other women there, local women of ill-repute so Garlanda didn't stand out too badly.

"I'll go get us some ale," Leon said.

"No need," Garlanda said demurely then bellowed, "Matey, get us some rum and gunpowder over here and make it bloody fast. We're thirsty!"

Leon's face was, for once, out of his control. He registered an expression of mixed horror and admiration that made it look as though his eyes might start out of his head. "My God!" he said in tribute and subsided into stunned silence until the barkeeper slammed down two grimy tankards of frothy drink. Leon handed him some coins then sniffed the concoction suspiciously. "Is this what we are meant to drink? What's in it?"

"Rum and gunpowder, naturally," Garlanda said as if she were giving a recipe for stuffed olives.

"And you *drink* the stuff?"

"Probably not without fatal consequences. Let's pour it out bit by bit back there in the corner. With a floor like this nobody will notice. Didn't you notice how your feet tend to stick to it?"

"My dear child, I cannot believe the extent to which I have underestimated you. I am, for the first time since the cradle, actually speechless."

Garlanda grinned. A rather harmless-looking individual was making his way toward their table. Garlanda's assessment of him as such was based on his posture. He was bringing his stool with him from another table, but he hadn't gotten off it to do so. He was shuffling along, bent over and holding onto the seat. Finally he reached them and sat himself and his stool down with a *clump!* Garlanda whispered to Leon, "Ask him about a captain named Roque."

"Just get in?" the man with the stool said conversationally to Leon.

"Mm-m-m-m," he answered noncommittally.

"You and the lady need some company?"

"Well, we might. I could use some information."

"Sure."

"I'm looking for a man named Roque. Used to be a captain. He owes me some money."

"Big guy, black hair? Manners like a swell and a fist like a cannonball?"

"The same," Leon said, shooting an inquiring look at Garlanda. "Know where he is these days?"

"Don't know as where he is now," their informant said, "but the other day he was here."

Garlanda bit back an exclamation.

"Don't pay him no mind," came a voice from the next table. "Crazy Dan *just* seen ever'body in the world. Leastwise, he says so. Thinks there might be sumptin' in it for him."

"I don't know 'bout that," someone else chimed in. "'Member that time he said he seen my uncle Willie on the road and we found him in that ditch the next morning?"

"Your uncle Willie *lives* in that ditch!"

"Hey, you can't talk that way about my family. They's god-fearing folk!"

"Sure, that's why your cousin Hattie bit off my little finger!"

"Yeah, but that was after she had those two little bastards of yours—"

"Where is Hattie these days?" A new voice came out of a smoke-clouded corner. "I haven't had a good woman for six months." Was the voice familiar, or did Garlanda imagine it?

"You don't want Hattie no more, she's gone fat."

"Then maybe this'n will do." A tall figure walked toward them and stood over Garlanda. "Yes, maybe she will." Suddenly Garlanda was yanked to her feet.

Leon made a quick move to defend her, but she put out a restraining hand. "I'm already taken, matey, but maybe a dance before we go," she said to the man who held her from behind in a viselike grip.

The others greeted this idea with enthusiasm and started clapping and singing. Garlanda was hoping to start a sort of musical free-for-all so that she and Leon could just dance out the door without being noticed.

But it didn't work out quite that way.

The man turned her around and held her closely. She could feel something hard pressing against her back and guessed it was a dagger, just a little added inducement to refrain from changing partners. She endured it as long as she could. He was drunk, staggering, and smelled abominably—and she knew who he was.

Finally she edged him close to the door and checked that Leon was near. She made a signal over the man's shoulder toward the door. Leon nodded.

"Now, you let go of me, Hawkins," she said, "or I'm going to tell everybody in this room at the top of my lungs how Sabelle beat you fair and square."

Hawkins staggered back and stared at her, slack-jawed with amazement. "You wouldn't da—who the hell are you?"

He lunged at her, but she knew how to deal with it. She'd seen it done to him once before. Garlanda balled her fist and with her sword-strong arm drove it into his belly. He doubled over and roared. She didn't stop to see how long it took him to recover. She and Leon were out the back door in seconds and leaping on their horses. Leon even had the presence of mind to fling a coin at the man sitting in the barrel. "We're riding *that* way," he said and pointed left. They rode out the alley and turned right.

". . . And then we rode off in the opposite direction," Garlanda finished a recounting of their adventure to Althea, who was helpless with laughter.

"Did they follow you?"

"Not for far," Leon replied. "They were too drunk to stay on horses. Two of them nearly decapitated themselves on the overhang as they came out of the alley."

"Well, I must say, I'm very hurt that you didn't tell me about this until afterwards. I would love to have been there," Althea complained.

"No, my dear, it would have been far too strenuous for someone of your delicacy," Leon said. "Why, I've seen you become faint from the effort of lifting a fork to your lips."

"Leon! Are you implying that I'm indolent?"

Leon chose not to hear this question. "There was one ruffian there that didn't even have a shirt on and

I would swear he had neither washed nor cut his hair for years, but he was wearing a ring with a stone that would have made the Queen jealous. A huge gem!"

Suddenly Garlanda stood up. "Do we have a few minutes before dinner? There's something I want to show you."

Leon put a thin hand to his heart, "What now, most amazing of women?"

"I'll show you." She said dashing up the stairs. She brought the box for the beauty patches down. She made something of a production of slowly opening the lid under Althea's nose.

Althea gasped. "My heavens! Are those real!" She ran her fingers through the jewels. "Oh, dear, it really does make me quite faint to think what you must have had to do to 'earn' these!"

"Nothing much. I let a man kiss my hand."

Althea put the back of her hand to her brow and closed her eyes. "I suppose I must believe it since I've heard it from your own lips."

"Why are you keeping these loose this way?" Leon asked. "You should have them properly cut and put in settings. If you'll allow me, I'll take care of that for you. I know an excellent jeweler."

"But they're much too showy for me to wear, don't you think?"

"Not at all!" Althea said. "And you could loan them to me anytime you wanted."

"But won't people ask where I got them—just as you wondered?"

"Naturally they will and you can just say they are your legacy from your dear father. No one knows anything specific about your father's work or the extent of his wealth. He was, by nature, a very private man."

A very private man, Garlanda mused. *So private that*

he got himself killed and left me no clues about his death.

A servant appeared to announce that the carriage had arrived to take them to the dinner party. The jewels were put away and forgotten about for a time. Leon promised to come by and pick them up the next morning.

The dinner was being given by some of Elaine and Renwick's friends and although Althea did a good deal of advance complaining about having to attend, she managed to dominate most of the dinner discussion with news of her forthcoming trip. "I'm leaving with a group of friends a few weeks after my niece and Sir Lawrence are married. I grew up in France, of course, but it's been a very long time since I've been there for any length of time. France ought to be just lovely that time of year. Of course, the worst part of traveling anywhere is crossing the Channel, don't you think so?" she asked a dreary-looking young woman across the table. "I always get *so* ill. Or at least I did until I found this wondrous powder. You mix it in a glass of wine just before you sail and you sleep all the way. Count Jareski–Yanoviak told me about it," she said, throwing the conversation at Leon, who was unprepared for it.

Instead of elaborating on Althea's theme, Leon turned on the hostess. "The dinner is absolutely superb, madam. I haven't had such a well-flavored roast in a very long time. I must send my cook around for the recipe, if you don't mind."

"I don't mind in the least, but the secret is simply in using ample spice. It's so difficult to get these days," the hostess answered.

"Yes, why is that?" another woman chimed in. "I thought for a while that my cook was cheating me when she kept insisting that the prices were going up so much. So I looked into it and it's terribly difficult to get anything—at any price."

"It's all this piracy," one of the gentlemen said. "I was at Whitehall the other day and I heard all about it. It seems that for the last several years almost every spice ship bound for England has been captured by pirates."

"Certainly not *every* one!" someone else said.

"Yes, sir. It smacks of treason, I say. And that's what they think at Whitehall, even if they don't say so right out."

"But what do pirates want with spices?" the woman across the table from Althea asked.

"Meggie, spices are a valuable commodity," the man next to her said with exasperation. "They steal them and resell them at inflated prices."

"Oh, I say," Meggie giggled stupidly. "I thought they just liked lots of flavoring in their food." No one else deigned to laugh at this inanity.

"Why treason?" her husband asked the man who had brought it up.

"Well, the way I understand it, the dates and means of shipping are generally kept quite secret to avoid the very problem. But someone who knows this information is feeding it to the buccaneers. This person is probably getting some sort of payment or percentage of the haul. The difficulty, of course, is finding out who's involved and proving it."

"This talk is getting much too serious for me," the hostess announced. "Ladies, will you join me? The gentlemen may finish their discussion over port."

The women obediently trailed off to the card room where the conversation turned to such things as clothing and hair styles. Garlanda sat apart, wishing she could be listening to the men. Their topic interested her a great deal more. And the more she thought about it, the more frustrated she became.

It was a warm night and the card room was quite stuffy. Garlanda stepped out of the French doors onto the wide balcony to get some fresh air. As she stood there, she realized that the undertone of voices she heard was the men talking. The balcony ran along the side of the house and apparently past the windows of the dining room. She looked back into the sitting room—no one seemed to have noticed her absence. She strolled along the balcony toward the dining room doors. The voices were still too muffled to understand. Suddenly one of the doors opened and Renwick stepped out. He saw her, but didn't speak. He turned toward the dining room. "I believe I'll have my cigar out here, if you don't mind. It's cooler," he said, presumably to the host.

Somebody inside made a remark about his "hot blood," and they all laughed. He closed the door behind himself and stepped into the shadow where Garlanda stood. "Were you waiting for me?" he asked with a smile that was part warmth, part sarcasm.

"Of course not. I was just—well, spying!" She laughed.

"Spying? Why?"

"I was just bored with the women's talk and wanted to listen to something more interesting."

"I can tell you someting more interesting," he said languidly and stepped closer. "You're a beautiful woman." He took her in his strong arms and kissed her. For a moment the rest of the world swirled and disappeared and the only thing that existed was the feel of his lips on hers. The blood pounded in her ears and he held her in a breathless grip.

Then she realized what she was doing. She tried to pull away and he began kissing her neck, her throat, her ears. She shivered with pleasure. "No, no, Renwick," she mumbled and was surprised at the panting quality of her own voice.

"You're so very beautiful," he murmured in her ear. Somehow he had his hand inside the low-cut neckline of her dress and was caressing her breast. The feeling it reawoke in her was almost terrifying in its power. She wanted to throw herself into his arms, to feel the hardness of his body pressing against hers. If she had never known a man, perhaps she could have resisted him more easily. But she had known a man, she knew how this feeling could grow and build until it exploded and she was shattered with pleasure.

But not here—or now! And certainly not with *this* man—her best friend's husband. "No!" she said more strongly and pulled back abruptly.

"You want me too," Renwick said. "Admit it. You can't marry Lawrence and be away from me. He'll take you off into the country and I don't know how I'd live without you. Please, my darling, break this engagement and we'll find a way to be together."

"No. That's not true."

"It is and you know it. You can't deny your passion anymore than I can."

"I can and I do!" she said and gathered her light shawl around herself protectively. "This will *not* happen again!" She turned and forced herself to walk with dignity back to the doors of the sitting room. She stepped inside without looking back to see if he was following her.

"Garlanda!" Elaine cried. "What is the matter? You are so flushed!"

"It's—it's nothing, Elaine. There were just two

coachmen having an argument under the balcony. They were so coarse—it was quite upsetting," she said hurriedly.

"Why, you poor girl, come sit. Take my place and I'll fix you some cocoa. That will make you feel better. Maybe you'd prefer a dish of tea?"

"No—no need, Elaine. I'm quite alright. Please don't be so kind." *Please*! she added silently.

"Garlanda, it's no trouble at all to do things for your friends. You know that."

Garlanda nearly wept.

CHAPTER 18

The wedding dress was nearly finished. It was an elegant gown of satin crepe the color of a winter sky. The sleeves were three-quarter length, ending just below the elbow in an edging of lush, snowy Venetian lace. Tiny seed pearls adorned the bodice. The skirt was full, draping over hoops and hip rolls in a cascade of softest, shimmering blue.

Garlanda hated it.

Never mind the fact that it was the ultimate in fashion for a bride—she was frightened of everything it stood for. As the time for her wedding drew closer, her feeling of imprisoned panic swelled until she thought she would burst. The wife of a baronet—would she be a good wife? Good mother? How *could* she be when her emotions were in such turmoil! In the beginning she had worried about marrying Lawrence because of her love for Roque. Now she was doubly confused because of Renwick.

She did not love him and yet her body's needs and wants were making it hard to resist him. There was no emotion in it—it was animal lust, the yearning of one smoldering soul for another. Her craven desire for sin made her blush and tremble. The dressmaker shot a questioning look at her, smiling from behind a mouthful of pins. "Miss is starting to like the dress better?"

"It's perfect," she said lifelessly.

What was she going to do—?

Lawrence's family gave a hunt in her honor at their estate near Staines. Garlanda was intimidated by the size of the house that she would soon be mistress of. She got lost the first time she tried to find her way back to her room and had to ask help of an extremely disdainful butler.

The day of the hunt dawned bright and cool and cloudless. She sprang eagerly from her bed and donned her violet velvet riding habit before going downstairs for breakfast. The other women were wandering into the dining room, yawning and trying to hide it. Althea was already on her second plateful of everything. She complimented her niece's perky appearance and told her she had eyes like twinkling amethysts this morning.

"And why shouldn't I?" Garlanda cried cheerfully. "It's a lovely morning and I'm the luckiest girl in the world." For a moment she believed it.

When Lawrence came into the room he was as handsome and chivalrous as ever, sending little ripples of conversation through the ranks of women. He bent to kiss Garlanda's hand with an observation on her beauty that made her blush with delight. The mood was strangled when Renwick strode in. Blondly Olympian, his eyes met Garlanda's and turned her knees to marmalade.

"Good morning, Ridgely! And where is the fair Elaine?" Lawrence asked, in a mood generous enough to allow him to compliment sweet, inept Elaine.

"She'll be on her way in a moment. I'm not sure she

should hunt—she's had a restless night. Quite pale. A head cold, perhaps."

"Maybe it's something else—something you have something to do with," someone ribbed good-naturedly.

"I beg your pardon!" Renwick said, the blood draining from his face.

"Isn't it about time you started a family?" someone else clarified.

"Oh, I see. Yes, I suppose so," Renwick answered, obviously ill-at-ease with the trend of the conversation.

Althea leaned toward Garlanda and said quietly, "With these gossips at work, Elaine will have been delivered of twins by the time the week is out."

"She can't have children," Garlanda whispered back. "The doctors have told her that already. She wants a family so badly and yet she can't conceive. Poor Elaine. I am very worried about her, though. She seems to be ill so much of the time lately."

Elaine joined them just before the start of the hunt. Her tall riding hat was askew and she was pale with feverish patches of pink on her round cheeks. Renwick immediately picked her up and returned her to bed to be cared for by her maid. He returned looking unhappy. She had insisted he not miss the hunt, he said, and he must please her.

Garlanda thought about Elaine as they were mounting their horses. Elaine would be happier not going—she had confided to Garlanda that horses frightened her. Garlanda patted the neck of the spirited black filly Leon had loaned her.

The horse was a bone of contention between her and Lawrence. He had flatly declared it was improper for her to be seen riding a horse belonging to a gentleman other than himself. If she was going to ride at all, it should be on a horse of her own or one that he, Lawrence, had given her. She had told him that Leon had wanted to give her the filly and was only dissuaded from doing so by her insistence that such a gift *would* be improper. The filly was the daughter of the count's big, black hunter and as such was a prize animal. Garlanda sighed. Such a fleet beast, spunky yet gentle. Maybe she could accept the horse as a wedding gift.

The hunt was on. Renwick and Lawrence rode together, shouting conversation over the baying of the hounds. Althea was nearer the front of the hunt than any other woman. *Drat him*, Garlanda thought with a determined toss of her head. *If I want this horse, why should he be allowed to refuse me her? He certainly won't find a better mount and when her hunting days are over she'll be a splendid brood mare. I want her. Leon was just short of offended because I wouldn't take her. And what's wrong in accepting a horse from a friend just because he happens to be a man? Perhaps if I buy her from Leon—oh, dear, he'd never settle for that. To offer payment to someone of Leon's refinement and breeding would be the ultimate insult and I certainly don't want to lose the count's friendship.*

She was lagging behind and touched her heels to the filly's ribs. They sailed smoothly over a hedge, landing with the maximum of grace. "Oh, you're a beauty. I must have you. You make all the other horses look like plough nags!" Garlanda complimented the horse with a laugh. She stroked the gleaming shoulder under her. They looked pretty together and she thought the filly knew it, too. A fire-haired girl in violet on a prancing black hunter!

She urged the filly on. *I shan't favor any other horse Lawrence tries to find for me.* She wasn't too worried. Lawrence was easy to handle with the proper amount of eyelash fluttering and feminine giggles at the first signs of wit from him. She was definitely going to giggle and flutter her way into having this horse.

She made a clucking sound, speeding the filly's smart canter. It dawned on her that she had completely lost the hunt and had been letting the black pick her own way through the fields. They splashed through a stream, Garlanda giving little peals of alarmed laughter and hitching up her purple skirts so they would not get water-spotted. She let the filly drop her head and drink in midstream. Soon they emerged on the sunny bank. Garlanda dismounted and tied the filly to a low stump. She spread her skirt to dry and removed the bit so her horse could nibble at long, tender shoots of grass. It was a beautiful morning.

"Lost?" asked a male voice. She looked up to see Renwick approaching, his gray gelding moving at a smart trot through the clearing.

Garlanda struggled to her feet. She replaced the bit in the filly's mouth and pretended to tighten the saddle girth. "No, merely resting."

She untied her horse and prepared to mount. Before she could stop him, Renwick was next to her. "You can't get up there without help, allow me to assist you."

"No, thank you, I'm quite alright."

His hands were at her waist, but he was not helping her up to the awkward sidesaddle. Instead he was turning her around and pressing her close to him.

"Unhand me! I told you we were never to do this again!" she cried.

Renwick stroked the copper hair flowing from under her high-crowned hat. "I can't help myself. Be merciful. You know I love you. Oh, Garlanda, it's as great a calamity to me as you, don't you understand? You are betrothed and I—I have Elaine by my side for the rest of my life. She is as dear to me as a little sister, but I can't help but love you. I shall never forget my first sight of you at the Marseille embassy. Never! Dressed as a boy, with your magnificent hair unbound, wielding that sword like some inflamed Valkyrie—I lost my heart to you at that moment. You are so spirited, so—kiss me a final time and then I shall never again trouble you."

She let him tilt her chin up and kiss her. It lasted far too long. Her body melted against his and she could feel his buttons pressing through her clothes. "Let me go, you must let me go!"

He would not. She pounded on his back with cries of protest. Renwick was whispering impassioned endearments and kissing her neck. The black filly shied back from their struggle. Garlanda's hat fell to the ground where the black stepped on it, grinding it into the ground.

"What's wrong with you? Why do you fight? I'm not trying to hurt you, I—"

"Sir! Unhand my fiancée!"

Renwick released her. There was a skidding of hooves as Lawrence reined in his bay hunter sharply, nearly breaking the animal's mouth. He threw himself down, rapier in hand. "How dare you force your attentions on *my* future bride!"

Garlanda's mouth hung open in angry amazement. He wasn't coming to her rescue because she *needed* help, it was simply that someone else was using something of *his*! His property! That's how they thought of her! As if they were arguing over a horse or a hound— or the boundaries between territories!

Renwick drew his rapier from the scabbard and lunged. There were cries of consternation that made Garlanda look around. The entire hunt was riding into the clearing, ringing them with spectators. A clash of tempered metal made her wince.

"Stop it, stop it, both of you!" she shouted. Garlanda Cheney screaming like a harridan at two men dueling over her—one of them married! Who would have believed such a thing could happen to her? Surely this was a nightmare! Please! It had to be a horrible dream from which she would wake in a moment.

Renwick was too good a swordsman. He fought with a tigerish ferocity, as if he thought by winning he could claim Garlanda for his own. This was no affair of honor, she could see, to be settled by drawing blood. Renwick was serious. Lawrence was bleeding from a dozen cuts and fighting back gallantly to avenge his pride, but he was losing.

Suddenly Lawrence slipped. He went down and his opponent, temporarily off-balance, also fell. Garlanda watched as her soon-to-be husband's rapier went flying into the tall grass. Renwick suddenly recovered and leaped back up. He gripped his sword with an expression of jealousy and insane passion that wiped all sense from his features.

Suddenly Garlanda knew that Renwick was going to kill Lawrence in his blind fit of anger and no one in the crowd was doing anything to help! No one! They were unwilling to stop one man from making a murderer of himself and a corpse of one of his friends.

Garlanda ran to where Lawrence's rapier had fallen in the grass. She caught it up and countered Renwick's raised weapon. He stared in shock, then, instinctively parried. Three quick strikes with her flashing blade and Garlanda had neatly disarmed him and brought him to his knees. He clutched at the bloody stripe she had been forced to leave on his sword arm. Then he leaned forward and buried his face in his hands.

A starched silence prevailed. Garlanda glanced up to see every face registering shocked disapproval of her. No, not every face—Althea was looking at her with pained pride in her strength and wisdom in stepping in.

The silence was abruptly shattered.

"Well," sniped a woman, "if she learned *that* from the pirates and said nothing of it, surely she's hiding other secrets as well."

"I never did believe she escaped them so easily," another joined in. "Everyone knows what pirates do with female prisoners."

Lawrence had struggled to his feet and approached Garlanda. She threw herself into his arms—perhaps she could physically shield herself from what they were saying. But Lawrence drew back. "Go back to the house, Garlanda," he said in a terribly quiet voice.

She was stunned. "But Lawrence," she nearly whispered, "I saved your life."

"Yes, and caused me more embarrassment than I would have believed possible for a man to suffer at a woman's hands. I should rather be dead. Go back to the house and we will talk about this later!"

Garlanda threw the sword down. "We will *not* talk about this later!" she said. She mounted the black filly and rode toward the house without a backward glance, not for Renwick, not for Lawrence, not for the entire crowd rolling about in smutty speculation about her. She kept her head up and nudged the black horse in the ribs with her toe. Althea joined her in another minute and they rode together in silence.

As they neared the house Garlanda turned to her aunt. "You're not saying 'I told you so.' "

"I haven't the heart, my dear. But I must tell you this: I've never been so proud of anyone in my whole life."

They went back to London immediately without even changing their riding clothes. They took Althea's coach and left Jolee behind to gather the rest of their belongings. Althea said nothing more all the way home. She asked no questions, volunteered no opinions, and Garlanda was grateful. She was far too upset to speak about what had happened and feared that she would break down completely if she tried to talk about the day's events.

There was no word from anyone that night. It was as if Garlanda had ceased to exist. Leon was summoned to partake of a quiet dinner with them and Althea must have warned him in advance of what had occurred earlier, so he tactfully said nothing until after they had eaten. "You know, Althea, I believe I'll plan my own trip to end up in Marseille at the same time you will be there. It would be pleasant to have one's closest friends near at hand."

"Oh, Leon, that's wonderful. I was really rather wondering what there would be to do at the end of the journey. I'd be delighted if you were there."

"I think I'll travel around France and Spain by

boat, however, I find long trips over land extremely tiring."

"You're looking terribly pale anyway, Leon. Are you unwell?"

"I'm perpetually pale. Acquaintances have been predicting my imminent demise since I was a child."

Garlanda couldn't resist joining in. "Leon! You were never a child, were you!"

"It isn't something I like having known, but—yes, I was a child once—but only for a year and a half. It didn't suit me." Garlanda laughed and Leon's expression softened. "Why don't you go with Althea on her trip across France?"

"Oh, no, I couldn't interfere with her plans that way," Garlanda protested.

"Of course, you could!" Althea said. "The Countess of Dinmore has been begging to be released from her obligation to accompany us. Her daughter is finally with child and she wants to stay here. You could take her place."

"—I don't know."

"Please say you will. I would enjoy so much having you along."

What have I to stay here for? Garlanda thought. *I know now I can't possibly marry Lawrence. I was simply an attractive acquisition to him and that scene today spoiled my value. Thank heaven! And I certainly don't want to ever see Renwick again. The news of what happened will be all over London by tomorrow morning and if the fact that a married man was fighting over me doesn't destroy my reputation, the information that I actually fought him myself certainly will.*

"Yes, I'll go!"

"Good!" Althea squealed. "First thing tomorrow

we'll have to start getting you ready to go. You positively *must* get rid of that frumpy wardrobe—agreed?" Garlanda nodded. "And Leon must make certain that your jewels are all finished with the cutting and new settings so you can take them along."

They spent the rest of the evening going over Althea's maps and planning what to take. In the morning Garlanda made a neat little package with the ring that Lawrence had given her and dispatched it to his country home. The messenger brought back a receipt signed in Lawrence's neat handwriting, but no other communication.

The only other person she saw before they left was Elaine, who had sent her a note expressing her sorrow that Garlanda's engagement had been broken. Having determined in advance that Renwick was visiting friends in the country, Garlanda called on Elaine. Feverish and fragile, Elaine was in bed. She would not hear any sympathy and did not elaborate on the cause of her illness. Garlanda broached the subject of the painful incident at the hunt and Elaine brushed it off. "Don't be silly. You were not in the least to blame, I'm sure. Men are just so foolish. I'm only sorry it proved to be an embarrassment to you," she said.

Garlanda crept away feeling like an ogre.

She remained in the house except for dress fittings and an occasional carriage ride with Althea and Leon. She passed from being unhappy at society's rejection of her to being actively, furiously angry. "How dare they!" she raged at Althea. "I played by all their rules."

Finally everything was ready and they joined the rest of the traveling party at Dover. Count Jareski–Yanoviak had accompanied them but refused to stand around until the boat sailed. He said that prolonged good-byes wearied him. So they went on board, chatted for a bit with the other travelers, and then Althea retired to their cabin with a glass of wine and Leon's powder, muttering her objections to taking this particular boat. Her fellow travelers had outvoted her and chosen to go from Dover to Cherbourg—a far longer journey than from Dover to Calais. It involved being on the sea overnight which Althea thought was almost as bad as dying.

The boat was small and elegant, catering to wealthy travelers. There was to be a dinner in the salon which occupied the central area around which the cabins were arranged. Garlanda found herself seated with some of Althea's friends and a few congenial strangers.

"If you will forgive me for making a personal remark, madam," one of the gentlemen said, "that is an extraordinarily beautiful necklace you are wearing."

"Thank you, sire," she said fingering the big ruby in the setting Leon had designed. He had instructed the jeweler to mount it with the teardrop pearls surrounding it. It was quite beautiful.

"There must be an interesting story behind a gem such as that," the man went on.

"There must be," Garlanda said pleasantly. "But I'm afraid I don't know it. It was left to me by my father and he didn't tell me its origins."

"If only inanimate objects like that could tell us about themselves—" he mused and the company took up the subject. The first course was being served by then and there were still a few passengers coming in late. Garlanda glanced up and noticed a man at the door.

It was Roque!

No! It couldn't be! She peered across the room at

the man. It was impossible! He moved toward a table nearby and their eyes met.

But there was no recognition in his expression. She watched as he sat down and greeted some of the men at his table.

No. It wasn't Roque. This man had a full beard and his unpowdered hair was heavily streaked with gray. Closer, she could see the lines of age on his forehead and when he spoke it was with a thick German accent and a much higher pitch than Roque's voice.

But it was uncanny how much resemblance there was. Perhaps this man was some relation to Roque—an uncle or even his father! She turned to her neighbor. "Do you happen to know that man? No, the one next to him with the gray hair."

"Not to say 'know.' I spoke to him for a bit before we sailed. Rather interesting chap. Said he was going back to Berlin. Name of Schimmer, Schiller— something like that. Watchmaker, he said."

"Thank you. I thought I recognized him, but he's not who I thought he was," she said. She kept glancing at the man throughout dinner. Maybe she was just losing her mind! Perhaps someday she would be daft enough to think every strange man she saw looked like Roque.

After dinner the passengers strolled about the deck enjoying the fresh, spring air, and Garlanda leaned against the rail watching the moonlight glitter on the waves. She could not help but remember the last time she had stood thus. It had been as they passed through the Straits of Gibraltar. Roque had been at her side and they had watched the moon-bathed rock jutting out into the sea. She had been planning that night how she could escape Roque and get back to the only thing in the world she wanted—England!

Now she was escaping England. The sad irony of it made tears spring to her eyes and she hurried back to the cabin where Althea was sound asleep and snoring quietly. Garlanda slipped out of her clothes and started to get in bed with Althea. No, she didn't want to risk disturbing her. She got some blankets out of the narrow wardrobe and spread them on the floor.

She was almost asleep when there seemed to be a light in the room. She opened her eyes. There was a sliver of moonlight cutting through the room and a man stood silhouetted in the doorway. He said nothing, but she knew who he was. He closed the door and walked silently toward her. He knelt at her side and she moved automatically into his open arms. The sea mist clung to his clothes and felt astringent against her sleep-soft skin. She ran her hands through his gray hair. It might have looked different, but the silky feel of it was as before. He kissed her tenderly. She pulled him down beside her on the blankets, and rubbed her face against his rough, unfamiliar beard. It was right that they should be together.

He had never been gentler. She gave herself up to his embrace and felt the fire seep languidly into her veins. Slow, gradually mounting fire, full of emotion and need. This would not be one of their rough, barbaric frenzies of crude satiation. His body was as hard-muscled as she remembered and she touched it admiringly. His fingers slid over her flesh smoothly, then she was yielding to him and he to her. Their fulfillment trickled through their veins and left them warm and gently broken.

At long last he pulled away. She wanted to hold him, but he dressed and gave her a final kiss. He stood and went to the door. As he reached it, he seemed to have an afterthought, for he turned back and hesitated.

"Fleur—my love—"

He was gone.

The boat docked shortly before dawn, but few of the passengers were awake yet to notice. Garlanda slept until the sun came in the tiny window. Had last night really happened? she wondered as she stretched lazily. Althea was still sleeping as soundly as ever so Garlanda hurriedly dressed and went out on deck.

The captain was standing at the rail smoking a pipe and enjoying a rare moment of leisure. "Excuse me, sir," Garlanda said, "the German gentleman—the one with the gray hair—"

"Already gone, Miss. He was waiting here with his luggage when we docked. Got right off."

"Did he say where he was going?"

"No, Miss. Not my job to inquire."

What had he been doing on the ship? Why had he been in England and why was he in disguise? The questions jostled and pushed against each other in her mind, but uppermost was the most important one: Would she ever see him again?

CHAPTER 19

Garlanda was not impressed with Paris. The other members of the traveling party oohed and ahhed over each building and monument they passed, but her heart was not in sightseeing. Her thoughts were evenly divided between the man who had made love to her during the crossing and the mystery of her father's murder, if such it was.

Roque, she thought bitterly, *do you think I was fool enough to fall for that disguise? Well, perhaps I was. And what if I should find myself with child in time? I was a fool!* She shuddered at the thought of pregnancy. Children should be wanted, born into loving families, not forced on single women who had things to accomplish.

"Garlanda, my dear? Garlanda?" Auntie Althea was regarding her with amused concern. "Come, my child, for the third time, what is your opinion on the subject?"

"Well, I—I agree with you, of course."

"Marvelous! Elizabeth, do you hear that? She thinks we should take the Pont Royal, rather than the Pont Neuf."

"Well, it might be more fun, but—"

Garlanda scowled openly. She had a murder to solve and the fear of pregnancy to contend with and these people were quibbling over which bridge to cross! Her scowl increased when a dirty female urchin ran up and tried to sell her a bunch of mangled violets. She threw a few sous at the child and rode on without accepting the flowers.

"Sometimes, my dear, I fear for your health," Althea said, nudging her bay mare over closer to her niece's prancing chestnut. "Are you feeling quite all right? You're a trifle pale and your expression is—shall we say—not radiant."

"I'm sorry, I seem to be somewhat tired from all this riding."

"You do ride beautifully, you know. Leon has taught you splendidly."

Leon—how much more pleasant this trip would have been if he had come along, Garlanda found herself thinking. She frowned, shifting the reins to her left hand so she could rub her forehead to ease the sudden tightness inside her head. The embassy. How was she going to get to the embassy without the entire entourage trailing along? She glanced over at Althea. "Aunt Althea, I must confess, there is something troubling me."

"Ah, I knew there was! Come, girl, tell me so I can help you."

"I've been thinking of dear Papa—he was very close to his staff here in Paris, his letters spoke so highly of them, particularly Sir James Wilton, the gentleman who has replaced him. I thought it would be nice to visit Sir James and speak with him about Papa. It would be so pleasant to be with an old family friend, but I do not wish to interfere with this journey or take anyone out of his way on my account."

"What nonsense!" Althea cried in such resonant tones that all the pigeons basking in the sunlight on the bridge rails took flight. "What utter rubbish! Disturb anyone! Why, my dear, it would be unheard of for you not to see the gentleman when your heart is set on it, and he such an old friend of the family. I shall see you there myself tomorrow if it suits you. I'll leave you to chat with Robert's comrade, and I shall lunch at one of the cafés nearby. One doesn't have to be so terribly careful of the proprieties in France as in England, thank heaven. Dear, dear girl, always reluctant to cause the slightest distress to others. I shall be glad to assist you!"

Garlanda looked at her aunt steadily for a moment. "Helping me will also serve to give you a little break from your friends, won't it?" she said slyly.

Althea cast her eyes up. "Yes!" she said fervently.

Since she knows I'm going, it will simplify the proceedings, Garlanda thought. She remembered the little white envelope and card in her baggage. "The ambassador regrets to inform Miss Cheney that he will not be in Paris when she arrives." Garlanda allowed herself a tight smile. She had already found out that the ambassador was very much present and would be so until the next ball at Versailles in two days. She wondered if Althea had noticed how long she had conversed with the "fruit vendor" in front of the hotel the night before. Sir James, try though he might to evade her, would fail. She was going to get some positive answers.

The important thing was not to let Althea remain at the embassy long enough to see Garlanda introduced to Sir James Wilton, or it would become evident that they had never laid eyes on each other, despite the gushing speech about "dear old family friend."

* * *

"The ambassador is not in."

Garlanda spread her skirts and seated herself prettily on a pierced-work rosewood chair. "Then," she said with false sweetness and a beguiling smile bound to charm even the embassy staff a little, "I shall be forced to wait until he returns."

"But, milady! He's gone to Versailles! He shall not return before—"

"That is alright. I can send my servant to fetch as many meals as it takes to sustain me until his return."

"Miss Cheney!"

"Jolee, would you run and purchase some fresh fruit and a loaf of that wonderful braided bread with the slightly sour taste from the baker's down the street— oh, and yes, a small roast fowl would be excellent, and of course, a little cheese."

The maidservant curtsied and took the purse Garlanda offered her. By now the ambassador's next-in-command was pulling at his collar. Beads of nervous perspiration dotted his forehead. He brandished a small handkerchief to dab at his face, making a show of what misery she was causing him. "I shall see what can be done," he said vaguely and went off, elongated nose skyward.

The tilt of his head caused his gray-powdered wig with its careful curls to slide back, exposing a head as bald as an egg. Garlanda found a grim humor in it. *Pompous ass*, she told herself. *I won't be sent away by the likes of him!*

A low murmur of voices was coming from the next room. "But, Sir James—"

He was there alright! The devious man. Why was he avoiding her? She leaped to her feet, skirts snaring an eagle-footed side table bearing a vase of daffodils. It crashed to the floor. She fought it off and ran for the

door to the next room. Even as she burst in, there was
the slam of another door elsewhere in the building.
The spear-nosed assistant was standing alone in the
room, wig askew, an expression of guilt on his face.

Garlanda heard the creak of carriage wheels and
the snorting of horses. She scurried back to the waiting room and looked out the window. A portly gray-
haired man with apple cheeks and knock-knees was
scrambling into a coach bearing an English coat of
arms. He glanced up furtively, his gaze met Garlanda's for a second, then he hoisted himself aboard and
shouted to the driver.

By the time she ran out onto the street, the carriage
was kicking up a trail of dust in the distance. She
turned back to the embassy door and found it locked.
She knocked sharply several times and even adminis-
tered an ineffectual kick with the point of her slipper,
but she knew it would do no good.

Garlanda sat down to await the return of her maid.
Until now she had wondered whether her suspicions
were merely chimerical, the product of an overactive
imagination. She had considered that perhaps her
mother's mind had become unhinged at the end when
she had whispered of murder. But now—it was very
clear that information was being withheld. For what
reason? Why would a knighted ambassador go to such
ridiculous lengths to avoid her?

It was tragi-comical at the best, infuriating at the
worst. How dare he run from her like a scared rabbit?
The surly little man! His mistake had been in turning
around and letting her see his face. She would not forget that.

What now? she asked herself. *He shan't defeat me
so easily. If the only way I can speak with him is to go
to Versailles and embarrass him, then I shall! The old*

*goat! I'll follow him to the court of the King of France
and—and—*

"How exciting! Wherever did you get the daring
idea to do this?"

The jolt of the carriage over pitted roads could not
dim Garlanda's determination. "From Sir James," she
told her aunt. Althea looked almost like a bride, glowing with health and excitement. From time to time she
pulled back the curtains and peeked out.

"We're nearly there! Oh, Garlanda, what fun! Inhale
deeply—smell the orange trees? Thousands upon thousands of them line the avenues and there are many
more indoors. On a warm day the orange blossoms
and the flowers in the gardens form such a heady
combination that—driver, slow down! That curve was
much too sharp!"

Garlanda stared at her in frank astonishment. "How
do you know so much about Versailles?"

"You shouldn't be so surprised. Your mother and I
were French, you know, of very good family. Before I
was married I was a minor lady-in-waiting for a while.
Not to the queen, mind you, only to Athenais."

"Aunt! You mean to Madame de Montespan?"

"Yes, the she-devil herself. Dear old Athenais. What
a charmer she could be when she was sure of getting
her way. Still that way, I hear. Why so shocked? Oh, I
suppose Minette, your *maman*, never told you about
that stage of my life. She was scandalized, positively
scandalized!"

"I'm not," Garlanda said breathlessly. "Not at all.
Tell me more." Sir James was momentarily gone from
her mind.

Althea inhaled and smiled. "Well, Athenais never could leave well enough alone. I truly believe she poisoned Marie de Fontanges, you remember the hair style named after her, don't you? She was out riding with the King's hunt one day and her hat blew away. Not wanting her hair to become totally disheveled, Marie yanked off her pretty garter, all lace and ribbon, and caught her curls up in it. His Majesty was enchanted with it and wearing one's hair à la Fontanges became all the rage.

"Poor Marie! So lovely and so utterly—well, let us say that behind the beautiful face there was no one home. She actually believed it when they told her that her son had died a month after his birth, but everyone knew better. It's said they smuggled him away, but whether the King did the smuggling for the child's safety or whether de Montespan did it for revenge no one knows."

"I don't understand."

"I keep forgetting about your convent background. Fontanges was the King's mistress, one of them, and the child was his. It was a boy and no one knows whether he is alive or dead. Who will ever know? If Fontanges had possessed a half a mind to go with that angelic face, she might be the queen now, not the pious old hypocritical Françoise Scarron, alias Madame de Maintenon."

"But Althea, it's not certain whether or not the King has actually married Madame de Maintenon, and even if he had, she will never be crowned," Garlanda marveled. "By the way, how long were you at the court?"

"Oh, ages, my dear. I knew all the people and all the gossip and—"

"How long?" Garlanda persisted.

"—And the Prince was—"

"How long?" Garlanda fairly shrieked.

Althea looked subdued. "Oh—two or three months, perhaps?"

"Althea, you are incorrigible!" Garlanda said with a whoop of laughter.

The other woman looked very pleased. "You honestly think so?"

"Versailles!" the coachman bellowed.

CHAPTER 20

The women pulled back the coach curtains. Trees lined the straight avenues and there were artificial lakes fed by the Seine. Garlanda gaped at the splendor of the palace. She had often heard that the French were extravagant. Being half French, she had always shrugged it off. Now she knew the accusation was well-founded. No English monarch would have built anything so ostentatious. And this was only the exterior!

She turned to look at the people in other arriving coaches only to remember that no one here would be the least familiar to her. There was bound to be a prince or two in the vicinity, perhaps one of those dapper dandies astride snorting warhorses over there. And the blonde woman in the blue-watered silk gown, dripping with pearls and velvet ribbons—surely she was a duchess at the very least! Gold and silver thread was woven through the rich fabric of her gown and her voluminous skirts were raised slightly at each side to show the satin chemise beneath sparkling with a rainbow of metallic threads.

Garlanda craned her neck to see more of the sumptuous ensembles of men and women alike. Like birds, the males of the species often outdid the females in gorgeous plumage. Needlepoint lace was much in evidence, festooning collars, cuffs, sleeves, hats, scarves, handkerchiefs, and gloves. It was on everything but the men's swords. Bright, rich fabrics gleamed in the torchlight.

Versailles! The court of the Sun King! Garlanda was so excited she could hardly swallow. She and Althea fastened on their masks, hooking the sidepieces over their ears and trying not to disturb their lovelocks and confidants, as the dainty curls in front of the ears were called.

The coachman stepped up to the side of the carriage, opened the door and lowered the little ladder attached at the side. The ladies stepped down in a swirl of velvet, yards and yards of the plush material. Young dandies loitered about the stairs, anxious to catch a glimpse of ankle should the wearer be indiscreet enough not to cling determinedly to her gown the entire time. Garlanda mastered her swaying hoops and descended smoothly. There were murmurs of disappointment at her graceful success.

They entered the palace and a burst of splendor nearly overwhelmed Garlanda. Thousands upon thousands of candles illuminated the building although it was not quite dark outside. Tiny gold flames flickered atop virginal white beeswax tapers set in jasper and gilt sconces. Crystal and silver chandeliers glittered with flames that sent iridescent rainbows bouncing off the trailing teardrops of faceted glass dangling from the ceiling.

The ceiling! Garlanda tried not to stare straight up like a country bumpkin, but she had never seen such excessive frescoing, such grand murals in her life. Everything that could be painted was laden with gilt or enamel or flowers.

Althea tugged at her sleeve. They moved on into a

crowd of dazzling people adorned in the finest satins and laces. In her befuddled haze, Garlanda nearly knocked over a heavy silver and lapis lazuli candelabra. Her aunt righted her and pulled her deep within the crowd before the blunder was noticed.

"This is amazing," Garlanda said, still staring about her, wide-eyed.

"My child, it's all hideous in a wonderful way, isn't it? Leon would delight in verbally dismantling the place!"

"That would be like turning a trained panther loose in a yardful of lap dogs!"

They giggled together, attracting the attention of several nearby gentlemen. "Brush up on your French. I believe you're about to be approached," Althea warned her niece.

"Not me! I want to look at this place." They linked arms and moved on, fluttering their ivory and ostrich plume fans. Blue, green, tawny, and rust marble surrounded them, all of it veined in snowy white. Garlanda leaned against the nearest column. Gold leaf cherubs winked down at her from below haughty Romanesque patricians immortalized in marble, jet, and silver. She winked back in a spirit of reckless gaiety.

I must appear as giddy and shallow as the others until I can accomplish my business. I will find Sir James and discover what all this nefarious dodging amounts to, she thought.

They wandered over to a refreshment table to pluck gleaming little stained-glass-colored bonbons from silver trays covered with semiopaque lace. Garlanda discovered that she was hungry despite her nervousness. She heaped her plate high with shiny pastries given their gloss by brushing egg over them in the final moments of baking. Then she moved on to delicate meat pâtés, wedge-shaped confections dusted in powdered cloves and sugar, and slices of fresh fruit from the King's own gardens. The orange sections looked especially tempting. They were fat and swimming in their own glistening, sweet juices. A pyramid of *escargots* rose at one end of the table, next to thin slices of ham and pheasant smothered in a savory glaze.

The best was at the last. Snow had been brought down from the mountains and was being served with ladles of fruit-flavored syrup poured over it. Garlanda discussed the making of the dessert with the servant dishing it up. He seemed only too pleased to tell her about the preparation and added the information that it was being served this night at the special request of the King's honored guest.

"And who is that?" Garlanda asked.

"To be honest, Miss, I don't know," the man whispered. "But he's standing just over there. He's some important Turkish king or something." He pointed discreetly.

Garlanda looked around and immediately saw who he meant. A swarthily handsome man in his late thirties was standing at the far end of the long food-laden table. His face was dark, but somehow soft and serene—made so by large, dark brown eyes. His costume was lavish, but not in the gaudy way of the men at court. She looked him over, fascinated. He wore a richly embroidered white shirt of the purest silk. Ornate red, bronze, and gold thread adorned the collarless neckline and the cuffs holding full, gathered sleeves back from his hands. His trousers were also full, composed of yards of rich, black material, knotted about mid-calf. From there on down soft leather heelless boots encased his legs. Over the shirt and panta-

loons hung a lavish print coat, collarless like the shirt,
heavy with metallic thread and tiny mirrors held by
embroidered birds stitched in glittering crimson. A
wide turban of the same fabric as his floor-length coat
was on his head.

Garlanda didn't realize how intently she was staring
at him until he smiled. He was scrutinizing her as
well. She felt a blush creep up her face. *How brazen
he must think me,* she thought furiously. She tried to
pretend she had been looking at something else then
quickly turned back to the servant whom she had
been talking to. They had drawn to the end of further
discussion of the dessert when he looked her in the
eye and announced calmly that Mam'selle was surely
English.

Is it that obvious? she wondered as she moved on,
Is it my speech or my clothing or what? She glanced
around, glad to see that other women were also
masked. Her dress was the height of French fashion,
so that couldn't be it either. Her accent then? It really
wasn't the gown, was it? Surely the pride of her wardrobe couldn't be at fault!

She passed a mirror. Was that really her—a blazing
creature after all those months of black in London?
Her new gown was a sumptuous creation of cranberry
brocade velvet. The low scooped neckline revealed
the top of her expensive Flemish lace-trimmed chemise and the heavy red sleeves of her gown were drawn
up to reveal more of the fragile undergarment. Cas-
cades of gold-edged lace and flocked velveteen ribbons
peeked from under the brocade. More ribbons caught
her sleeves and held them back, permitting the creamy
chemise to show, along with a flash of soft skin. Her
feather-topped gloves, in the same shade of cranberry

as her dress, covered her arms from fingertip to elbow with a line of small pearls forming the buttons on the gloves.

Black satin "frogs" held the front of her bodice together. She drew her breath in and was startled at the way the curve of her breasts showed at the top of the neckline. Too daring! There was far too much flesh showing between the lace of her neckline and the choker of the enormous ruby and teardrop pearls circling her throat. *How Sabelle would like this dress!* she thought.

She fussed a little with her hair—the lure of a mirror was irresistible. Black embroidered ribbons, velvet bows, and gold lace decorated her bounding, laboriously crimped hair, each flourish sporting pearls. She had refused to put feathers in her hair as Althea had advised and looking around the roomful of feathers half-wilted in the heat and crush, she was glad she had.

She tugged at her "favorites," the wispy forehead fringe, then rearranged a dangling lovelock. "The orchestra is beginning. Would Mam'selle perhaps wish to dance?" a male voice said.

She whirled to face a handsome gentleman of middle age. His wig was a masterpiece of chestnut curls, falling in a riotous tumble down his broad back. At least he wasn't one of the leering young fops on the front staircase!

"Why, thank you, that is—if you think it's entirely proper for us to dance without an introduction. I don't want my papa to scold me for being too silly at such an important fête."

"Mam'selle is English," he announced in the same all-knowing way as the manservant with the flavored ice.

"Yes, however did you know?"

He bowed over her hand. "And who is your dear papa?"

"Why, he's Sir James Wilton, of the British diplomatic corps. He's ambassador to Paris and I can't seem to find him anywhere. So many people—I'm sure he'll worry about me if I don't find him soon." *There,* she thought, *just the proper amount of country girl innocence. If he doesn't fall for that I'll have to find the elusive Sir James myself.*

The duke—for she had decided that he must be a duke at the very least—informed her that he would take her to her father. He offered his arm with grave dignity. Garlanda laid her gloved hand on the offered elbow with the lightest of possible touches. What a nice man—so dark and so stately. He seemed a little familiar, was he—!

She stealthily took a peek at him from under her thick veil of eyelashes. The proud set of his shoulders, his robust swarthiness, the lines of wisdom and age and the slightly beaked nose—"Oh!" she gasped.

He bestowed a paternal smile on her. "There's no need to fear, there is your papa now."

"B-but—you are the k-k-k—"

"Sir James, your daughter."

She was delivered to the arms of the man who least wished to see her. Her presence of mind returned in time for her to give a low, graceful curtsey. The ambassador bowed with a sweep of his tricorne. The tall man in the chestnut wig moved on.

"Why the mask? And who are you?" the little man demanded.

"I am Garlanda Cheney, daughter of the late Sir Robert Cheney, as you well knew when you lied to me, sent me that spurious note, and later fled the embassy with me watching through the window. You're a clever man, Sir James, but I believe it's high time to speak to me."

"Sir James? I am not Sir James! And who is Robert Cheney?"

She could have wept with disappointment at his stubbornness. "Please! Why must you persist in this charade? All I want to know is where my beloved father is buried and what he died of. If you do not tell me," her eyes narrowed threateningly, "I shall throw a scene and weep and fling myself on the floor saying I am your mistress whom you have gotten with child. You are deliberately trying to confuse me. Why! Why shouldn't a girl want to know what happened to her beloved father while she was away at convent school."

"You!" he snorted with derision. "At convent school?"

Garlanda felt color crawl hotly up her face under the half-mask. She knew she looked none too convent-reared in her blazing gown.

"You harp on this father," Sir James said. "I know not of what you speak, girl!"

She stood up to her full height, which was not much, even with the extra inch gained by her silver-buckled dancing shoes. "If you do not know, then you are a madman. I saw you run out of the embassy with my own eyes. And if you do not know of what I speak, why are you so pale and quaking?"

"It must be the ague," he said with a moan and pulled a handkerchief from his pocket to mop at his steaming brow. "Let me think—no, I cannot recall a Robert Cheney being of my acquaintance. I am sorry."

"Sorry? I'll wager fifty crowns that your only sorrow is in not being able to completely escape this.

Very well, sir, eat, drink, and be festive—but know that I am always near you this evening."

He stormed off. Garlanda found herself standing next to the servant who had served the iced delicacy. She nodded tightly at him and squeezed through a pack of heavily powdered ladies in order to keep an eye on Sir James. She thought of Freddie, and wished she had brought him with her to London as part of her household staff. How easily he could have slipped through this assembly. No one would even look twice at a servant running an errand. But instead of him, there was only her, conspicuous as a cardinal in her red gown. *I shall probably fall down the stairs and disgrace myself with a great show of starched petticoats the moment I go aspying on Sir James,* she thought. But she was determined to harass and annoy him by dogging his footsteps until he told her something.

Althea was approaching. She swirled to a stop, looking girlishly becoming in her sprigged white gown. "Garlanda! That was the King you were with!"

"Yes, I found that out myself mere seconds ago. What a shock!"

"He's still a fine figure of a man, although greatly aged," Althea said softly. "Such noble features, such a great mind!"

"Why, Althea, you speak as if you're fond of him."

"Well, he's my motherland's sovereign. What do you expect me to do? Berate him?"

Garlanda could have sworn she had detected more than patriotism in her aunt's voice, but perhaps Althea merely felt about France as she herself did about England.

"Who was that stubby little knave and why was the

King taking you to him?" Althea asked. "It didn't seem to be a very polite conversation."

Garlanda mumbled something about not catching the man's name and steered her aunt to the refreshment table, where she practically forced a goblet of wine at her. They sipped their drinks, then observed as most of the gathering headed toward the closest ballroom. Elegant music was floating on the night air. They set their glasses down and went to the ballroom.

Garlanda was still being careful to keep Sir James in sight and it was clear that he knew it. From time to time he gave little birdlike jerks of his head, peering about until he sighted her. She would smile at him, a gleam of white teeth between her reddened lips, and stare at him until he turned away. Garlanda hoped he could feel her eyes searing holes in the back of his brain, forcefully reminding him that he was not alone. She was ready to pounce.

She was asked to dance. Althea gave her a suspicious look as Garlanda immediately feigned a foot injury. She couldn't keep an eye on Sir James if she was promenading about the dance floor. Her would-be suitor then swept Althea off. Sir James was on the dance floor as well, executing a clumsy step with a highly painted lady of little or no underwiring. It was obvious that the woman wore no stays or boning. Her bosom, not unlike the prow of a ship, heaved and swayed with each mincing step. Garlanda winced. He was going to dance his way out of the nearest door at the first opportunity—ship-woman and all!

The King was leading the dance with a young woman. Garlanda asked the wobbling relic of a female next to her who the girl was and was told that it was one of his daughters by de Montespan, who had wed the Duc de Chartres only the year before. None

of that made any sense to Garlanda, but she feigned a
knowing air and kept a lookout on the exits. The old
woman began to talk to her so quickly and in such
flawless French that Garlanda lost all track of what
was being said. She tried to keep an eye on Sir James
while inserting an occasional "m-m-m" into the conversation.

Althea floated by having the time of her life in the
arms of a very handsome young man. Her tall, slim
figure moved gracefully through each elaborate step
of the dance, drawing admiring glances from the men.
Garlanda forgot herself for a moment between seeing
her aunt and listening to the old woman.

When she next looked for Sir James, he was gone!

CHAPTER 21

She slipped out the side door and ran through the hall. Not a sign of him! "That wily rogue! I shall pin his ears to the wall," she said aloud. She went back to the ballroom and sighted the lady of the impressive prow standing to one side looking bewildered. "Madame, your dance partner—where did he go?"

The woman regarded her blankly. Garlanda realized that in her excitement she had forgotten and spoken English. She hurriedly repeated the question in French. The woman shrugged and said the little man had scurried out the nearest door and that if Garlanda found him she was to tell him he was a lout, a knave, and a despicable dancer. Garlanda went out the door the woman had indicated. It seemed hopeless. How could she find him?

"Mademoiselle?"

She gasped and whirled to face the manservant who had instructed her in the making of flavored ices. "The gentleman you were conversing with earlier made an assignation within my hearing. Perhaps it is not the proper thing to do, telling you this, but I could not help but overhear you demanding news of your father. It is not a good man who keeps a young lady from her papa. He agreed to meet another English gentleman in the north wing of the palace, the Nobles' Wing."

Garlanda paused only long enough to thank him then charged off in the direction he pointed. She didn't stop to think, then, that Versailles was huge beyond words and an entire army could easily be lost in the halls, let alone one man.

The Nobles' Wing was a twisting leviathan of interlocking corridors. Garlanda heard voices from behind a closed door and knelt to look through the keyhole. Inside, a white-haired woman sat rocking herself in a chair, talking in one voice and answering herself in another. She was clutching a china doll to her heart. Garlanda crept on guiltily. Who was the old woman and who knew she was there? Was she fed? Visited? Cared for in any way whatsoever?

Someone was coming down the dark hall. She flattened herself into a niche in the wood paneling. Two young men brushed past without noticing her. Both of them held drawn swords as if prepared for action. So hers was not the only intrigue afoot this night—

She waited until they had rounded a corner and disappeared before creeping out of her hiding place. It was far from still in the north wing tonight. Further down the hall were more voices, filtered through heavy wooden doors. Garlanda sneaked on her way, lifting her skirts so they would not rustle against the floor and betray her presence. A light was showing from under a door, a thin strip of illumination in a hallway with thick gloom relieved by a feeble candle flame every fifty feet or so.

"Do you really know, or is this a jest?" a man's voice cried. "Give me proof of what you know. I must have proof!"

Aha, Garlanda thought, *I've got him now! Caught*

in the act of trading information! She flung open the door. A blond couple entwined in a state of partial undress greeted her shocked gaze. She muttered, "wrong room," and slammed the door shut in embarrassed haste.

After that she took a candle down from the wall and, cupping a hand about it to keep drafts away, she went on investigating. The place was an endless labyrinth. There seemed no end to the corners, doors, whispered secrets coming from dark compartments. The lascivious atmosphere of the gilt decadence made her catch her breath. It reminded her too much of Roque somehow. On such a night as this, heady with the scent of fruit trees, the air sultry and delicious—no, don't think about it! The difference was that there was no innocence or affection here. These people were coupling and plotting like savage beasts, mindless of all except their own satisfaction.

I must find Sir James, she thought. *He could be gone by now. Gone—or as lost as I am.* The latter thought gave her hope. She leaned against a bronze bust on a pedestal to catch her breath. A door creaked open behind her. "Ah, my beautiful Marie, I thought you would never arrive."

Strong hands caught her and dragged her back into a dark room. "Unhand me! I'm not Marie!"

"No? But you'll do, anyway."

She cuffed her molester across the head and dropped her candle. Before he could defend himself, she stomped down on his toes with a heeled slipper and gave him a shove. She did not wait to see how he fared. There was a muffled cry of pain from her victim as she ran from the room.

Where now? Where? She glanced about her in despair. Oh, no, this was the same place she had started.

Garlanda ran down the hall on her toes. She passed a young man running from the opposite direction. Both of them were panting. She rounded the corner and stumbled over the body of a man contorted in agony. There was no mark of violence on him, but Garlanda caught a sickly smell as she bent over him. She stood up. Poison! He was beyond being helped—dead!

I must get out of here—forget about Sir James, I only want out of this wretched place! I must flee, she thought wildly. She ran. Pearls fell from her carefully crimped coiffure and went rolling along the slick floor. She ran and ran until she could not run anymore. Her heart was pounding and her stays were abbreviating her breathing. She could not get enough air—air!

Garlanda fell. She clutched a brass doorknob and pulled herself up. The door opened. She staggered inside and tried to steady the swimming blackness threatening to overwhelm her. For some minutes she remained like that, a heap of flounces, cranberry velvet, and lacy petticoats, her pretty copper curls disarrayed. At last she sat up and began to rearrange her hair with shaky fingers.

Footsteps were coming down the hall. They stopped a mere breath away. From the other direction came the demented scrambling stride of a frightened person. "You are late, Sir James! Now tell me what this foolishness is and make it fast. You have damnably interrupted my schedule!"

Short, gasping breaths. "Forgive me. It's the Cheney girl—Sir Robert's daughter. She's here suddenly, asking any number of awkward questions. Wants to know where her father died and of what."

"Can't you send her home with a stern rebuke?"

"Not this one, she's a very determined miss. How can I hide the truth from her? She has kept in my very footsteps all the night! She even threatened to make a public scene—accuse me of—oh, never mind."

There was a sharp, bitter laugh, then an intake of breath and a disturbed exhalation. "She must not learn about her father. It would endanger a great many of us. Good Lord, couldn't Bramson in London dissuade her? Feed her some facts, false as they may be? And you!"

"What could I do? I don't know a thing about his death myself! I was merely told to keep silent regarding it! This girl is being a complete nuisance! It's natural that she should be curious."

"Natural? It's not natural for a female to do anything but remain at home and bear sons! Wilton, I shall have to consult my superiors."

"B-but," Sir James sputtered. "Give me something I can tell her. Tell me where he went after he left Paris."

"He went to Nice, but she mustn't find that out. If you see her again send the troublesome minx to Rome or someplace where she'll wander about blindly and run out of time and money. She'll eventually long for the sound of English voices and go home."

Their voices trailed off. She waited until their footsteps had faded into the distance before emerging from the room. She would show them! Nice, eh? She would certainly pay the embassy in Nice a call!

Garlanda smoothed her curls, straightened her gown, and blundered around until she was at long last able to escape the mazelike north wing. She returned to the ballroom. All her spying had awakened her appetite. She checked her appearance in a mirror on her way to the refreshments. No one would ever suspect she had been involved in dangerous eavesdropping and almost witnessed a murder only a few minutes before.

A flock of brightly clad, giddily gossiping women had descended on a food table en masse. Garlanda picked up a crystal plate and began to dish up delicacies. The gossip item currently under fire was the Man in the Iron Mask. "You know what they say, don't you? They say that the Iron Mask is a twin of the King—either a relative or an unfortunate peasant."

"That makes no sense," insisted another woman. "He is a noble gentleman—far too important to be executed so he must be imprisoned in solitary confinement in the Bastille." She noticed Garlanda listening and smiled at her, silently inviting her to join the group.

"What is this?" she asked. "A mask of iron?"

They instantly clustered around her, delighted with virgin ears to pour their theories into. "There is a man in the Bastille," the loudest of the group said, squelching the others. "He wears an iron mask at all times. He can't take it off!"

"Surely that means his face is well-known then," Garlanda said.

"He appears to be of good breeding, I hear. He is allowed no visitors. He is examined occasionally by a doctor—not the regular prison doctor—and even then the mask remains bolted on. He is kept alone and no one may speak to him."

"Perhaps this man is not anyone recognizable," Garlanda suggested. "Perhaps he is merely guilty of some horrendous crime and the worst punishment is to keep him alone for years and years, locked in an ungodly mask." She was suddenly depressed. What an absurd thing to gossip about! It was too bizarre to be entirely fiction. The French were such strange people, she thought, denying half her heritage. No English king went around locking people up in private torture devices. King Louis was not only ostentatious while children ran hungry in Paris, but he was cruel as well, living and entertaining this way where one found corpses in the hallways. She wondered if this was really any better than the back streets of Port Royal.

She looked around frantically for Althea. She wanted only to leave this place. She noticed the exotic foreign gentleman for the second time. He was still standing near where he had been earlier. His eyes met hers. He touched his right hand to his forehead, lips, then heart in a spiraling gesture and bowed to Garlanda. She dropped a curtsey and continued her search for Althea.

When she glanced back over her shoulder, the strange man was talking with several other men who were dressed like him, albeit more simply and less expensively. They were all watching her with polite interest. Garlanda turned to a woman standing nearby. "Who is that very dark man?"

"The one in the turban?" the woman asked, fanning herself with a Chinese paper fan. "He is a Turkish pasha. That's something just below the rank of sultan. He's an emissary from Sultan Ahmed. The title of 'pasha' has territory that goes along with it, but I'm not sure what this one is pasha of."

"Oh, I see. He's like a duke or a governor in America. He controls a certain area."

"Exactly. And I daresay he's looking at us in a very disconcerting manner. We had best lose ourselves in the crowd. It's very dangerous to have one of them take too great an interest in you."

"Dangerous? Why?" Garlanda asked, but the

woman merely cocked an eyebrow as if Garlanda were making a joke in poor taste and disappeared into the crowd.

Althea was nowhere to be found. Garlanda spent long hours seated next to a Hungarian woman who spoke terrible French and even poorer English. At long last, as exhaustion and boredom were making her nod, Garlanda spotted Althea. She looked fresh and radiant. She practically skipped to where Garlanda sat and rapped her affectionately on the head with her folded fan. "My dear child, where have you been? I've been frightened half to death, wondering what had become of you."

Garlanda sat up drowsily. "Been? I've been wondering the same about you!"

"Oh, I've run into dozens of my old friends and we've been having the most delightful chats—catching up on old times. I suspect we rambled on far too long. But you! Where have you been off to?"

"I've been all over looking for you. In the meantime I received a first-rate education on Turkish dukes and political prisoners in metal headdresses."

Althea chucked her under the chin. "What? You must be silly from lack of sleep. You make no sense at all! Come, up with you, let's go!"

Garlanda was dragged for the nearest door. Was it only her imagination or was there a streak of watery color in the east? She rubbed her eyes, heedless of her rings. One caught on her eyelid, sending a little stab of pain through her eye. She let Althea propel her into their carriage.

Her last waking thoughts were of getting to Nice and the fact that she didn't think Althea believed for a moment that Garlanda had spent the evening sitting around innocently listening to gossip.

*　*　*

They visited Rheims Cathedral. "Althea, must we see this place? It's old and smells stale."

Domrémy, home of Joan the warrior maiden, was interesting, but only for what had happened there. It was a sleepy little village, placid until Althea's troops swept in. Garlanda found the forest where Jeanne d'Arc, La Pucelle, had first seen her visions. Fascinating. The ancient oaks seemed to harbor countless secrets, especially those of the young girl who had led her uncrowned king's forces to victory.

"—And she perished at the stake, you know," the guide said.

"Is that what comes of guarding one's virtue?" Althea muttered.

Lyon was lovely, the churches, the shops of the lacemakers. Everyone in the band of travelers bought as much lace as they could, and sent it back to their homes in England.

The Rhone River was blue as sapphires as it wound through the lush green countryside. "Ye gods! What is taking so long? Must we stop to examine every stone and lichen-covered cemetery gate on the way?" Garlanda protested.

"Niece, you are getting peevish."

They were nearly to Aix. "Althea, I'm not going to Marseille. There's someone I must see in Nice."

"Another friend of your father's?"

"Yes."

"Then I'm going with you. We'll split from the group in Aix and there we'll find travelers who are going to Nice. Quit fidgeting! Why are you so nervous these days? Are you having trouble? Female trouble, perhaps?"

"Yes."

They were rained in at Aix. The aged inn was cold and uncomfortable and drove Garlanda to distraction. She paced the floor at night and it was during one of these walks that she finally felt the twinge of discomfort in her lower abdomen that signaled the start of her monthly courses. She had not had them since leaving England.

It was normal, not a miscarriage, but a plain, common course of nature, delayed by her overwrought nerves, perhaps—but not by pregnancy.

"So this is Grasse. Let's hurry through it."

"Garlanda, calm yourself!"

At long last, Nice!

CHAPTER 22

A warm Mediterranean breeze laden with memories wafted in the windows of the Place de Casini. Garlanda stood breathing it in and wishing she did not remember so well the last time she smelled the salt scent of that sea.

"I cannot imagine how I shall exist in this positively torrid air!" Althea complained in the background as she reclined on a couch and patted a cologne-scented handkerchief on her brow. "I can't fathom why I let you talk me into this. I don't even like Nice, and that silly story you told everyone about Nice being the center of the perfume industry—as if you cared!"

"Of course I care. Stand here and lean out and smell the market below. I think it's lovely."

"All I can smell is dead fish, but I haven't got your delicate sensibilities. We're not staying here long, you know. I mean, I don't mind that much being dragged away from our traveling party for a little side trip, but I don't intend to remain here for more than a week at the most. I want to get to Marseille. The rest of them are probably there by now, along with most of our clothes, I might add," she said.

"You brought enough clothes to Nice for a dozen people, Althea," Garlanda said calmly. She had grown accustomed to her flighty aunt and knew that she was almost all bark and no bite.

"Be that as it may, I am anxious to see Leon. It's been so long and I must confess I've missed him. You're not nearly as much fun to argue with."

"I'm so sorry," Garlanda laughed.

"You're getting better, I'll admit."

"Do you really think Leon has arrived in Marseille yet?" Garlanda asked. She was suddenly aware of how much she, too, had missed Leon's cool wit and remote realism. *I wonder if there's some way we can sneak away in Marseille and give my sword arm some practice?*

"I don't know if he is or not. Possibly not. His health was so poor when we left, I'm worried about him. I think that's why he was taking the sea route later. It's easier travel than by land; that is, for some people."

"Do you think he was seriously ill?" Garlanda asked with alarm. It hadn't crossed her mind that someone so aloof should even be subject to ills of the flesh.

"Who could tell? Leon is the sort who could walk around for days with a broken arm without mentioning it to anyone." Althea strolled over to the window to test the aroma from the market. She took a deep breath, coughed ostentatiously, and staggered back to her couch. "Wretched," she muttered. "Wretched."

"Would you like a glass of wine or something?" Garlanda offered.

"That would be very nice. Ring for the maid."

"No need, I'll just run downstairs and ask for it."

"Nonsense, that's what servants are for."

"I don't mind. Anyway, I thought I would see if there were any letters for us," Garlanda insisted. How was she going to get out of here?

"I checked when we came in. Don't you remember?"

Temporarily defeated, Garlanda pulled the rope to summon service. She pulled a chair near the window and sat, staring out until it appeared that Althea, full now of wine, was napping. Then she quietly gathered up her cloak and crept furtively toward the door. She was pulling it open when Althea opened one glittering eye and said clearly, "Where are you going?"

Garlanda yelped with surprise. "Just out on the balcony for a little air," she said, trying not to sound as guilty as she felt.

"There is a great deal of what you insist on calling 'fresh' air in this room now," Althea said coldly.

"Althea, I just need to get out for a little while. To stretch my legs," Garlanda said, making a valiant attempt to mask her exasperation. She didn't succeed very well.

Althea regarded her with one of her rare, serious expressions. "Have I somehow been unfair to you, or cruel?"

"Why no, of course not. Why would you even ask? You have been wonderful to me!"

"Then why can't you just tell me where you're going and what we're doing here?"

"I told you. I'm going out for a little exercise, and as for being here, I just wanted to see what Nice was like," Garlanda answered. She didn't even sound convincing to her own ears.

"Then have a nice walk," Althea said and closed her eyes.

Garlanda tried to sort out her thoughts as she went down the hall. Why not just tell Althea she was seeking information about her father's death? Because she'd laugh? Possibly. Because she'd interfere in Garlanda's investigation of the matter? Surely. But why not? Perhaps Althea *would* take her interest seriously and be of some help.

Yes, she decided as she fastened the light cloak at the neck and adjusted it around her slim shoulders. *I will tell Althea all about it as soon as I find out where he is buried. And I should be able to find out here. Certainly Nice will be the end of this search.* As she descended the stairs wrapped in her thoughts there was a hint of movement in the corner of her vision. She glanced about just in time to see two small, dark men going through a door.

They were dark sleek men such as those with the pasha at Versailles. She had all but forgotten about him. A handsome man and undoubtedly very cultured in an un-European way. It had all been rather flattering the way he looked at her, even if he was the next thing to a barbarian. Of course, this far east and south in France was rather near the Ottoman Empire. Not surprising to see dark, exotic pagans in Nice, she supposed.

The hotel was not far from the shady little side street that housed the embassies. She drew herself up very straight and turned up the ruff at her throat. She walked along briskly, not looking to either side lest someone attempt to talk to her or mistake her nature. Nice women, after all, did not customarily wander about in strange cities (or even familiar ones) unescorted. But the situation demanded extraordinary measures.

She tapped on the door of the embassy and stood waiting. She had the eerie feeling that she was being watched, but attributed it to the fact that she was uneasy about being out alone. She looked around, but no one seemed to be showing the least interest in her.

An old peasant couple were prodding a dilapidated horse pulling a wagon piled to tottering with cabbages. Two young mothers sat on a stoop opposite, rocking their babies and gossiping contentedly. Three well-dressed men strode purposefully down the narrow avenue, talking with animation in a dialect she didn't understand. There were knots of children in assorted sizes plotting or enacting various mischiefs. Why then did she have such a strong feeling that someone was watching her?

Finally the door was answered and she was shown into another ambassador's office. This one was so like Bramson's in London that she felt returned in time. But the man standing behind the desk was not trying to be the elderly featherbrain that Bramson projected. The English ambassador at Nice was a heavyset, unsmiling individual with a bluish upper lip that wanted to have a moustache. He spoke in a deep, resonant voice. "How may I be of service to you, madam?"

"I am Garlanda Cheney," she said, removing her gloves and watching him for a reaction. Either he didn't recognize the name or he was a master at concealing his surprise. "My father was Sir Robert Cheney. He died here and I wish, while passing through, to visit his grave and make arrangement for flowers to be put on it." Would this work any better than her previous inquiries? She had learned not to just ask questions—they didn't get answered. This time she was simply stating her intentions and pretending that it was a verified fact that he had indeed died in Nice.

"Oh?" the ambassador said. Then he waited for her to go on. She had hoped that she wouldn't have to. "I'm afraid the letter giving the name of the cemetery has been lost in a tragic shipwreck, so naturally I came here," she said. Still the ambassador regarded her steadily, without a sign of answering. Garlanda could play that game too. She leaned back in her chair slightly, folded her hands, set her jaw and stared back at him.

"I don't know that I have that information," he said finally.

"Then I shall be very glad to wait while you find it, sir."

"It may take some time." He was hedging now.

"I have a great deal of time."

"Very well!" The man was clearly angry. She no longer cared. He rang a bell on his desk and a young man came in. Plump, and embarrassed about it, he tended to slump in dejection and looked like a dressed-up cream puff. "Charles," the ambassador ordered, "I want you to look up the location of Sir Robert Cheney's grave."

"But, sir—" Charles whined.

"Look it up!"

Poor dispirited Charles vanished and the ambassador sat drumming his fingers on the desk and looking into the middle distance as if Garlanda weren't there for a moment. Then, without a word, he got up and went out as well. Garlanda could hear furious whispering in the hall, but she couldn't make out the sense of it.

The ambassador came back. "I'm afraid my information is not very exact, but my records show that he was buried in the cemetery on the Rue St. François de Paule. That is a block to the south and you will need to follow west then for several blocks. It is quite large." He clamped his mouth shut, obviously through giving out information.

"Thank you," Garlanda said. There was nothing

more this man would tell her. Not now, anyway. She put her gloves back on very slowly, taking painstaking care with every wrinkle and hoping that he would be forced into additional conversation to fill the void. It didn't work. The man seemed to positively thrive on silence.

The dumpy young man named Charles escorted her to the door and looked up and down the street for her carriage. Not seeing one, he looked at her questioningly. "My servant must have wandered off," Garlanda said and pretended to be scanning the road for the imaginary servant.

"Scoundrel!" Charles said, deeply affronted at the thought of a young woman being left to fend for herself. "I should be glad to escort you myself, if I may be so bold?"

"I should be charmed. You're sure I'm not taking you away from your work?" Garlanda asked, positive that she was and that he was enjoying it.

He summoned a passing hire carriage and as she stepped in, Garlanda looked back at the windows of the ambassador's office. He was standing just back from the window and glowering at her. She waved gaily. They understood each other. Information was what she wanted—information was what he didn't wish to part with. And each knew that the other was determined.

"How long have you been in Nice?" Garlanda asked lumpy Charles with a coquettish flutter of her eyelashes. If he knew anything about her father, it would certainly be fair for her to try to get it out of him.

"W-w-well," Charles answered, stricken with a sudden fit of stuttering, "Two, almost three, years now."

"And where are you from, sir?"

"Maidstone."

"Oh, my," she cried girlishly, "that's very near my home. Perhaps my father spoke to you of it. Our families might even know each other."

"Well, no—he didn't," Charles volunteered reluctantly.

So! Father had been here; it wasn't simply a pointless chase after a rumor.

"You knew him well?"

"Not to say 'well,'" Charles said. His discomfiture was making unattractive beads of oily sweat stand out on his forehead. "In fact, hardly at all."

"My mother, God rest her soul," she said, lowering her eyes prettily, "didn't tell me much about Papa's death before she too died. What exactly *did* he die of?"

"I—uh—I don't really know." He almost whimpered. She decided it was better not to push him too hard right now.

"Oh, there's my hotel. My aunt is waiting for me, you needn't see me in. Perhaps," she said, holding his sweating hand a moment longer than necessary when she descended the carriage steps, "we will have the opportunity to see one another again."

The poor man looked as if he might start drooling in another second. She turned away, concealing her feelings of contempt. *He wouldn't last long on Roque's ship*, she found herself thinking. *Sabelle would run him through a spit for dinner.* She hurried into the hotel but didn't go to her room. She asked the proprietor to locate her maid.

She didn't feel like taking the risk of traveling alone again. The feeling of being watched still lingered. As silly as she knew it to be, it made her uneasy. Finally Jolee appeared cloaked and ready to accompany Garlanda.

The cemetery had been used for many years.

Crowded, both with graves and ancient trees, it gave Garlanda a green, underwater feeling. Jolee almost balked at entering the premises, but in the end her training and loyalty held and she accompanied Garlanda. At intervals she made the sign of the cross, but so nervously that it appeared to be random twitching. Garlanda lost her fear in her irritation with the girl. "Stop waving your arm around like you've got a nervous affliction!" she ordered, "and help me look for the right grave. It will be relatively new and should be easy to find. You take that path and I'll take this one."

A few minutes later she found Jolee literally treading on the back of her skirts. "Did you find it?" she asked the girl.

"Find what?"

Garlanda put the heels of her hands to her temples and counted to ten. "Never mind," she said through clenched teeth. "Let's go look over there."

Half an hour later they were sitting together on a lichen-covered stone bench next to a fountain upheld by a sad-looking cupid that reminded Garlanda of Charles at the embassy. "It isn't here," Garlanda said aloud, to herself more than to Jolee. "They must have known I'd come here and discover they were lying!"

That evening they had an invitation to dine with friends of Althea's. Garlanda went along willingly—in hopes that she could find someone who knew her father. Unfortunately, none of them did, but the visit did prove a benefit in one way. Althea was feeling particularly festive and stayed very late, drinking prodigious amounts of sherry in tiny sips. The result

of all this merriment was that she slept very soundly
and was still sleeping when Garlanda awoke and crept
out in the morning. She roused Jolee, who came along
protesting that they "didn't have to go to another cemetery, did they?"

She left Jolee sitting in the carriage while she
marched up the embassy steps and showed herself
boldly into the ambassador's office. He looked up at
her in confusion for a second then came to his senses
and said, "Miss Cheney, I'm so glad you've stopped
back in. You didn't leave your address and I've been inquiring everywhere for you."

"All you needed to do was ask your assistant," she
shot a look at Charles, who had trailed into the office
in her wake. "He delivered me to my hotel door yesterday. Why were you looking for me?" she asked sarcastically.

"Why, to apologize for the trouble we might have
inadvertently caused you. You see, I told you the
wrong cemetery. Can't imagine how I could have
made that mistake—"

"Neither can I."

"You see," he ignored her interruption and went on,
"I told you to go to the cemetery at the west end of
the Rue St. François de Paule and I have since found
out that he is interred at the cemetery near the cas-
tle—at the *east* end of the road. You see what an easy
error that is to make. Allow me, please, to send you
there with an escort from my office. Charles—"

"No, thank you. I can go quite well on my own. I
would prefer a private moment there."

"I beg you—"

"No." Garlanda flung the door open before Charles
could waddle across the room and open it for her. She
stepped out and slammed the heavy door with a thud

that made the windows rattle. She walked heavily—
noisily—to the end of the hall. No one was about, so
she tiptoed back to the ambassador's office. She bent
over as if examining the heel of her shoe, just in case
someone should come out and find her there.

"I didn't expect her to be here so early," the ambassador's low voice grumbled. "Why in hell didn't you
warn me that she was in the building before she burst
in my door?"

"She dashed in without saying a word. I didn't
know she was here until it was too late." This was
Charles in his usual whine. "Sir, why don't you just
tell her the truth?"

"Am I now expected to explain foreign policy to my
clerks? Your job is to do as you're told, not to ask
questions. Have you done what I instructed you to
do?"

"Yes, sir," Charles's beaten voice was nearer the
door.

Garlanda hurriedly fled down the hall and out to
the waiting carriage. So, Charles *did* know something,
but probably, judging from the ambassador's attitude,
not much. Time enough to deal with him later. Poor
dumpy Charles, dragged into the middle of a battle of
wills, and not even knowing the rules of play.

She gave directions to the driver, quelled Jolee with
a cold look, and sat back to think. Certainly they
wouldn't have the nerve to send her on another chase
after a nonexistent grave—but if the grave was actually in the cemetery they were heading for now,
why hadn't they simply told her the right place yesterday?

If she had ever had doubts that there was something sinister about Papa's death, they were gone now.
She had upset too many people by asking questions.

Apparently they were questions that no one ever thought would be asked, for all the diplomats she had come in contact with seemed to be feeling their way along and trying to guess what the others might have told her.

It took a great deal of patience to get Jolee into another cemetery without the girl having unseemly hysterics, but Garlanda's strong will prevailed. This graveyard was considerably smaller than the other, and there were many headstones with distinctly English names. Finally she found it.

SIR ROBERT CHENEY
A Loyal Servante
Of Hisse Countrie
1648–1691

Garlanda stared at the headstone standing bravely in the French graveyard. So this was where her father's body would spend eternity. At long last, one of her questions answered—the "where." Now she must still find out the "why" of his death—murder—she was sure now. She knelt before the newly polished gray stone and said a heartfelt prayer. She sent Jolee back to the carriage and sat there for a long time contemplating. How unutterably sad this place was. Even the flowers growing next to the grave marker looked wilted and unhappy.

"So! This is what it's all been about!" Althea said, breaking the peace of the cemetery.

Garlanda whirled around in shock. "What are you doing here? How did you find me?"

"You leave a trail as subtle as a cavalry parade, and so do those men who are following you."

"Men following me? What do you mean?"

"Come back to the carriage. I'm not in a position that I have to explain myself. You are! You are my ward, young lady, and if I don't have a full explanation of what you have been doing, I shall cart you back to England so quickly it will make your little red head spin."

Garlanda was astonished at Althea's attitude. She had never seen her truly angry. "I was going to explain everything to you tonight."

"Do you expect me to believe that? Perhaps you really do take me for a fool!"

"No, I have never thought you a fool. You are my dearest friend and relative, Althea," Garlanda pleaded.

"Next you'll be writing me sonnets. Pick up your skirts and get back to the carriage. You aren't safe here," she said and added in an undertone, "you're not going to be truly safe with me either!"

"Wait, let me at least pick a flower from the grave to press." Garlanda bent to snap a flower stem, but it did not break and she inadvertently pulled up the whole plant. She and Althea stood and stared in shocked confusion at the roots of the little plant.

They were perfectly formed in the shape of a pot!

CHAPTER 23

Garlanda and Althea stared at the little plant, mounting horror showing on their faces. Finally Althea said in a strangely quiet voice, "There's something very wrong here."

She knelt and began to delicately scrabble around in the growth surrounding the grave. All the plants came up, the soil below was freshly turned. "This grave hasn't been here long. Only since the last rain. Garlanda, what is this about?"

"I—I don't know," she said on the verge of tears of fear and frustration.

"Come on, let's get out of this place," Althea said. She grabbed Garlanda's arm and dragged her, unresisting, back to the carriage. They did not speak on the way back, but the atmosphere in the vehicle could have been sliced with a fish knife. Even Jolee looked like she would rather be back in the graveyard than riding with these two women who seemed on the brink of open warfare.

Once back in their room, Althea was calm—the same deadly calm as the center of a hurricane. She removed her cloak, dismissed Jolee, and poured herself a small glass of wine. Sitting down in the most regal-looking chair in the room she said, "Well?"

"I don't know quite where to start," Garlanda said uneasily.

"Anywhere you want." Her voice had frost on it.

Garlanda told her everything—about the shipwreck and her mother's last words. "Hadn't my mother ever mentioned her suspicions to you?" she asked her aunt.

"She left almost immediately after your father's death notice arrived. She said nothing to me of the matter. It seems to run in the family."

Garlanda went on to explain about her interview with Lord Bramson in London. "Jamie Bramson said the letter was lost?" Althea asked incredulously. "Why, that old buzzard never lost anything. He still keeps his milk teeth in his vest pocket. Why, in the name of heaven, didn't you tell me about this? I would have gotten some information out of him. We've known each other a long time and I—I know a few things about him that I could have brought to bear."

"I had no idea whether he really lost the letter or not. You see, I felt such a fool about the whole thing. I really thought I might just be imagining everything and going on Mama's ravings. She was terribly ill when she told me."

"Go on!"

"Well, Lord Bramson let slip that the letter had supposedly come from Sir James Wilton so I sought him out at Versailles. He pretended not to know who my father was."

"That's patently absurd. Everyone knew of your father!"

"Yes. I followed Sir James and heard him later talking with another man about me."

"Who was the other man?"

"I don't know. I couldn't see him and neither did I recognize his voice."

"What did they say?"

"They said my questions could endanger them and that I was to be sent to Rome or someplace else since my father had actually gone from Versailles to Nice."

"Ah, that explains this jaunt."

"Yesterday I went to the embassy here—"

"Yes, I know."

"How do you know?"

"I followed you, of course. Even into the dingy cemetery you went to. Gloomy place That silly Jolee nearly tripped over me. I should have just risen up in all my glory from behind a tombstone and scared the wits, such as they are, out of her."

"Thank heaven you didn't. I'd have had to carry her home!"

"What were you doing there?"

"The ambassador told me my father's grave was there. It wasn't. When I went back today, his whole manner had changed. He apologized for having sent me to the wrong place and directed me to the cemetery where you found me today."

"Standing in front of a new grave," Althea said thoughtfully. "They deliberately sent you to the wrong place so they could hurriedly erect this grave you found today. Undoubtedly a fake. I do wonder why."

"I listened at the door before I left. I heard the ambassador's assistant asking why they didn't just tell me the truth."

"And?"

"The ambassador just asked him if he'd done as he was told. I must assume now that he meant setting up that false grave."

"But this assistant knows the truth?"

"I think he may know something."

"What is his name?"

"I don't know. Charles somebody."

"Well, we shall have to extract some information from him. I'll work something out. Now, who are these men who have been following us?"

"I haven't the faintest idea—unless they've been hired to see what I'm up to."

"They've been right behind us ever since we left Versailles. They're an exotic-looking pair, unlikely for English spies—Versailles, m-m-m," her eyes narrowed suddenly. "Garlanda! During your adventures at court you didn't go and make eyes at that Turkish pasha, did you?"

"No! Of course not."

"But you did notice him?"

"Yes."

"And he noticed you?"

"I suppose so. He bowed to me once."

"Then that must be it. I imagine he took a shine to you and wants you for a wife."

"What!"

"He probably sent his underlings to keep an eye on you and report on whether you were suitably refined and cultured," she said matter-of-factly.

"But that's absurd! What will we do about it?"

"Nothing. If he gets a favorable report, he offers for your hand, you turn him down, politely, of course." She went to the drawer, carefully selected a fan and said, "Now, here's what we'll do about this Charles."

An hour later Garlanda was once again in the ambassador's office. This time she had Althea with her, mother hen-ing. "I can't adequately express my gratitude for your kindness to my niece. I think now she will be able to find peace, having visited her father's final resting place. Such a hard thing for a young girl—to lose both parents in such a short time. She's been so distraught that I—well, frankly, I've been rather worried about her. But now—" she patted Garlanda's hand with exaggerated affection. "Now I'm sure everything will be just fine."

"I'm glad to hear that. We're always happy to be of whatever service we can to visiting Englishmen—or women," the ambassador said.

"Oh, and you have been of the greatest help. We shall go on now and not take up anymore of your time. Thank you again," Althea rose. "No, no, don't bother seeing us to the door, we've bothered you quite enough already."

The ambassador gestured to Charles, who was standing in the doorway, to accompany the ladies to their carriage. Garlanda hurriedly descended the steps, but Althea latched onto Charles's arm at the top step. "My niece told me how kind you were to bring her back to the hotel yesterday," she said in an undertone. "She's far too shy to express her gratitude. I thought maybe I could plan a little surprise for her if you would agree to help me."

"Oh, yes, certainly. Anything I can do!" Charles said.

"She spoke so very highly of you. I thought perhaps you could join us for dinner tonight—our last night here in Nice. Let's not tell her. How pleased she'll be and what a fun surprise!"

"Oh, yes, I'd be happy to do that—if you think it would really please her."

"Wonderful!" Althea clapped her hands together. "Why don't you meet us at the hotel at eight and we'll have a nice little dinner—just the three of us?"

Garlanda stood by the carriage pretending that she couldn't hear Althea's discussion with her plump victim. Althea joined her and Charles, red-faced and a little breathless, handed them into the carriage and stood gaping after it as they drove away. Althea gave a repulsed shudder. "He reminds me of something I found in a salad once."

"What time did you tell him?"

"Eight," Althea answered, but she seemed preoccupied with something outside the window of the coach. "I certainly wish I could be sure who they're working for."

"Who?"

"Those men who are following you. I wish I could get a better look at them. I may be wrong about them being harmless. Until we know, you must be especially careful."

"Yes, of course," Garlanda agreed, but privately she thought Althea was letting her imagination run away with her. "Did you tell Charles we are leaving tomorrow?"

"Yes, I said we were leaving, but I didn't tell him for where. We'll have to go to Marseille from here before we follow whatever information we can get out of him."

"What if we need to go in the opposite direction?"

"Garlanda, we must go to Marseille first. There are a great many people expecting us there—not only the people we've been traveling with, but that young man—what was his name? Sir George something?"

"Sir George Young-Brookes?"

"Yes, I wrote ahead and notified him we were coming. He will be planning on our arrival, as will Leon, if he's there yet."

"Oh, very well." This was what Garlanda feared

would happen if Althea knew what she was doing. She had a dreadful tendency to regard the rest of the world as incompetents sitting around in huddled masses waiting for Althea's advice. Still, she was right. Their friends and acquaintances would become alarmed if they failed to arrive at the appointed time. She might as well allow herself to be swept along in Althea's tide for a while; she hadn't learned much by herself and perhaps Althea could help unravel the mystery.

They were sitting in the dining room when Charles arrived. Althea nudged her viciously and hissed, "Look surprised."

Garlanda threw her hands up in an exaggerated expression of glee and said, "Oh, Charles! What are *you* doing here?"

"That is adequate," Althea said coldly and turned a serpentine smile on Charles. "Do join us!"

Charles had come to dinner with the misapprehension that they wanted to hear all about him. They had his childhood with the hors d'oeuvres, his education with the fish, his entire family history with the main course, and some rather slurred hunting stories with dessert. It was all paralyzingly dull, but Althea and Garlanda sat firm with frozen smiles all the while. Althea, who could consume enormous amounts of sherry without any ill effects, kept drinking in little sips and insisted that he join her, glass for sip.

By the end of the last hunting saga, which was a confusing chronicle of somebody laying a false scent and someone else ending up in a stream, they were all nodding—Charles with inebriation, Althea and Garlanda with boredom. Finally the older woman stood up and said she thought they should all go upstairs to their sitting room and have a pleasant drink together before they parted for the evening. Charles staggered to his feet, tipping over two chairs in the process. The women pretended they didn't notice.

They practically had to carry him up the stairs. Althea tactfully propped him up in a chair in their elegantly appointed sitting room. Suddenly Althea swooped in on him. "Where did Robert Cheney go from here?" she asked bluntly.

"Marseille," he blurted out. His piggy, bloodshot eyes widened with the shock of what he'd done, and he looked for a moment as if he might actually cry. He clapped a chubby hand over his mouth. "Washn't supposhed to tell you that," he giggled.

"What did he go there for? What was he doing?" Althea shot at him, no doubt thinking she should strike while the iron was still hot.

"Need a little drink—" he muttered.

"Very well, you may have a little drink, then we'll all talk, won't we?" Althea said. "You can tell us *all* about Sir Robert—what he was doing, and where in Marseille he went." She poured a drink and handed it to him.

"Washn't supposhed to tell," he gurgled before tossing the liquid down his throat. He set the glass down on the little walnut table at his side, closed his eyes, and almost gracefully toppled forward onto the floor.

"Damnation!" Althea said. "We'll have to call the servants to haul him out of here."

"Don't you think we can revive him and get him to talk?"

"My dear, the next time he wakes up he's going to think he's died and gone to hell. He will not be anxious to confide secrets into our shell-pink ears. Best to get him out of here. He may not remember what he's told us. Just in case, I think we had better leave first thing in the morning. I'll tell Jolee to put out our traveling clothes and pack the rest so we can make an early start."

Leaving wasn't that easy, however. Jolee insisted that there was a traveling case missing and Althea, only half-dressed, insisted that she had already sent it down to be put on the carriage. Finally Garlanda offered to go down and check for herself whether it was strapped on top. "Speaking of things getting lost," Althea said, "I wish you would carry this necklace of yours on your person instead of turning it loose with the luggage. Here, wear it."

"I can't wear something like this around in the middle of the day, I'll look ridiculous," Garlanda said, feeling the silky weight of the great ruby in her hand.

"Put it down the front of your dress, then. It *ought* to be safe enough there!"

Garlanda slipped the necklace down her bodice and went to check on the missing traveling case. It was, as Althea had said, on top of the carriage. She was about to return with this news when she noticed that the morning breeze was laden with a heavenly floral fragrance. The market was just across the street and she decided to take a moment more and find the flowers that made the delightful scent. She could take a bunch along in the carriage and it would make the long ride to Marseille much more pleasant.

She traced the smell to a small booth at the far end of the market place. A shriveled little peasant woman was sitting on a blanket selling waxy, white flowers. Garlanda asked what they were and the woman merely shrugged as if giving them a name was unnecessary. Garlanda purchased a large bunch and buried her face in the blooms.

The smell was almost intoxicating—that, and the hot morning sun beaming down on her, made her feel faint for a second. There was a narrow alleyway between buildings next to the booth and she stepped into the shade for a moment to enjoy the coolness. How pleased Althea would be with the flowers!

Suddenly a smooth, strong hand clamped over her mouth and she was dragged back into the alley. She tried to bite or scream, but the grip was too forceful and suffocating.

She clutched insanely at her flowers as she was pulled back into the darkness.

PART THREE

SAFIYE

CHAPTER 24

Garlanda did not join the harem willingly.

The pasha's men had been courteous as they traveled across France and had been eager to impress upon her what an honor it was to be kidnaped by them. She had replied to their fine manners by stabbing one in the hand and doing another considerable damage with her knee. They were none too sorry to unload her on the harem guards when they arrived, at last, in Turkey.

Garlanda threw a scene that would have done an enraged lioness credit. She took a look at the other women who had been captured and added to the collection as they'd traveled along. The fools! Why didn't they move? She slapped the nearest eunuch and kicked one of her captor's horses. The animal shied straight up and in that second, she managed to get her hand on the rider's scimitar. She pulled it free and swung to face the guards, shouting for the other women to back her up: They stood and stared stupidly.

Someone grabbed her from behind. The sword was wrested from her hand, but that didn't stop her. She bit, kicked, screamed, punched, clawed, and in the end, was subdued by no fewer than five men who looked embarrassed at having to jointly pile on such a little woman to control her.

She joined the harem.

The seraglio was not one building as she had expected. Instead the women's quarters were an intricate marble maze of buildings and pavilions. There were lush gardens and ornate fountains and beyond them, the tiled road separating the women from the men's world. Sheer silk curtains and beaded streamers hung in the doorways and swayed lazily in the sultry breeze. The Turkish women in the harem immediately named her "Safiye"—The Light One.

She soon learned how the harem hierarchy operated. The pasha ran his household on the same pattern as the Grand Hareems of the Sultans. Eunuchs guarded every door of the seraglio and jealously waited to report the least indiscretion on the part of the women.

The order of the women was the hardest thing to bear. Newcomers such as herself were crowded into rooms by the dozen where they slept on mats on the floor and awaited the day they would catch the eye of the pasha. Whether they waited in dread or anticipation—they waited together. Next up were those who had been favored by a night in the pasha's bed, but had not borne children. Then there were those who had given birth to daughters, then those who had borne sons—the *khadins*. Their stature was great. The pasha had few favorites who had proved themselves worthy of recall after the birth of a male child.

Garlanda struggled to learn the rudiments of the Turkish language so she could better understand what was going on around her. The first fact that she became aware of was that she and the others were considered legally and permanently slaves. The second was that over half the women in the harem were Europeans. Apparently the pasha preferred them to his dusky, fiery beauties with their gold nose rings. He seemed to particularly like blondes and redheads.

She talked to the other European women and found that they were from such places as Venice, Krakow, Carcasonne, and Naples. They had all been kidnaped after meeting the pasha at a social occasion. Garlanda's fastest friends became the other Englishwomen in the harem—one from Brighton, one from London, and one from York. They all confessed to being embarrassed, not only by their situation, but by the clothing they had to wear. The gauzy veils and divided garments, actually pantaloons, caused them endless upset. None of them had been called to the pasha's bed yet, but there was constant worried speculation.

"Savages, these Turks! We'll be utterly debauched," Maiselle said with a shudder.

Wilma cocked her head to one side. "Oh, do be reasonable. I met him at an embassy ball and he seemed a civilized sort."

"What will we tell our husbands and children if we ever get out of here?"

"The truth," Garlanda said drily. "We were spirited away and had no choice in the matter."

"I wonder," Wilma said calmly, "whether we should put up token resistance when our time comes. I have no wish to be decapitated by the guards. On the other hand, dishonor—?"

"Who's to know of our dishonor?" Betty asked. "We'll never get out of here. No one saw us taken, our families haven't the slightest idea of our fate. The only disgrace is in our minds."

Garlanda ground her teeth. "No one's raping *me*! I'll carve out his lungs first."

They laughed at her—the smallest of them was the most defiant.

Bath time was called. They filed down the hall to the marble room full of wet bodies, steam, and towels. "This is the part I hate—being herded in here like animals after the chief *khadins* have gotten the only dry towels and used most of the soap. They have scented oils and slaves to scrub their backs. They even have their own hairdressers," Maiselle complained.

"What do we get? Leftovers at dinner *and* in the bath."

"Don't complain," Wilma advised. "We may be lowest on the ladder, but it's because we haven't been sent for. What would you prefer—leftovers and soggy soap or facing the pasha?"

"Wake up! Wake up!"

Good. The harem was only a dream! Garlanda sat up, sleepily rubbing her eyes. Maiselle was shaking her. "The pasha's decided he wants to see the new girls. Hurry and get ready, Safiye!"

So it wasn't a dream after all. It was real life and she was going to be herded in front of a man like one of the heifers on market day. She crammed her fire-hued hair under a headdress to hide it, veiled her face, and donned the shabbiest garments she could get her hands on. The women were hurried down the road that divided their quarters from the men's, and into the throne room. Garlanda skulked around at the rear of the procession, shoulders slumped to distort the lines of her body. She needn't have worried. Barely five women had been shown to him before he pointed out the one he wanted.

Wilma was dragged out from the ranks of women. "Flower of Winter," whispered a eunuch to the pasha. "She is new."

"Well," Flower of Winter (recently Wilma) said bravely, "it's something to tell John and the children about if I ever go home."

The women were sent back and the preparations begun. What the preparations consisted of, no one was sure. Wilma was whisked away to join the Turkish governor. She was round-eyed when she returned in the morning.

"Are you alright?" Maiselle asked her.

She nodded, speechless. A few of the Turkish girls sneered at her, resenting the competition. "He was—something of a gentleman. He—he even gave me the choice of having the child or not if I should discover I'm—you know. It seems they have a doctor here who sees to such things."

She fainted very gracefully.

I have got to get out of here! Garlanda thought. *I have much to do! I can't fritter away my youth in some foreign brothel and that's what this is!*

It was a hot afternoon, like most afternoons, and there was nothing better to do than take turns fanning each other and making lazy conversation. The *khadins* had taken to persecuting the lower harem girls whenever the two groups came in contact with each other, so Betty was on watch by the window in case of a sneak attack. "One more rotten apple in my face and I swear I'll strike Khurrem. That woman! You know she is Prussian? Yes! And from a good family! And here she is, living exactly like one of these people, pretending she's one of them. She's not at all ashamed about bearing that man's child."

"They're vicious, every last one of them. Is there no way to make them leave us alone?" Garlanda asked, nibbling a honeyed nougat.

"Not unless we join them on their level," Maiselle said.

Betty, at the window, hushed them with frantic waving of her ostrich feather fan. "Sh-h-h, here comes Jealous George and he's got something!"

They sat up. Jealous George was the biggest, meanest eunuch in the entire complex, and for that reason he was in charge of the newcomers' section of the harem. He could quell a resistance faster than any other guard on the premises. Garlanda stayed where she was, enjoying the breeze Maiselle was creating by waving her fan as if her life depended on it. "Betty! What's he got?" Maiselle asked.

"Another victim for our ranks, tied hand and foot. She must have put up a terrible struggle."

"Avast, ye swarthy cad!" bellowed a lusty female voice. "Unhand me else I'll have your ears. They've already gotten everything else of value from your worthless carcass! Poltroon! *Sacre Bleu!*" A stream of gutter French followed. Garlanda leaped to her feet.

"I know that voice!" she ran to the window. "Quick, girls, help me get her away from George." She shouted out the window, "Alright George, bring the hussy up here, we'll break her in."

Hazing the new girls was a popular sport, but Garlanda and her friends never engaged in it. They joined her at the window now, looking puzzled, but they assisted her in slinging verbal mud at the most recent addition to their house. The buxom black-haired woman was slung down on the cobblestones.

"George" shouted in Turkish that she was all theirs. Garlanda ran out and untied her.

"Christ, little one," Sabelle said with a rich laugh. "We get ourselves into some damnable situations, don't we?" She stood up, massaging cramped wrists and ankles.

Garlanda tried to hug her and was pushed away with a scowl.

CHAPTER 25

Life became a great deal more interesting after Sabelle's arrival. First she led a raid on the *khadins'* quarters. This provided the newcomers with some fine clothes to wear, along with some minor pieces of jewelry, glass figurines, hand mirrors, and oriental fans. Garlanda's troop covered the exits while Sabelle's women overcame the *khadins* then Garlanda and Betty swept in and gathered up everything they could get their hands on. By the time the eunuchs were alerted, the attackers were back in their own building, fanning each other and looking amazed at the eunuchs' accusations. They didn't need the spoils, it simply enlivened their dull existence.

The *khadins* were not ones to let such a breach of the law go unpunished. They convinced Jealous George to toughen up on his reprimands. Beatings were handed out for the mildest of infractions. But still, Garlanda refused to be humbled. She and Sabelle together were more than a match for any adversary, or so they hoped.

"What happened to you in Marseille anyway?" Sabelle asked one languid afternoon as they lazed in the bathhouse.

"I thought Roque was going to ransom me so I jumped ship."

"I thought as much. The cap'n kept rantin' and ravin' that you'd been kidnaped, but I noticed that your little friend the cabin boy was missing too, so I figured it must o' been a joint effort. Funny boy, that one. Didn't seem to get used to the sea."

"He wasn't at sea willingly. He said you found him in Tortuga and bought him for *La Doña del Fuego*."

"Aye, I bought him, and he bought himself back less'n a year later. What happened to Freddie after the two of you got away?"

"He stayed on in Marseille to work at the embassy."

Sabelle seemed to be considering this. "He speaks damn good French for a boy calling himself 'Freddie.' I ladled rum into him one night and he talked about Paris like he really knew the place. Speaks like a little swell when he's in his cups!" She laughed. "So, you've turned him into a pint-sized ambassador, ha, ha. Poor little thing was crazy about you."

"Don't be cruel. He was like a little brother," Garlanda said.

Sabelle shrugged. "As you wish, Fleur, but if you was smart you'd wait for him to grow up. He's not shifty like Roque."

"Roque! You know, I met him crossing the Channel one night. He tried to pretend he didn't know me. He was in disguise."

Sabelle took a swat at a fly with her fan. "That's what I mean, shifty. Always creepin' around in costumes and pullin' a devilish disappearin' act. Something unnatural about a man so sneaky. He's up to no good, that one. Intrigues and spyin' and runnin' off at odd times—it adds up to no good in my book. He must have connections in high places."

"Why do you say that?"

"Haven't you heard? English vessels are gettin' picked off like—like these flies." To prove her point she killed another one. "The Spanish and French and Portuguese are being raided like always, but not like the English. Somebody's passing around the word of what's sailin' when, and that's pretty difficult information to get usually. Rumor is that there's an Englishman betraying his own country. Even *I* don't hold with that! Who'd be in a better place to do that than a captain who's English and knows every trading center and smuggler's inn like the back of his hand? It's damned queer, too, that Roque never gets caught. That's why I say he has mates in high places."

"Roque—a traitor to England!"

Sabelle waved the issue—and a fly—off. "When do you 'spose we meet this pasha?"

Garlanda ignored the attempted change of subject. "Do you really think Roque could be involved in something like that?"

Sabelle wouldn't be drawn in to discussing him further. "Who knows?"

"You haven't told me yet how you got here," Garlanda said.

"Oh, Roque went creepin' off to port and left me in charge. As quartermaster I had to see to the loadin' of supplies on the ship. Damned if I wasn't snatched in a dark cul-de-sac and here I am."

"Where did this happen?"

"Constantinople. Roque's really spreading out his territory. He has two ships working the Caspian, another in the Black Sea, and the *King of Rhye* and a fighting corsair are in the Caribbean. Say, I hear this pasha's away on business. Wish he'd hurry and get back."

"Why?"

"'Cause it's been too damned long since I had a man and all this layin' around in hot baths is gettin' me blood coursin'. What do they have for entertainment around here? Any good-lookin' slave boys?"

"Uh-h-h, Sabelle, not only would it be impossible for the male slaves to, uh, complete your wishes," Garlanda said, blushing, "but any harem girl caught with a man is killed rather messily."

"You mean that lily-livered, landlubbing grubworm keeps us *all* just for himself? Some stallion, eh?"

"Bellè, he doesn't get around to all these women. In fact, fewer than half of them have ever—"

"All show and no go, eh? Does he like boys? Never mind. Now, how do I get to be a *khadin* so I can spit on them old birds on top?"

"To be a *khadin* you have to give birth to a son."

Sabelle whistled and shook her head. She reached for her clothes. "Not for me, little one. Having the last one fair killed me. I won't be havin' no more—couldn't even if I wanted to. Maybe I could fool the old dastard, put a pillow under my—no, in these skimpy clothes you couldn't hide even a toothpick."

"He's not old. In fact, he's nice-looking in a foreign way."

They dressed in silence, then, as they turned to go Sabelle looked at her with a distressed expression. "Are all the guards and page boys except him . . ." Garlanda nodded. "All the men in this court?"

"Yes. But look at it this way—the lack of opportunity will keep you alive whether you want that or not."

"Lot o' comfort that is," Sabelle returned sourly. "Well, if I can't have men, I guess I'll adjust me energies to gettin' out of here."

At the next parade of the concubines, Sabelle was chosen. She went off to the preparations with a smile on her lips and the next morning she was as fresh and pert as a two-year-old filly let loose in a field after a long winter indoors. "Cagey bastard, but lively— lively! A real gentlemanly sort. I don't know where he learned all that, but he's got it down right well." She went whistling on her way. By nightfall the rumor was that the pasha looked like a house had fallen on him. Sabelle had, and that was enough.

That night Sabelle was called back—and the next night and the next. She was elevated to the *khadins'* quarters although she was not of their level. "Squalling cats, all of them. You're going with me as my maid. 'Course you don't really have to wait on me. I don't hold a grudge for the way Roque made me give you my red dress. It didn't fit anyway," she told Garlanda. "Grab your things and let's go."

The Bearers of Sons squawked that it was improper and unfair that a childless slave should be allowed preferential treatment. They breathed a loud sigh of relief when the pasha went off on business and did not take Sabelle along to further infatuate him.

"There's our chance," Garlanda whispered one night. "The next time he goes you must convince him to take you and your faithful serving maid. Then we can escape."

"He's not a man one can sway with convincin', but that's an idea. Why do you keep slinkin' around in those tatters? Why not dress yourself up and risk a visit to the pasha?"

"Sabelle!"

"I keep forgettin' you like to play the lady. Oh, well, it's your loss. Say, I like them Janissaries the sultan loaned the pasha. You know, the men in yellow and white uniforms. I hear they're Christians who are stolen at an early age and most of 'em don't even know their real names or families. They breed Circassian slaves on farms like horses. Ain't that odd—? Christians being the right-hand men of the sultan? I particularly like that one Janissary with the blond hair and big shoulders. They don't fix them, do they?"

"Surely not, but Sabelle, you'd better stop thinking like that. You know what the penalty is."

Sabelle sighed. "I was just thinking, little one, don't fret."

The pasha returned and Sabelle was again favored. Garlanda was concerned about her. Sometimes lately she had turned very quiet. When asked what was wrong, she simply shook her head. Garlanda wondered if it was the children she had mentioned having. Did she have a family somewhere? A husband or parents? And what of the child—or children?

She couldn't ask, of course. They had been comrades on the high seas and Garlanda had learned that privateers never questioned each other on their backgrounds. It took strange twists of fate to make pirates of such diverse people as spunky Sabelle, gentle Sebastian Sim, temperamental William Kidd, and especially Roque, with his air of better days and fine family showing through the facade of a rapscallion corsair captain.

What crime, what disaster had forced a gentleman to flee to the rough, unstable life the sea provided? Had he killed someone? Been wrongly deprived of a fortune by a scheming relative? Or had he merely been seduced by all that pirating had to offer? It was indeed suspicious that he had never been captured in his plundering. He fit the role of genius-traitor well with his smooth manners and flair for convincing disguise.

The pasha went away once more, this time to quell a rebellion in an outlying province. While he was gone Sabelle did the unthinkable. She spoke of her past.

CHAPTER 26

"When I lived in Martinique," Garlanda said in a lazy voice, "Grandmother's cook used to make jelly on the hottest day each summer."

"Good!" Sabelle said sarcastically.

Garlanda was undisturbed. She wasn't really talking to Sabelle anyway. She was talking to herself just to while away the day. It was far too hot to do anything *but* talk. Even the effort of walking around was devastating in the heat. The two women had taken some blue silk cushions and found a place in the courtyard that was in the shade of a small formal grove of olive trees. It was infinitesimally cooler than the rest of their small world.

"I think she knew in advance which would be the hottest day," Garlanda continued as she languidly fanned herself with a brightly colored paper fan, "and she did it then so that Grandmother would feel sorry for her. Cook thought jelly was nasty, English stuff. I can't see why she never came to like it. She made wonderful combinations of tropical fruits and we loved it.

"She had a little cook house and she would build up a big fire and make the jelly in a hugh iron pot. She'd stand over the pot for hours, sweating in the steamy air and I'd go in the little house and watch her—just to see how long I could stand the heat. But Sabelle, even that little house was never as hot as it is here."

"Hell itself couldn't be any hotter than this god-forsaken country!" Sabelle said. "I remember doin' the same sort o' thing. Seems stupid, now that we're here, wantin' to be hot—but my mother made bread for some neighbors to make a little money, and I recall seein' how long I could stand close to the fire. Kind of a game—"

Garlanda struggled to picture Sabelle as a child with a mother. "What was your mother like?" Garlanda asked, her curiosity overcoming her respect for the pirates' unspoken code of privacy.

"I don't recall that much about her," Sabelle said, then cast a bitterly amused look at Garlanda. "I guess it don't matter if I tell you about myself now, seeing as how you've been itchin' to know. I never met anybody as nosy as you!"

"You know I wouldn't talk to anyone about anything you tell me," Garlanda assured her.

"I 'spose that's true." Sabelle seemed to be thinking it over—weighing whether she should expose any of her life to this inquisitive young woman with whom she had become friends in spite of herself. She took one of the blue pillows in her lap and absently picked at the fringe. "I grew up in Paris—in an awful poor part of Paris—and there was only one way for a girl with looks to get along. There was a brothel down the street and when I was twelve my mother took me there and sold me to 'em."

"Sabelle!" Garlanda gasped. "How awful! How could your own mother do that to a twelve-year-old?"

"Aw-w-w, it wasn't really her fault. We didn't have no money at all and my two sisters was both ugly as dung—no way they could make a livin' for my mother,

and she was always sick, anyhow. There weren't much
choice—I didn't really mind. I've always sorta liked
the men—not all of them, but then everybody's got to
do some things they don't like. I could think of
worse!"

Garlanda looked skeptical.

"Sure, I could have been making jelly in Martinique," Sabelle said with a laugh. "Anyhow, I'd been
livin' at the brothel for a while and this rich swell
came in and one of the girls gave him a bad time, and
the next day some soldiers came bustin' in and arrested everyone. 'Cause I was so young I was took off
to this convent in Paris where they locked up 'sinful'
girls and tried to beat the sin outta them. There must
of been fifty or sixty of us and they'd die of the beat-
in' 'bout the same rate that new ones was brought in."

"Why, that's barbaric!"

Sabelle looked surprised. "Sure it was. Lots of
things are. Haven't you noticed? The nuns gave me a
real bad time, 'cause I was so pretty. Seemed to make
'em real mad. Most of the girls was sorta draggle-
tailed rickety things, and they had a mite easier time
of it. So, one day the sisters bundled us all up and
dragged us down to the docks and put us on a boat."

"On a boat? Why?"

"Nobody would tell us where we was being taken.
But one of the girls who could read had been snoop-
ing around in the Mother Superior's office and had
found a letter sayin' that King Louis wanted a load of
women sent off to a place called Tortuga, so we figured we was the boatload. They gave us each a hun-
nert lashes 'fore we left. And us just kids! Still makes
me mad to think 'bout it. Some of the girls had these
puny little babies and—"

"Please!" Garlanda said. She couldn't bear to hear what happened to the babies. "Why Tortuga?"

"That's what we wanted to know. 'Course, none of us had ever heard of such a place. Turns out, it was an island near Hispaniola and it had nothin' but men—pirates who'd settled there and wanted some women. King Louis figured, I guess, that he'd make friends with the pirates and get rid of an awful lot of whores at the same time. It was a rare day when we got there!" Sabelle laughed at the memory.

"'Bout fifteen of the girls died afore we got across the ocean, but the rest of us was eager for the sight of dry land and men! There was this governor there and he made us all parade off the boat and let the men look us over. He didn't want us all just belongin' to everyone, so one by one he let the men come up on this platform where we was standing and pick out his own woman. Then before he could take her off, they had to be married. Right then and there! They had a whole passel of priests rippin' through the vows fast as they could! Funny as anything."

"Were you chosen?"

Sabelle looked at her like she was joking. "Was I chosen? I was one of the first! I was a real beauty then, real young and soft lookin'. Remember the girl the pasha's men brought in last week?"

"The young one with the dark hair?" Garlanda remembered her clearly. She was very young and striking, not only in her dark, delineated features, but in her proud, defiant manner.

"Yeah, I looked like her, only better."

"Who were you married to?"

"Oh, a young fella they called Peg-leg Willie. Not that I'd ever wanted a husband, but he wasn't a bad one. He tried to beat me once and I blacked his eye—

after that we got along real good. In fact, after the
young 'uns came along he got to like me a lot and
would bring me jewels and spices and pretty cloth
when he came back from sailin'. He taught me t'
speak English."

"Children? Where are your children now?"

"I don't know," Sabelle said curtly and clamped her
lips shut, seeming to indicate that she'd already said a
great deal more than she had intended. She had
picked most of the fringe off the pillow and threw it
down to start demolishing another.

Garlanda wasn't about to let the story stop there.
"Did they die of a tropical fever or something?" she
persisted.

"I don't know that they died of anything."

"How could you not know?"

"They was taken from me and sold as slaves, just
like I was. My little ones—my treasures!"

"Who took them?"

"Bunch of sailors and natives from Hispaniola came
over one night when most of the men was gone and
burned the villages. Lots of the women was killed.
They spared me 'cause of my looks, I guess. They took
my young 'uns away in a different boat. I never saw
them again. After a while I was sold. Some sour-
breathed old bastard bought me. He thought he was
gonna take me back to his big house and keep me in
the kitchen and his bed. He didn't make it," she added
ominously.

"What happened?" Garlanda asked, fearing that she
knew the answer.

"Oh, I killed the old buzzard. I didn't exactly mean
to, but I didn't mind much that I did, either. Then I
was afraid someone would come after me for it, so I
sneaked down to the harbor and stowed away on a

ship that was gettin' ready to sail. Lucky for me it was Roque's old ship. I had a hell of a time convincin' him I was worth takin' along, but finally he agreed to let me make one trip and see if I paid my way—it was bed and a kitchen again, but at least Roque had teeth. He even made a stop in Hispaniola for a couple a days so I could look for my family, but they'd been taken elsewhere by that time and no one could tell me where."

"Couldn't tell you or *wouldn't?*"

"That's about it. That sea scum knew they'd been sold somewhere, but I didn't have no way of getting it outta them. I've been back a couple of times and sent friends to look, but they just seemed to disappear without a trace. I 'spose maybe they're all dead by now, but I hate not knowin'. I know the buccaneer what led the raid, and someday—someday!"

She broke off angrily. "Don't know why I'm tellin' you this. Heat must be rottin' my brain!" She threw down the second mutilated pillow and took hold of Garlanda's arm in a tight grip. "If you ever breathe a word of this, I'll rip that pretty face off you."

She got up and stomped off. Garlanda watched her go, knowing her curiosity had once again gotten the better of her and led her into information that she might have been happier not knowing. How tragic for Sabelle, forced to be a child prostitute, then flung to a husband she had never seen before. They had found some degree of happiness, only to be torn asunder, their children auctioned off on the block. What had happened to the husband, Peg-leg Willie? Sabelle hadn't said. Probably came home, heard news of the calamity, and went on his way. Garlanda knew pirates well enough to realize that their lives were full of upheavals. They were a breed familiar with the winds of change.

Later that evening, when it was cooler, Garlanda sought out her friend. "I'm sorry I pried, 'Belle."

"Pried? You didn't do nothin'," the older woman said with attempted lightness. Their eyes met and locked in mutual understanding. The subject was never to be reopened unless by Sabelle. Her past was a secret gift she had shared with a fellow pirate woman, an outcast like herself—Fleur, kidnaped for a harem and detained from investigating what had become of her family—much as Sabelle. They shared hurts and common cares despite all appearances.

Two nights later, Sabelle was discovered in a compromising situation with the blond Janissary who had caught her eye days before. She was clapped in chains in the bowels of the dungeon to await the return of the pasha.

Their lord returned. Garlanda accepted the news with a rigid face, knowing what she had to do. Only as a favored concubine could she ask a favor, only then could she approach the pasha and plead for her friend's life. It would mean groveling, subjecting herself, losing her dignity, and abandoning her beliefs. And for what? Once again she saw Sabelle's face—defiant, proud, and yet full of passionate motherhood, saying, "My little ones, my treasures!" It took a brave woman to rise above such sorrow—and good friend.

With Roque she had given herself out of love, Garlanda told herself bitterly. Now it would be sheer prostitution. She washed and trimmed her hair, then donned the collective best of the newcomers' clothes and lined up with the others to go make her bid for the bed of the pasha.

"You can't do it," Wilma whispered.

"I can and I will!" Garlanda held her head high, shoulders back, spine stiff. No longer dressed in tatters, she stood out among the other women. When she drew close to the chair of the man who owned them, she went down on her knees, crossed her arms on her chest in an attitude of subserviency and smiled.

"Ah, the woman from the court of the French king! Why has she not been brought to me sooner?"

A eunuch prostrated himself on the floor. "Oh, Most High, Safiye has been here many fortnights but has not been at the front of the line before."

"Why not? Someone take this dog out and flog him. Come here, Safiye."

She approached. The pasha did not look cruel. There was wisdom and a trace of humor in the droll curve of his sensuous mouth. He studied her at great length. "This is the one I will have tonight. Prepare her."

She was taken away to undergo the ritual of purification and preparation for the bed of the pasha.

Garlanda was shaking when they took her to the pasha's quarters. She had never been cleaner or more mortified in her life. A cluster of old women had massaged and pummeled her with oil and then left her to sweat in a steam bath. After that she had been given a

cold bath, been yanked from it, and had her body
subjected to a humiliating shave of all body hair. Next
she was plastered with mudpacks, scrubbed until her
skin was raw, and dried off so vigorously her skin tin-
gled. Rich scents were applied all over her body. Her
fingernails were dyed, her eyes outlined in kohl, and
her lashes darkened. A reddish stain was dabbed on
her lips.

They worked on her hair next, removing the final
traces of crimping she had done to it in London.
Heated irons were used to smooth her coppery mane
to make it straight. It was trimmed and then brushed
a hundred strokes until it gleamed.

They brought her splendid clothes of Brusa silk and
gauze. She was dressed and taken, at last, to face the
pasha. Just short of the door one of the old women
paused and inquired in faulty French if she was a virgin. Garlanda nodded. It was not hard to lie when she
was so worried about Sabelle and the ordeal she herself was about to submit to. Her value would be much
more enhanced if he thought he was getting undam-
aged property.

"My Exalted Lord Mustafa, the girl is here for you
and she is a virgin."

"Ask her if she wishes one of you to wait outside the
door for her," came the bored-sounding voice from
behind the door. Garlanda nodded and clung to the
nearest woman's hand. As frightened as she was, she
could easily believe it to be her first time.

They pulled her inside the room. Braziers of delicately scented incense swung gently in the breeze and
soft candlelight flickered about in the room. The
pasha was lounging on a great gilt bed covered with
satins, furs, and pillows. He took a leisurely puff from

his hookah before sitting up. "Do not look so frightened," he told Garlanda in perfect French. "Ask anything you wish of the women before they leave."

The fat old harridans who had done such wretched things to her were suddenly her best friends. She took one's hand and said shakily, "What do I do?"

"You will find that if you relax it will be much easier," she said. They forced her up, sat her on the bed, and left.

"You were not, I think, so shy this afternoon when you smiled at me," he said without a trace of the mockery she expected.

"I thought if you saw me you might recognize me from Versailles and let me go."

He laughed. A short, kind sound. "I am not going to harm you. I find you interesting as well as beautiful. I might even find you witty. Where were you educated?"

"Martinique. It's an island—"

"In the Caribbean."

She blushed.

"You see," he said, "we are, neither of us, savages. I was schooled in Rome for a great many years. Come closer."

"I'm afraid to," she answered with just the right maidenly duck of her head. It wasn't going to be easy to convince this man of her virtue without playing the fool.

He grasped her wrist and drew her closer. "Relax, Safiye. I am gentle and patient in taming wild mares. I will be no less than kind to you, but you must be willing. I do not force women."

"Oh? I was under the impression—you mean if I want to walk out I can? But what would happen to me then? I'll have to go back to being buffeted about by the *khadins* and mocked and—oh, I don't know what to do!" Because she was already upset and her nerves overwrought to the breaking point, she had no difficulty crying. Suddenly she found herself sobbing on his shoulder while he patted her back. She managed a few more dry sobs while he dabbed at her nearly nonexistent tears and held her until she stopped shaking.

"Better now?" he asked, removing her veil and headdress.

"Yes. You won't hurt me, will you? Whatever you're going to do is wrong and I'm not supposed to—but I am your slave and—" *Oh, Lord,* she thought, *Althea would be getting sick if she could only hear me now! But if I could fool them in London, I can fool them here. It isn't really so difficult to be a convent girl again. All I have to do is look back—*

He was stroking her hair now. His hand slid down over her shoulder, then he was unbuttoning the front of her short, sleeveless jacket. He threw it to one side and cupped her full white breasts in his hands. Garlanda uttered a frightened sound that he hushed with a kiss.

"No, no—" she said.

He laid her down on the satin bedcovers and removed their clothes. In spite of herself she moaned with arousal. It had been too long since she had been with a man. "No—I shouldn't enjoy this," she said aloud. He stroked her with experienced hands. It was all she could do to remain still and play the role of an innocent. Shame boiled in her blood as she realized how much she wanted to return his gentle caresses.

His hands fondled her breasts and then slid down over her hips to between her legs. He kissed her and moved down. He kissed her white throat, her shoulders, her taut nipples, her stomach. And still he moved lower.

"No!" she cried, but it died in her throat. His mouth was on her, searing her flesh, driving her to unexpected new peaks of pulsating ecstasy. She had never known this experience with Roque. Again and again she spiraled upward in a vortex of sensual fulfillment and crashed back to earth spent and yet yearning for more. It took every bit of her willpower to remember to act as if it were painful when he first entered her.

Through her mindless haze she was confused and embarrassed. How could she feel this way? She was no better than a whore, writhing under any man who chose to make her do so, and yet—yet, there was something wonderful in knowing she could experience such pleasure. Roque was not the beginning and end of all sexuality. It was not, she told herself, necessary to feel guilt and shame at what her body could give her.

The pasha stopped, saying he did not wish to hurt her, new as she was to erotic sensation. Garlanda did not need to playact. She nodded and drifted off to sleep.

CHAPTER 27

Sabelle was alive, but for how long? Garlanda asked herself that every day when she crept back from visiting her friends. She would have been a *khadin* after a short time had it not been for the skills of the court doctor. Every time she thought of that, Garlanda gritted her teeth. Would it be worth the sacrifice of having a child to save Sabelle? What if it was a girl? What if Sabelle was executed before Garlanda's time came?

But she had been saved making the decision. When the pasha first discovered that Garlanda was pregnant he had sent for the court abortionist, saying he did not want a child to interrupt their time together. Argument would have done no good.

Tonight they had an important dinner and she was required to be there, along with the chief *khadin*, Khurrem, mother of the principal heir. Khurrem and Garlanda hated each other fiercely and the fact that Garlanda had free access to move between the pasha's quarters and the newcomers', did not make things any better.

Garlanda moved along the corridor with her shoulders slumping dejectedly. Tonight she would have to tolerate sitting silently at the pasha's feet while another European caller tried to convert him or bribe him or whatever else was left on the list. Last week it had been a Viennese ambassador, followed by two priests from Madrid. Monday someone from France had been at the palace to discuss the corsairs in the Mediterranean.

It was terribly frustrating—being so close to these Europeans who were in no position to rescue the non-Moslem women. Even if they had wanted to help, which most of them probably didn't. They were there to get specific favors, not to get into disputes with the pasha.

Garlanda sighed. At least she learned things at the dinner parties. Later on when they were alone the pasha would sometimes discuss affairs of state with her. He would call her his tawny mare, tug her hair, and laughingly ask her opinion on things such as state protocol or raising his cut of the profit he took from the pirates he allowed to operate in his territory. At first he only laughed affectionately at her questions and replies, but before long he began to think over what she said, mulling her words as if she were an equal and not a "mere woman" as most Eastern men seemed to believe.

She had gradually come to have great respect for him. Sometimes she could forget for a little while that he held her prisoner against her will and in these moments she found him strong but gentle, wise, witty, and exciting. And yet when she was in his arms she pretended he was Roque. He was really the one she made passionate love to.

"Safiye?" She turned, accustomed by now to that name. It was the pasha. He strode toward her, silent as always, on feline feet. He had a grace European men would never master, a lithe, light tread that brought him, soundlessly, through the passageways.

"Yes, master?"

"Why does my favored Safiye look so unhappy?"

She bowed her head, hands crossed over her bosom as she had been taught to do in the harem. "Because the person next dearest to my humble self after you is sad."

"And who is this person?" he asked, hands clasped behind his back.

"It is she who was once the favored of your sight and was called the Raven."

There was an uncomfortable quiet. Then, "Know you, Safiye, that I have not made the law. It is from the sultans themselves and says that any concubine proving unfaithful to her lord shall meet with death. It is kismet—the fate that is written on the woman's forehead."

She dropped on her knees before him. "Then slay me as well, for surely my kismet says I cannot live without my dear friend."

"Woman, you vex me. I cannot break the law."

"Forgive me, I had only hoped there was some way—forgive me. I will not speak of it again if it displeases you." Tears came to her eyes, big tears that made her violet eyes shimmer with grief. He couldn't let Sabelle be executed! He couldn't! Surely he could find a way to pardon her.

He touched her cheek. "Your eyes are like great amethysts when you are troubled, Safiye. I have something I want you to wear tonight." From the folds of his clothing he produced a carved sandalwood box and handed it to her.

She opened the box and the familiar beauty of her ruby and pearl necklace winked and sparkled. "I would like to return this to you," the pasha said.

"Thank you," she whispered. "It means a great deal to me."

"You must not thank me, not for this. It is not a gift, it is simply a return of your own. But these," he said, pulling out another, smaller, matching box, "are a gift."

She opened the other box and gasped with surprise at the sight of the earrings. They were an exact match of the necklace. Each was a large ruby suspended from a diamond setting hung with teardrop pearls. "Oh! Most generous lord!—"

"It was not an easy thing to find jewels the equal of that which you brought with you. No more than I could match the jewel I have in you, Safiye."

She fell to her knees and kissed his hand. "I cannot express my gratitude, Oh, gracious lord, but as much as my heart is touched by these gems, I would happily give them up to have my friend freed." She closed her eyes, almost cringing in anticipation of his wrath.

But he merely took her hand and pulled her to her feet. "The sages say that a kind heart and a quick mind are more than the gods dare grant a man in the same woman. You disprove the sages, my lovely one. I shall see what can be done. Now, go, and prepare yourself for the feast."

The ambassador was a boor. Khurrem was asleep in no time, head leaning against a pillar, while Garlanda struggled to remain open-eyed and alert-looking. She kept her hands demurely folded in her lap as the pasha, noticing the ambassador's peeks at the women, told him a harem girl would be sent to his suite. "But not," he added politely, "either of these." He stood and snapped his fingers for Garlanda to follow him.

She did so, rubbing her eye and smudging the careful application of kohl.

"Your jewels were noted by the ambassador," the pasha said proudly. "You do me credit."

"I am glad, Most Exalted One."

They were in the corridor, walking toward the pasha's rooms. "My fire-haired mare, I have news of interest to your ears."

"Yes, master?"

"There has been an inquiry into the charges brought against your Raven. It seems that the witnesses of the accusers cannot be found. I cannot allow her to stay imprisoned when there is no proof of her guilt. Very untidy of the witnesses to disappear, don't you think? One is inclined to believe that they may even be dead."

Garlanda squealed, flinging her arms around his neck. He picked her up and carried her to their bed. Garlanda covered his face with grateful kisses until his mouth found hers and he dragged her down into explosive darkness.

"—So I see it this way. With both of us runnin' free we should work on our escape plans. Unless you don't wanna get out of this overdecorated conch shell they call a palace," Sabelle said suspiciously.

"I—I still want to leave," Garlanda said wistfully.

Sabelle signaled a slave boy to peel her another grape. "They talk funny around here, but they sure have good food. Boy! Get yourself over there and hunt me up a nectarine, you little varmint or I'll have you keelhauled!"

The boy did not speak English and Sabelle didn't speak Turkish, but her general gesture was fairly clear. He scampered to obey.

"Cute little monsters, the lot o' them," she said. "He's got no call to treat them like animals and fix 'em so they can't have women when they grow up. Most of them are kidnaped Christians, not that I hold much store in religion, but it does seem nasty of him to have such a what-you-call-it—"

"Fetish," Garlanda offered.

"Yeah, fetish for Christian people and such. Poor little children, they've got no call to do them like that, make slaves of them."

"You seem to forget. We're slaves too. And any children we might have here will be slaves as well."

"You aren't, are you?"

"No."

Sabelle patted the littlest boy on the head and stuffed a grape into his mouth. "Poor little savages— say, did you say himself trades with pirates?"

"Yes, they apparently pay him a percentage to trade in his jurisdiction and promise to keep away from his own ships going out."

"We're damned near on the water, you know. See if you can't get him to take you down to the docks some time so you can see how accessible a ship would be."

"Sabelle!" Garlanda said scornfully, "How are the two of us going to steal a ship? We'd need an experienced crew and—"

"Yeah—well, it was just a thought. We gotta get outta here some way!"

"We'll think of something. *I'm* not going to spend the rest of my life here!"

* * *

Quite late that night after the pasha had made gentle, skilled love to Garlanda, she said, "Most Honored Lord, you seem tired. Have you been suffering from the heat?"

"The heat? Certainly not. I am accustomed to it and it doesn't distress me as it does my pale northern beauties. In France I have seen what they call 'hot houses' where they keep plants that cannot endure their cold winters. Perhaps I should build a 'cold house' from blocks of ice from the mountains for you pretty flowers who wilt and droop in the sun." He laughed lightly. "But you are right. I *am* tired. I have been overseeing the loading of my largest spice trader. It is to sail later in the week and I want to make sure that its cargo is properly stored. Many delicacies can suffer in the hold of a ship if they do not have sufficient space and—how would you say it?—dryness? I ordered that the ship be doubly sealed, caulked twice with great care. But I had to check myself to see that it had all been done properly."

"That is why you have been absent so much of late, then. Tell me about the ship."

"My dear blossom of love. That could not possibly interest you."

"Why not? Have you not often noted yourself that I have a mind?"

"Ah-h-h, you have thrown my own words back at me. Yes, you do have a mind. Would that the women of my own world had such. I hardly know how to tell you about the ship—there is so much to say."

"Why don't you take me to see it?"

He drew back in alarm—whether it was genuine or pretense Garlanda couldn't tell. "Take you to the docks? Unheard of!"

"But, my lord, you are known throughout the world

for doing the 'unheard of.' You are a law unto yourself and the world echoes of your exploits—the things you have done that lesser men never dream of doing!"

The pasha roared with laughter. "You make it sound as if taking you to the docks would be on the same level as inventing the wheel. But you are so charming! Your hair reminds me of a sunrise I saw once when I was a child," he said, fingering her red locks. "It was so beautiful it frightened me and I wept. I was beaten for my weakness, but it made no difference. The memory of that sunrise could never be erased."

"Then you will take me to see the ship?" Garlanda asked, not to be diverted by compliments.

"Why do you want to see the ship?" he asked with a hint of suspicion.

"It's not so much that I want to see the ship. I want to see something different. Anything other than the walls I see every day and the same women and eunuchs. You must realize how boring it is for us—when you are gone," she amended, fearing that she had taken her complaint too far. "Besides, I wish to share some part of your life other than your bed."

"The women of my country would never wish for anything more," he said.

"That must be why you populate your court with them?" Garlanda said coquettishly.

"My own words come flying back at me once more. Very well, I shall possibly take you to see the ship before she sails. But it cannot be tomorrow—later in the week, perhaps. And I cannot take you alone, you must have other women with you and everyone must be more heavily veiled than ever. A pasha's women are *never* seen outside the harem and if I am going to flout convention to please my fire-haired beauty, I must do so as tastefully as possible."

Garlanda kissed him gratefully. She yearned to fly from the room and tell Sabelle, but she must not appear to be the least bit eager to leave the pasha's presence. She lay back against the coolness of the silken sheets and let the pasha make love to her once more before he fell into a sound sleep. She rose and paced across the cool mosaic tiles until almost dawn, her mind whirling.

Later she sought out Sabelle. "You told me yourself what a silly idea it was," Sabelle scoffed. "The two of us sailing a ship! The crew wouldn't listen to us for a moment. They'd just tie us up and bring us back to him."

"The pasha's crew would, but we're going to have our own crew!"

"What do you mean? Have you lost your mind!"

Garlanda made a sweeping gesture to include all the European women in the compound. "Don't you think we can teach them to sail?"

"Them! They wouldn't know how to launch a paper boat!"

"Not now, they don't. But they can learn! Sabelle, you taught me to fence—you're a good teacher! You can look over the ship, determine what we would need to know to sail it—please, at least consider it."

"Well, it still sounds like a barnacle-brained idea to me, but you're right. We might as well think about it. We ain't got any better ideas."

She was silent for a long time then said so softly as to be almost inaudible, "I want to find what became of my children, and I can't do that without me own ship to command. If we could fight our way out, get a ship and sail, I'd drop you and your friends wherever you wanted to be. Whoever had a taste for adventure on the high seas could stay with me. You haven't stopped to think that if most of us got our scurvy carcasses outta this iniquitous bilge, some wouldn't be welcome at home after dishonorin' at the hands of the heathens."

"Sabelle, don't be silly," Garlanda said, scooping herself another dish of sherbert flavored with tangerines. "Of course their families want them back!"

"You don't know a pile of seaweed's worth about men if you believe that, Fleur."

"Don't I though," Garlanda asked, licking her spoon. "We'll see what there is to say about that once we get the pasha to take us to the docks."

It was three days later before the pasha announced that they were going to see the ship. In that time Sabelle's interest had mounted, and she had schooled the other ladies as to what they were to look for and note. The rest of the European ladies went along with the idea as well. It wasn't that any of them necessarily believed it could ever be done, but their lives were so extraordinarily empty that they seized greedily on anything new to divert them. Sabelle wanted to know how many men manned the ship, how many sails, how many ropes anchored it to the dock, what kinds of charts, what sort of instruments were on board—every detail they could possibly note and store up.

Finally they were dressed, veiled, reveiled, and herded like cattle into a docile little herd. Jealous George and his biggest, strongest accomplices were to go along with them and one look at their sullen faces told how much they resented this break with tradition. Not only that, it was extra work for them, and they were happy only when they could be silent, glar-

ing sentries positioned strategically around the harem
and expending no energy.

The women were taken in twos in covered litters
and were allowed to see nothing of the route—
theoretically. Naturally, all of them sneaked peeks out
of the muslin fabric that draped around them claus-
trophobically. When they reached the docks, there
was quite a wait and a great deal of confusion before
they could go aboard. A plank had been run from the
ship to the dock and posts ran the length of it on both
sides. From post to post were more draperies. Each
litter in turn was brought to the end of the plank, and
the women emerged from their muslin cocoons into a
fabric tunnel, open only to the sky and the ship. This
way the public could not get so much as a glimpse of
them. The ship, likewise, was draped on the land side.

There was one fortunate aspect of the enforced
modesty. The entire crew had been dismissed for the
day so that they could not look upon the pasha's
women. Therefore, they had the ship virtually to themselves. The eunuchs were with them, of course, but
they were not chosen for their brains and were in unfamiliar territory as well. They could not keep as close
a watch as they would like and one by one the women
managed to slip away and investigate whatever aspect
of the ship they had been assigned.

Garlanda nearly forgot for a moment what they
were there for. The ship was overwhelming. The smell
was so strong, so sensual, that her mind ceased to
work for a bit. The pasha himself showed her around
with some of the other women trailing along respectfully. In the vast dry hold there were crate upon crate
of exotic goods. There were boxes of crystallized musk
and barrels of civet, pure and nauseatingly pungent.
Barrels of olives in another area glistened with the oil

that could not be contained by even the snuggest staves.

The pasha opened a large wooden box to show Garlanda. It was full of dirty-looking gummy balls of some sort of resin. She pulled one of the sticky objects loose and smelled it. It had a pleasant, astringent odor. She looked questioningly at the pasha.

"It is frankincense. I am told that it was among the gifts presented to one of your primary gods." He closed the box and led her to another part of the hold. There, in locked metal chests, were jewels. Each box contained a different sort—one very large box contained only pearls. Thousands of them! Garlanda ran her fingers through the silky contents. "Where is all this going?" she asked the pasha.

"Many places. Some of it will go only as far as Marseille, having come from as distant places as China. Most of the cargo, however, will sail out around Spain and Portugal and be delivered to France and England— if it makes it." There was bitterness in his tone.

"Is there much chance it won't?"

"I believe I have planned adequately for problems. Come, I'll show you some of my precautions, my curious little mare."

Garlanda made rapid mental notes on the ship. Lateen-rigged, that meant it was fast. Narrow-beamed—built for speed as well as carrying cargo. The pasha showed her dozens of cannon and again as many swivel guns. She twisted her mouth in thought. Those swivel guns would come in handy, considering that a favorite trick of robber vessels was to come in behind a ship where her cannon could not reach. It was a ship to do Sabelle proud.

Sabelle seemed to think the same. Her eyes were glowing over the top of her silver-trimmed veil. Garlanda felt an emotion akin to hers—sailing lust! To feel the pitch and roll of decks under one's feet, to see the sails unfurled, racing a storm, the lash of salt spray— she could almost taste the sea on her lips, a hale, hearty sensation after this indolent, pampered life. The untamed waves, the wind—

"You grow faint, Safiye?"

"No," she told the pasha. "Only excited. I have thought of a silly game to amuse your lordship."

"And what is that?"

"Anthony and Cleopatra once sailed up the Nile on a gilt barge, did they not? And you have a birthday soon, I have heard that all over the palace. For your birthday would it please you to have your women take you sailing? It would be so pretty! We would wear our best silks and act like sailors scurrying up and down those ropes and perhaps even rowing. On a big, decorated barge!"

"But," she added, as if she just thought of it, "We would have to learn something about real sailing, not just playacting, and some of the women are so terribly silly I fear it would be beyond them. Oh, dear. And it would have been such great fun for you. We should have lolled about on great cushions and fanned you with peacock feathers and fed you delicacies—but that's out of the question, I suppose."

He affectionately tugged a copper wisp of hair that had escaped her hat. "I should be the envy of the sultan's court if I had such lovely sailors. Yes, I believe I shall have the men teach the females the barest basics of handling a small vessel, but not you, Safiye. I would not have you injure yourself on such work."

That's alright, she thought, teeth tensely gritted behind her excited smile. *I'll learn what I need to know.*

CHAPTER 28

"Another big dinner tonight."

"Not the Viennese ambassador again," Garlanda said and groaned. Betty shook her head. The women were all tired from the subversive planning and practicing they'd been doing. They found that the only thing harder than working, was working without looking like they were doing anything. Every time the eunuchs' backs were turned they were busy learning to handle swords, tying knots, or being schooled in sailing. But as soon as a eunuch or one of the *khadins* appeared they had to suddenly fall idle. Maiselle and Wilma had been practicing sword fighting one day with the curtain rods when Khurrem strolled through. Suddenly both of the European women began to examine their "weapon" as if it were a strange object that they were trying to identify.

"I don't know who the honored guests are tonight," Betty said, "but they have already arrived and you and Raven have to sit at the pasha's feet and look enthralled."

Garlanda sighed and signaled for her slaves to stop brushing her hair. "I'm awfully tired after my ride this morning. I think I'll take a nap. This heat is stifling and I feel shrewish from it. I'm sorry I haven't been good company today, Betty."

"You're not—in the family way, are you?"

Garlanda shook her head, the smoothly plaited copper hair swinging about her curved shoulders. "No, luckily." She snapped her fingers at the slave boy. "Fetch the Raven for me when she returns from the baths."

Betty hugged her and left. Garlanda lay back on the plush bed and stared up at a smiling gold cherub. *I will escape*, she told herself. *I will! I must cease this slothful life and get out of here so I can track my father's murderer. Althea—Leon—surely they must think me dead by now.*

She conjured up a mental picture of Althea, bristling, on the stairs of the Nice embassy. "What do you mean, sir, disappeared? Young English ladies do not simply disappear! You shall find my niece or I shall—" Shall what? Garlanda drowsily wondered what Althea would threaten the ambassador with. Her body, lulled by the sluggish torpor of the day, sagged on the feather mattress. Presently she slept.

She dreamed of nightingales and birds of paradise serenading her. The only problem was the birds were off-tune. And the song was wrong. She tossed uneasily, trying to escape the sound. Familiar—it was somehow familiar.

Garlanda sat up with a start. She shook her head, trying to clear it of her dreams, but the sound persisted. Someone was whistling a song far below in the courtyard the visitors had access to. It was a song she'd heard before—when she thought about it she was able to hum along and even remember a few words. "—Strung him up tight—fought with terrible might—over and under clutching a bottle of rum—" How did she know that?

The image that trickled into her mind was that of

warm ocean breezes on board ship and a rollicking crew, their voices slurred with rum. Realization slapped her full in the face.

It was the song Roque's crew often sang, and Sabelle sometimes, too. A song known to all seafaring men—"The Keelhauling of Black Jack Bowers."

"Who is it? Who?" Garlanda hissed through her veil.

"It could be any old brigand. Ain't necessarily one of ours," Sabelle said with a shrug.

"Safiye! Raven! Quiet thyselves," an old slave woman chastised. Garlanda attacked a dish of *Rahat Lokum*, Turkish Delight. She wished for a large helping of cool peach sherbert to help her through the hot evening, made hotter still by her excitement.

"Listen, Fleur, if there *is* a sailor here maybe we can get news of what's afoot on the high seas. That piddling barge o' the pasha's ain't gonna get us across the Mediterranean, let alone to the Carribbean. We need a big ship, that big spice cargo beauty."

"Who said anything about the Caribbean? I'm going to Marseille to look for my aunt and the count. Why the Caribbean?"

"I've sworn to get my own ship and use it to find my children. I'm gonna take revenge on them what sold my little ones like they was common slaves. I know who the men was what did it and I won't rest easy 'til they been paid in full. Goddam cushions! Why don't they have chairs like real civilized people 'round here? Scurvy dastards, sissies, the lot. Me legs ache fair to burstin' what with layin' on this damned floor on these goddam cushions. *Sacre Bleu!* Broke another fingernail! I want to get outta this damn sissy outfit!"

Garlanda could tell that Sabelle was excited. She didn't normally waste that much swearing.

The pasha entered the room. "Safiye, Raven, I bid you a good evening. Our guests are about to arrive. They have traveled from Marseille. You are about to meet—"

"Sir George Young–Brookes," Garlanda whispered hoarsely to herself. And behind him, hands defiantly crammed in his pockets, was Renwick.

The pasha turned to Garlanda and Sabelle, "The ambassador, Sir George Young–Brookes, and his assistant, Renwick Ridgely, Fourth Earl of Puden."

Garlanda drew her second and third veils hastily, glad her coned hat hid her hair. Who knew what sort of disastrous scene might ensue if Renwick recognized her!

"You know them blokes?" Sabelle asked in a whisper.

"No-o-o."

"That big blond earl is the finest portion of male I've seen in many a moon, Fleur. Sure you don't know him?"

"Oh, God, Sabelle! Not *him*!" For a fraction of a second it struck her as almost funny. They had shared Roque's "favors" and the pasha's, now Sabelle was ogling Renwick!

Renwick swept in the doorway with his usual frosty arrogance. His gold and iron presence filled the room, even blotting out the understated mastery of the pasha. Sir George, between them, was as floridly British as ever—stocky, well tailored, and dull.

Freddie brought up the rear. Garlanda almost didn't recognize him until she heard a suppressed gasp and felt Sabelle's fingers dig into her arm. Freddie was refined, polished, and impeccably groomed to the ideal model of an ambassadorial assistant. His smoky gray eyes took in the room with a glance, missing nothing, except, apparently, the identity of the heavily veiled women. It was incredible that this boy was the same person as the ragged ruffian Garlanda had brought from Roque's ship with her.

She wasn't sure yet that she wanted Sir George or Renwick to recognize her, but Freddie was a different matter. Surely he had been the one whistling in the courtyard earlier. He had seen her at her worst, he was an old comrade from her sailing days. The humiliation of facing Sir George or Renwick was too much to think of.

"It is most auspicious, your presence here," the pasha was saying calmly. "Sir George, greetings. And the Earl of Puden, you have only recently attained the title, is this not so? The death of one's brother is always a tragic loss. I had seventeen brothers. I regretted losing each of them, but there was a great malady involving the throat that year. Tragic."

Renwick paled. Garlanda noticed that he was in mourning. It set off his splendid gilt hair and tiny, neatly trimmed moustache. *Black becomes him,* she thought. *He's looking well. I wonder how dear Elaine is. Renwick an earl!*

"—A carriage accident," Renwick was saying. "My brother and his son, the heir. Quite sad, but this is not a time for sadness."

The pasha signaled for them to seat themselves. He clapped his hands for the slaves to bring in the first course of dinner.

"Your wives grace the room," Sir George said, bowing in the direction of Garlanda, Sabelle, and Khurrem, who were seated well away from the visitors.

"Thank you, but they are not my wives. They are my concubines."

"Calls a spade a spade, that one—or a whore a whore," Sabelle whispered, but Garlanda blushed to the roots of her hair. The men settled down to dinner.

Freddie was looking in her direction. Garlanda smiled, then remembered he couldn't see it through her veils. Her hair was covered, eyes heavily outlined in kohl, the lower half of her face obscured. How could she get his attention without alerting her other friends and causing an international incident? If they recognized her, Renwick would doubtless demand her release and cause all of them trouble. The pasha would think nothing of having a visitor run through with a eunuch's scimitar if there was a scene. No. She'd have to be subtle, catch the boy's attention.

She stared into the gray eyes. If he knew anything at all about harem women, he would know her conduct was unusual. And if he watched her long enough he would surely see that she was not a Turkish woman. Her skin was fair, her eyes violet. But from a distance did her eyes look dark?

Freddie noticed her stare, raised an eyebrow, gave her a bored, forcibly polite look and turned away. Garlanda dug her fingernails into the palms of her hands. He's been trained too well. They'd probably told him not to have any sort of prolonged eye contact with the Infidel's women.

She suffered through the sherbert, agonized through the broiled oxen on rice, bit her nails between bites of honeyed pastries, and braced herself for a move during the bread. She caught the pasha looking at her. So he had noticed her fidgeting. She dropped her hands demurely on her lap, eyes downcast. If only women were allowed to speak with the men!

Sabelle nudged her sharply in the ribs. "If it wasn't for these scurvy hats and the heathen way we got to cover our faces, Freddie would know who we was. How can we get his attention without gettin' all of us killed?" she whispered.

"Stare at him. If both of us do it, he's bound to notice."

It didn't work. He was trained too well. Finally, in desperation, when she was sure no one was watching, Garlanda threw a walnut at him. It bounced off his head. He put a hand up and glanced around. Sir George glared at him, and the boy sat still once more.

Sabelle took the hint and palmed an almond.

After that, Freddie had to endure a veritable barrage of food. Every time he flinched, Sir George gave him a stern, questioning look. Freddie retreated behind Renwick where Garlanda could see him furiously rearranging his food. "What ails the boy? Is he daft?" Sabelle hissed. Khurrem cuffed both of them, forcing a return to silence. Freddie was still scrabbling his food around with fierce dedication. He trounced the rice into submission, smeared in some honey, and held the plate at an angle, tilted slightly toward the women.

"What the devil is that little bastard up to?" Sabelle demanded in an undertone of Garlanda. "He's made a picture with his dinner of a damned flower and it's dripping all over."

"Sabelle!" Garlanda gasped, heart hammering joyfully. "It's the fleur-de-lis, the lily of France. Fleur-de-lis, *Fleur*! He knows us!"

They gripped each other's hands under a fold of fabric, unable to do anything else to celebrate. Thus occupied, they did not see a pair of almonds come flying across the dining area with precise aim. A double *thunk!* sounded in the women's corner of the table, then Freddie returned to his food with a satisfied grin.

Sabelle rubbed her forehead regretfully. "Wurra the day I taught that deckswabbin' little varlet to throw!"

"We've got to get a note to him!"

"Too dangerous, Fleur. And what good would it do? It 'ud just get him in as bad a spot as we are—maybe worse."

The pasha was staring at them disapprovingly. They sat up and stopped whispering. They folded their hands in their laps. No one was remotely fooled by this display of exemplary behavior. "If it pleases your august self, I shall send the women and servants away and we can talk business," the pasha told Sir George.

"Yes, we must discuss the business of your Lord Ahmed and mine, Their Majesties William and Mary."

"Oh, yes, a woman assists in ruling your nation," the pasha stroked his moustache thoughtfully. "And yet, my women have sat here and indulged in petty little games to amuse themselves and bring entertaining dishonor to my table by tormenting your young man there. Do you think it wise for a woman to rule when they all harbor such whimsical traits? Whereas my jewels are dear to me, I would hesitate at giving them the reins of government."

Sir George turned on Freddie. "I knew you were up to something. Shameful behavior!"

"Oh, he did nothing to provoke it. My jewels are merely frisky tonight. Do not punish the boy. I think the Raven and Safiye need to ride the matched mares from the Barbary Coast and disperse thusly of their overabundance of spirit."

"You have Barb mares? Why, they are worth their weight in gold in England, Sire, and this miserable young man of mine is good with horses. If he can make up for his misbehavior somehow—"

"I will have my women race for you. Would that be amusing before we sit down in conference? Yes? Let us see if the boy can catch the mares. That should also entertain as they are proud animals," the pasha said amiably. "This way we shall see our perpetrators of mischief exhausted and humble once more."

CHAPTER 29

Freddie caught the mares. He was bitten, kicked, tossed through a fence, and shorn of half a sleeve, but he captured the two fiery dappled gray mares eventually and brought them to the eunuch who was to saddle them.

Garlanda pretended interest in her mount's bridle. She kept her voice low. "Freddie, don't look up. Just remain as you are and stroke the mare as if seeking to gentle her. Listen to me. I was kidnaped and brought here, as was Sabelle. Do not tell Sir George and Renwick. They would only try to negotiate for me and bring unwanted attention to me. The pasha will never let me go willingly—"

"But Miss Fleur, someone must get you out of here."

"No! Shh! If I am to get out of this place," she said, speaking very quickly and quietly, "it must be by means of escape. Sabelle and I think we have such a means."

She told the eunuch in Turkish, very loudly, to adjust the bridle of her mount, then went on talking while pretending to check the saddle. "Freddie, I have something for you to take back to Marseille with you. There is a Polish nobleman who is a very good friend of mine, Count Leon Jareski–Yanoviak. Give him this!" She slid her hand under the mare's belly and handed the young man her ruby necklace. "He'll recognize it and tell my aunt, if she is still in France, where it came from. Tell him with any luck I'll be home to Althea within a year. They are *not* to come for me, the pasha would kill me before he would let me go. I can get free by myself."

"But, how?"

"Never mind, we have a plan and if it fails—if it fails, I won't be here for anyone to' worry about. Please, you must find him and give him the necklace. Please, Freddie!"

"Miss Fleur, I—I'd do anything for you!"

There was an awkward pause in which she pitied him for baring his heart. "Here," he said, pretending to tighten the saddle girth for her. "Take this in case— well, in case something goes wrong and we don't see each other again. We're leaving in the morning. I'll get the necklace to your count. I won't fail you."

"I believe you. Now be sure and tell him *not* to come for me or to send anyone. I won't leave without Sabelle either, Freddie. We go together no matter what we do. What is this you've given me?" There was no time to look at the ring on a chain he had handed her. She straightened her tight bodice and skillfully dropped what he had handed her down the front of it.

"It's something of mine from my mother, I've been told. Will you keep it safe for me, Miss Fleur?"

She was about to answer that she was the last person in the world in a position to keep anything safe, but she had no time to answer. Sabelle poked her and hissed that they were taking too long. The women mounted up. Garlanda glanced back to see Freddie watching her with shining eyes. He'd grown so much taller in the two years since she last saw him. Two years! Could it be that long? Yes, of course it was. Sometimes it seemed much longer, lifetimes ago when she and Freddie had jumped ship and ended up on the embassy steps midfight. It seemed like even Sir George treated him now like a young man of some consequence and not just riffraff from the docks.

Would he find Leon? Leon had said he was going to Marseille to stay, she could only pray he meant it. And Althea? Where was she now? Had she given her last relative up for dead and gone back to London? Or was she still in France—Nice, perhaps, searching for word of her niece? Well, if Freddie could find Leon, at least her loved ones would know where she was, if not vice versa.

They rode to where the pasha stood chatting with the Englishmen. Garlanda caught a fragment of conversation concerning pirates operating in the pasha's territory. She presumed Sir George was attempting to convince him he could profit more from trade with the British than by taking cuts of the privateers' booty which they gave in tribute for being allowed to ply his seas. Pirates, pirates, pirates! She thought of Roque and felt a queer tightness in the pit of her stomach.

The men noticed their presence and the conversation abruptly switched. "Raven! Safiye!" the pasha said sternly, "are you prepared?"

Garlanda nodded, afraid her voice might be recognized. She glanced at Renwick—so handsome, so aloof, never guessing that two yards away stood a woman he knew—well. *Roque, Renwick, the pasha. What a puzzle my life has become because of men.*

She spurred her horse.

In the morning, stiff and sore from a fall that had enabled Sabelle to win the race as well as the pasha's favor for the evening, Garlanda wearily raised her head from a satin pillow. The rousing notes of "The Keelhauling of Black Jack Bowers" came jauntily sailing up from the courtyard. She hastily donned a thin, emerald-hued wrapper of Brusa silk and ran to the window.

Freddie was down below, holding the reins of three horses and kicking a pebble around the paving. Garlanda leaned on the cherrywood sill and whistled along with him. He gave a nervous start, then looked up, smiling. Together they finished the song, then he sang a chorus of "Greensleeves" in honor of the verdant gown she wore. Sir George emerged from the visitors' quarters, looking as if he had experienced too much Grecian ouzo the night before. He barked at Freddie in a gruff tone and even tried to cuff him on the side of the head, an effort that Freddie dodged effortlessly.

"Shut up, can't you! My head's on fire and I don't wish you to cause an international incident with your warbling."

Garlanda plucked a rose from the cut-crystal vase near the bed and flung it down to her young friend. She ducked back as Sir George glanced up, blinking in the sunlight. "What the devil! Where did you get that? Renwick? Renwick, blast you! I believe some woman up there is throwing flowers at me. Give me that, boy!"

Garlanda threw on a veil and a scarf to cover her hair. She leaned out the window and threw Freddie another four roses. Her aim was quite good. Once she'd made clear who the object of her affections was, she tossed one to Sir George and another to Renwick for good measure.

Renwick was breathtakingly handsome this morning, unbefogged by liquor as was the ambassador. His honey hair gleamed as if gilt in the early morning light and his eyes were blue as sapphires, even at such a distance. For a moment she nearly shouted to him, tore off her veil, cried out her identity, and begged him to get her out of this indolent, scented prison. Her hand trembled at the corner of her veil, then, with an effort she lowered her hand and turned away for a minute.

How is Elaine? she wanted to shout. *Have you seen Althea or Leon? Did Lawrence Jennings's terrible mama find him a suitable wife?*

She looked back. Renwick was still staring up at her window. "You've a great deal of explaining to do, Freddie," he said in a good-natured tone, never looking away from Garlanda.

"Yes!" chimed in Sir George, checking his saddle girth and bending in order to do so, which made him flinch from the pressure in his swollen head. "My entire head hurts! I daresay that fellow can drink like an Englishman."

"Better than some Englishmen," Renwick said. He continued to stare coolly at Garlanda. "Is there something you'd better tell us, Freddie?"

It was a situation she couldn't resist. She let out a high-pitched giggle then ducked back. A moment later she stripped off her smaller rings and began dropping them to the former cabin boy. His face was redder than her concealed hair.

"I—uh—no, sir."

A small string of pearls followed and more giggles. Next she started on a vase of daisies, showering her unfortunate friend, much to his flattered humiliation, the astonishment of Sir George, and the mild curiosity of Renwick. "I *said*, is there anything you had better tell us, Freddie?" he repeated.

"Oh, Ridgely, be serious! He's little more than a boy."

"He's old enough. I hardly thought him the sort to catch the eye of a harem girl, though—let alone being stupid enough to do something that could get us all beheaded. We must be on our way. Throw a farewell kiss to your impassioned mistress and let us be on the way. But first, pick up all the favors she's flung you."

"The hell I will!" Freddie blurted out.

"You must have done *some*thing to earn them, so fetch them and let's ride before every Janissary in the Ottoman Empire comes swooping in here to take our heads apart from our bodies." Unexpectedly, Renwick gave Freddie the ghost of a grin and cuffed him lightly on the side of the head. "You little rake! Get your jewelry and let's ride. The flowers, too."

Freddie gave Garlanda a furious glare, then obeyed. Just before they rode through the gate, the boy turned and waved. Sir George swung at him, missed, and tumbled off his horse. Renwick hooted with laughter while Sir George righted himself and remounted with awesome dignity. The gate closed behind them.

Garlanda sighed and removed her hat. Oh, to be going with them. It would be the grandest thing in the world if she and Sabelle could have ridden out, free, with their friends. But there was no use thinking about it. Wishing would not help.

"I think, Safiye," said a low voice behind her, "that we had better go to the pasha and tell him how you have spent your morning so far."

She turned to face a felinely smiling Khurrem.

Garlanda fingered the ring in her pocket, the one
Freddie had given her. She hadn't had time to look at
it closely yet, but now she clasped it over and over as
if it could protect her from Khurrem's lies.

"Safiye, have you nothing to say to these charges?
You must admit you acted suspiciously at dinner and
your conduct this morning was deplorable. What are
we to think of this? Is it true this young man was your
lover?"

She shook her head. Why couldn't men believe that
there could be something in a male-female relationship besides lovemaking? Couldn't they see it was
possible to have friends of the opposite sex? She
thought of saying Freddie had been her brother, but
there wasn't the least resemblance between them, not
hair color, not eyes, nothing. He didn't even look like
Sabelle, although he was of an age to be one of her
children—which was why she supposed Sabelle had
taken pity on him and purchased him.

"He's me son!" Garlanda's head jerked up. Had her
thoughts burst forth of their own accord?

Sabelle entered the room, idly munching a pome-
granate and spitting the seeds on the floor. "At least, I
think he's mine. Me children were stole from me years
back. Safiye and me, we was on a ship together. I
bought the boy in Tortuga a few years after me own
little ones was stole in a pirate raid. He's her friend,
helped her escape from the pirates. And, like I say,
there's a good chance he's my son."

"You aren't old enough!" Khurrem scoffed.

Sabelle shrugged this off. "Just 'cause I ain't agin'
as fast as you—! Me husband Willie had gray eyes and

dark red-brown hair," she told the pasha, ignoring Khurrem fuming and hissing. "Freddie thinks he was born in '78 or '79—so was me son. I taught me son French. Kid speaks it like a native. He's got Willie's color of hair and eyes. At any rate, he's Fleur's friend and the idea of bedding down with that slip of a boy when she's got a man such as yerself is downright silly. Khurrem's just jealous, is all. Don't like the thought of another woman cuttin' in on her territory."

"Your tale makes sense in a strange, rambling manner," the pasha said, stroking his short beard thoughtfully.

"Your lordship! Do not listen to that woman," Khurrem insisted.

"Woman, you weary me! Go elsewhere and trouble me no further. All of you—go! Leave now!"

It wasn't until they were alone in Sabelle's room that Garlanda spoke. "You seriously think he's your son? Then does this mean anything to you?" She extracted the ring. Together they examined it. It was a heavy metal thing with no stones and bore a raised insignia of a rose and a fleur-de-lis entwined with thorns. On the inside was the inscription "L.R. à M.A."

"It's like one a'them rings they stamps in sealin' wax on letters and such. I never seen it. Where'd ye find it?"

"Freddie gave it to me to keep until we see each other next. He thinks it's from his mother. If it is, it couldn't be you," Garlanda said gently, hating to break such news.

Sabelle gave a rich, warm molasses laugh. "Don't fret ye none, little one. Peg-leg Willie were as blond as a beach at noonday and his eyes was green like yer gown. Freddie ain't mine."

"Why, Sabelle!" Garlanda exclaimed, feeling a little

foolish. "You're a very skilled actress then. You should
be on the stage! I believed every word you said."

"Yeah?" she asked, scratching her shoulder. "I already been on stage, don't particular want to go back.
Say, how do you suppose the kid was able to hang
onto this?"

"Probably because it's of no value, except sentimental. No jewels, just some dark, worthless metal. He
wore it on a chain around his neck. What are you
doing? Give that back!"

Sabelle was jabbing the ring with the little gold
toothpick she had taken such a shine to. She scratched
the dark surface of the raised emblem and whistled.
"*Le Bon Dieu*! Worthless, it it?" She showed Garlanda
where the gleam of solid gold showed through the
scratch she had made.

"No!" Garlanda said, backing away. "No more mys-
teries! If you want to find your children, fine. If Freddie wants to find out who his parents were, 'tis none
of my affair. But I will find the murderers of my father, and I'll not be waylaid by other people's kidnap-
ings! I'm not going to think about what stories this
ring could tell us if it could talk—I'm not going to ask
you how in the name of the merciful Lord you were
ever an actress. I do not care if Freddie is Khurrem's
twin brother and you're the Queen of Sheba! It's none
of my business! And I don't want to know why Sir
George was here or Renwick, or why they were negotiating behind closed doors. I'm not even mildly curious about the pasha's seventeen brothers with the
throat afflictions. I just don't—"

Sabelle threw her head back and laughed. "You see,
Fleur? I knew all it'd take would be a heap o' uncon-
nected information to cure you o' that infernal curios-

ity! Yer on the road to bein' a right proper uninvolved sort! It'll only take ten years or so to finish the job.

"But don't you wonder," she said with a slow diabolical grin, "what Roque's last name is?"

"NO!"

CHAPTER 30

The escape plans were going well. They were almost
beginning to believe it might work. Garlanda's friends
were becoming quite adept at running the little gilt
barge they would take the pasha sailing on—or so he
thought. Once they had mastered the art of sailing,
they would work out in more detail how to get out of
the palace. Wilma had already smuggled large
amounts of laudanum from the apothecary to drug the
guards with. Betty, Maiselle, and a few others were
proficient with curtain rods and presumably proficient with swords, although Garlanda hoped they
wouldn't have to use them.

The *Nightbird*, the beautiful ship they had visited,
had returned from delivering its precious cargo, had
been in port for repairs, and was now ready, though
not scheduled, for sailing. Garlanda managed to convince the pasha to take them aboard again on the pre-
text of curing their boredom—actually to further their
knowledge of the ship. She was even able to investigate the captain's quarters and determine that he had
the charts and maps they needed.

Sabelle kept merciless order among the ranks.
Women who had never done harder work than thread-
ing a needle suddenly found themselves doing strenuous exercises at daybreak with Sabelle supervising

with prods from a riding crop. Sabelle would not tolerate anyone becoming slack from their languid life. Garlanda knew it was of vital importance that every woman among them be in prime physical condition, or their performance on board ship would suffer—thereby endangering every last one of them.

Garlanda herself would be quartermaster to Sabelle, the captain. Wilma would be ship's doctor. Betty, who had no stomach for sailing and could get queasy just watching the splash of the fountain in their courtyard, announced to the glee of her companions that she would be chief cabin boy, just so long as she didn't have to get anywhere near food or the odors thereof.

Their plans were sent awry one night as the ten of them most involved in the plans huddled around a map of the *Nightbird* under the gnarled olive trees in the garden. "It shouldn't be hard—the rope ladder is left down," Garlanda explained, pushing a lock of hair back from her face. "A few of us will swim over there and scale the ladder and the rest is in the laps of the gods. My God, some of you can swim, can't you?"

Four of them said they could. Garlanda breathed a sigh of relief and turned to Wilma, who rested her head against the nearest tree and didn't seem to be listening. "Wil? What is it?"

"Oh, a multitude of thoughts. These trees are ancient, probably they stood here in the days of Our Lord. We seem so insignificant in relation to them. We have so little time and yet so much to accomplish. How many other plots have been discussed here, I wonder? Why isn't Sabelle here?" she asked jumping from the philosophical to the practical.

"I don't know, she—"

The awesome bulk of Jealous George loomed over

them suddenly. "We will go to Mustafa Pasha now, women of the harem," he said in Turkish.

Garlanda felt her stomach lurch in a spasm of sudden terror. "Why?" she demanded in polished Turkish, "Are we forbidden to sit in the gardens of the Mustafa Pasha on a hot night?"

"It is forbidden to plot rebellion, O, Safiye," he answered gravely and in *English!*

What happened next occurred so quickly that Garlanda could not at first understand it. There was a whizzing sound, then the massive eunuch staggered and crashed across her feet. Almost before he was down a crouching shape came shooting across the courtyard.

It was Sabelle! She bent over the eunuch in the near darkness, made a twisting motion, and caught him under the arms. "Hurry! Wilma, go engage Khurrem in a game of cards! Betty, go find the pasha," she ordered. "Get him in bed any way you can! Fleur, help me. I can't carry this whale alone."

They all stood, dumbstruck. Finally Garlanda spoke, "What are you talking about?"

"I killed him with me knife, ye damned fools. Now move yer arses! The pasha suspects somethin's afoot. This could mean the end of all of us, lasses. Hurry, our lives is at stake, ye great, blithering poop deck scrapers. Don't stand there chattering like a pack o' scared sheep. Maiselle, go with Betty! Wilma, if Khurrem's seen anything—kill her!"

Wilma picked up Sabelle's little mother-of-pearl dagger and wiped the blood off on Jealous George's garments. Then she tucked it into her bosom. "I will, Raven. I will." Her eyes were clear with determination.

She dragged Betty and Maiselle off with her. Garlanda took the heavy corpse by the feet and assisted the huffing Sabelle as best she could. "Where are we taking him? Oh, God! If we were to be stopped so close to freedom—"

"Shut up, Fleur. Ain't no one can stop you and me. In under a week we're sailin' outta here in the fastest, prettiest ship in the Mediterranean, and ain't no connivin' sissy half man gonna get in the way. C'mon, *chérie*, to the garden. The shrubber been diggin' a lot and the ground's soft and wet there. We'll drop ol' Jealous in there as deep as can be and by the time anyone finds the *insensé bâtard* he'll be old bones and you'll have a hold full o' grandbabes."

They fell silent while they dragged Jealous George to the garden. As hoped it was deserted. They picked the lock on the tool shed—another of Sabelle's hidden talents recently come to light—and got out shovels. They set to work furiously. "Is this enough?" Garlanda asked, muscles burning with fatigue.

"No!" Sabelle snapped. "Fall to, there. If that moon breaks through them clouds before we're done, we might's well dig two more and jump in t' save 'em the trouble. They ain't blind 'round here. I been listening at more 'n me share of keyholes lately and they know somethin's goin' on. Hurry, Fleur, hurry!"

Garlanda's shoulder and back throbbed, but this could mean their lives. She dug with renewed vigor. They were lifetimes older when they finally rolled their victim in the hole and smoothed the dirt around. Both of them were panting and grimy as they hurriedly washed down their burial instruments and replaced them. She could feel no guilt at being an accessory to murder, only relief that they had gotten away with it, and that Jealous George was no longer a danger to them—at least not until his presence was missed.

"'Belle, you were smart to stay behind and spy for us. If you hadn't we'd all be in the dungeon by—"

To her complete astonishment, Sabelle flung her to the ground. "Yeah, matey? Don't you put on no airs with me, or I'll sling ye down again and finish thrashin' that pretty lil' face to a pulp," Sabelle bellowed mightily, then added, in a whisper, "Hit me. Hurry. We've been discovered."

"Get off me, you wretch! Get off or I'll hit *you* again." Garlanda feigned a punch to her friend's face. Sabelle fell screaming as if hit with a boulder and not one small fist.

"Don't you tell the likes o' me what to do, Red, or I'll have yer liver for breakfast—on toast!" Sabelle roared, then whispered, "Ye gotta really hit me." To prove her point, she punched Garlanda in the stomach. The girl fell backwards with a cry of indignation and pain. She got up quickly, threw herself at Sabelle and they grappled fiercely, rolling in the mud and herbs. Handfuls of hair were loosened, eyes puffed, lips bruised.

"*Aux armes, mes amis!* Help me subdue this bitch!"

"I'll kill you!" Garlanda screamed. Sabelle was really hurting her. She wished someone would step in and break it up, but no one did. A crowd of concubines and guards had gathered and were placing bets as to the outcome.

"*Sacre merde!* Don't hit so hard, little one," Sabelle hissed.

"You're scalping me, Frenchie," Garlanda roared. "Shameless vixen!"

"Sissy!"

They rolled over. Garlanda knelt on Sabelle and pretended to pummel her in the stomach. Sissy! All right, then! She'd show them some of the words she'd learned as a pirate. Words she certainly hadn't *meant* to learn, but now struggled to get out. "You call me an uppity English bitch again and I'll scuttle you, you diseased strumpet! HA! You French whores are all alike—cesspools from the seas. I'll carve out your lungs, so help me! The thought of sharing a man with the likes of you fair makes me want to puke—Christ knows what I'll catch for my troubles!"

Sabelle's face creased into an admiring grin before she seized her little friend by the throat and threw her in the nearest fountain. Garlanda staggered out, gasping, and slung a bucket of icy water over her foe.

"Drown *me*, will you, you poxed bitch," she said triumphantly.

"Yer hair ain't even really red!" Sabelle shouted.

"Why, you filthy—"

They went tumbling down in the mud again. Finally strong hands forced them apart and held them at bay. They pretended to spit on one another, but they seemed to have deplorable aim since they always hit the eunuchs restraining them.

"Scrawny English slut!"

"Fat French sow! You've got saddle sores on your backside!"

"Raven! Safiye! Calm yourselves," came the voice of the pasha. He was standing with Maiselle and Betty on either side of him, each clutching at gaping bodices and doing their best to fade into the crowd. The pasha's voice was tinged with amusement. "If you could see yourselves looking as do the harridans of the earth's lowest gutters, I believe it would cool your heated disagreement. Cooling? That is precisely what

they need. Into the fountains. The *khadins* will supervise your cleansing. Khurrem?"

Garlanda and Sabelle groaned in unison.

A stifling air of deadly calm prevailed.

There was no wind, no motion, no stirring of life.
Garlanda was on the other side of the bed from the
pasha, shifting uncomfortably in a puddle of her own
sweat. It had been three days since her "fight" with
Sabelle and the bruises had begun to fade. Jealous
George had been missed, but Garlanda drew attention
to her missing necklace at the same time. The court
was thoroughly searched, the necklace (which had
gone with Freddie) was not found, so it was assumed—at least officially—that the big stupid eunuch
had fled with it.

And tomorrow night they would flee, if all went
well. Tomorrow night—if the wind returned. If! She
was sick of the word! *If* they could drug the guards, *if*
they could get to the ship, *if* the wind returned, *if*
they were not becalmed in the harbor, *if*—

The pasha was awake. He leaned on his elbow and
stroked her damp hair back from her face. "My blossom of love, you do not sleep well. You are not, alas, a
hothouse flower."

"I should have grown accustomed to the heat in
Martinique, but I never did. It's so very still it is un-
nerving. The trees do not rustle, I hear no sound at
all." She rose from the vast bed and crossed the room
to lean on the windowsill. She did not bother to don a
wrapper in the butter-melting heat. No breeze wafted
in to cool her flushed face nor dry her heavy hair.
"When did the new ships arrive?" she asked idly.

"What new ships, my tawny mare?"

"The two in the bay a short distance from the *Nightbird,* my lord."

He was instantly out of bed and at her side. "There should be no—"

They heard a drawn-out gurgle in the olive grove below. The pasha moved swiftly, donning his clothes and seizing his sword. Garlanda dressed too. She needed no one to tell her that the sound was that of a man's throat being slit.

"ATTACK! To your posts!"

A deafening explosion filled their ears, rocking the floor under their feet. The seaside wall of the palace exploded in flame and a shower of rubble. There was screaming and sounds of scrambling feet all over the compound.

"They were asleep, the fools! I shall have them smeared with honey and left to the ants," the pasha said as he dashed from the room.

Garlanda took the other swords down from the wall and raced to the women's quarters. "We're under attack! Arm yourselves!"

"But this could be salvation, couldn't it?" one of the women asked, a small, scared voice in the darkness.

Garlanda swung on her. "Do you consider being sold as a whore to the highest, dirtiest bidder salvation compared to the pampered life we live here? Sabelle? Where is Sabelle? Oh, Sabelle! The guards have been overcome, that means the palace has been infiltrated. Arm yourself with anything you can—"

Eunuchs burst in, heavily armed. They began blocking off the doors. Sabelle whirled to face Garlanda. "I been spoils of someone else's war once too often, we all have! Are we gonna sit here and let these bastards carry us off? I say we take our chances like

people and not just women to be sold off to anyone
with enough gold. You was willin' to sail outta here.
Now," she said to the other women, "are ye willin' to
fight like I taught ye? There's enough of us to make
plenty of reinforcements for the pasha. And if our side
wins we can barter our freedom from there on out."

There was a nervous shuffling of feet and a downward casting of glances. "Look, lasses, we're in the
middle. Whoever wins gets us—and I know what kinda
men they are out there. Fleur knows somethin' about
it, too."

"She's right," Garlanda said. "Please believe me, we
can't fall into the pirates' hands. You will suffer horribly—unspeakable things will be done to you. We must
come to the pasha's aid."

Another explosion rocked the buildings. Sabelle and
Garlanda stood shoulder to shoulder. "Very well,
then," Garlanda said, as their friends stepped forward.
"They'll take us dead or not at all. Come on, it seems
we have a man-sized job to do."

There remained one door that the eunuchs had not
yet barricaded. The European women ran out and
crept along the stone wall to where the pasha's men
were struggling with the heavy guns. *Nightbird* had
been cut adrift and was out in the bay, away from the
line of fire. *Of course*, Garlanda thought bitterly, *no
pirate would risk damaging such a prize.*

The attackers were armed with cannons on every
deck. Even as she watched, one of the pasha's sloops
began settling into the water, a hole torn in her hull.
Sabelle grabbed her arm, shook her, and handed her a
ramrod.

Load, prime, flint, fire.

It became a litany. In front of them the savage sea
hurled death and about them were the sounds of

hand-to-hand combat. The pungent stench of smoke and blood assailed their nostrils.

The barrage of artillery was too great and yet they fought on. When Garlanda was well enough acquainted with the cannon, she shooed the other woman onto another. There was a roar of color and light as the wall erupted into a volcano of mortar and stone a few yards to her left. She winced as falling debris struck her, but she fired again.

The pirate's sloop was listing to one side. She double-loaded her weapon and lit the fuse, then stood back, hands over ears. The recoil from the cannon sent her reeling, but when the smoke cleared she saw that the one-masted vessel was taking in water. How stupid of them to attack in a sloop! A sloop only carried guns on one deck.

"Sabelle!" Garlanda shouted. "Help me. Blow that sloop out of the water. I overloaded this cannon and now it's too hot to touch."

"Aye, aye, little one. By the way, there's a one-eyed rascal with a saber creepin' up real careful like on your small self. Move to yer left, *chérie!* Ah-h, that's it." Sabelle fired a musket she had picked up.

Garlanda whirled around and saw a pirate dropping like a stone in a lake. There were more coming up the walls where he had been. " 'Belle! Hold them off while I sink that sloop! We've got to get her down before they can salvage the men and guns!" She shouted to the eunuchs and few remaining Janissaries in Turkish, crying the need to sink the crippled sloop rapidly. There was a hail of fire from the trim brigantine that rode the turbulent waves just out of their range of fire.

"One, two, three—FIRE!"

She knew her command of the language was suffi-

cient when the wall cannons roared as one thunderous
voice. The sloop staggered at the starboard bow, then
there was a pause. The explosion that followed
sounded like the trumpets of Jericho tearing down the
walls for the Children of Israel.

They had hit the powder magazine! A red and orange explosion rattled the very ground under them as
the sloop burst into thousands of flaming pieces. Garlanda peered through the fiery fog at the brigantine.
Crewmen were climbing the riggings and beating out
sparks that had landed in the sails. Behind them she
could make out the ghostly triangular sail of the
Nightbird, bobbing serenely on the sanguine waters.

The sea wall was nearly depleted of gunners. She
looked about and saw only three eunuchs remaining,
all of them wounded. *Where was the pasha?* Garlanda
wondered. The one Janissary still on his feet was
helping Sabelle fight off the pirates trying to scale
the walls. There was a high-pitched cry of "Follow
me, girls!" and then small figures in brightly colored
garments swarmed over the men on ladders.

Whether it was fatigue or the sight of a swarm of
European harem concubines armed to the teeth and
howling for blood that did it, Garlanda was never
able to ascertain. She only knew that the badly out-
numbered men didn't stand a chance.

"The guns! Help me!" Garlanda shouted when the
men who weren't slain in the harem onslaught had
been led off to the dungeons. "One ship is out of com-
mission and I believe we can get the others if we are
swift. Hurry!"

Wilma and Maiselle joined her and were quickly
taught the rudiments of gunning.

"Sabelle! Where is Sabelle?" Garlanda cried. No one
answered. *Dead? No, not dead! She couldn't be! I'll*

kill the swine that harms her, Garlanda thought. *I'll send them to hell this very night! A braver woman and truer friend never walked the earth. I'll even the score with those—*

The barge had caught fire and its ghostly orange glow illuminated something that made her heart, pounding madly as it was, skip a beat. The figurehead on the sleek warship in the harbor had red hair!

La Doña del Fuego! Roque's ship!

Why hadn't she recognized it before? Only one ship had such a graceful, sharklike smoothness of line. Worm-proof, of Bermuda cedarwood and square-rigged, she rode the waves as lightly as a debutante in a lace gown, bowing to her first beau. The beauty of the ship made it hard to realize it was one of the fastest, most dangerous vessels on the high seas.

There was a lull in the battle. She waited, eyes bright with unshed tears. She knew that it was up to her. The way the cannons had fired on her command told her that. But suppose she gave the order to run up the white flag and then found out that the ship no longer belonged to Roque? That would send all her friends to the slave block, if not directly to death under the pulsing bodies of sailors starved for the touch of a woman.

"Cease fire!" she said. The order echoed along the wall.

Why wasn't Sabelle here? Sabelle would know what to do. No, she had always counted on others, like Sabelle, Althea, Mother, to pull her through. Now it was her choice and hers alone. She looked down and saw a mortally wounded man thrashing in agony. With leopardlike litheness she descended the ladder and knelt at his side. "Your commander—what is his name? Your captain! The name of your captain!" she shouted.

"Ro——" he said and his head lolled sideways, blood gushing from mouth and nose.

Ro——what? Roque, surely? Suddenly she heard footsteps behind her. She whirled to face a burly buccaneer with an outstretched hook for a hand.

"A weapon! Throw me a weapon!" she shouted up at whoever might be above to hear her. He was almost upon her. She ducked and went rolling, then sprang up and faced him, armed only with a broken branch from a shattered fruit tree. "If your captain's name is Roque, you'd be a fool to kill me!" she shouted at him.

He came to a halt. "Captain Roque! You knows him?"

"Hell yes, I 'knows' him. If you can describe him to me we've got a truce."

The man looked uncertain, then he spoke. "Big fella, black hair, manners, foreigner."

She nearly wept with relief. "Foreign, alright. Let's go up on the wall and run up that white shirt of yours so he knows we're not his enemies."

There was a sudden bombardment and screams. Garlanda had only a second to look up before the wall crumbled above her, folding in on them like a heavy, bloody cape.

CHAPTER 31

They thought she was dead and so they left her lying among the rubble. She realized that she was not covered by the stone, though she could feel sharp weights resting on her legs. She must have been thrown out of the way of the worst of it. She could not open her eyes, their weight was as great as the stones, but hearing required no effort. She drifted in and out of consciousness for a while, aware that she was hurt and not knowing or even caring how badly.

She could hear the other women being rounded up into a subdued herd, all the fight ebbed from their souls. She heard someone say that Maiselle was dead, and Khurrem who had gone down fighting at Maiselle's side.

Marching feet, the wailing of babies, the broken whimpers of women who faced rape and worse. Laughter—raucous, coarse, horrible male laughter. The clink of coins and swords.

A cool, compassionate hand on her forehead. "Fleur?"

She tried to say "Sebastian" but couldn't make her lips move—it came out a moan. The stones were being lifted from her legs and strong, competent hands were feeling for breaks. She was lifted easily, head against a shirted shoulder ripe with smoke and the odor of medicines.

Then, another voice, not quite so close. "Damn you, men! Don't touch those women! They're not our prisoners, they are our guests until their families ransom them. The first man to molest one of them will be hanged, no questions asked."

It was Roque's voice. Impervious to the will of others, cool in the knowledge that his lusty subordinates would not disobey. "Where's the pasha?"

"Doan know where the rest of him is got to, but we saved his head for you."

There was fury in Roque's voice, "He was to be taken alive! Those were my orders! Who is responsible for the flouting of discipline? Who?"

Mumbling. Pleading. The throaty voice of a musket. A body slumping to the paving. The reek of flint smoke and salty blood.

"Ye say we can't handle the women. Do that include not cuffin' a little common courtesy inter 'em after they killed more'n a score of our mates outright with swords and blew the rest to Hades with guns? These women is downright vicious!"

"Aye, cap'n, they's regular A-may-zons! Fought like furies, they did."

"Small wonder, two tigresses taught them, didn't they, Sabelle," Roque said.

"If you killed little Fleur I'll make a eunuch outta you with me bare hands!"

"She's just stunned. I have her right here," Sebastian said, walking slowly. Mustafa dead, Maiselle dead, Khurrem dead. But 'Belle was alive. What of Wilma, Betty, and the others? More muscular arms took her.

A voice near her ear said, "Smallest damn gunner I've ever seen."

"—And the best," Garlanda said loudly enough to bring laughter to the listeners. "Ransom, my foot. I'll see you in hell first."

The women cheered. Roque had taken on a little more than he bargained for and this was just a hint of things to come.

They took the *Nightbird* with them. Part of Roque's crew and half the prisoners were transferred to the Turkish ship. Sabelle was livid. "She's *my* ship and I'll get 'er back, I will. Ye just wait, little one. Our chance'll come. No matter how nice a prison is, it's still a prison whether it's a palace or someone else's ship. I ain't gonna serve on this ship. I'm gonna be a prisoner like the rest o' ye."

Garlanda shook her by the shoulders. "No! Don't you see that you've got to serve? You've got to be one of the crew again. Battles are better won from the inside. With you on the crew we've got a spy and a friend and hope."

"I'm a mite tired o' all this spy malarky."

"You want the *Nightbird*? You want your own ship? Then you must play their game and make them think you're one of them. Fight from the inside, Sabelle."

"I said I were an actress, I didn't say I wanted to go playin' at Drury Lane," Sabelle muttered, puckering her forehead in a worried frown as she walked off.

Garlanda was well enough to be up and around, but she hid that fact for as long as possible because it delayed the inevitable confrontation with Roque. When a week had passed and she could no longer fool Sebastian, the old doctor shook his head and warned her the captain was growing suspicious. That very afternoon Roque strode in without knocking.

"This isn't Versailles, sir, and I'll thank you not to come barging in here unannounced."

"You haven't learned yet—this is *my* ship and *my* cabin, you feisty little wench!"

"And I'll chew your hands off at the wrist if you try to touch me! Oh, Roque!" she said closing her eyes. "Sit down. I'm sorry. Let's talk like civilized people; we both are, somewhere down underneath."

Roque pulled a chair next to the bed where she sat, plucking at the new blue moire coverlet. "My God, you've developed spirit and brains!" Roque said. "How long since the island? Two years and more, I'll wager. Our paths have not been easy since then and yet you've become a better person for it."

"And you?"

"I wonder," he said, shaking his head wearily. She noticed that fine lines were trying to mar his handsome visage.

"Did you know Sabelle and I were at the palace?"

"Did you think in truth I attacked only to ransom a silly lot of women I've never beheld before, lass? I ran across our former cabin boy, Freddie, in Naples. I asked if he'd seen you and he told me he had and that you and Sabelle were both captives of the pasha. I tried to bargain with the pasha. I even tried to steal you, but my men were caught and foully murdered."

"And in return your men 'foully murdered' a just and honorable man. He was wise and as fair as his culture would allow. His people live with death much more easily than do ours. It is their belief in kismet— the fate written on the forehead of all men. Kismet—I wonder, is that what has brought me here?"

"Not kismet, but rather, my ship."

She looked up at him, remembering the power in those broad shoulders, the texture of his thick black hair under her fingers. "So, you shelled a palace to save me?"

"You and the best quartermaster I have ever had," he tossed back cockily. "Don't be so flattered, lovely one. After all, I have only attacked one small palace. Helen of Troy had an entire war fought over her and it lasted years." His tone was jesting, they both laughed.

"Oh, Roque," she said fondly, "so we have both changed, have we not? We are able to talk now as adults, something that sore tried our patience before. Why did you leave so early after that night of the Channel crossing?"

"Business, Fleur. I had tarried too long as it was."

"Roque—" her fingers played faster over the blue coverlet, eyes downcast. "There is talk of ships to England being stopped—betrayal—"

"Let us not speak anymore of spies and pirates," he said abruptly, bitterly. "I know that for all there is between us, you love England and would be glad to believe the worst of me."

"Then convince me otherwise," she pleaded. But he said nothing, merely walked to the cabinet and poured himself a drink. "You're in a position of enough power to be the man betraying the English ships," she said and waited for a rebuttal. None came. "It is a fact you are a master of disguise who flits around most mysteriously. You have never been caught."

"Ha! Little you know, Fleur!" he said. "I've served in galleys in chains that tore my flesh, I've been hunted and—"

"Hunted? Why?"

"Because of who I am. It is amusing, isn't it? What I feel and what I do does not matter. It is the blood coursing in my veins that causes *my* kismet and nothing I can do will change that." He flung his glass at the wall and his anger seemed to fade as the liquid dripped down the paneled walls. He kissed her lightly on the top of her head and walked out without another word.

She had missed the sea.

Garlanda stood, a hand on the rail, watching the swell of blue water unfolding for miles around the ship. She had not realized that she had missed sailing so very much. To be standing on deck now with the salt spray in her face and a hearty wind playing with her hair was something akin to complete, mindless happiness. With the familiar pitch and sway of *La Doña del Fuego* she could feel years away from her adventures and misfortunes. It was as if she had always been here aboard ship and could remain safely so forever. A nice, hopeless fantasy.

But it could not be. *I have mourning to do and battles to win,* she thought. *I have my own heart to conquer, my father's murderers to track, and I must find Leon and Althea and reassure them that I am safe.*

The sea spray tickled and chafed. She stepped away from the rail. Where would they dock? Marseille was too much to hope for. Italy, perhaps, or Lisbon. Roque refused to tell her. *I love him,* she thought, *but he will stand between me and my goals. And he is a traitor, he must be. He could easily deny it, and he does not.*

"What are ye thinkin' about, little one?" Sabelle asked, leaning on the rail. The older woman's skin was fast regaining the healthy tan she had lost while confined in the harem. Some of the fabric the two women had bought so long ago in Port Royal had still been in the bottom of a chest in Roque's cabin and Garlanda had made Sabelle a bright scarf to hold back her ample ebony curls and a matching bandana print skirt. Sabelle had a knife tucked into her belt and she wore the sleeves of her fine white linen shirt rolled up to allow freer movement. A smattering of pale scars showed on her nicely plump arms.

"Hello, Sabelle, I'm planning insubordination and rebellion, as always."

"Is that all? I was afeared you was thinkin' up somethin' difficult. We're gettin' good at this sort o' thing by now, matey. Oh, you might like t' know Wilma still has that heapin' supply of laudanum with her. Enough to send the crew of the *Doña* sleepin' real peacefullike, should we find a chance to escape."

"Are you planning to cast them adrift and steal *La Doña?*"

"Ain't ye got any sense at all in that pretty lil' head? Settin' adrift is a terrible thing to do!"

"So is ransoming a shipload of helpless women who were kidnaped to begin with."

Sabelle shook her head. "Not helpless, for sure we ain't helpless. If I knows Roque, we'll make port at some outta the way place where we'll drink and loaf and he'll leave the women with a few guards while he goes and sends out his ransom demands. While we're there we'll have our revolt. We dope 'em and sail off on the *Nightbird*. I've got a powerful hankerin' for that ship. She's a beauty, ain't she? Anyways, wherever we stop, we dope the crew and bolt for it. I'll even drop you off where you want to go, s'long's it's sensiblelike and not sailin' up the Thames or such."

"Marseille," Garlanda said firmly. "Marseille is where I have unfinished business."

Sabelle shrugged and gave her a resigned smile. "I was sorta hoping you'd want to come sailin' with me."

Garlanda swung around to face her. " 'Belle! I should like nothing more. Do you mean it? But—but I can't come—not yet, anyway. I have to track my father's murderers."

"Why? If he's dead, he's dead. Ain't gonna bring him back, findin' out who done it."

"I know. That's true, but he was a good man, a valuable man—to his country and to me. And someone took him from England and his family. No one had the right to do that, and they *must* pay!"

"I 'spose I can see that," Sabelle admitted. "But you'd make a fair quartermaster—"

"Fair?" Garlanda laughed.

"Good, then! 'Ceptin' o' course, yer on the small side and you'll never learn to bellow at the crew like I can."

"I did pretty well the night we buried Jealous George, didn't I?"

"Aye, you did! Me sides hurt for days after from tryin' not to laugh. You was great! I wish you could come with me."

"To find your children? You'll find them, I know it."

"Not unless I gets me own ship and crew."

Sebastian approached them. They tried to look nonchalant. He gave Garlanda a close look. "Last time, Miss Fleur, you escaped with the best cabin boy on board. This time you'll take the finest quartermaster the ship's ever had."

The women eyed each other, then the kindly older man. "I'm afraid we don't know what you're talking about," Garlanda said, but she couldn't suppress a grin.

"Of course not, but when it comes to dosing the crew, Wilma could use a bit of advice. She has the makings of a good ship's surgeon in time, in fact when I started I knew less, but until then you don't want her putting the crew to sleep permanently. She's been working with me in the 'pothecary and I'm afraid her questions have been none too subtle. Good day, ladies."

Garlanda and Sabelle raised delicately plucked eyebrows at each other and smiled.

That night Roque came to the cabin. Garlanda, seated on the bed, hesitated with her hairbrush raised over her long copper waterfall of hair. When he said nothing, she resumed brushing. He poured himself a glass of brandy and gestured to Garlanda questioningly. She smiled and shook her head 'no.' "How are you feeling?" he asked.

There was genuine concern and tenderness in his voice. *Why not?* Garlanda asked herself. *I'm not an innocent little convent girl anymore. He's due for some bad surprises—why not a good one?* "I'm much better," she answered, "but you look tired."

"Mm-m, a little. Keeping my men away from your women is a full time job."

"Does that include keeping yourself away from me?" she asked and was pleased to see that he looked a little disconcerted. "Here," she said, patting the blue coverlet, "sit down and let me rub your back. That will make you feel better."

He sat beside her, turned slightly away. She dropped the hairbrush on the floor and began to lightly knead the muscles of his wide shoulders with her fingertips. She moved slowly down his back, delicately prodding him to relax. She felt his tenseness loosen, and she moved back up to his shoulders, then his neck. She ran her fingers gently over his collarbones then down the front of his shirt. He straightened up a little but said nothing.

She began to unlace the ties of his full-sleeved shirt and slipped her hand inside the fabric to stroke his chest and play with the silky hair growing there. Roque leaned back a little and she gripped the sides of the shirt opening and tore with all her strength. The shirt came away in her hands with a loud, rending sound. He tried to turn and face her. "What the—" Garlanda pushed him down. His eyes were wide with astonishment. "Fleur—"

"If you must speak," she said, running light fingers down his muscled abdomen and around the silver buckle of his belt, "why don't you tell me my little convent stories? You swore you'd memorized them when we were on the island together."

He laughed, eyes following her every move. Garlanda hummed to herself as she struggled to remove his boots. "Now, you just be quiet and let me take care of you. You're tired, remember?" she said cheerfully, dropping the last boot to the floor. Then she rose and blew out the lantern, leaving only a fat beeswax taper flickering on the desk. "Finish your drink, Roque. Shall I pour you another?"

He obeyed and then laid back, anticipation and a small shadow of disquiet in his gray eyes. Garlanda fluffed up the pillows and popped them under his head. She bent to plant teasing little kisses all over his throat. He tried to stop her when she reached for his belt buckle. But Garlanda, with a sweet smile but strength in her grip, forced his hands back down to the satin bed coverlet. She unfastened his trousers and removed them with light flicks of her fingernails on his stomach and thighs. When she had accomplished this she stood back and regarded him calmly. "You used to do this to me," she said. "I always wondered what it would be like to reverse roles."

She gave a quick toss of her head to get her long hair back from her face. Roque grinned lazily. Garlanda gave him a brief, perfunctory smile and crossed over to the cabinet where he kept his liquor. She poured herself a half glass of fine port and sipped it, looking him over at length. Her expression was that of a woman trying to decide whether or not to buy the item for sale. "Hm-m-m," she said in a thoughtful voice.

Then, as if the decision had been made, she set the glass of port down and began to unbutton the front of her dress. Another sip of her drink, then she slowly slid first one shoulder down a little, then the other, before letting it slip off. Wearing only a lacy chemise of the sheerest fabric, she picked up the dress and carefully folded it. She walked across the cabin with slow, languid strides and put the dress in the walnut wardrobe. Then back again to take yet another sip of her drink.

Roque's eyes followed her every move, but he said nothing. She suspected it was because he couldn't think, for once in his life, of anything to say.

Suppressing a smile at his surprise, she yawned and stretched her arms over her head seductively. The pasha had told her that anticipation is half the pleasure and during her time with him she had come to understand and appreciate what he meant. She was going to share this knowledge with Roque, whether he was a willing student or not. She glanced over at him and could tell that he was, indeed, willing!

She slowly unlaced the ribbons that tied the front of the chemise, then, one strap at a time, she shrugged her shoulders out of the lacy garments exposing her pale, full breasts in the flickering candlelight. She smiled at Roque as the chemise fell around her ankles. Then she stepped out of the circle of discarded lace and walked over to the bed. Staring down at him, she began to trace a light design on his thigh with her fingertip.

She felt his muscles instantly contract when she touched him, then he smiled at her again and relaxed. He started to reach out for her, but she moved aside slightly and with the other hand touched his arm. Running her hand along the smooth brown flesh, she bent and kissed his lips, letting her breasts brush lightly across his chest. She swayed slightly, enjoying the feel of him against her excited nipples. She still had one hand on his thigh—now she moved it up farther. She felt him shudder involuntarily as she moved down and took him in her mouth. Roque's hands gripped her thick hair.

Garlanda teased him with long, hungry strokes of her tongue. It pleased her to see how incredibly aroused he was. Loving him as she did, his enjoyment heightened her own. Suddenly anticipation turned to painful desire. She knew that neither of them could prolong lovemaking any longer. She sat up and quickly straddled him. She lowered herself onto him and gasped at the sweet madness that flooded her with fire.

Roque sat up, clasping her by the hips and pulled her long legs around his waist. They moved together in a frenzy of hot eroticism. Their bodies, soaked with perspiration, surged together again and again until the completion of their passion overwhelmed them.

Garlanda cried out a long, wordless sound that spiraled as the first spasms took her. Wave after wave of throbbing fulfillment shook her, tore her, left her spent and mindless. A warm afterglow settled on her and she collapsed into Roque's strong arms.

He kissed her face, her pointed chin, dainty nose, flushed cheeks. "My compliments," he murmured in a husky, spent voice, "to the pasha!"

CHAPTER 32

They dropped anchor in Cold Harbor at Levanzo, an island off Sicily so small that it was on few but the most exacting maps. *"Merde!"* Sabelle muttered upon first setting foot ashore. "Whadda they got here besides rocks and too many bunnies?"

There were, indeed, rabbits popping up all over the place. Garlanda stiffled a giggle and glanced around her. The island did not look like much, a conglomerate of bald cliffs and a few small trees randomly scattered about as if a massive hand had flung them to the wind to fall where they might. "Surely it cannot be large enough to support all of us, even for a short time."

Roque was talking to a group of local fishermen, among them a grizzled old bulldog of a man with knotty muscles on his furred forearms. He seemed to be the leader of the group and an old acquaintance of the captain. There was much handshaking, backslapping, and lecherous laughter. Garlanda wondered how Roque was explaining his boatloads of women, most of them still in harem clothes, a few in striped shirts and trousers bought, in one way or another, from sailors.

Sebastian stepped up behind Garlanda and Sabelle. "He wouldn't have stopped here if it would not support us. There are citrus and olive trees, an over-abundance of rabbits, which the locals would be happy to see thinned out, prickly pears, some grapes, and plenty of fish."

"I'm fair sick to death at the thought o' fish," Sabelle grumbled.

"Even lobster, octopus, and mullet basted in butter and herbs?" he asked.

"Well, I could force meself to eat somethin' like that."

"Look at the mountain," Garlanda said, gesturing at the hulking blue giant across the water, its peak crowned in motionless, ivory clouds that rested like a proudly won laurel wreath on the brow of a victorious athlete.

"Mount Eryx, or Erice, as it is now called."

"What's the matter with ye," Sabelle demanded crossly of the surgeon. "Ye get real educated overnight or somethin'?"

"Safiye! Raven!"

A rowboat from the *Nightbird* had just unloaded and Garlanda saw Betty and several other of her friends. She had not seen some of them since the night of the shelling of the palace. They flung their arms around each other, laughing and crying a little for happiness. Before long they fell to whispering in little knots.

"I have something to show you," Roque said. Was he handsomer by moonlight? Garlanda studied him. His thick black hair was straight except for a wave at the broad temples and, untied, spilled over the collar of his creased white shirt. His muscles rippled like waves when he shifted position as he did now, leaning back against a carob tree.

The silvery-blue night lighting played along his hair. Garlanda smiled at him to make him smile back so that she could see the little laugh lines ease the face near hers, a face too often tense with the duties of command. His fierce, hawklike gray eyes softened. "By the Blessed Virgin, that's a winning smile," he said taking her chin in his hand. "Don't you want to see the surprise?"

"Of course I do, Roque! How mysterious you can be and such a tease."

He stood up and helped her to her feet. "Let's borrow some clothes from one of the boys so you can make the climb. Aren't you curious? Will you be angry if the surprise isn't jewels or fripperies?"

She put her hands on her hips and laughed. "Angry? Of course not! Whatever adventure you have in mind sounds like a—Roque, my darling Roque!" She flung her arms around his neck and kissed him hungrily.

"Delightful, Fleur, but we'll never make the hill if you continue to provide such delicious distraction."

It was more than an hour later when they finally set off, Garlanda in borrowed clothing and contentedly munching an orange.

"How can you look so devilishly beautiful in a cabin boy's clothes?" Roque inquired with irritated fondness. Garlanda swung the lantern she carried and clucked at him, tarrying long enough to spit out orange seeds.

"I think I make a marvelous cabin boy. Freddie thought so, too, the night we escaped your ship."

"Ah-h-h, so that's how you did it, he smuggled you out dressed like one of the boys. How that ever deceived anyone, I'll never know."

They hiked along through wildflowers that dappled the moonlit hill. "So you don't fancy me as a cabin boy?"

"Well," Roque said, pretending to seriously consider the situation, "we could smudge some dirt on your face, cut your hair, and make you look like a scoundrel, but I'm afraid we can't hide these." He made a grab for her breasts. Garlanda ducked, laughing and swooped under his arm.

"But, captain, there would be scandalous rumors if you were seen chasing a cabin boy around the decks!" she said.

"Hardly! How do you think many of the men tolerate long voyages without women?"

She decided he was trying to shock her. He wouldn't succeed. "In Turkey it is quite acceptable for men to have relationships with other men." She went him one better, drawing on the gossip she had heard in the harem. "And a great many women in a seraglio get bored without men and they seem to make do quite nicely with one another."

Roque's face was in defenseless ruin for a second, then he laughed. "And you a convent girl, telling things like that! What would the sisters say?" He folded his hands in an attitude of prayer and raised his face toward the heavens in a mute posture of supplication.

Garlanda hit him with the last of her orange peel and they continued up the hill. "Voilà, Fleur!" he said at last.

She looked about. "Surely you did not bring me here for the view! Why, it's as black as pitch, Roque, and I'm not at all impressed by those three ragtaggle bushes you're standing in front of."

"Are you afraid of the dark or of tight places?"

She gave him a dour look. "I've spent half my life in whalebone stays—find me a tighter place than that, sir. You mean we're going to explore a cave? What fun."

What fun? she asked herself later as she crawled along behind Roque on her hands and knees. Pebbles bit through the thick, clumsily knit fisherman's stockings encasing her legs. "I don't like these things hanging down from the ceiling. They're dripping and they look like fangs."

"Where's your sense of adventure?" Roque's voice floated back. She considered pinching the part of him nearest her, but restrained herself. A moment later they were able to get up. "Isn't this exciting? You can write to the good sisters all about it?"

"No, thank you. Midnight excursions in dirty tunnels full of reeking bats would fail to enthrall them as it fails to enthrall me."

"*Touché*, my love. You've learned to fence with words. Who taught you?"

"My love," he had said, but was it only a term of colloquial conversation? Her breath caught and hung suspended for a moment before she realized that he had asked a question and was waiting for an answer.

"Fencing with words? I learned from my aunt and her best friend, a gentleman who also improved my real fencing. A Pole, a count—Leon Jareski–Yanoviak."

"Leon!" he said and laughed. "I've heard of him from mutual acquaintances. When next you see him, tell him his friends Sledgeski and Koniecyzska—never mind, they don't know me as Roque."

"That's quite alright, Leon doesn't know *me* as Fleur. He knows me by my real name."

"Your real name?" he said, obviously perplexed.

"What do you mean? Why did you tell me your name was Fleur?"

It was her turn to laugh. "I didn't tell you that was my name! You just called me that on the island and never gave me the chance to say otherwise."

"Then what is your name?"

"We all have our little secrets, don't we," she said lightly. "Now, why are we here? This place is so—oh!" They had stopped walking. Roque's lantern, when raised to a wall, showed a painting so realistic she gasped and started back, thinking she was confronting a real animal.

"Roque! Good heavens, what is this?"

He held the lantern further aloft. "Paintings by men long dead. The interesting thing is that this island is so small it can't support animals such as these."

She raised awed fingers to the flanks of one of the tawny deer fleeing in a herd across the uneven surface of cave wall. Brawny bulls, magnificently horned and muscular, challenged stick hunters. "They must be very, very old," Roque said thoughtfully. "Odd, isn't it, how the animals are so realistic and the men are like something small children would scrawl— meaningless stick figures."

"For being so badly drawn, the male figures are certainly—male," Garlanda muttered, cheeks aflame at the defiantly unnatural phallic drawings.

Roque roared with laughter that chased itself, head over heels down the winding corridor. "So, part of the little nun remains in you after all! I knew it! But I didn't bring you here to embarrass you. I thought these would intrigue you as they did me. What ancient hunter painted these? Why is he so shadowy and his prey so real, so alive. Where, living on this tiny island, did he learn of animals such as these! Come on. Further back is a female."

Deeper and deeper they went into the bowels of the dark cavern. At last the beams of the foully burning lantern picked up a flickering specter. Garlanda cried out and clutched at Roque. "It's just a painting, too, Fleur. Come see her. She is ugly as sin, some primitive fertility goddess perhaps."

"She *is* ugly," Garlanda said, stepping closer, "but fascinating."

"I only hope for the sake of the fellow who painted her that she wasn't typical of the women he knew."

"We shouldn't joke about her. Somehow back here, away from the other paintings, she seems—different. Sacred, perhaps."

They joined hands and left at a much faster pace than they had entered. When they emerged, it was dawn. Garlanda was surprised that so much time had elapsed while they were in the cave. She gave a mighty stretch, still feeling haunted by the featureless white goddess in the depths of the stagnant, bat-infested stone corridor. She looked down at the shimmering waters of the Mediterranean, molten in the rose and peach glow of the newborn day. Across the narrow neck of sea rose a fog-shrouded Mount Erice, its bulk like an anchor in this fairy world of freshness and light. She inhaled deeply, hugging herself.

"It's good to see that you remember you're young and beautiful," Roque said softly.

"Beautiful? With lantern soot on my face and scraped hands and knees? You, sir, are a poor liar." She began to peel off her soiled clothing, letting it drop to the lichened rock at her feet. The morning wind fanned her silky copper hair about her shoulders. "A poor liar," she said, drawing Roque down into her arms to lie on the pile of discarded garments, "but a wonderful lover."

She removed his clothing even more deftly than she had her own.

CHAPTER 33

The women announced they were throwing a party for their captors.

"It's an irresistible offer, sir-r-r," the first mate, a Scotsman named Buchanan, told Roque.

The black-haired man frowned. "I know. That's why I don't trust it."

"Hoot, cap'n, yerr no thinkin' the lasses'll be oop to some mischief, air ye?"

"I dinnae know, laddie, but I'll be postin' the guarrrds, same as any oother naught."

"Ye do a prroper brogue," Buchanan said, frankly unoffended. They watched Sebastian, nearby, winding bandages.

"There's something damned suspicious in this friendliness. Buchanan, if you were being held for ransom, would you drip with sweetness and plan festive little parties?"

"But mon, they're oonly lonesome and farr from theirr hoomes. Might make 'em feel good, fixin' us a feast, eh, Sim?"

Sebastian looked up, squinting in the early morning Mediterranean sunlight. "I don't see what harm it would do to eat real cooking instead of Raoul's slop," he said.

"Very well, then, I'll put you in charge of supervising the culinary preparation," Roque said sternly. The ship's doctor gave him a bewildered look and protested that he knew nothing of food preparation. "You're a surgeon, aren't you? Cut the meat, then!" Roque said and stalked off.

"It couldn't have gone better if I had gone to him and asked to be in charge. Then he would have been suspicious. But this way—" Sebastian said.

"Yer a canny sort for a man," Sabelle said admiringly. "What do ye want to help us for anyway?"

"I told you. I know you're going to do it anyway and I'd rather be in on it then have you kill half of them by overdoing it."

Garlanda twisted her mouth into a grimace, wiping the back of her hand across her sweaty forehead. "Enough talk, Sabelle. Help me turn this piglet." The older woman lent a hand. Together they managed to get the spit over the fire. The glare of bronze and gilt flames dazzled their smoke-wearied eyes. "The wine's all been laced with laudanum, then?" Garlanda asked.

"That it has, little one." They watched Sebastian move off toward the tables. Wilma and another woman approached him with a plate of seafood basted in herb butter.

"I don't know," Garlanda said wistfully. "He helped Freddie and me escape from the ship in Marseille, too."

"Nice old sort like that ought to be home wi' a family, 'stead of out to sea with cutthroats and the like. Wonder what he was before he signed on as a doctor."

"You mean he's not a doctor?" Garlanda said, half

her mind on whether the piglet had been placed too close to the fire.

"Not to start with. What kinda real doctor would want a job like this? Man with schoolin' got no call to be wastin' his life."

"But he isn't wasting his life, he's saving the lives of others—even if some of them aren't the best people in the world. And anyway, why do you talk as if all privateers are scum? Roque's educated—so is Freddie. And look at you!"

Sabelle craned her neck, glancing at her attire. "Why? What have I got on that I shouldn't?"

Garlanda laughed merrily, "No, no, 'Belle! I meant look at you as an example of how a buccaneer can be a fine person. In the battle at the palace, who did I want at my side? Who's a better companion, braver or wiser about the sea?"

"Well," Sabelle grudgingly admitted, stopping to inhale the wonderfully greasy reek of grilled pork, "you could have a point there, Fleur."

They both laughed. Garlanda rolled her sleeves up to above her elbows and wiped her forehead again. "Before I eat, I've got to slip off and take a dip in something other than butter."

"Fleur, it's tonight or never. If you falter, if the cap'n weakens your will, we'll have to leave you behind. We can't have no loitering nor foot-draggin'. We ain't gonna hurt the men except maybe to kidnap a few for long enough to teach them other women more about sailin', so don't you go gettin' no notions 'bout warnin' Roque. We ain't gonna harm a hair on his head."

"You needn't doubt me, I'll be the first on board ship. I have the plans in my mind."

"Aye, plans in yer mind and a man in yer arms, that always makes it a mite hard."

"No, Sabelle," she said angrily. "There are too many things between us. I wouldn't stay with him even if he asked me to, which he has *not* done!" She scowled and stomped away.

The lush odors of cooking food followed her as she headed down to the beach. Meat drippings were being stirred into thick, dark gravies, fruit was being sliced, fish smoldered in pits of basil and lime leaves, octopi hung spitted over low fires or broiled in carrageen and butter. Sweet purple wine sloshed sluggishly in wooden vats and goatskin bags.

The women attended busily to their chores, sleeves rolled up, skirts caught up in makeshift aprons. Bright ribbons tied up their long hair, stray locks tumbling down, here a gold wisp of curl over a red-moired shoulder, there a fat tea-brown curl resting on its owner's creamy throat.

Garlanda went to a secluded cove she had found earlier. As she walked, she unlaced her gown bodice, feeling safe from prying eyes. When she reached the tiny, cloistered spot she shed her skirts and blouse and waded into the water until the waves were at her waist. She lay back and floated around for a while until she felt rid of the smell of food and intrigue.

She came out of the water, shivering a little, hair plastered to her shoulders. She rubbed her arms, teeth chattering. It didn't surprise her when Roque stepped from behind a tree, applauding. "I'm freezing," she told him. "Quick, I need that blanket."

He strode over to her and scooped her up in his arms with the heavy woolen blanket around her. Garlanda threw her arms around his neck and said, "What might you be doing on the beach, sir?"

"Ravishing foolish maidens who wander out alone when it's so nearly dark." She tripped him and they fell in a tangle of arms, legs, and blanket. Wrapped in Roque's embrace and the blanket, Garlanda did not stay cold for long. What started as a huddle to keep her warm ended as an impassioned interlude in the moonlight. Their soft murmurs mingled as did their bodies. It was with great reluctance that they at last moved apart and dressed. Roque pulled Garlanda close to him and said, "Isn't the sea beautiful tonight? So calm and steadfast."

"Beautiful indeed," she agreed, her head nestled against his shoulder. "Never stopping, never slowing down. The water keeps moving and nothing stops it. Would that I could be so resolute."

"What do you need to be resolute about? We have each other and a feast to attend. That's all we need."

"For the moment." Had he said those three words or were they in her head? Everything was lovely, the night sky, the sea, the lovemaking they had just shared under the crescent of smoky moon, but it would not last. They would go in different directions after tonight. Until then they were together.

The feast was underway when Garlanda and Roque returned. Wooden platters of meat, seafood, and fruit filled the makeshift tables. The wine had not been passed around yet, but soon—the sight of it jolted Garlanda. The drugged wine! In the joy of being with Roque she had tried to forget the dangerous adventure ahead of her. Now it all came back in a dizzying rush of fear and pain. He wasn't her enemy, he was her lover, but she would leave him. She must.

It would be a bloodless coup unless the watchmen on the *Nightbird* proved difficult. Earlier in the day she and Sabelle had talked about the ship. They had agreed that *La Doña del Fuego* was much closer than the *Nightbird* but neither of them would dream of stealing Roque's ship.

"She's to him what the *Nightbird* will be to me," Sabelle had told her. "You don't come 'cross a ship like that often. He can't be as he is—the best, without *La Doña*. She's his ship and his friend and his lady. Besides, I likes the *Nightbird* better."

Garlanda returned to the present with a jolt as Wilma passed them a tray bearing cups of wine. The women had prepared some grape juice that looked like wine for themselves so they could keep clear heads through the trying night ahead.

Roque speared half a roasted fowl and a hunk of glossy golden-crusted bread from a passing tray on the end of his rapier. Garlanda laughed appreciatively and pulled the food free. Everyone around them had begun eating. Garlanda smiled at Roque with a sick sense of hypocrisy and fed him a piece of chicken then offered to get some more wine for him.

I love him, she thought, heart hammering fiercely. *I love him and here I sit, plotting against him.* But she knew what she was doing was right. They were women, her friends, not just commodities to be traded for ransom. Many of the women had expressed grave doubts since they had been on the island that their families would want them back and even more of them were sure the money for ransom couldn't, or wouldn't, be found.

What life was left for them, these women who had learned to sail a ship and fight a duel and fire cannons and make love as if it were an art and not a duty? How many husbands would welcome them back? Yet they could not forget and go back to being mere housekeepers for husbands who might have found other charms more entrancing in their absence. But neither could they be left with Roque. In spite of his own standards they might well end up as slaves, playthings for the crew, or worn-out old women existing on what they could beg in foreign ports.

No, what she was doing was right, even if it cost her the greatest price she had ever paid. She fed Roque another bite of bread.

The moon was no longer a dusty white sickle. It rested low on the horizon and glowed gold through clouds as black as Sabelle's hair.

She had wasted that bit of poetical thought on Sabelle, Garlanda told herself wryly. "It went too easy," Sabelle said gruffly.

"Ha!" Garlanda countered. "For you, maybe. *I* was the one who had to knock Billy out with a bottle and tie Raoul to a tree. You seem to forget the trouble we had getting rid of the watchmen on the *Nightbird*."

"That's only on account of you wouldn't let me run the rogues through. It would o' saved a pile o' trouble. There wouldn't a been no fighting and Wilma gettin' knocked overboard and fair drowning and Veronica got herself cut up by that sailor and she's plenty mad, but not much hurt. *None* o' that woulda happened if you'd let me knife 'em."

"Captain! You're needed!" a feminine voice called out. Sabelle took off in answer. She had already settled into the role she had sought so long and so hard. Garlanda followed the older woman's example and set to work. There was much to do since it was the first actual time the women had been able to put their training to actual use. They were doing amazingly well.

They'd burgled Roque's cabin, taking his astrolabe, portolani, charts, armillary sphere, and cross staff. That left him with a magnetic compass. Sabelle said it wouldn't take him long to get replacement navigational instruments in Sicily, but he would be unable to trace them for the time being. They planned to be out of the Mediterranean by the time Roque's sailing tools were fully replaced.

The sails unfurled to the wind, taking the ship swiftly through the glassy waves. Garlanda led the safety check of riggings and shrouds. Leaving Roque had been difficult to begin with, but the fact that he had barely touched the wine had critically worsened the situation. Garlanda had pressed him to drink and he had shaken his head, telling her a good captain never let his guard down. "Suppose we were ambushed by a rival crew or attacked by wild animals?" he'd asked her. "Wild animals?" she'd repeated. "There's nothing on this island bigger than a rabbit!" Roque had given her a solemn look and said, "Well, perhaps they are very large and sinister rabbits."

Garlanda climbed down the riggings, teeth clenched. She had hated having to hurt him, but as time went on and most of the other men were snoring or getting lured to secluded spots, she knew it was looking suspicious. Too many men were "falling asleep" or not returning from their romantic rendezvous.

Roque had grown uneasy. It had taken a heavy wine bottle smashed across the back of his head to knock him out. Once she'd done it she became nearly hysterical because she thought she'd killed him. Sabelle had slapped her smartly, tied Roque up, and pointed out that he was still breathing. She'd allowed Garlanda time for a quick farewell kiss on the unconscious man's brow before hauling her off to finish the night's work.

She had been thinking the rest of the night of the innocent days when they were first together. The days on the island when they were all there was. And even if she could turn back time, would she? Garlanda shook her head, knowing she would not trade naiveté for the hard-won knowledge of life she had now.

She knew herself, her potential, her resourcefulness, her limitations. She had learned more about other people and how to deal with them. Life no longer took her by the nape of the neck and flung her about to the winds of fate. She was in control of her own destiny, and she would not trade that for anything, not even the love of a man.

Not that Roque had once spoken of love to her. She tossed her head proudly. He was a pirate, doubtless a traitor to the crown. It was better that Roque did not love her. With that fact, she could hold her head high and say he was warm, bright, clever, attractive, understanding, but he was still only a buccaneer and would come to a bad end. There was no future in her love for him; therefore, she would put all thought of him aside. No future, no chance—

My love, my love. Tears trickled from her violet eyes, beading her long lashes and stinging her face in the wind. *Good-bye, good-bye.*

PART FOUR

THE COUNTESS

CHAPTER 34

Marseille again.

Garlanda assembled the best of her wardrobe from the clothes that had remained on *La Doña del Fuego* after her escape in this very port—how long ago? Two years or more, perhaps three, she could not remember. She took only the clothes she needed and left the rest for Sabelle's "crew."

Respectable women one day, harem girls the next, then captives of pirates, and finally, sailors. The women who were leaving to return to families had already disembarked. A great many, however, were staying on with Sabelle. A rap sounded on the oaken door. "Fleur? You ready?" came Sabelle's voice from outside. "I'm leavin' to get supplies and a few sailors to fatten up the crew, and I thought if you was ready I could take you ashore with me."

Garlanda struggled to fasten the bodice of a hopelessly unfashionable muslin gown. "Yes, I'm ready." She stepped out and smiled at Sabelle. The older woman was hardly recognizable in the pine-green moire dress Garlanda had sewn her from a bolt of fabric in the hold. The gown was stylishly lowcut and bereft of frills, fitting snugly through the bodice and flaring over the full petticoats. But the greatest change was in Sabelle's hair. Her usually wayward raven curls were smoothed up into a chignon, with a few curly wisps allowed to dangle free. Her only concession to frippery was a pair of long jade eardrops in her pierced lobes. She was beautiful, and yet wholly businesslike, which she would need to be.

"Ready to round up new crewmen and find buyers for the spices?" Garlanda asked. Sabelle nodded, then stopped to hitch up a silk stocking. There was, of course, a dagger tucked in the lacy garter over her dimpled knee. Garlanda repinned a rebellious strand for her newly dignified friend and looked her over. " 'Belle, you are stunning. A real lady. No one would know that you aren't a Parisian blueblood who had recently inherited the family shipping business. But they'll find out there's a sharp mind behind all the kohl and lipstain when they come to bargaining."

"That's for sure, little one. Well? Shall we go? This damned sun is trying to melt me eye paint!" She looked at Garlanda for a moment. "Yer sure ye won't stay?" she asked softly.

"I'd love to, but I've got business to—oh, Sabelle! Do you suppose we'll ever see each other after today?"

She was surprised to see tears well up in the dark-haired woman's eyes. In the first physical gesture Garlanda had ever seen her make, the first sign of affection not hidden behind blustering words or a cuff on the head, Sabelle put an arm around her. "Of course we'll see each other again, Fleur. The sea has a strange way o' throwin' people together."

Garlanda hugged her and let unashamed tears flood her eyes. "I hope so, Sabelle. I genuinely hope so. You'll find your children and I'll find my father's murderers and—and the best of luck to you, the first lady captain."

Sabelle released her. "Naw, don't say the first, *ma petite*, say the best. That sounds better, don't it?"

Garlanda's return to Marseille was a surprise amounting to shock to her friends. She didn't know where Althea might be living or if indeed she had given up hope and returned to England, so Garlanda presented herself first at the English embassy. The first person she saw inside was a secretary, an impeccably dressed young man in yellow satin breeches and a loose-sleeved white shirt. He stopped on his way down the stairs and gaped at her as if she were a ghost. "Fleur!" he said, then corrected himself, "Miss Garlanda, is it really you?" He came up to her and took her hands.

She had to look up into his face for a moment before she realized that it was Freddie! How he had grown. He was no longer a boy, but a well-dressed, sophisticated young man. "Freddie!" she cried and embraced him.

"I've been trying to find a way to get you out since I saw you. You can't imagine the plans I've made that have not worked out. How did you—"

"Well, well, well," Sir George Young–Brookes's hearty English voice boomed out. "I do believe it's Miss Cheney!" He elbowed Freddie aside who winked at Garlanda and mouthed "later." "I can hardly believe my eyes. We'd given you up for lost. Everybody but your aunt and that friend of hers, that is."

"Is my aunt here in Marseille?"

"Oh my, yes. She comes here two or three times a week for news of you, which unhappily we've not been able to give her. I'll send my footman for her."

"No, I don't want to wait. Just give me her address, if you please."

Sir George obliged and added, "We must hear all about how you got here."

"Perhaps later, sir. All I want now is to see my aunt."

"Could I take Miss Cheney to her aunt, Sir George?" Freddie asked. "I've finished with those papers. All they need is your signature."

"Very well, but do come right back. I have some other work for you to complete before tomorrow."

Once outside, Garlanda slipped her arm through Freddie's. "You've gotten so tall," she said. "You got my necklace to Count Leon, didn't you?"

"Oh, yes, immediately upon returning from our voyage I sought him out. Told him you were in good enough spirits to harass me half to death in front of my associates. He made me tell him all about it and laughed quite hard about you throwing your jewelry at me. Your aunt was frantic. I did my best to assure her that you were in no danger and, in fact, lived like a queen, but she was not very relieved to hear it. The count was quite calm. He said he believed you could escape." He signaled a sleepy coachman on the embassy buggy and assisted Garlanda up into the vehicle.

Once they were on their way Garlanda said, "Freddie, I have something to discuss with you. You told Roque where I was and the villain came and shelled the palace. People were killed. I could have escaped without harming a fly."

"Yes, I know. I'm sorry that I took him into my confidence and he abused it so. I don't care for the thought of so many innocent people dying under siege. But still, you might not have been able to carry out your own plan, you know."

"Under siege? How did you know that?" she asked abruptly. His gray eyes avoided hers.

"Did I say that? Well, rumor reached the embassy."

"Rumor, my foot! You haven't severed any of your old ties, have you? My god, you're still in league with the privateers! How many ships have you turned over to them?"

"I haven't!" he said angrily, the first time in their friendship he had raised his voice to her. "You haven't any right to say that."

"Then what the devil are you doing associating with them?"

"I—" he opened his mouth, then shut it again and turned to look out the open window of the carriage. The breeze stirred his dark red-brown hair.

"Here—take your ring," she said in a soft voice. "I carried it with me these many months looking forward to the time I would see you again."

" 'Tis no good, Fleur. Wheedling will not get you where shouting would not. You may think ill of me if you see fit to do so, but I will tell you this: I have betrayed no one, no one of good intentions." She stared at him, aghast. "The jewelry you threw at me is with your aunt," he continued. "I couldn't keep it. The only thing I did not return was the ruby you gave me when we first escaped *La Doña*. I'm attending the university on that. I had hoped it would please you to hear the use to which I have put the stone. Fleur— Miss Garlanda—let's not part enemies."

"Freddie, I'm glad about your schooling. I just wish I knew—" she took his hand in hers. "My friends come after my country, you know." She clasped his hand tightly, but he was unmoving. He wasn't her adoring little cabin boy anymore, and she wasn't sure what had wrought the change, or whether it was for the better.

Garlanda's meeting with Althea consisted mainly of a great deal of giggling and crying on both sides. Althea was plainly incoherent with joy at having her niece back. "I kept telling them about those men who'd been following us, or rather, following you," she said. "After the trouble you'd given the ambassador at Nice I thought perhaps he'd abducted you. I just didn't know, so I accused everyone! Finally I got that silly fat boy—what was his name? Charles?—from the embassy at Nice and questioned him, rather brutally, I'm afraid. I actually reduced him to tears, but he genuinely didn't know anything about your disappearance, so I ruled that out. Then I went and badgered Sir George about the pasha's men."

"What did he say?"

"Oh, he admitted that a number of European women had been kidnaped and seemed sort of vaguely sorry that you might have been as well. Silly, pompous ass! Told me all sorts of diplomatic reasons why nobody could barge in there and see if you were there. Kept talking about the possibility of starting a war and endangering trade agreements."

"He was probably right," Garlanda said.

"Then I tried to hire a boat and crew and come get you myself."

"No! You didn't!"

"Of course I did. But when the captain found out where it was I wanted to go, he backed out and must have told every other captain in the western world because from then on, none of them would even talk to me. Well, tell me, how *did* you get away?"

Garlanda told her story. This time she was completely honest with Althea about what had happened. To her surprise Althea neither gasped nor swooned. "Have you been able to find out anything about Father while I've been gone?" she asked when she had finished the account of her own experiences.

"Your father! Good Heavens, child! I've made a fulltime job of just trying to get you back! You aren't still interested in pursuing that, are you?"

"Yes. But we can talk about it later. What about everyone else? What about Leon?"

"Ah, Leon," Althea sighed. "Poor Leon."

"What do you mean, 'poor Leon'? He's not ill, is he?"

"I'm afraid he *is*—very, very ill. Consumption, I think. He grows weaker and his tongue grows sharper by the day."

"Is he here?"

"Yes, in Marseille. He's far too weak to travel back to England, even if he wanted to. It's not really his home, anyway. He says he's come here, to his favorite villa to die. And I'm afraid he's quite correct."

Garlanda felt tears running down her cheeks. "I must see him!"

"Yes. We'll go first thing in the morning. He retires quite early and we might disturb him if we went now. You must get some rest, too."

As Garlanda got ready for bed Althea chattered about what else had occurred in Garlanda's absence. Renwick's brother and nephew had both died and the titles and estate had gone to him, she said.

"And what about Elaine? Is she better?" Garlanda asked.

"Didn't you know? No, of course not, how could you? Elaine has died."

"Oh, no!" Garlanda said, genuinely sorry. "What did she die of? I thought surely she would recover, perhaps just because I wanted so much for her to get better."

"No one knows what she died of. She was ill when we left, you recall, then later, when Renwick came back to Marseille, he told us she had slipped gently away. The doctors said it was a stomach ailment. They apparently did all they could, and she just wasn't strong enough to throw it off."

"I should have guessed. She was so frail."

"Renwick took it quite badly, I'm told," Althea said. "Wouldn't even go to the funeral or leave the house for weeks. Very hard on him, losing so many loved ones in such a short time, though I don't suppose he was as close to his brother and nephew as he was to his wife. Those deaths were compensated for, in a way, by his inheritance."

"Poor Elaine. I can't bear the thought of the additional suffering I must have caused her," Garlanda said.

"What do you mean? Oh, that scene at Lawrence's estate! I'm sure Elaine didn't blame you, and you know you were not at fault. Don't dwell on such things. Just rest now and we'll talk tomorrow."

Leon was feeling better than usual the next day when they went to visit him. He received them in great style, and for Leon, exuberance. Althea had sent a note ahead, asking his leave to bring Garlanda. She had feared that the shock might not be to his welfare if they just showed up, unannounced. Leon was, as

usual, austerely but richly attired and had insisted on
providing them with luncheon. He folded Garlanda in
his lean arms and kissed her forehead. "I knew you
would come back. Unlike me, you are indestructible,
dear lady."

"I had to come back," Garlanda said. "I couldn't
persuade the pasha to kidnap you and Althea for me."

"Does this pasha person really have eunuchs?" Althea suddenly asked. "Are they—how do they—I
mean—"

Leon lifted a thin eyebrow. "If you are going to become anatomical, Althea, I think I may have to go
rest. An intimate little discussion of the physical defi-
ciencies of eunuchs hardly seems a suitable topic for
luncheon."

"You just say that because you're a man and know
all about such things."

"What has *being* a man got to do with being *half* a
man?" he said, then relented to give Althea a brief,
learned lecture on eunuchs. He touched rapid-fire on
processes, method, results, side effects, and ended
with life expectancy. It left Althea gaping and, for
once, stunned into silence. "Now then, Garlanda, tell
me all about yourself," he said, leaving Althea to di-
gest her new knowledge as best she could on her own.

Once again Garlanda told her story. And once again
she left out one thing—the most important thing. But
she wasn't sure yet, perhaps there was some other reason. Once before, traveling in France, she had worried
like this and it had proved to be needless.

Garlanda could see that Leon was tiring during
lunch. His pale, thin face became even paler with
bright spots of pink on his angular cheeks. His breath
seemed to have a slight rasp and his eyes were im-

measurably weary. "Althea, we must go now and let Leon rest," she said quietly.

But not quietly enough. "Don't go yet," Leon said. "I have the most awful greedy need for your company."

"Then we shall stay, but you must go rest for at least an hour. We will amuse ourselves in the garden," Althea said.

Leon agreed and the two women spent the time strolling among the beds of carefully tended gardens behind the huge villa. The grounds were extensive and set high on a hill overlooking the city and sea. In exactly an hour and five minutes Leon reappeared looking almost as healthy as ever, except for his increased thinness. They had a long afternoon of conversation. Althea was very grand and witty, Leon matched or beat every witticism, and Garlanda simply enjoyed it all. It was early evening before they returned to Althea's home. A carriage stood in front of the house, unfamiliar arms on the doors. "Renwick," Althea explained.

"Oh, dear!" Garlanda wasn't quite ready to meet Renwick, especially after an afternoon with dear, beloved Leon. She remembered Renwick with some embarrassment. She had been caused considerable unhappiness because of the physical attraction between them—as much, she had to admit, on her part as his. Now that seemed laughable. After having been with both Roque and the pasha recently, the memory of Renwick seemed rather pale and silly.

But the memory of Renwick and Renwick in the flesh were two different matters. He was in the drawing room and swept her into his arms as if they were long-lost lovers. "My dear Garlanda," he said and kissed her on the lips.

"Do you know this man?" Althea muttered, then issued the obligatory invitation to share a light supper with them. Renwick accepted and Garlanda expressed her sorrow at his family losses. Renwick replied with exactly the right mixture of sorrow and courtesy. *He always says and does the proper thing,* Garlanda thought and somehow it made her a little uneasy. Worse yet, he managed to imply, without a single word that was not strictly proper in front of a lady's aunt, that he intended their relationship to take up just where it had left off before the duel at Jennings's estate.

"Please, Garlanda, if you can bear to talk about it, tell me—well, about everything—" he said.

Garlanda gave him an impersonal and very abbreviated account of her life in the harem, managing to say absolutely nothing about her own role in the pasha's household. Nor did she mention which of the many Turkish pashas she was talking about. It sounded, in her own ears, like a travel lecture, given by someone who was repeating it at second hand.

After supper Althea attempted to escape their company, thinking no doubt, that it was what Garlanda desired, but her niece waylaid her and developed a sudden, devastating headache. Renwick had no choice but to bid them both good night. He promised to return the next day and asked Garlanda if she would accompany him on a carriage ride if the weather was fine.

She agreed and he turned up the next morning in a beautiful open landau. He had a picnic lunch along and had the coachman drive them along the high escarpment above Marseille that looked out over the Mediterranean. It was a breathtaking view. They left the coachman to his solitary lunch and went to sit on a grassy area that seemed to overlook the world. "It almost takes your breath away, doesn't it?" Garlanda asked. But her mind was not here with Renwick; it was back with Roque, listening to him talk about seas as women. This was the sea he loved most and he was probably out there somewhere right now.

"*You* take my breath away," Renwick answered.

"You mustn't say such things," she protested.

"Why not, it's true. I have always thought you the most beautiful woman I've ever seen."

"You should not speak to me this way, Renwick. You are so recently widowed, it is merely your grief speaking."

He laughed. "I mean no disrespect to my late wife, but even you must admit she was not a beautiful woman."

"But she was loving and sweet."

"Yes, she was. Garlanda, please—"

"Renwick," she said firmly. "Allow me to speak my heart to you. The last two years of my life have been very troubling to me. I have changed, my attitudes have altered, and I'm not sure of what I think about anything right now. I'm very flattered by your attentions, for I—well, I find you very attractive, but—"

"But what?"

"I don't want to be forced, I suppose. I feel like other people have had more control over my life than I have. It's my turn." She laughed. "Does that make any sense?"

"I suppose so, but I want to help guide your life. God made men to look out for their women, didn't he?"

She had her doubts about this, but it was not worth discussing right now. "I don't think you can guide my life right now. No one can. I have—I have things to do, things to find out about."

"What kind of things?"

"I'd rather not say. No, don't look hurt. I shouldn't have put it that way; it was very rude of me. But it— oh, how frustrating. It's like—" she searched for the words to explain. "It's like when I went home to my parents' house in England. I needed time just to roam around and remember where I'd put things so long before. I didn't even remember what things. That's how I feel about my own mind right now. I have been away from home, away from Garlanda. I have been Safiye, a slave in a harem. Now I need to get used to being me again."

She wondered at herself saying this. It was true, of course, but it was only part of the truth. Why couldn't she just tell him about her quest for her father's murderer or murderers? Because he was so strong a personality? For fear that he would not allow her to pursue her own goals if he had control over her life? Or was it that she was afraid of falling in love with the small things in him that reminded her so much of Roque?

"Then you do not wish to see me," Renwick said.

"Oh, Renwick, that isn't true. I just need time to think. You're being patient with me, really you are, and I thank you for it."

"Patient?" he asked. "I am far from patient. I will try to respect your wishes, but you must understand it will be difficult. I cannot promise I will give you time to think. I have thought it out and I think I know what is best for both of us."

CHAPTER 35

Renwick managed to stay away for all of three days, after that he showed up everywhere Garlanda went. Leon was her only salvation. She spent much of her time visiting him and he primed his butler with a wealth of excuses to give Renwick whenever he stopped by Leon's villa looking for her. "Miss Cheney? I believe they are picnicking along the shore," he would say. Or, "I believe she and the count have gone to the maritime museum for the day."

Althea gracefully ignored the whole situation for the first few days, but after that, her curiosity could not be contained. She broached the subject one evening as they worked on their hobbies. "Tell me, dear, has Renwick done something to offend you?"

Garlanda looked up from her needlepoint pillowcase. "Oh, no, he's a perfect gentleman."

"No gentleman is perfect."

"Oh, Althea, you know what I mean. Renwick has said and done nothing wrong, but Elaine was my friend. I think he wants to marry me and I cannot. She was my friend and marrying her husband would not be right. Anyway, I do not love Renwick."

Althea wielded her paintbrush, brow furrowed. There was a loud "splat" on the canvas and an immediate backwash of cerulean blue on her smock. She

looked pleased. "Love? What has love to do with a
happy marriage? Marry for convenience or money or
name—and love for pleasure. Whom do you love?"

"A pirate," Garlanda said miserably.

Althea's eyes lit up. "A real pirate? Does he wear an
eyepatch and have a wooden leg and carry a knife in
his teeth and—"

"He's well educated and can recite the works of
Shakespeare and Jonson from memory."

"Oh," Althea said, voice flat. "Not even a parrot?"

Garlanda withered her with a sour look. "Althea,
what I need is you to stand between me and my ardent suitor. I don't wish to be alone with Renwick. I
like him, but I don't trust him—or perhaps I don't trust
myself."

"I think you are imagining the entire thing," Althea
said, gleefully desecrating the canvas even further,
"but if you want a duenna I shall be obligated to
comply."

"Thank you," Garlanda said. She had solved one
problem, but the largest problem was looming larger
and larger on her horizon. What could she do about it?

For the next week Althea and Garlanda managed to
be as one, as far as Renwick was concerned. They
continued to spend most of their time with Leon. Garlanda's return seemed to have a salutary effect on
him. He improved daily, showing more strength and
better appetite. There were bad days naturally, and
those times Garlanda would have his servants set up a
comfortable chaise on the wide balcony overlooking
the gardens and they would sit there in the sun—
Garlanda reading, Leon listening or napping.

But Leon's mind was never feeble, no matter what traitorous tricks his body played on him. He determined that Garlanda should know Polish and for two days he addressed her only in that language. With sufficient gestures and facial expressions, she was able to understand a good deal of what he was saying in a remarkably short time. He also made her don dueling gear and give him an exhibition of how much she remembered.

One evening as she was leaving Renwick caught her alone. He had dismissed his coach so that she could not be forewarned of his presence when she arrived home. Althea was out, so there was nothing to do but see him privately. It was as she had feared. "Your modesty becomes you, my love," he said, "but you are no longer a virgin child who needs a chaperone every minute."

"I can't imagine what you mean?"

"Have you forgotten how well we know each other? You cannot playact with me. I want you and there's no reason why we should not have each other now."

"Is this a proposal?" she asked, trying to avoid contact with him by busying herself pouring two glasses of sherry. He took the decanter from her hand. He set it on the table and wrapped her in a bruising embrace. Garlanda regarded his kiss with cool analysis. Not as moving as she remembered. Had he changed? No, it was her—her experience with the pasha, more specifically. She pulled away. "Would you care for some sherry?"

"I want only you."

"Then you *are* proposing?"

"Yes, I am. The loss of Elaine—I need your sweetness, your courage to heal me."

"Then I will consider it," she said, further disengaging herself from his grip.

"Consider! What is there to consider?" *If you only knew*, she thought bitterly. "You are free to wed and so am I now," he went on. "There is nothing to stop us."

"But you are still in mourning for your wife."

He snapped his fingers. "Only for a short time more. I am traveling to Paris next week and will be gone a month. When I return we will be married."

"If I accept."

"You will accept. I assure you."

You would not assure me if you knew me as well as you think. "I will let you know my decision when you return from Paris," she said.

"Garlanda, darling, why are you being this way? I can't understand it. Ah, well, never mind. If you wish to play this role, go ahead. But do have your wedding dress picked out when I get back." One more kiss with more force than tenderness and he was gone.

Garlanda was awake long that night, weighing and considering what to do. Finally she decided to talk it over with Leon before deciding.

"Has Althea told you about my father's death?" she asked him the next morning when she visited him.

"Well, she has attempted to, but Althea's version is, naturally, rather garbled."

"Do you mind terribly if I explain it all to you and get your impressions?"

"I should be charmed," he said, motioning to a servant that they would take their tea on the balcony.

Garlanda told him of her mother's dying words, the letter in the secret drawer, and her visit to Lord Bramson who claimed to have lost the letter from the ambassador in Paris.

"I presume you went back to see him?" Leon said.

"Not in person. I wrote to him several times. He always answered me very politely but claimed that the letter never turned up."

"Do you not find that a little strange?"

"More than strange. A lie, I'm sure. The odd thing is that I have always thought of Lord Bramson as an honorable man, and I still do in spite of everything. I think he's lying, but for what he considers a very good reason. I want to know what it is. Anyway, when Althea and I got to France—" she began and related the story of the night at the palace at Versailles and their subsequent journey to Nice.

"You are certain that the grave was new?"

"Absolutely. The stone could not have been in place for more than a few hours—the plants at least. In fact, it was not a grave, just a headstone. We dug around a bit and the soil was not disturbed except at the base of the marker."

"So the trail has now led you back here? Have you talked to Sir George yet?"

"No. I wanted to think of the right approach. I think there is a conspiracy among the ambassadors to keep information from me. In all this time I've been gone Sir George was almost certainly told of my questions and also told how to answer them. They are answers that would not be real truths, no doubt."

"Assuming that any of them thought you would ever find your way back and the chances of that were not good."

"Tell me, Leon, is this all my imagination? What would you do?"

"I don't believe it is your imagination, no. As to what I'd do, that would depend on how badly I wanted the truth."

"Very badly."

"Why?"

"I don't know why. I've asked myself that many times. But I *must* know. The truth has a value of its own, doesn't it?"

"I've always felt that it did, but you may be getting yourself into a great deal more distress by pursuing this, and I'm not sure the truth of the matter will be sufficient reward. Suppose, for instance, that your father got into a common brawl in a pub over a woman and the government is simply covering up the truth to save embarrassment for everyone."

"It couldn't be anything like that!"

"But, my dear, it *could* be. You've said yourself that you hardly knew your father even when you were a child and haven't seen him since you were four or five. Besides, I meant that only as an example of what I mean when I say that the truth may not be worth knowing. It may be something sordid and ordinary that you'd be happier not knowing.

"But," he went on with a suggestion of a twinkle, "if it were me, I would want to know anyway. And, next to myself, you are the most curious person I know."

"Thank you, Leon, for understanding. You are the only person who does. What can I do next, though?"

"Let me consider it for a day or two and do some asking about among my acquaintances."

"Leon, there is another problem." She got up and walked to the balcony rail and gripped it until her knuckles stood out white. "Time, you see, is suddenly in short supply to me."

"Why? Is there something wrong?"

"Renwick Ridgely wants me to marry him."

"And you don't want to? That's an easy problem. Just turn him down, prettily. You can do that."

"I'm afraid to marry him. I'm rather afraid of him altogether, in fact, and I don't know why. But I *need* to get married. Right away."

"What do you—Oh, I see. When are you due?"

"Six months," she said.

"Who is the father?" Leon asked coolly.

"That's the very worst! I don't know." She turned to face him. He didn't look the least bit shocked for which she was grateful. "It could be the pasha—or Roque—I—I can't tell."

"M-m-m, I see. What do you think is the solution?" Leon asked.

"I suppose I must marry Renwick, but he will know soon that—no, I can't do it. But I can't have the child without giving it a name. I don't care anymore for my own sake. The strictures of society have been proved empty, but I cannot force that judgment on a child. I want to pursue the matter of my father's death and no husband would condone a wife wanting to spend her time harassing embassies, even if he would want to be responsible for another man's child. Oh, Leon, I don't know what to do! There doesn't appear to be any solution. I should not have bothered you with all this, you are a dear, but not a miracle man."

Leon leaned back and took a long sip of his tea. Finally, he said, "Oh, but I am! I thought you knew that by now. There is a very simple solution."

"What!"

"Marry me, of course."

Garlanda stared at him is disbelief. "You can't mean that!"

"Why can't I? Jareski–Yanoviak is a perfectly respectable name to give a child—unspellable, but respectable."

"But, Leon, you don't want to marry me!"

"Why shouldn't I? I haven't long to live, no heirs that I know of," he added with a laugh, "and I think you and I have always been congenial companions. Marry me and in a short time you will be a rich young widow."

"Oh, Leon, don't talk this way, please. You aren't going to die. You're better every day."

"It is only temporary, I can tell. There is no point in being a silly romantic about it. I'm dying and it remains to me to do one worthwhile act. You cannot deny me that. If you and your child do not inherit my earthly goods, there will be a dozen Polish second cousins fighting over it for the next fifty years. By that time it will all be dissolved in legal fees. Incidentally, it would be a purely Platonic marriage. I do not need to exact payment of the usual kind."

"I don't know what to say."

"Say yes. You have no other choice, as you told me, and this solution would be to your advantage and to mine."

"How would it be to your advantage?"

"Why, you could read to me in the middle of the night, when I can't sleep. Isn't that to my advantage?"

"Leon, you are so dear. How can I possibly thank you?"

"By reading to me. Get out that book we were working on yesterday, and I want to hear the Polish poem you were to have learned by today."

Althea didn't believe her at first, then she passed into a stage of hysterical laughter and only later was able to admit that it was really a very sensible idea. Garlanda explained the circumstances to her and she,

like Leon, was not the least bit shocked by Garlanda's
pregnancy. The wedding was the next week and very
small, just Father Gacom, who officiated, Althea, and
a few of Leon's friends who lived in Marseille. They
had waited until Renwick left for Paris for fear that
he would hear about the wedding and make a scene.
He was capable of doing so, Garlanda thought. The
count's wedding gift to her was the beautiful black
Andalusian filly she had ridden in England. Garlanda
named her Kismet.

True to his own prediction, Leon's health did begin
to decline. But he never complained and someone
who did not know him well might not have even suspected he was ill. Oddly enough, it was Garlanda
whose health concerned them more of the time. Her
pregnancy was going badly, with cramping and slight
occasional bleeding. Leon's physician examined her
and ordered complete rest. Althea moved into the
villa with them to take care of Garlanda. Though
Leon and Garlanda spent most of their time sitting in
the sun on chaises, the conversation was always as
bright and healthy and entertaining as it had been in
happier times in London.

Garlanda sent a short letter to Renwick when he returned from Paris. She told him she was married and
said that, owing to ill health, she was unable to invite
him for a visit. There was no reply.

Leon had instructed Garlanda that she was not to
leave the villa during her pregnancy nor for three
months afterward. By that time she could simply
emerge with a well-developed infant and no one
would know just how long after her marriage the
child had been born. There would be gossip, of
course, but there was always gossip. The child would
not have the official stigma of bastardy attached to it.

The arrangement suited the three of them ideally. Leon and Garlanda were both quite content with only each other for company. When his friends called upon him, Garlanda would slip away before they were shown in and Leon made her excuses. Althea, who liked company, was entirely free to visit her friends in Marseille. She came home one day with the news that she had met Renwick at a party and he refused to speak to her. She was very amusing about it all, but Garlanda's replies were weak and listless.

"What's wrong?" Althea asked. "Are you feeling unwell?"

"Yes. I think—I'm afraid—Oh, Althea, I'm going to lose the baby!" she cried.

"No, you won't! Just rest and I'll send for the doctor right away."

She hurried out and a few minutes later Leon entered the room. "Althea told me," he said and pulled a chair to the bedside. "Is there anything I can do?"

A sharp spasm of pain tore through her body. She could only gasp and hold to Leon's hand desperately. Finally the wave of agony ebbed a little and she said, "Leon, stay with me, please stay with me!"

"I shan't leave you, my dear girl." And he stayed with her through the night, allowing her to crush his hand when the pains came, mopping her sweating forehead with eau-de-cologne and helping to gently turn her to her side from time to time so that Althea could remove and replace the blood-soaked bedding.

The doctor could do nothing and after the first hour or so, admitted as much. He gave her a draught of bitter-tasting liquid for pain. She vomited it up. He put cold compresses on her abdomen in a desperate effort to stop the bleeding and it only made her so cold that her teeth chattered violently and she bit her tongue. "I'm going to die!" she cried out.

"Don't be silly, you're not!" Althea said. But even through her mad haze of pain, Garlanda could see the look Althea exchanged with the doctor. He nodded.

I am dying, Garlanda thought, *and they don't want me to know. I won't die! I can't die now. There is too much to do and Leon needs me. Leon!*

"Please, Garlanda, stop thrashing!" Althea said.

In a brief lucid flash Garlanda realized something. Leon was dying too and he was not behaving like this. He, too, must be in pain and have the same fear she felt now. "Leon," she whispered, "Hold me, please. Let me have some of your strength and courage."

Leon lifted her slightly and sat on the bed with her head against his chest. He stroked her hair and murmured in Polish. She felt a strange sense of calm. After a while he lifted her head and said, "You must drink some of this again and you must keep it down this time." There was tender determination in his voice. She took a sip and gagged. She could feel a renewed rush of blood. She swallowed the rest of the liquid in one awful gulp and forced herself not to gag again.

It wasn't long before it started working. She felt the pain diminishing and a devastating sleepiness came over her. Leon still held her and crooned foreign comfort. She fell into a deep, dreamless sleep from which one sharp, endless pain half-awakened her, but could not keep her conscious.

When she finally awoke the late afternoon sun was casting warm orange shafts into the room. She looked around, barely able to move her head. Leon was in a chair beside the bed and Althea was asleep on a small cot by the window. "Leon?" she whispered.

His eyes were instantly open. "You're awake at last," he said and came to her side.

"The babe—?"

He shook his head sadly. "I'm sorry—"

"Leon, you should be resting. You look as bad as I feel."

"No, I'm fine. Just cramped from sitting in that chair. I'm having it burned in your honor tonight. I had no idea how uncomfortable it was."

"Darling, you're awake!" Althea said sleepily. "How do you feel?"

"Althea, that's ridiculous," Leon said. "How do you think she feels?"

Garlanda fell back asleep to the sweet music of Leon and Althea arguing amiably.

CHAPTER 36

"We thought we were going to lose you as well as the baby," Althea admitted later. She was taking Garlanda for a short and very slow walk in the gardens. It was the first time Garlanda had been outside. Althea had adjusted herself to the invalid pace that was the best that Leon or Garlanda could do.

"I wouldn't have lived except for Leon," Garlanda said, taking his hand and noting how hot and dry it felt. He said nothing.

Althea hung back for a moment conferring with a servant who had run up behind them. "Excuse me, won't you?" she said. "There is some sort of tempest in the kitchens that needs my attention." She rushed away.

Leon gestured wordlessly to a stone bench next to a cool, splashing fountain and they both sat down. Garlanda sat staring at the sparkling water dancing in the sun. How peaceful life was. How utterly serene she felt. Her recovery was taking a long time owing to the great amount of blood she had lost, but it had served to slow life to a dreamy standstill. "You are almost recovered," Leon interrupted her thoughts.

"Yes, thanks to you."

"I had nothing to do with it," Leon brushed off her gratitude. "What are you going to do now?"

"Do? I don't know. Have luncheon and resume our reading this afternoon and there's always mending—"

"I don't mean today. I mean what are you going to do with your future?"

"Oh, Leon, I don't want a future. I just want it to stay today forever and ever. Must I decide on something? We'll just go on as we were before—won't we?"

"No. There's no reason for you to stay here."

"What do you mean?"

"Well, our marriage was created to help you out of your social difficulties regarding your pregnancy. Unfortunately, you no longer have to consider that."

"Are you throwing me out, Leon?" She laughed.

"I'm simply giving you the opportunity to leave. The marriage can be annulled, or you can simply go on your way and be a widow shortly. Whichever you prefer."

She looked at him sharply. "Leon, are you serious?"

"Naturally I am, my dear."

"Why Leon, I wouldn't leave you."

"You must, Garlanda. I am a dying man, it won't be pleasant—"

"I do not ask life to be pleasant anymore. Staying by me was not enjoyable to you, I'm sure, but you did it."

"Because I cared for you."

"And what makes you think I care less? I'm staying, Leon, and that's that! You shall have to die to get away from me."

He rose and took her hand. With enormous stateliness he kissed it and actually smiled. "Shall we go rescue the cook from Althea?" he asked.

"If we don't, she may give notice and we'll all go hungry tonight."

"I've been thinking about your father," he said as

they strolled toward the house. "The fact that he came to Marseille is significant, I think."

"Why is that?"

"Marseille is known all over the world as the 'jumping off place' of Europe. It is said that more men change their names here than anywhere else."

"Change their names?"

"Yes, anyone who wishes to leave their wives or debts or reputations behind comes here to assume a new identity. Very possibly that's what your father was trying to do—trace someone who was attempting to disappear. But apparently whoever he was following caught on and killed him before leaving."

Leon sat down on another bench for a moment to catch his breath. "I don't think you need look anywhere but here for information of what he was doing, who he was trailing."

"How shall I go about finding out then?"

"As flattering as it is to be looked upon as an all-knowing sage, I must admit that I haven't got the answer to that. I do suggest, however, that you regard anyone who tells you where he went from here with the gravest suspicion, for I don't believe he got anywhere from Marseille. I have had visitors from time to time while you were ill, and I have been trying to bring up the subject of his death and see if anyone reacts."

"Have they?"

"So far—no. But there is a large semipermanent English community here and I am certain that someone among them knows something."

"I should check the cemeteries," Garlanda said.

"I've already done so, or rather, my servants have. There is no headstone with his name, but that means little. You don't murder a prominent man then draw attention to the fact by putting up a monument to him."

"Then what can we do?"

"We can continue to keep our ears open. Unfortunately, I'm going to have to drop out of the search shortly."

"Leon!"

"I'm not really even well enough now to receive visitors, but I will be gone soon and I wish to discuss the actions you must then take."

"Please don't talk like that."

"Garlanda, you are not a silly girl. Don't behave like one," he said sharply. "We know that I am dying and I propose to do so in a dignified way. That means dropping this silly social pretense of acting like it isn't happening. I know your protests are designed to convince me of your fondness for me, but it is unnecessary to do so. Now I will not discuss your plans any further unless you promise me that you will stop pretending to believe I will recover." He stood up, ready to return to the house.

She put her arm around his waist and smiled up at him. "Alright. You are dying, Leon. I admit it—I don't like it—I abhor the idea for all sorts of selfish and a few *unselfish* reasons, but I admit the reality of it."

"Now," he said in a let's-get-down-to-business voice, "if we accept the premise that all your clues are here in Marseille—"

"Yes?"

"And that therefore someone among the English in Marseille holds valuable information."

"Yes."

"Then it is necessary for you to make yourself acquainted with as many of those people as you can—become a social butterfly, in other words."

"Me! How absurd. I won't be accepted—not after all that's happened to me."

"Nonsense, you will be a very wealthy, very beautiful young widow with an exotic past. Social judgment is not so harsh here as it is in England, not even among the English. You will not have rich dowagers begging you to marry their only sons, but there will be men lining up at your door, and where men want to go, their women make sure they go as well."

"You haven't any idea who might be most useful?"

"Not in the least yet. It will be necessary for you to become friendly with as many people as possible and my funeral will be a grand place to start."

Garlanda bit back an exclamation. How could anyone be so horribly realistic? She remembered the nearly hysterical fear she had of dying only a short time before. "You will delay it as long as decently possible," Leon went on, "so that everyone knows about it and attends—a sort of grim 'coming out,' you might say." Leon went on to detail what she must do when he died. He had it all planned in detail and drilled her after the explanation.

The next day Althea discovered Garlanda in her room dressed in black from head to toe. "Heavens, child! Why are you in that?"

"I'm practicing for Leon's funeral," Garlanda answered, matter-of-factly adjusting her hat.

"What a positively *awful* thing to say! Poor Leon, if he knew—"

"Oh, he does know. Come along, I am supposed to model this for him."

"Have you lost your wits!" Althea fairly screamed. "This is madness!"

"No, it's not. Come with me, you'll see."

Althea trailed along, exhorting Garlanda to return

to her room and forget this insanity. At the door of Leon's bedroom Althea was still begging in a suppressed hiss.

"Come in," Leon called at Garlanda's light knock. "Ah, the dress. Here, get into the light, let me see. Hm-m-m," he considered to the accompaniment of Althea's wordless sputtering. "The veil is far too heavy. Your lovely face can hardly be seen, and the dress doesn't hang right. I suppose it's all the weight you've lost. You must either eat like a pig or get the seams taken in. And you must look—well, more wistful than sad. Absolutely *no* crying. It will make you look like a groggy frog. Now I've got the guest list made up for the ball. Althea!" he said. "You know everyone in Marseille. Look this over and see if there's anyone we've left out." He handed her a number of papers inscribed with his neat, even handwriting.

"But what is this for?" Althea asked.

"It's a guest list for a grand party. Everyone who is the least bit important must be invited," Leon explained.

"A party? But Leon, you are not well enough. Won't it be an awful strain on both of you?"

"Don't worry, Althea my sweet. I'm not going to the party."

"Then why have it? Where do you think you're going that you won't be here?"

"I'm going to my grave. I'll probably be roasting merrily in hell by the time the party is given."

"Now look here, Leon, you are a grown man and not well, and I suppose you must be allowed your whims, macabre as they may be. But Garlanda! How can you participate in this kind of—"

"It's to be a masquerade, Althea. Perhaps you better start thinking about your costume," Leon cut in.

"This is positively vile and despicable!" Althea raged. "I cannot even stay in the room with this sort of talk." With that she went to the door, walking hard on her heels.

"She'll be back within half an hour," Leon whispered to Garlanda, then louder he said, "Don't forget the guest list, Althea."

She stomped back to the table beside the bed, snatched up the handful of papers, favored them both with a splendid glare, and stormed out of the room, slamming the door violently. Leon chuckled and Garlanda laughed until tears obscured her vision and her sides hurt.

Leon's death was like Leon's life—dignified, tasteful, and at his own leisurely pace. He gradually weakened, but made no mention of it. He accepted the ministrations that were necessary, like trays of food in his room and rejected all others, like sympathy, with cutting wit. When he was able to read aloud to Garlanda on the terrace without coughing, he did so. Other times, she did the reading. They worked their way through Shakespeare's sonnets, and several Restoration comedies, which Althea and Garlanda took turns reading and acting. A slim volume of Polish verse was turned up and they read that.

One day, after discussing the final form of the guest list for the postmortem party and selecting the script style for the invitations, Leon asked Garlanda to find the Polish poems and reread a few of them for him. While she was reading, he closed his eyes.

This was not unusual. He frequently took short

naps and Garlanda laid the book aside and watched him sleeping. He would awake in a few minutes. Wouldn't he? She wasn't aware at first that he was growing paler and his breathing was becoming more and more shallow. She rose and put her hand to his brow. Instead of the usual feverish warmth, his skin was cool. She touched his shoulder. "Leon?" she whispered. "Leon, wake up now. You're getting chilled, you should be inside."

There was no response. His breathing, faint as it was, did not change. "Leon!" she said a little louder and aware of the thin edge of hysteria in her voice. "Leon, *please* wake up."

Still nothing.

She knotted her fingers together, closed her eyes, and took a deep breath. *Calm,* she told herself, *stay calm. Do not make a scene.* She stepped into the cool interior of the villa and pulled a tapestry cord to summon the butler, then sat by Leon holding his nearly lifeless hand until the servant arrived.

"Billings," she said very calmly, "please help me get the count to his room."

Billings, who had been the count's servant for many years, took in the situation in a glance and was blinking back tears. "Yes, madam."

They took him upstairs and for almost two days Garlanda sat by his bed. Althea joined her for hours at a time and the servants would tap lightly at the door at frequent intervals to inquire if he was any better. They were red-eyed and begged to relieve her of her vigil so she could rest, but she would not leave his side. Sometimes he would stir slightly or mumble something unintelligible and hope would spring up in her heart, but then he would slip back into the quiet state for hours and Garlanda would have to fight down the impulse to shake him and scream at him to wake, please wake.

Leon had become such a vital part of her life that she couldn't imagine going on without him. It was during this long wait for the inevitable that she realized that, of all men in her life, she loved Leon best— Leon who had never touched her except in friendship or comfort. A very different sort of love, for Leon was a very different sort of man, but a sort that could have lasted her the rest of her life, had it been allowed her.

As she sat there in the darkened room, listening to his shallow breathing and staring at his thin, distinguished face, she remembered all the ways he had touched and changed her life. She chuckled aloud at the memory of their adventure at the Mermaid and the look on his face when she bellowed for rum and gunpowder to drink and of their wild ride out of Rye with enraged pirates chasing them. It was Leon who had taken her jewels and had them set, Leon had encouraged her to go with Althea to France. He had spent many hours of his time teaching her the fine points of the art of fencing. He had made a gift of his native language to her, his name, his fortune, and his own ebbing strength when she had needed it the most.

She knelt on the floor at the side of the bed and took hold of his cool, thin hand. "Please, Leon," she wept quietly, "please don't die. Please. Please live. I can't go on without you. You are too good to die. We need you. I need you."

Tears ran unheeded down her cheeks and her breathing was ragged with sorrow. "Oh, God, please let me keep him. Don't take him. Another year, just another week." She had known this was coming, she had thought she was prepared for it, but she had been wrong. She could not have imagined how much of her was being torn away from her soul. Leon had been so good to her, so good for her. It was wrong, it was unfair, unjust!

"Leon, Leon, Leon, stay, live. Oh, Leon, please don't die. Don't leave me."

She felt the tiniest of pressure on her hand. She lifted her face and looked at him. His eyes were open slightly and the corners of his thin mouth were curved up ever so slightly, maybe it was just her imagination. "Leon!" she said, and it came out in an incoherent sob.

His lips moved. "Frog," he said in an almost inaudible voice. Then he closed his eyes. He meant she must not cry, she looked like a frog, she realized. But she could not stop.

"I'm sorry. I'm sorry," she said, trying to stop the tears.

"Sh-h-h," his voice trailed off into a sibilant whisper. Then it stopped.

It stopped.

His breathing stopped. His eyelids flew open and he looked straight at her for a moment in defiant farewell. In that second she realized what he had known. That he was not leaving her. That the essence of Leon—the wit, the love, the curiosity, the dignity that was Leon would remain with her forever.

The hand she held was limp now, the nails going bluish. She folded his hands over his chest and gently closed his vacant eyes. Then she wiped her hands across her eyes, trying to dry the tears. She looked down at him once more. He was at peace. She had been unaware of the lines of pain and weariness gath-

ering in his face over the months, they had come so
gradually. Now they were gone in a minute. He was
at peace.

"Good-bye, Leon," she whispered. "Thank you." She
kissed his forehead then put her face to the side of his
and said again, very quietly, "Thank you."

CHAPTER 37

In a strange way Garlanda almost enjoyed Leon's funeral. It was as if Leon were at her side, silently praising the way she was carrying out his instructions and from time to time whispering, "Didn't I tell you it would be this way?"

She had sent word to the English embassy of his death with a private note to Sir George Young–Brookes saying that she was too distressed to get word to all of Leon's friends and would he please do so for her. Sir George, of course, had little idea of just who Leon's friends were so he told practically everyone. Coming from the ambassador, most of them regarded it as a request to come. This was just what Leon had predicted would happen.

He was buried with great pomp and an enormous headstone with his coat of arms carved on it. The cemetery was packed to overflowing with Leon's real friends and a wealth of curious acquaintances.

"Had he any children?" Garlanda heard a good-looking young man ask his companion.

"Not that I know of."

"Then that pretty widow must be a rich woman now?"

Garlanda smiled to herself behind her veil.

"Very handsome, he was," a diamond-bedecked crone said.

"—Excellent horseman—"

"—Old family—some sort of break—"

"—Only son—hundreds of thousands of pounds—"

Leon had predicted it all so accurately. The funeral was like sharing a private joke with him. When it was over she went back to the big villa that was now hers and began her preparations for the next stage of her life—as planned by Leon.

Two weeks later a dozen of Leon's friends received invitations to have tea with the Countess Jareski–Yanoviak. It was something they wouldn't have missed for the world and were further startled when the bereaved widow appeared in a low-cut yellow satin gown. "You must excuse my appearance," she said. "But I am following my dear late husband's" (how odd that sounded in her own ears!) "last wishes."

"Indeed, madam," Count Koniecyzska said.

"Yes, he despised the idea of lengthy mourning and demanded that I dispose of my widow's weeds within a fortnight. He said I would do his memory greater honor if I would move back into the world and among his friends." She had rehearsed this speech to Leon, and she felt that he would be pleased with her delivery and the reception it got.

"Very sensible and also very much Leon," an old gentleman named De Bohun said.

"But do you think it's quite proper?" his wife worried.

"No, it's not at all—at least not if we were back in England," Garlanda admitted to the woman. "But my husband held strong views of such things and out of my love for him, I am bound to respect his desires in this matter."

"Of course you are, my dear," the woman said and patted her hand.

"My husband had also requested that I hold—well, a ball—in his honor. You see, this is all rather awkward for me and I thought, as his friends, you might be willing to come to my aid."

A chorus of assent went up.

"You see," she went on, "he prepared a guest list for this ball and asked that it take place one month after his demise. All of you who knew him well can understand—or at least accept that, but I must depend upon you to make the other guests know that I do this out of respect for him, not callousness."

"You can depend on us," De Bohun answered.

"You certainly can!" his wife seconded.

"Then I shall send out the invitations at the end of the week and I hope you will help defend my action to those who did not know Leon as well as we did." Garlanda then served them tea, chatted pleasantly with them about the weather, and sent them on their way.

"Well?" Althea asked when the guests had left.

"Just as Leon said," Garlanda answered. "I grow more impressed every day with how well he knew human nature."

"De Bohun's wife stopped me on her way out and raved about what a sweet, brave girl you are."

"I'm glad."

"You should be. She's as much an eccentric in her own way as Leon was, I suppose that's why they got along, but she's the final arbiter of what is acceptable in Marseille. If she likes you, you will have no problems. Just why are you having this party anyway, if you don't mind my asking?"

"Because Leon felt it was the best way to fling my-self into the lap of society."

"And just why do you wish to do such a thing? I would have thought your experiences in London would have cured you of wanting to sit in the 'lap' of society, as you put it."

"It did, but this is for a particular purpose. Leon felt that the key to Papa's death was hidden in the English sector of Marseille, and I must get to know all those people to find anything out."

"And the party is a way of meeting them?"

"Yes. Every guest at my party will be obligated to return an invitation. The ball will also serve to announce my somewhat precipitous return to society."

"That's rather more calculating than I would have thought you capable of," Althea said.

"Someone murdered my father," Garlanda answered. "That's rather calculating, too, don't you think? Would you unlace me?" she said, turning her back on Althea. "According to Leon, the news of the forthcoming invitations will have spread by the end of the week. The ladies will all be scandalized, but will nevertheless wave their invitations under the noses of their less fortunate friends."

"That sounds like Leon!" Althea laughed.

"He really did enjoy planning this."

"I'm sure he did. I doubt that many men have left this life on such a wave of smug self-congratulation as Leon did. I do miss him terribly."

"I don't. I mean, he seems to still be here. I sometimes feel that he's just stepped out for the afternoon and will soon be back. But, of course, he won't." She embraced her aunt. "Oh, Althea," she cried, "I *do* miss him."

* * *

"Countess Jareski–Yanoviak."

"Countess," Sir George said politely, rising from his chair to take Garlanda's hand.

She smiled and rustled to a stop, watered silk skirts brushing the walnut parquet floor. "Sir George, I do hate to disturb you, but I would like to ask you about my father's death."

"Your father was—"

"Sir Robert Cheney," she said still smiling although behind the friendly facade she was frosted with tension.

"Yes, of course. What do you want to know? We received a notice saying he had expired in the spring of '92. That was four years ago."

"Did this notice say where or how he had died?"

He frowned. "No. Odd, isn't it? I had never stopped to consider that before, but no, the notice did not say where or how he died. Most irregular. Shall I write the home office in London and inquire for you?"

"I have already been there," she replied, tapping her feather fan impatiently on his desk. Anger sizzled underneath her cool exterior. "I am most upset with all this," she said. Leon would disapprove, could he but see her now. She was being too unsubtle, losing all stealth.

Sir George asked her to be seated while he checked his files for further information. He went in the next room. There was a clicking sound then two giant dogs burst in the room.

The clerk at the nearest desk looked up. "Zeus! Jove! Leave the lady alone! Be careful, madam, they are very fierce, but they will not bother you if you ignore them." He excused himself and returned in a moment with a tray of tea and biscuits for her then went back to work.

The massive, rough-coated wolfhounds never looked away from Garlanda. As the minutes ticked by she peered into the next room and saw that Sir George was still digging through the files. She looked back at the dogs. Their stares were utterly unwavering. She began to talk to them in a low, soothing voice. "Hello, Zeus, hello, Jove. I wish you would stop burning holes in me with your eyes. Nice doggies, nice doggies. Want a biscuit? Here, have a biscuit."

The dogs stood up, sniffed her outstretched hand and gave her austere looks that said she must set the two biscuits down before they would accept them. She did. The tea biscuits vanished as if by canine magic. She held out two more biscuits. This time the dogs crowded in close and let her pat them. By the time Sir George returned the tea biscuits were gone and the dogs were her best friends.

"Countess! Please! Those are savage animals! They are meant to guard the embassy and must not be treated as pets or it will break down their discipline."

"I'm sorry," she said with feigned meekness. "Were you able to find anything?"

"No, I didn't," he said rather abruptly. She sensed that his attitude had changed. Before, he had seemed as perplexed as she was, now he was cutting off the inquiry. "I shall be happy to look into the matter further at a later time, but for now—"

"Thank you," she said politely, feeling as she left that she was being swept out the door like last night's dinner crumbs. What had caused the change in Sir George? What was in those files?

She could not follow Leon's advice and wait. She was too impatient to simply wait for news of her father. She decided to break into the embassy. She wanted to see those files of Sir George's.

She crept from the villa one dark night, dressed in black clothing that had once been Leon's. She had a feeling Leon would have been amused had he been able to see her in his clothes, hair pulled up under a hat, riding her black mare, Kismet, through the night streets of Marseille. Although it was late the streets were not entirely deserted. But no one approached Garlanda. She wore a brace of dueling pistols and carried a dagger under her jacket. The pistols undoubtedly contributed to the fact that a seemingly effeminate "youth" such as herself was not bothered by the street people who flourished in the side lanes after decent citizens were abed.

Kismet picked her way over the brick streets as evenly as the dirt lanes. When they were nearly to the embassy, Garlanda reined the mare in and stopped to think out her plan. There was an alley behind the embassy, perhaps she would not be so noticeable there. It would take some doing to scale the fence that surrounded the building. That still left the dogs to contend with. She hoped they had not forgotten the petting and biscuits she had lavished on them a few days earlier.

Garlanda nudged Kismet with her toes. The trim black hunter turned down the alley with dainty hooves clopping. That would never do—far too much noise! Garlanda stopped behind a building and rummaged in a barrel. She located some shabby garments and set to work tying them on the mare's steel-shod feet. When they moved on, Kismet's footsteps were muffled.

The alley was deserted with the exception of a few greasy rats who peered out from behind moldering rubbish with furtive, cunning eyes. The sight of their anxious greediness and twitching, reptilian tails made Garlanda shudder with distaste. She had the morbid thought that she might have them for cellmates soon should she be caught. Could a countess be thrown in jail?

Kismet came to a halt at the embassy fence although her rider had not signaled her to. "Easy, *ma petite*, easy Kismet," Garlanda soothed, patting the mare's sleek neck and clinging to the fence. "I've got to stand on your back now, don't buck. Easy, easy—"

Garlanda looped the reins around an iron post and stood up on the saddle. Amazingly, the mare let her do it, but she laid her ears back, snorted in disgust at the entire adventure and stood still. Garlanda balanced precariously, seized a metal rail, inhaled sharply, and sprang up. She was too short to make it to the top in a single try and now she hung limply, black-gloved hands sliding on the smooth iron surface. Her muscles went slack with nervous fear, then she looked down. The alley floor was broken cobblestones and hard, packed earth. A fall would break an ankle or leg easily. Kismet had moved a few feet away.

Fear gave her impetus she needed. Her body tightened. She gave a sudden, almost spastic lurch that brought her to within a handspan of the pointed iron caps that marched across the top of the fence like brutal sentinels. Garlanda hung, scrambled, found a place for her small booted feet. She surged upward, seizing hold of the metal points. Another lunge and she was on top, standing over the vicious spearheads of the fence.

There was the sound of hurrying paws and big bodies crashing through the brush below. A wary "woof" sounded. Two enormous shaggy wolfhounds burst through the flower hedges and began a round of angry barking. "Zeus! Jove! It's alright, it's only me. Zeus, hello, remember me? Do you, old boy? Here—this should help your memory." She dug tea cakes out of her deep pocket. The dogs stood upon their hind legs, front paws pressed against the fence. Garlanda pitched them a few of the delicacies and while they ate, she slid down the fence, landing somewhat clumsily on her left ankle. The dogs jostled against her but there was no hostility in it. She fed them more cakes calling them by name. They made no attempt to keep her away from the embassy building, but fell all over themselves to escort her.

The building was as dark and menacing as a feral beast crouched in the dark awaiting the approach of its prey. The thought made the fine hairs on the back of her neck stand up. What if there were guards? More dogs? She might be shot, killed, imprisoned. Or—she might discover the truth.

That thought emboldened her. She crept to a window. Locked. She tried several more, all to no avail. At last she backed up and tilted her head back. A window was open on the second floor, if she could get up there. But after the dangerous fence, scaling a building with only vines, tiny toeholds between bricks and her own strength to pull her up seemed natural. She began to climb.

It was Sir George's room and he was snoring soundly in the big, high-postered bed. She pulled herself through the window and crossed the room. The snoring neither slackened nor abated. She winced as the door handle creaked in her trembling hand.

The snoring caught and hovered on an inhalation of impressive magnitude. Garlanda dropped silently to the floor and waited. There was a sound of restless tossing and a long noiseless interval that made her stomach contract with sick fear. The tension was almost painful; every nerve in her body tightly stretched as a bow being fitted with an arrow.

And then the ambassador loudly exhaled with the force of a whale. Garlanda exhaled, too, feeble with relief. Sir George resumed his hearty snoring and Garlanda tried the door again. It creaked still, but this time he did not stir. She slipped out into the hall, knees banging together as she struggled to close the heavy door.

Now, downstairs to the files.

It was easy to tell Sir George was a bachelor—the dust between the stair rails was wooly with age. He probably paid little attention to what the household staff did as long as a semblance of dinner made its nightly appearance. She wondered where Freddie's room was.

Her mind wandered as she crept slowly down the steps. Freddie. Suppose he was really guilty of treason and had been feeding information to the pirates? Surely not. But if he was innocent, why hadn't he defended himself when she brought it up? Oh, men were all so stiffly silly when their pride was at stake!

A stair squeaked. She hesitated. When there was no sound of movement anywhere in response, she continued. The embassy offices were abustle with nothingness. She looked about. Books, ledgers, furniture, desks, the place was so packed she fully expected to see people working despite the hour and lack of light. An aura of phantom business hung in the room like a pall of smoke.

She shut the door and fumbled for a lantern. It lit with the minimum of resistance and the maximum of stench. She had to hold her breath for a moment at the reek of rank whale oil. The filing cabinets were huge and endless. "C" for Cheney. Where were the "Ch"s? She put the lamp on a desk beside the "C" drawer and started to dig through. It was packed.

There! A file titled "Cheney." It was full of correspondence to and from her father. Misty tears came to her eyes at his letters and notes, even though they were impersonal business missives. She recognized his clear, flowing script on sheet after sheet of paper the color of old lace with the embassy letterhead stamped on it in crisp, clean black. Bills, requests, reminders, orders—all there, written by her dead father. It seemed to bring him closer despite the passage of time.

For the first time her patriotism faltered. She tried to tell herself he had died in the service of his country and that was the finest death a gentleman could have had. But still, doubts bit at her annoyingly. She swallowed and went on wading through the fat file on her father. She skimmed over account after account until at last she found what she sought. Her eyes smarted from the strain of reading so much in the ill-lit room, but she knew that this was what she had come for.

An official communication from Lord Bramson was the last entry under "Cheney." She held the thick textured parchment envelope open, fingers shaking. It took her three tries to pluck the neatly creased paper from the envelope and unfold it.

4th February, 1692

The Honourable Sir George Young–Brookes, K.G.

Lord Bramson has instructed me to inform alle ambassadors that Sir Rbt. Cheney is to be considered deceased. It is your Responsibilitie to publishe Notice of this accounte in the Newsheetes of your Citie. Any inquiries shoulde be addressed to Lord Bramson.

Respectfullie
Jonathan Fixley, Clerke

Considered deceased? Considered?

What did that mean? How could anyone be *considered* deceased? It made no sense unless it was an error of grammar. Or unless—

There was no time to think. The door opened behind her and the bright beam of another oil lamp glared in her eyes.

"Since you presume that my having friends who are pirates brands me as treasonable, might I think the same of you? Most well-bred young widows are not caught robbing embassy files in the middle of the night."

Garlanda's knees sagged with grateful relief. "Freddie! How you startled me! Get that light out of my eyes, would you? It's blinding me."

The light did not move. She shielded her eyes as the disembodied voice continued, "I think you owe me an explanation," he said frigidly. "You would not find prison agreeable. What are you doing here? Make it convincing so I don't have to call for the servants or Sir George."

"I'm trying to find out about my father's death. None of his associates will give me a straight answer."

"So you burgled the files? Give me what you're holding."

She handed the letter toward the brilliant circle of light. There was a pause as he read it, then the lantern was abruptly extinguished. Footsteps sounded on the stairs. "Quick, put the letter where you found it," he said.

She did. "Are you turning me in?" she asked, preparing to fight him if the need arose.

"This way, up the back staircase. I'll hide you somewhere until he goes back to bed. Then I'll let you out, not that I believe a word of your tale," he hissed and dragged her out of the room and down the hall to the rear staircase. They raced upstairs on tiptoes. The stride of the other person was coming closer.

"Where is your room?" she asked.

"I beg your pardon!" he sounded as dignified as a stately octogenarian instead of a teen-age boy in danger of losing his job.

"Your room. We'll let them think you've smuggled in a girlfriend. They can berate you for it, but that's better than both of us going to prison."

He gave her an infuriated glare and led the way. She removed her hat as they went, and dropped her headscarf on the floor, releasing her thick hair. "What are you doing?" he demanded. "Leaving a trail?"

"Precisely," she said with a grim smile. She dropped a bracelet outside his door. Once inside his room she made a flying dive under the covers on his narrow bed. "Hurry! Take your shirt off and get in here with me!"

"I will not! Suppose you're recognized. That hair of yours—"

"Be quiet! I hear footsteps!"

He tore his shirt off, flung it on the floor, and got in bed with her. A heavy tread pounded up the corridor. It came to a halt at the headscarf, hesitated, hurried on, and stomped to a halt directly outside the door. She shrank down under the covers with her back to the door.

"Clever plot, countess!" Freddie said with caustic courtesy.

The door banged open emphatically. "What the devil!" boomed Sir George. Freddie sat up and Garlanda buried her face in the pillow, shaking with unexpected mirth. What if Sir George came barging over to the bed and ordered her out. Before his eyes she would be forced to rise, fully clothed, and in men's clothing at that—the recently widowed Countess Jareski—Yanoviak in bed with the ambassador's assistant! She wondered impersonally which of the three of them would be most embarrassed.

"What the devil!" Sir George blusteringly repeated. "You've got a woman in there with you! This is highly irregular, very much against the rules! Isn't it enough that harem girls throw jewelry at you and Baron de Gwynne's daughter disgraced her entire family chasing you and my niece—must you bring women *here*! This is unheard of! I won't have it!"

"Not all of us," Freddie said with glacial calm, "get invited to weekend hunts with Spanish comtesses. However, we make do."

Sir George let loose with the enraged bellow of a wounded bull. "You impudent pup, why I—"

"Sir, this will not happen again. But if she could slip through the defenses of the embassy, perhaps the precautions we have are not enough. Security needs to be stepped up."

"I'll thank you not to tell me my business! Who the devil is the wench, anyway? That hair—"

Freddie drew the covers up closer around Garlanda. "Sir!" he said in a tone that conveyed the greatest possible insult to the laws of chivalry.

Sir George snorted. "I'll see to you in the morning, boy. Spanish comtesses indeed!"

"*Married* Spanish comtesses," Freddie murmured.

"Harumph! Well, perhaps we'll let it pass this time, lad. But never again!" He slammed the door.

Freddie collapsed, falling straight back on the narrow bed. "I ceased breathing twice," he said. "He recognized you just before he left. I saw it in his eyes. You're as good as ruined. Now what are you really doing here—or is that preposterous story true?"

"Oh, Freddie, it's such a long story," she said sitting up. "It's nearly dawn and I must hurry back to the villa before my aunt wakes and discovers I'm gone."

"You burgle government files and are discovered in a compromising situation with a member of the embassy staff and yet you worry about your aunt knowing you are out too late?" he asked.

"I suppose that doesn't sound sensible, does it?" She handed him his shirt. "Please, help me find my way back out of here."

She was nearly home when she finally realized what the letter in the file meant.

Considered deceased.

Garlanda absently knotted the reins around her hands.

Her father was *not* dead!

CHAPTER 38

Everyone in Marseille society came to the ball thrown by the recently widowed Countess Jareski–Yanoviak. Leon's friends, true to their word, came to show their support of her entertaining so soon after her bereavement. Count Koniecyzska was there early with Lord and Lady De Bohun. The entire Letourneau family, including all their eligible daughters, came as did the Saniuks, the Dowager Lady Freiler, Father Gacom, and countless others.

Garlanda and Althea stood at the entry to the great ballroom and greeted the guests as they were announced by the major-domo. There was one bad moment when Sir George Young–Brookes arrived with Renwick at his side. Garlanda had, of course, included him in the invitation list—it would have been grossly and publicly insulting to leave him out, but she never dreamed that he would actually come to the ball. She had not seen Renwick since before her marriage, nor had she had any communication from him. He came in with the same elegant swagger that had always fascinated and sometimes angered her.

"Ah, countess," he said blandly, correctly. "What pleasant weather for a party." It was as though they were casual acquaintances, to judge by his tone, but something in his eyes, the way he looked at her, was not casual. Garlanda could almost hear the air crackling around her.

Sir George stepped in with some more innocuous talk about the climate and the two of them moved on without a backward glance. Garlanda let out an audible sigh of relief. She had long dreaded another meeting with Renwick and had certainly not expected it to happen tonight. She had been sure he would not accept the invitation. But it had not been so bad, after all. Perhaps he had genuinely lost interest in her. Perhaps.

People who could not secure invitations were not disappointed at the gate—the doorman had been instructed to let in anyone who looked respectable and Garlanda spent the next hour making introductions and pointless chatter with bejeweled dowagers and young rakes. She took a certain satisfaction in seeing people's shock at her costume. She had saved her harem clothes and wore them now—gauzy trousers, abbreviated jacket, exposed stomach, and a topaz in her navel. Her veils floated down from her cone-shaped hat and her hair gleamed. She was liberally draped with jewelry, but the highlight of her costume was her ruby, pearl, and diamond necklace, and the dangling eardrops to match.

The guests were trying not to swoon over her brazen attire. A few of the women regarded her with a haughty moralistic disdain which masked, insufficiently, their jealousy and the men were frankly pleased. Leon had suggested the costume because, he said, gossip lost its bite when the facts are admitted, even flaunted, rather than concealed. She hoped he was right.

So she stood, a little embarrassed, with Althea and greeted the guests. Althea made a fetching Greek goddess with her long blonde hair unbound. A somewhat immodestly draped gown of white silk kept people in almost as great a state of shock as her niece's costume. Freddie from the embassy waved and kept going as he arrived. He made an attractively tousled Mercury being pursued by a none-too-virginal Artemis—Baron de Gwynne's ardent daughter. Garlanda shot a knowing grin at him. The sour look that he returned said he didn't find it humorous, which only increased Garlanda's appreciation of the situation.

Most of the guests had arrived, though a few were still straggling in, so Garlanda left Althea to greet them and went to look over the crowd. She tried remembering the many unfamiliar names to attach them to some of the unfamiliar faces. Over by the pillar was Miss Worthington surrounded by swains. Her name was easy, she was heavily jeweled, and must be "worth" a great deal. There was a grand dame near her named Marjorie Culver, who had been among the last to arrive. How to keep her name in mind—not that the woman herself could easily be forgotten.

As she scanned the costumed crowd another familiar face caught her eye and stopped her name game. She stared for a moment, disbelieving. And yet, it wasn't so strange. Leon had told her that there would be those who would come without an invitation.

Ironic that on the one occasion that called for a disguise, Roque hadn't worn one. There he stood, not even masked, wearing an eyepatch, headscarf, and cutlass—a barefoot stage pirate. As she watched, he seemed to sense it and turned to look at her. The expression in his face reflected hers—surprise, then pleasure. She stood rooted to the spot while he made his way through the mob toward her. She lost sight of him for a moment, then he was at her side.

"Good-bye," he said with a smile.

"Good-bye?" she repeated.

"Well, we didn't get to that part of the conversation last time we spoke. You do recall, do you not? One moment we were talking and the next thing I knew it was morning. Oh, but you don't know about that part. You were gone by then, weren't you?"

"Now that you mention it—"

"You thieving minx! Where's my ship? And what the hell are you doing at this party?"

"I'm giving it," she said and tried very hard to keep her voice from showing the excitement she felt at seeing him.

"You're giving—? My God, do you mean you're—"

"Countess Jareski–Yanoviak." Roque seemed stunned by this, but said nothing.

"What are *you* doing here?" Garlanda asked.

Roque just looked at her, not speaking for a moment, carefully weighing what to say. "I will have to tell you privately, if I don't wring your deceitful neck first. When I think of the way—well, will you look at that!"

She followed his gaze. There, by the door at the far end of the ballroom, was Sebastian. It took Garlanda a minute to recognize him, dressed as he was. He had on an embroidered waistcoat, satin knee breeches, fine silk hose, silver buckled shoes, and a plumed hat set on a powdered wig of the latest fashion. On him, it seemed like a costume. If she hadn't known better she'd have thought he really was a gentleman and not just a pirate ship's doctor.

"I wonder where he stole that getup!" Roque said with a chuckle.

"Didn't he come with you?"

"No. He said he had something to do and told me

he'd come along later, but I had no idea he was going to dress up like that!" He took her elbow and steered her forcefully across the room to have a word with Sebastian.

"Why, Miss Fleur!" the older man said, "how nice to see you."

"Miss Fleur is the hostess of this party," Roque explained from between clenched teeth. "Our little ship-stealer is an aristocrat now. Isn't that nice?"

Sebastian seemed as jolted as Roque had been. "I hope you don't mind our coming, Countess," he said politely.

Before Garlanda could reply, a new group of guests rushed up to her and by the time she extricated herself both Sebastian and Roque had disappeared. What were they doing here? She found that her heart was still beating faster than usual from the excitement of seeing Roque. She looked around and started mentally recounting the names of people she had just met. It was an almost automatic exercise that kept her mind off Roque. She was staring, unseeing, into the middle distance, her mind on making memorable associations between names and faces when she realized she was watching Renwick.

He was acting somewhat strangely. One of her liver-ied servants was standing next to him and with an oddly intense look Renwick was folding a piece of paper and putting it into an envelope. He put the envelope on the silver tray that the servant held and said something to him, then they both started looking around the ballroom. For her? Perhaps. She slipped behind a pillar.

Was Renwick sending notes to one of the ladies? Perhaps he had found someone else upon whom to focus his romantic interests. She certainly hoped so. She had not seen him, until tonight, since before she married Leon, and was still surprised that he had come to this party.

Lord and Lady De Bohun found her lurking behind the pillar. "Lovely party," he said. "I think Leon would be pleased."

"I would like to think so, sire."

"We explained everything to our friends," his wife said. "I think they all understood the circumstances, at least as well as you could expect anyone who did not know Leon, to understand."

"You see, they're all here," De Bohun said.

A discreet cough at her side preceded the servant's quiet, "Pardon me, madam." He held out a silver salver with a small, white envelope. Garlanda's hand trembled slightly as she reached out for it. Why not just tear it up? Certainly it was from Renwick and she didn't want to read anything that Renwick wrote to her in private little notes. And yet, she couldn't do that. Her curiosity was far too strong to make a decision like that, even though she knew it would be best.

She opened it. There was no heading, just a curt message in a quick scrawl: "Meet me in the garden. Urgent.—R."

Why would he send this? Just to get her alone? What if it were truly urgent? No, it was just a ruse, it must be. "Is there a reply, madam?" the servant asked.

"What? Oh, no. No reply."

"Is there something wrong, dear?" De Bohun's wife asked solicitously.

"Not at all," Garlanda replied, putting on a bright smile that would not have deceived anyone who knew her well. She slipped the note into the pocket of her harem breeches. "Will you excuse me? I must have a word or two with my aunt. I can't imagine where she's gone. I haven't seen her for a while." She got away from the De Bohuns and started searching for Althea, with the idea of getting Althea to go with her to the gardens. She knew that she would go to the gardens, in spite of a small, sensible being at the back of her mind telling her not to.

But there was no sign of Althea. Garlanda thought darkly that her aunt had probably slipped away to some secret little rendezvous of her own and was currently hoping no one would notice her absence. She considered taking someone else along, perhaps Lady De Bohun, but that would be the ultimate affront to Renwick. No, she would go alone. After all, the garden was only a short walk from the ballroom. If Renwick proved a nuisance she would simply walk away.

She stood by the French doors for a while as if merely enjoying the fresh air, then slipped outside when she felt sure no one was looking. After the bright, candle-lit ballroom it was difficult to adjust her eyes to the dark garden. The sky was overcast and only a few feeble strands of moonlight managed to filter through the clouds. With her vision at a temporary loss, her other senses heightened in acuity. The scent of the garden was overwhelming. Leon had ordered orange trees planted and their heady scent, mingled with tuberoses, hyacinths, and jasmine, filled the languid air with an aroma so sensuous as to be almost tangible.

She was taken back to Versailles or the garden of the pasha. The music and laughter from the ballroom seemed an intrusion in this sheltered oasis of peace and beauty. There was no sign of Renwick, or anyone else. Garlanda sat down on a stone bench and tried to blot out the garish sounds of civilization grating harshly on her ears.

She waited for a long time, mainly because it was so pleasant to sit here, then she decided he must have changed his mind and wasn't coming. That was a relief, that he had thought better of whatever he had intended to say to her, even though she did feel a bit the fool, answering Renwick's summons, only to be stood up. Yet, she had done worse to him, he deserved this little victory over her. Perhaps that's what he intended. So be it.

She couldn't bear to go back yet. She strolled down the brick path, inhaling the thick, softly sweet air. The garden was fresh with the odor of green plants and trees bursting into glorious life all around her. If only life could be this lovely all the time. Somewhere in the darkness a bird trilled, disturbed in its late night calm. Grandmama in Martinique had told her once it was the sound of a bird having a nightmare. *Poor bird,* she thought, *what have you to have nightmares about?*

A little farther along the brick path was another bench by a fountain. This was where she and Leon had spent so many hours reading to each other. Tears involuntarily filled her eyes. She went and sat in her usual place, eyes tightly shut as she remembered those tranquil times. It must have been the sound of the splashing water that prevented her from hearing footsteps. She didn't know anyone was there until a hand closed on her arm like a vise and a voice hissed, "So you *did* come to meet him!"

Garlanda stifled a scream. "Renwick! What do you mean, creeping up on me like that? And whatever are you talking about? I came in response to the note I saw you put on that tray for me."

"I was reading it and putting it back. I decided to

wait and watch what happened, but I didn't see you leave the ballroom."

"As if the matter were any of your business," she said huffily. "A lady's correspondence is her own business. Let me go, Renwick." It must have been Roque who sent the note. How stupid of her. "R" for Roque.

"No, I *won't* let you go." He drew her to her feet with a painful, powerful grip. "You've made me wait long enough while you played your silly games. You wanted me one night and I can't forget the way you responded, so spare me your virginal blushes. You were no maiden then and you certainly haven't reverted now. You knew from the start I wanted you. You with your courage and fire and beauty. And all that time I was saddled with pathetic, mousey Elaine—"

Even in the near darkness she could see enough of his face to be horrified at the expression there. She had seen this look before, or at least a hint of it. That one horrible instant when she had known that he was going to kill Lawrence Jennings in cold blood if someone didn't stop him. She hadn't put a name to it then, it was indefinable, hinted at by the twist of an eyebrow, crease of a forehead.

But now it wasn't a hint, nor was it any longer indefinable. It was madness, his face was a map of jealous insanity. She swallowed and said timidly, "Poor Elaine." Anything to keep him talking. Once he stopped talking—what then?

"Yes," he sneered. "Poor little Elaine. It took quite an effort to rid myself of her, but I did it. Quite a picture. The impassioned would-be lover slowly poisoning his unwanted wife and then chasing the woman he wants cross-continent only to find she's been kidnaped into a harem. I was at last free to marry you and you were gone."

Murdered Elaine! This was no sudden madness, no momentary loss of control. The man had been planning for a long time. He had murdered one of the dearest people in the world—for her—for "love." Love! How could he think of it?

More important, how could she get away from him? She was in as much danger right now as Elaine had been!

CHAPTER 39

Garlanda tried to gently pull away from him, but it was futile. He drew her into his iron grip. "No, my dear, you won't escape again. Our little scene with Baronet Jennings happened just in time. I'd have killed him if you'd become his wife," he said, echoing her own thoughts. "I've even got a title and money now and we're both free from our other marriages. By God, you'll marry me now, or I'll break your pretty neck."

Garlanda did not doubt that he meant it. She must try to remain calm, to do the right thing. She must not allow him to sense the horror and revulsion she felt. Her only chance of escape was to play along, keep him talking until she saw an opportunity. Where was Roque? If, as it seemed, *he* had written the note, not Renwick, then he must be somewhere near. But it had been some time since she came out. Perhaps he was looking for her by the ballroom where she had been sitting earlier. By now he might have given up looking for her at all. *Stay calm,* she told herself again. *Stay calm.*

She affected a cool air in opposition to his crumbling nervous clumsiness of speech. Renwick, the calmest and iciest of men, falling apart? Even if she had not been in danger, this would have been terrifying.

"Really?" she said in a voice she hoped sounded casual. "You really poisoned Elaine? Why didn't you tell me sooner? I avoided you because I believed you truly loved her. How did you do it, Renwick?"

He laughed with a demented cackle. "It was amusing. She liked me to bring her breakfast tray up to her and talk awhile. I just slipped the poison in before giving her the tray. You mean you were only waiting because—my darling!" He embraced her passionately.

Garlanda's stomach floundered in the grip of frightened nausea. Her mind fought for control over her trembling body. *Keep him talking, then catch him unprepared and run,* she told herself. "You're so clever, Renwick. And your brother and nephew. How did you get rid of them?"

"So, you figured that out too? I paid the coach driver to send the horse off a sheer cliff, then he jumped off at the last minute. It was wonderful! The coach tumbled over and over like a toy, down and down and down."

"You were there?"

"Of course I was—behind some bushes. I had to be."

"Why?"

He looked exasperated. "You didn't think I could let the coach driver go around telling what had happened, do you?"

"Oh, I see. You killed him too."

"Of course I did. Then I threw him off the cliff too. No one ever questioned that it was just an unfortunate accident."

He spoke of the deaths as coolly as if he were discussing the latest sporting event about town. It made Garlanda feel like her bones had turned to ice. She forced herself to smile at him and say, "Renwick, I think we really are free now. There's no one else in our way. Come, come back to the house. We have no one to fear."

He held her so tightly that her breath nearly ceased. "Garlanda, my beautiful, fiery darling! It isn't that easy. I'm afraid my partner and I have figured out that you were in the harem we visited. He wants to kill you, but I've convinced him you won't talk. Of course, we'll have to kill the boy."

"What partner? What boy?" she asked, rigidly muffled against his shoulder.

"The boy has to die. Yes. He's been spying and has learned far too much. Sir George told me he found you in bed with the boy one night. He said there was no mistaking that copper hair of yours, and I'm afraid I have to believe him. So, you see, we'll have to kill Freddie for spying on my—my business transactions—" the awful laugh again, "as well as for bedding you."

"But he hasn't!" she cried out. What *was* he talking about? Business transactions—the harem—spying— Freddie—? Was this talk just part of his madness?

"We'll announce our engagement tonight just as soon as our betrothal is consummated."

"Oh, no!" she cried, then caught herself. "I mean we can't announce it so openly. It's too soon after Leon's death. It wouldn't be proper, do you think?"

"But I won't wait!" his voice was rising again. "And you haven't anything left to be proper about. You in that outfit!"

"Oh, I didn't mean to wait. I just meant it wouldn't be right to have a big wedding so soon after—after my husband's death and if we announce it to all these people we will have to invite all of them to the wedding." Soothe him, say anything he wants to hear! Pretend to go along with him.

"Maybe—we will marry tomorrow then. I will stay

here, with you, until then. I cannot bear to have you out of my sight again. Here and now. I've waited too long. I will have you!" He grasped the scarf around her hair and yanked her head back so roughly she could feel the bones in her neck snap in protest. He pressed his lips on hers and she could feel his teeth biting into her skin. She could taste blood.

Suddenly he was enraged with thwarted passion. He dragged her to the ground and threw his body on hers. "I will have you now—and forever!" He moaned in her ear. She tried to turn away, but he was too strong. She could hardly breathe and felt herself going faint. She screamed and the edges of her vision started to go red.

Then there was activity. The weight was gone. Someone was shouting—two voices, she thought. She drew one heavy hand up and put it over her eyes. She must not faint, she must not. With a great effort of will, she forced herself to her knees. In the dim moonlight she could see a horrible, writhing shape. No! It wasn't one being—it was two. Two men locked in combat. They said nothing, but she could hear them breathing in broken syncopation, and she could almost feel the pain of the murderous blows they exchanged.

The clouds cleared for a brief moment and she could see them. It was Renwick, of course, and Roque—he had found her! Roque was the larger and stronger of the two, but Renwick had the advantage of unleashed madness. He lashed out violently and she could see Roque stagger back. She held her breath as the clouds again crossed the moon and blotted out the light.

She must go for help, but could she? She didn't think she could even stand without losing consciousness. Her neck was still shooting shafts of pain up the back of her head from the wrenching and even her limited view of what was happening kept dissolving into a blurred image of four men fighting in pairs. But she must try!

She got partly up and had almost managed to stand when there was the sound of another blow meeting flesh and a body hurtled toward her. The man, whichever he was, struck her and fell sideways into a heap. She raised her head and looked at the figure standing over her.

Who was it?

It was dark, so dark. She couldn't make her eyes focus properly. She heard the man's sucking rasp of breath and time crawled. If it was Renwick he might well kill her on the spot and she hadn't the strength to fight him off.

Slowly, ever so slowly, the man leaned over her and took her chin in his hand. Was he going to strangle her? Or strike her? She tried to pull back, away from his touch, but could not move.

"Fleur, are you hurt?"

She collapsed, sobbing into his arms. He let her cry until her breathing became more even, then he held her back a little and looked at her. "Are you injured?"

"No, I don't think so," she said, putting a hand to the back of her neck. "It's just twisted, I think, and my head hurts. Are you alright?"

"Just bruised and scraped." He rose and went to where Renwick lay sprawled on the grass. Roque turned him over and peered into his face in the near darkness. "He'll survive—long enough to get to the gallows."

"The gallows! You heard, then, about Elaine and his brother and nephew?" she shuddered as she said it. It was too awful to contemplate. Poor Elaine, trusting him and loving him so deeply while he slowly poisoned her.

"Yes, I heard, but he was headed for the gallows anyway. I'm sorry I didn't get to you sooner. I wanted to hear all he would say, but I misjudged him. I didn't think he would attack you that suddenly and when he did—well, I fell in some damned hole back there in a flower bed."

As intriguing as this vision of her hero floundering in a hole in the garden was, Garlanda was not about to be diverted. "What do you mean, he was headed for the gallows?"

"It's a long story. Remember when you asked me what I was doing here? Well, your 'friend' Renwick is part of the reason."

"I don't understand, but shouldn't we go back in? You can tell me later. I'm the hostess, I should—"

"No! I don't want you in there. That's why I wrote the note."

"I thought Renwick wrote it," she said without thinking.

"Then why did you come out here?" Roque said.

"I don't know. Just incurably curious, I guess. I thought he might have something important to say."

"And he did, didn't he? You idiotic—"

"That still doesn't tell me why you wanted me out here—aside from the obvious," she said, snuggling back into the warm protection of his arms.

"Well, I don't know quite where to start. You see, for the last several years, nearly every spice ship bound for England has been—"

"Intercepted. Yes, I know about that."

"You do? How?"

"Oh, Sabelle, and other people. But will you please, please tell me your own part in all this?"

"*Now* I can. I wish I could have earlier. I was asked by Lord Bramson."

"Bramson! I know him!"

"Do you? I suppose everyone does. He's got a pinhead for a heart, but he's smart. Anyway, he asked me, or rather, paid me generously to abandon the honest life and go into piracy."

"You're working for Bramson? For England?"

"Yes. That surprises you, doesn't it? You really believed I was the traitor, didn't you?"

She hung her head and tried to think of some denial that would sound convincing. "I don't know whether to be insulted or flattered," he went on, "at having persuaded you by my excellent acting."

"Then you've been trying to find out who the traitor is?"

"Yes. I'd just been in London reporting on my progress to your friend Lord Bramson when I met you on that boat—the one going to France. That's when I realized that I loved you, by the way," Roque said as if this were an inconsequential side issue.

"Why?" Garlanda asked, completely abandoning interest in the topic of traitors.

"Because I suddenly saw you as a woman, a confident, independent being, not just a sweet little convent girl with nothing to talk about or think about but life with the sisters. I could tell the moment I looked at you that you had changed. Something in your eyes and your bearing, I don't know, it's impossible to describe. Even at that, I was frankly astonished at the further transformation when you came out of the harem. It was too good to be true." He kissed her—a long, lingering kiss that blotted out the pain in her head.

"We must go in," she murmured weakly.

"No. Not yet. It hasn't happened yet."

"What hasn't happened?"

"That's what I was trying to tell you. I went to Lord Bramson with the information I had and told him of my suspicions. He said he had to have concrete proof and gave me the name of a woman in Marseille, an old laundress. Since then I have been gathering various documents and testimony, some of it from your friend Freddie, in fact, and leaving it with this woman to give to Bramson's other man."

"Other man? Who is that?"

"I have no idea. I never see who gets the papers, it's just someone Bramson trusts to carry out the arrests when the time comes and the proofs are sufficient. Which, as I'm trying to tell you, they are now."

"Then you know—you know who the traitor is?"

"Yes. And he will be arrested momentarily. That's what we're doing sitting out here in the damp grass."

"What!"

"The laundress gave me a message from Bramson that his representative would make the arrests tonight. Your ball was a perfect opportunity to find all the malefactors in one place, at one time, and unarmed. You could not have helped us more if you had been working for Bramson. Although, if I had known that the grand widowed countess was my own Fleur, I wouldn't have allowed it."

"All the malefactors?" Garlanda said, looking uneasily at the unconscious form of Renwick Ridgely.

"Yes. That's what I meant," Roque said. "I'm sorry. You didn't really care for him, did you?"

"No. I thought I did, once or twice in England, but

it was always just the things in him that reminded me of you."

Roque opened his mouth to reply, but before he could speak, the sounds from the ballroom changed. First the music stopped, dying with a half-hearted squawk. Then it was very quiet for a few seconds before the quiet was split by the sharp *crack* of a pistol shot. Feminine squeals of alarm wafted across the night air along with raised masculine voices.

"Can you walk now?" Roque asked urgently.

"Yes," Garlanda said, not at all sure it was true, but determined to see what was happening. She couldn't make her legs cooperate very well, but Roque supported her when she stumbled and they hurried awkwardly along the garden path. A low buzz of conversation had resumed in the ballroom and Roque pushed their way through the people by the doors. Everyone had drawn back toward the perimeter of the dance floor, leaving the principal actors in this drama to themselves in the center.

Garlanda stared, then blinked her eyes, sure that she could not be seeing properly. There were three men with their hands tied behind them and a small, still-smoking pistol lying on the floor. Two of the men were strangers to Garlanda—men she had met for the first time only tonight. But the third—the man standing glowering in the middle of the group—was none other than Sir George Young-Brookes!

Sir George—England's own ambassador! Incredible that such a man would turn on his own country. And yet, who had a better opportunity to know what was going on both in England and in the Mediterranean? He was in a perfect position to betray information for the material gain it could bring. And to think, she had been his guest—worse, she had placed Freddie, her friend, in his household! He was the sort of man whom people trusted and he had taken advantage of that.

Everything fit so well. Why hadn't she seen it before? And yet, she had a nagging feeling that something else fit, something she must know, but didn't yet realize she knew.

The man making the arrests had his back to them, conferring with two other gentlemen who were apparently helping him. Roque took Garlanda's hand and led her up to the group. "Ridgely's out in the garden, unconscious. My God. You!"

"Sebastian!" Garlanda exclaimed. "What are you doing?"

"I'm sorry, Fleur. I mean, Countess. Captain, I didn't like deceiving you."

Roque threw his head back and roared with laughter. "God in heaven! Are *you* Bramson's man? Do you mean that all those times I spent the day evading you to take my information to that woman, you just followed along and picked it up?"

"I'm sorry," Sebastian said with a sheepish smile. "You see, Bramson didn't entirely trust you. He's never trusted anyone, so he asked me to get as close to you as I could and keep an eye on your activities. You can't get much closer than being a ship's doctor."

"Damn! That's typical of the old bastard," Roque said, still laughing. "Then you weren't a doctor?"

"Not until the day I joined the crew, but I learned fast, didn't I?"

The crowd had gradually drawn closer to listen in and there was now a bustle of activity. The three prisoners were being removed and someone else was apparently trying to push through the crowd. Finally Althea emerged, disheveled and casting a baleful look over her shoulder at whoever had impeded her progress. "What is all this about?" she demanded of Garlanda. "I heard a commotion—are you alright?" Her eyes raked the group then suddenly she clutched Garlanda's arm and seemed to sag. Her mouth hung open for a moment as she stared at Sebastian.

"Althea!" he said and held open his arms. "It's been so long!"

Althea put a shaking hand to her forehead and in a whisper that was strangely reverent and angry at the same time she said, "But—but, you're dead!"

Sebastian looked puzzled. "What are you talking about? Dead? You can see I'm not. Where did you get an idea like that?"

"Minette got a letter from Bramson—"

With awful suddenness Garlanda understood. She covered her mouth with both hands to hold back the hysterics.

Althea noted the motion and turned to her. "Garlanda—"

"Garlanda?" Sebastian echoed. "*This* is Garlanda? Fleur—the countess?"

He stepped closer and said, "Daughter!"

Garlanda slipped to the floor before anyone could catch her.

CHAPTER 40

"Start at the beginning, please," Garlanda said in a quavering voice.

The man she had to start thinking of as her father sat down and took her hands in his. It was remarkable how much younger Sir Robert Cheney looked than "Sebastian Sim." He had removed the gray dye from his hair and stood straight and tall without the stoop he had adopted as the ship's surgeon. Instead of looking like an aging grandfather, he now gave the truthful appearance of being a pleasant man in his forties with a lightly lined face that easily broke into smiles. "Garlanda, my own dear child, I must assure you that I never dreamed of what scheme Lord Bramson had devised to hide the truth. To tell you and your mother that I was dead! Unforgivably cruel! The man is a fanatic patriot, however. He would not consider any individual's unhappiness when it came to the national welfare. I suppose he thought when my work was completed, it would all be straightened out. Alas, it wasn't to be. Poor Minette!"

Althea took Garlanda's hand and spoke to Robert. "The truth then. What is the truth? What about the letter that Garlanda tells me you wrote to Minette?"

"I was doing very dangerous work for the King and Queen," he said and in his eyes it seemed she could see the dim reflections of that day so many years ago when he had first begun to live as a hunted spy. "You have heard that there was a traitor revealing English shipping plans to anyone with the money to buy them. Two good men, friends of mine, had been on the track of this traitor and both died violently. Bramson asked me to assume a new identity in order to investigate these deaths. I was not supposed to write to your mother at all. Bramson told me," his voice now became very bitter, "that it would all be explained to her. I knew that he would not explain the *whole* truth but—"

He walked to the window, turning his back on them while he fought to contain his anger. Finally he said, "I was being followed and I was afraid someone might try to harm you and your mother. I suppose Bramson, in his own warped way, thought he was protecting you both with the story of my death. No one knew of my assignment but Bramson and his clerk."

He stopped and inhaled deeply with a slow shake of his head. "Bramson had a man he thought would be able to spy on the spies, so to speak. A man with years of sailing experience who could operate as a pirate— Roque, of course. He took his orders directly from the King and stopped at various ports to gather his information. He thwarted ship after ship from being taken. He has risked his life countless times for England."

Garlanda gripped her father's hand. "Why did he not know you were working for the government?"

"Because Bramson doesn't trust anyone. I was to do my own work, spy on Roque and, whenever necessary, provide him with assistance. There were many times when he was in danger, and I was able to help without him knowing it."

Althea interrupted. "What about that young man at the embassy?"

"Freddie?" Sebastian said. "I arranged for Freddie to escape the ship with Garlanda in the hopes that he would find employment at the embassy. It worked out that way and I contacted him later. I realize now that he must have known that Fleur was actually Garlanda by the time I next saw him, but I didn't ask who she really was and he had no reason to tell me.

"It was Freddie," he went on, "who first noticed Sir George carrying on peculiar correspondence. You see, one of the things puzzling us was how the traitor seemed to move about in different countries. We knew that only a man high up in the service of England could be passing on the information, but ambassadors do not travel extensively—not without notice."

"Renwick?" Althea asked.

"Yes, Renwick Ridgely. He was working with Sir George and doing most of the actual running about to sell the information."

Garlanda frowned, teeth catching on her lower lip in an expression of deep thought. "But why? What did they get out of it that was worth betraying their country and running the risk of discovery and death?"

"I can tell you that," Althea said. "After the arrests the ballroom was absolutely alive with it. Money! Both of them had apparently inherited enormous debts along with their fine titles. It's all come out now. Renwick was a heavy gambler—"

"And a murderer!" Garlanda added with a shudder.

"So it seems," Althea added sourly. "He was certainly a good actor, though. I never liked him very well, but I would never have guessed he was capable of that! He always seemed so utterly controlled and courteous."

"Not always," Garlanda said. "I saw the real Renwick once, for just a second. I should have known."

"What do you mean?"

"That day he nearly killed Lawrence. But please, let's don't talk of him. Father, I still cannot believe you were alive all the time I was running about France learning to ride and fence so I could find your murderers and wreak vengeance."

"And I thought you were dead as well," he said. "Bramson sent me word of the slave insurrection and the supposed deaths of you and your mother. Naturally he did not bother to correct the error when he found out you were alive and well. He has *much* to answer for!"

"Oh, but Papa, it doesn't matter now. All that matters is that you are alive and Roque is not a traitor. I've misjudged him so horribly."

Her father's blue eyes twinkled. "Not only is he not a traitor, but he's been pacing outside the door ever since we carried you in here, I imagine. I'm surprised he hasn't broken the door down yet."

"Oh, please send him in," she said.

Her father stood to go. "I think you have things to talk over with him. You and I will talk more later. Althea!" he said rather sharply. "They do not need either of us. Come along."

Althea hung back for a moment, then allowed herself to be removed from the room, and a moment later there was a light tap on the door. Garlanda smoothed her hair and called, "Come in."

Roque stepped in with his usual careless grace. He seemed to fill the room. Garlanda motioned to him to sit down. He remained standing. He cleared his throat. Nothing happened. He cleared his throat again. "What a shock for all of us, Sebastian being your father. For you, most of all."

"It is wonderful to have a father again. Roque, do you think that you could tell me now of your family? You have spoken once or twice of them, but I didn't understand what you meant."

"I suppose you should know," he said softly. Then he was quiet for a minute, as if organizing his thoughts. "My father is an illegitimate son of King John of Portugal. King John was married to Queen Luisa, but in love with my grandmother, a woman of ordinary birth. When he died his legitimate son, Afonso VI came to the throne and Queen Luisa made a little 'arrangement' with France."

"Arrangement?"

"Yes, a treaty of sorts—some of it official, some of it not. Afonso, a demented, deformed man, got a French bride and France, in return, kept my father—whom Luisa regarded as a threat to Afonso's throne—locked up for the rest of his life. My English mother died when I was an infant and I was a small boy when the soldiers came to take my father. I hardly remember what he looked like, but no one else will ever know that he had the Braganza looks."

"What do you mean? Is he dead?"

"No. But his face is never seen."

"You can't mean—"

"I do. He is the Man in the Iron Mask. It is a cruel fate, but I suppose I should be grateful that Queen Luisa didn't just have him killed outright. But Afonso had no heirs, and neither did his brother Pedro when he came to the throne. I was about twenty then and Pedro found out about my existence. My life became a series of flights. I came to France, thinking to some-

how see King Louis and implore his mercy, and ask to
see my father."

"Did you see the King?"

"No. Pedro's agents were right behind me. I had to
act fast, death was dogging my every footstep so I did
the one thing I knew they would not expect. I had
myself arrested. They never looked for me in the gal
leys. I was a galley slave for three years. By that time
Pedro had a new wife and two sons, so he had los
interest in me."

"And when you escaped the galleys, the King o
England gave you sanctuary—?"

"Yes, my nosy little nun. That's how I became a pi
rate for the King with your father spying on me!"

There was an awkward pause. Garlanda felt a
swimming fogginess fill her eyes. She ducked he
head.

"Are those tears?" he asked, and drew her to her
feet. "Fleur?"

She pressed her head to his chest, crying
ashamedly. "Oh, Roque! I have my father back, but
I'm losing you! All that time I held my heart back because I thought you were a traitor! How stupid I've
been! I knocked you out and helped steal your ship so
I could look for news of my father—and he was there
all the time. I've been so wrong. Ever since that day
you told me you liked me and that was all—"

He laughed. "I liked you then and I like you now."

"Oh," she said in a small wounded voice.

"However," Roque continued with a mischievous
glint in his eyes. "You've grown up since then. You're
not a silly little convent girl full of other people's rules
and petty regulations. You are a woman now, strong
and stubborn and beautiful. Have I ever told you how
beautiful you are and how much I love you?"

The words she had wanted to hear for so long brought a renewal of tears. "What!" he asked in mock alarm. "I bare my heart to the lovely harem girl and she cries?"

"I'm crying because I love you, Roque. I've loved you for so long—"

He kissed her then held her close, her head nestled against his broad shoulder. "I'm so relieved to hear that, because I would have felt such a fool walking out there alone and unloved after telling your father and aunt that we are getting married."

"Are we?" she said and kissed him again. "But we can't. You love the sea too much, it is a part of you and I will not have you unhappy on my account."

"Sebastian—I mean, your father—and I have been talking. We both have commissions coming from the King and your aunt has no interest in the plantation in Martinique that your grandparents left to you and her. Your father and I want to retire to Martinique and become wealthy, safe, dull old shipowners and builders."

"And Althea?"

"She says she is going back to London. It seems all her beaux are clamoring for her return. She is taking Freddie back with her to supervise his education, or she thinks so. I don't know that Freddie has been consulted."

"Everyone seems to have worked this all out quite nicely without a single sentence from me. Where do I fit in?" Garlanda asked a trifle crossly.

"Well, who else would rechristen my ship as founder of a new line? I'm afraid my Lady of Fire is incomplete without the real Lady."

Garlanda toyed with the lace-up front of his linen shirt. "Perhaps before we settle down to family life and running a business we could take a final trip on a pirate ship. Maybe we would even find ourselves stranded on a remote island, all alone. I hear it can be wonderful to be stranded like that with one's lover."

He kissed her hungrily. "Say 'husband,' Fleur. It's a word you must grow accustomed to."

"If I must call you husband, you must call me Garlanda. Fleur is not my name, you know."

"I do not care. Safiye the harem girl, Fleur the pirate, Garlanda the proper English miss, Countess Jareski–Yanoviak—you're still the same woman to me—the woman I love."

She surrendered herself to his arms.

By the author of Scarlet Shadows

THE BURNING LAND

EMMA DRUMMOND

Judith: A proud English beauty, she left the glitter of London society to pursue Alex across two continents.

Hetta: Gentle, tender, she gave her love boldly, without thought of the past or the devastating future that threatened to separate her from Alex forever.

Two women from different worlds, their passions blazed for one man across THE BURNING LAND!

A Dell Book $2.50